Praise for the novels of
BRUCE STERLING

HOLY FIRE
"A HAUNTING AND LYRICAL TRIUMPH."—*Time*

"*HOLY FIRE* IS A BOOK MADE ENTIRELY OF
IDEAS . . . BIG, FAT, JUICY TECHNOLOGICAL
EXTRAPOLATIONS, PRESENTED WITH FLAIR
AND ENTHUSIASM. AN INTELLECTUAL FEAT,
IT IS ALSO A TREAT FOR THE SPIRIT AND
THE SENSES."—*Wired*

"A PATENTED STERLING EXTRA-SPECIAL."
—*Newsday*

"STERLING IS THE BEST AT SERIOUSLY
TRYING TO PREDICT FUTURE TRENDS. IN
HOLY FIRE HE HAS COMBINED HIS
PREDICTIVE TALENT WITH A SYMPATHETIC
AND COMPLEX HEROINE WHO CAN BLEND
THE OLD AND THE NEW."—*The Denver Post*

"THE SOCIAL DIMENSION IS HIS BAILIWICK,
AND WHILE STERLING HAS ALWAYS HAD A
SENSE OF HUMOR, PARTICULARLY IN HIS
STORIES, HE'S NEVER WRITTEN ANYTHING
WITH THE SATIRICAL ZING AND LAFF RELIEF
OF THE FIRST 70 OR SO PAGES. INDEED, NOT
MANY HAVE—THIS ENGLISH-HONORS BOY
WILL TAKE IT OVER ANY NATHANAEL WEST
OR EVELYN WAUGH HE KNOWS."
—*The Village Voice*

HEAVY WEATHER

"BRILLIANT . . . FASCINATING . . . EXCITING . . . A FULL COMPLEMENT OF THRILLS."—*The New York Times Book Review*

"A REMARKABLE AND INDIVIDUAL SHARPNESS OF VISION . . . STERLING HACKS THE FUTURE, AND AN ELEGANT HACK IT IS."
—*Locus*

"SO BELIEVABLE ARE THE SPECULATIONS THAT . . . ONE BECOMES CONVINCED THAT THE WORLD *MUST* AND *WILL* DEVELOP INTO WHAT STERLING HAS PREDICTED."
—*Science Fiction Age*

"SHARP . . . INTRIGUING . . . A NEAR-FUTURE THRILLER."—*Publishers Weekly*

THE DIFFERENCE ENGINE
(with William Gibson)
"BREATHTAKING."—*The New York Times*

"BURSTING WITH THE KIND OF DEMENTED SPECULATION AND OBSESSIVE DETAILING THAT HAS MADE BOTH GIBSON'S AND STERLING'S WORK STAND OUT."
—*San Francisco Chronicle*

"HIGHLY IMAGINATIVE . . . [A] SPLENDID EFFORT."—*Chicago Tribune*

"SMARTLY PLOTTED, WONDERFULLY CRAFTED, AND WRITTEN WITH SLY LITERARY WIT . . . SPINS MARVELOUSLY AND RUNS LIKE A DREAM."—*Entertainment Weekly*

ALSO BY BRUCE STERLING

Novels

THE ARTIFICIAL KID
THE DIFFERENCE ENGINE
(WITH WILLIAM GIBSON)
HEAVY WEATHER
INVOLUTION OCEAN
ISLANDS IN THE NET
SCHISMATRIX
HOLY FIRE

Stories

CRYSTAL EXPRESS
GLOBALHEAD

Nonfiction

THE HACKER CRACKDOWN:
LAW AND DISORDER ON THE ELECTRONIC
FRONTIER

Editor

MIRRORSHADES: THE CYBERPUNK
ANTHOLOGY

DISTRACTION

A novel

BRUCE STERLING

BANTAM BOOKS

New York Toronto
London Sydney Auckland

This edition contains the complete text
of the original hardcover edition.
NOT ONE WORD HAS BEEN OMITTED.

DISTRACTION
A Bantam Spectra Book
PUBLISHING HISTORY
Bantam hardcover edition / December 1998
Bantam mass market edition / October 1999

ISBN 0-553-57639-9

Published simultaneously in the United States and Canada

PRINTED IN THE UNITED STATES OF AMERICA

OPM   10 9 8 7 6 5 4 3 2 1

DISTRACTION

1

For the fifty-first time (according to his laptop), Oscar studied the riot video from Worcester. This eight-minute chunk of jerky footage was Oscar's current favorite object of professional meditation. It was a set of grainy photos, taken by a security camera in Massachusetts.

The press called this event "the Worcester riot of May Day '42." This May Day event did not deserve the term "riot" in Oscar's professional opinion, because although it was extremely destructive, there was nothing riotous about it.

The first security shots showed a typical Massachusetts street crowd, people walking the street. Worcester was traditionally a rather tough and ugly town, but like many areas in the old industrial Northeast, Worcester had been rather picking up lately. Nobody in the crowd showed any signs of aggression or rage. Certainly nothing was going on that would provoke the attention of the authorities and their various forms of machine surveillance. Just normal people shopping, strolling. A line of bank customers doing business with a debit-card machine. A bus taking on and disgorging its passengers.

Then, bit by bit, the street crowd became denser. There were more people in motion. And, although it was by no means easy to notice, more and more of these people were carrying valises, or knapsacks, or big jumbo-sized purses.

Oscar knew very well that these very normal-looking people were linked in conspiracy. The thing that truly roused his admiration was the absolute brilliance of the way they were dressed, the utter dullness and nonchalance of their comportment. They were definitely not natives of Worcester, Massachusetts, but each and every one was a cunning distillation of the public image of Worcester. They were all deliberate plants and ringers, but they were uncannily brilliant forgeries, strangers bent on destruction who were almost impossible to notice.

They didn't fit any known demographic profile of a troublemaker, or a criminal, or a violent radical. Any security measure that would have excluded them would have excluded everyone in town.

Oscar assumed that they were all radical proles. Dissidents, autonomen, gypsies, leisure-union people. This was a reasonable assumption, since a quarter of the American population no longer had jobs. More than half of the people in modern America had given up on formal employment. The modern economy no longer generated many commercial roles that could occupy the time of people.

With millions of people structurally uprooted, there wasn't any lack of recruiting material for cults, prole gangs, and street mobs. Big mobs were common enough nowadays, but this May Day organization was not a mob. They weren't a standard street gang or militia either. Because they weren't saluting one another. There were no visible orders given or taken, no colors or hand signs, no visible hierarchy. They showed no signs of mutual recognition at all.

In fact—Oscar had concluded this only after repeated close study of the tape—they weren't even aware of one another's existence as members of the same group. He further suspected that many of them—maybe most of them—didn't know what they were about to do.

Then, they all exploded into action. It was startling, even at the fifty-first viewing.

Smoke bombs went off, veiling the street in mist. Purses and valises and backpacks yawned open, and their owners removed and deployed a previously invisible arsenal of drills, and bolt cutters, and pneumatic jacks. They marched through the puffing smoke and set to their work as if they demolished banks every day.

A brown van ambled by, a van that bore no license plates. As it drove down the street every other vehicle stopped dead. None of those vehicles would ever move again, because their circuits had just been stripped by a high-frequency magnetic pulse, which, not coincidentally, had ruined all the financial hardware within the bank.

The brown van departed, never to return. It was shortly replaced by a large, official-looking, hook-wielding tow truck. The tow truck bumped daintily over the pavement, hooked itself to the automatic teller machine, and yanked the entire armored machine from the wall in a cascade of broken bricks. Two random passersby deftly lashed the teller machine down with bungee cords. The tow truck then thoughtfully picked up a parked limousine belonging to a bank officer, and departed with that as well.

At this point, the arm of a young man appeared in close-up. A strong brown hand depressed a button, and a can sprayed the lens of the security camera with paint. That was the end of the recorded surveillance footage.

But it hadn't been the end of the attack. The attackers hadn't simply robbed the bank. They had carried off everything portable, including the security cameras, the carpets, the chairs, and the light and plumbing fixtures. The conspirators had deliberately *punished* the bank, for reasons best known to themselves, or to their unknown controllers. They had superglued doors and shattered windows, severed power and communications cables, poured stinking toxins into the wallspaces, concreted all the sinks and drains. In eight minutes, sixty people had ruined the building so thoroughly that it had to be condemned and later demolished.

The ensuing criminal investigation had not managed to apprehend, convict, or even identify a single one of the "rioters." Once fuller attention had been paid to the Worcester bank, a number of grave financial irregularities had surfaced. The scandal eventually led to the resignation of three Massachusetts state representatives and the jailing of four bank executives and the mayor of Worcester. The Worcester banking scandal had become a major issue in the ensuing U.S. Senate campaign.

This event was clearly significant. It had required organization, observation, decision, execution. It was a gesture of brutal authority from some very novel locus of power. Someone had done all this with meticulous purpose and intent, but how? How did they compel the loyalty of those agents? How did they recruit them, train them, dress them, pay them, transport them? And—most amazing of all—how did they compel their silence, afterward?

Oscar Valparaiso had once imagined politics as a chess game. His kind of chess game. Pawns, knights, and queens, powers and strategies, ranks and files, black squares and white squares. Studying this tape had cured him of that metaphor. Because this phenomenon on the tape was not a chess piece. It was there on the public chessboard all right, but it wasn't a rook or a bishop. It was a wet squid, a swarm of bees. It was a new entity that pursued its own orthogonal agenda, and vanished into the silent interstices of a deeply networked and increasingly nonlinear society.

Oscar sighed, shut his laptop, and looked down the length of the bus. His campaign staffers had been living inside a bus for thirteen weeks, in a slowly rising tide of road garbage. They were victorious now, decompressing from the heroic campaign struggle. Alcott Bambakias, their former patron, was the new U.S. Senator–elect from Massachusetts. Oscar had won his victory. The Bambakias campaign had been folded up, and sent away.

And yet, twelve staffers still dwelled inside the Senator's bus. They were snoring in their fold-down bunks, playing poker on the flip-out tables, trampling big promiscuous heaps of road laundry. On occasion, they numbly rifled the cabinets for snacks.

Oscar's sleeve rang. He reached inside it, retrieved a fabric telephone, and absently flopped his phone back into shape. He spoke into the mouthpiece. "Okay, Fontenot."

"You wanna make it to the science lab tonight?" said Fontenot.

"That would be good."

"How much is it worth to you? We've got a road-block problem."

"They're shaking us down, is that it?" said Oscar, his brow creasing beneath his immaculate hair. "They want a bribe, straight across? Is it really that simple?"

"Nothing is ever simple anymore," said Fontenot. The campaign's security man wasn't attempting world-weary sarcasm. He was relating a modern fact of life. "This isn't like our other little roadblock hassles. This is the United States Air Force."

Oscar considered this novel piece of information. It didn't sound at all promising. "Why, exactly, is the Air Force blockading a federal highway?"

"Folks have always done things differently here in Louisiana," Fontenot offered. Through the phone's flimsy earpiece, a distant background of car honks rose to a crescendo. "Oscar, I think you need to come see this. I know Louisiana, I was born and raised here, but I just don't have the words to describe all this."

"Very good," Oscar said. "I'll be right there." He stuffed the phone in his sleeve. He'd known Fontenot for over a year, and had never heard such an invitation from him. Fontenot never invited other people out to share the professional risks he took; to do that countered every instinct in a bodyguard. Oscar didn't have to be asked twice.

Oscar set his laptop aside and stood up to confront his entourage. "People, listen to me, here's the deal! We have another little roadblock problem ahead." Dismal groans. "Fontenot is on the situation for us. Jimmy, turn on the alarms."

The driver pulled off the road and activated the bus's inbuilt defenses. Oscar gazed briefly at the window. Actually, the campaign bus had no windows. Seen from outside, the bus was a solid shell. Its large internal "windows" were panel screen displays, hooked to external cameras that scoped out their surroundings with pitiless intensity. The Bambakias campaign bus habitually videotaped everything that it perceived. When pressed, the bus also recorded and cataloged everything that it saw, exporting the data by satellite relay to an archival safe house deep in the Rocky Mountains. Alcott Bambakias's campaign bus had been designed and built to be that kind of vehicle.

At the moment, their bus was passively observing two tall green walls of murky pines, and a line of slumping fence posts with corroded barbed wire. They were parked on Interstate Highway 10, ten miles beyond the eldritch postindustrial settlement of Sulphur, Louisiana. Sulphur had attracted a lot of bemused attention from the krewe of staffers as their campaign bus flitted through town. In the curdled fog of winter, the Cajun town seemed to be one giant oil refinery, measled all over with tattered grass shacks and dented trailer homes.

Now the fog had lifted, and on the far side of Sulphur the passing traffic was light.

"I'm going out," Oscar announced, "to assess the local situation."

Donna, his image consultant, brought Oscar a dress shirt. Oscar accepted silk braces, his dress hat, and his Milanese trench coat.

As the stylist ministered to his shoes, Oscar gazed meditatively upon his krewe. Action and fresh air might improve their morale. "Who wants to do some face-time with the U.S. Air Force?"

Jimmy de Paulo leaped from the driver's seat. "Hey, man, I'll go!"

"Jimmy," Oscar said gently, "you can't. We need you to drive this bus."

"Oh yeah," said Jimmy, collapsing crestfallen back into his seat.

Moira Matarazzo sat up reluctantly in her bunk. "Is there some *reason* I should go?" This was Moira's first extensive period off-camera, after months as the campaign's media spokeswoman. The normally meticulous Moira now sported a ratted mess of hair, chapped lips, furry eyebrows, wrinkled cotton pajamas. The evil glitter under her champagne-puffed eyelids could have scared a water moccasin. "Because I *will* go if it's required, but I don't really see why I *should*," Moira whined. "Road-blocks can be *dangerous*."

"Then you should definitely go." This was Bob Argow, the campaign's systems administrator. Bob's level tone made it icily clear that he was nearing the point of emotional detonation. Bob had been drinking steadily ever since the Boston victory celebration. He'd begun his drinking in joyous relief, and as the miles rolled on and the bottles methodically emptied, Bob had plunged into classic post-traumatic depression.

"I'll go with you, Mr. Valparaiso," Norman-the-Intern piped up. As usual, everyone ignored Norman.

The twelve staffers were still officially on salary, mopping up the last of Bambakias's soft campaign money. Officially, they were all taking a richly deserved "vacation." This was a typically generous gesture by Alcott Bambakias, but it was also a situation specifically arranged to gently part the campaign krewe from the vicinity of the new Senator-elect. Back in his ultramodern Cambridge

HQ, the charismatic billionaire was busily assembling an entirely new krewe, the Washington staff that would help him to govern. After months of frenzied team labor and daunting personal sacrifice, the campaigners had been blown off with a check and a hearty handshake.

Oscar Valparaiso had been Bambakias's chief political consultant. He had also been the campaign's Executive Director. From the spoils of victory, Oscar had swiftly won himself a new assignment. Thanks to rapid backstage string-pulling, Oscar had become a brand-new policy analyst for the U.S. Senate Science Committee. Senator Bambakias would soon be serving on that committee.

Oscar possessed goals, a mission, options, tactics, and a future. The other campaign staffers lacked all these things. Oscar knew this. He knew all of these people only too well. During the past eighteen months, Oscar had recruited them, assembled them, paid them, managed them, flattered and cajoled them, welded them into a working unit. He'd rented their office space, overlooked their expense accounts, given them job titles, managed their access to the candidate, even mediated over substance-abuse problems and romantic entanglements. Finally, he'd led them all to victory.

Oscar was still a locus of power, so his krewe was instinctively migrating in his wake. They were "on vacation," professional political operatives hoping for something to turn up. But the esprit de corps in Oscar's entourage had all the tensile strength of a fortune cookie.

Oscar fetched his oxblood-leather shoulder satchel and, after mature consideration, tucked in a small nonlethal spraygun. Yosh Pelicanos, Oscar's majordomo and bagman, passed him a fat debit card. Pelicanos was visibly tired, and still somewhat hungover from the prolonged celebration, but he was up and alert. As Oscar's official second-in-command, Pelicanos always made it a point to be publicly counted on.

"I'll go with you," Pelicanos muttered, hunting for his hat. "Let me get properly dressed."

"You stay, Yosh," Oscar told him quietly. "We're a long way from home. You keep an eye peeled back here."

"I'll get a coffee." Pelicanos yawned, and reflexively clicked on a satellite news feed, erasing a bus window in a gush of networked data. He began hunting for his shoes.

"*I'll* go with you!" Norman insisted brightly. "C'mon, Oscar, let *me* go!" Norman-the-Intern was the campaign's last remaining gofer. The busy Bambakias campaign had once boasted a full three dozen interns, but all of the campaign's other unpaid volunteers had stayed behind in Boston. Norman-the-Intern, however, an MIT college lad, had stuck around like a burr, laboring fanatically and absorbing inhuman levels of abuse. The campaign krewe had brought Norman along with them "on vacation," more through habit than through any conscious decision.

The door opened with a harsh pneumatic pop. Oscar and Norman stepped outside their bus for the first time in four states. After hundreds of hours inside their vehicle, stepping onto earth was like decamping onto another planet. Oscar noted with vague surprise that the highway's patchy shoulders were paved with tons of crunchy oyster shells.

The tall roadside ditchweed was wind-flattened and brownish green. The wind came from the east, bearing the reek of distant sulphur—a bioindustrial reek. A stink like a monster gene-spliced brewery: like rabid bread yeasts eating new-mowed grass. A white V of departing egrets stenciled the cloudy sky overhead. It was late November 2044, and southwest Louisiana was making half-hearted preparations for winter. Clearly this wasn't the kind of winter that anyone from Massachusetts would recognize.

Norman alertly fetched a motorbike from the rack on the back of the bus. The bikes were designed and sold in Cambridge, Massachusetts, and were covered with union labels, antilitigation safety warnings, and software cheatsheet stickers. It was very typical of Bambakias to buy motor bicycles with more onboard smarts than a transcontinental airliner.

Norman hooked up the sidecar, and checked the battery. "No hotdogging," Oscar warned him, clambering into the sidecar and placing his hat in his lap. They tugged on dainty foam helmets, then pulled onto the highway behind a passing electric flatbed.

Norman, as always, drove like a maniac. Norman was young. He had never ridden any motorized device that lacked onboard steering and balance systems. He rode the motorbike with intense lack of physical grace, as if trying to do algebra with his legs.

Dusk began to settle gently over the pines. Traffic was backed up for two kilometers on the east side of the Sabine River bridge. Oscar and Norman buzzed up along the road shoulder, the smart bike and sidecar scrunching over the oyster shells with oozy cybernetic ease. The people trapped within the stalled traffic looked stoic and resigned. The big road professionals—eerie-looking biochemical tankers and big, grimy, malodorous seafood trucks—were already turning and leaving. Roadblocks were a sadly common business these days.

The state of Louisiana's office of tourism maintained a roadside hospitality depot, perched at the riverside just at the state border. The tourist HQ was a touchingly ugly structure of faux-antebellum brick and white columns.

The building had been surrounded with fresh, razor-edged concertina wire. The highway into Texas was thoroughly blockaded with sentry boxes, striped barriers, and nonlethal clusters of glue mines and foam mines.

A huge matte-black military helicopter perched on its skids at the side of the highway, mechanically attentive and deeply bizarre. The black copter lit the tarmac with searing bluish spotlights. The colossal machine was armed to the teeth with great skeletal masses of U.S. Air Force weaponry. The ancient air-to-ground weapons were so insanely complex and archaic that their function was a complete mystery to Oscar. Were they Gatling fléchettes? Particle accelerators? Rayguns of some kind, maybe? They were like some nightmare mix of lamprey fangs and sewing machines.

Within the brilliant frame of helicopter glare, small squads of blue-uniformed Air Force personnel were stopping and confronting the cars attempting to leave Louisiana. The people within the cars, mostly Texan tourists, seemed suitably cowed.

The Air Force people were engaged in an elaborate roadblock shakedown. They were pulling white boxes out of refrigerated trishaws, and confronting travelers with their contents.

Norman-the-Intern was an engineering student. He tore his fascinated gaze from the copters' appalling weaponry. "I thought this was gonna be a party roadblock, more like those cool gypsy bikers back in Tennessee," Norman observed. "Maybe we'd better just get out of here."

"There's Fontenot," Oscar parried.

Fontenot waved them over. His advance vehicle, a sturdy all-terrain electric hummer, was straddling the roadside ditch. The campaign security manager wore a long yellow slicker and muddy jeans.

It was always reassuring to see Fontenot. Fontenot was a former Secret Service agent, a security veteran of presidential caliber. Fontenot knew American Presidents personally. In fact, he had been serving as bodyguard to an ex-President when he had lost his left leg.

"The Air Force flew in around noon," Fontenot informed them, leaning on the padded bumper of his hummer and lowering his binoculars. "Got their glue bombs down, and some crowd-foamers. Plus the sawhorses and the tanglewire."

"So at least they didn't destroy the roadbed?" Norman said.

Fontenot cordially ignored Norman. "They're letting the lane from Texas through with no problems, and they're waving everybody with Louisiana plates right through. There's been no resistance. They're shaking down the out-of-staters as they leave."

"I suppose that makes sense," Oscar said. He put his helmet aside, adjusted his hair with a pocket comb, and donned his hat. Then stepped carefully out of the bike's sidecar, trying not to dirty his shoes. The Louisiana bank of the Sabine was essentially a gigantic marsh.

"Why are they doing this?" Norman said.

"They need the money," Fontenot told him.

"What?" Norman said. "The Air Force?"

"Got no federal funding to pay their power bills at the local air base. Either they pony up, or the utility cuts 'em off."

"The continuing Emergency," Oscar concluded.

Fontenot nodded. "The feds have wanted to decommission that air base for years, but Louisiana's real mulish about it. So Congress wrote 'em out of the Emergency resolutions last March. Kinda dropped a whole air base right through the cracks."

"That's bad. That's really bad. That's *terrible*!" Norman said. "Why can't Congress just have a straight-up vote on the issue? I mean, how hard can it be to close down a military base?"

Fontenot and Oscar exchanged meaningful glances.

"Norman, you had better stay here and mind our vehicles," Oscar said kindly. "Mr. Fontenot and I need a few words with these military gentlemen."

Oscar joined Fontenot as the ex–Secret Service agent limped up the long line of traffic. They were soon out of Norman's earshot. It felt pleasant to be strolling slowly in the open air, where technical eavesdropping was unlikely. Oscar always enjoyed his best conversations when outside of machine surveillance.

"We could just pay them off, y'know," Fontenot said mildly. "It's not the first time we've seen a road-block."

"I don't suppose it's remotely possible that these soldiers might shoot us?"

"Oh no, the Air Force won't shoot us." Fontenot shrugged. "It's nonlethal deployment and all that. It's all political."

"There are circumstances where I would have paid them off," Oscar said. "If we'd lost that campaign, for instance. But we didn't lose. We won. The Senator's in power now. So now, it's the principle."

Fontenot removed his hat, wiped the permanent hat-crease in his forehead, and put the hat back on. "There's another option. I've mapped us an alternate route. We can back off, head north up Highway 109, and still make that lab in Buna by midnight. Save a lot of risk and trouble all around."

"Good idea," Oscar told him, "but let's have a look anyway. I think I can smell an issue here. The Senator always likes issues." People were glaring at the two of them from within the stalled cars. Fontenot was easily passing for a native, but Oscar was drawing resentful and curious stares. Very few people in southwest Louisiana dressed like Beltway political operatives.

"It's a big stinkin' issue all right," Fontenot agreed.

"This local Governor is a real character, isn't he? A stunt like this . . . There must be better ways for a state politician to provoke the feds."

"Green Huey is crazy. But he's the people's kind of crazy, these days. The State of Emergency, the budget crisis—it's no joke down here. People really resent it."

They stopped near the searing glare of the copter lights. An Air Force lieutenant was addressing a pair of daytripping Texan civilians through the open window of the couple's car. The lieutenant was a young woman: she wore a padded blue flight suit, a body-armor vest, and an elaborate flight helmet. The helmet's screen-crowded interior was busily ticking and flashing as it hung from her webbing belt.

The Texan man looked up at her cautiously, through the driver's window. "It's *what*?" he said.

"An Air Force bake sale, sir. Louisiana bake sale. We got your corn bread, your muffuleta bread, croissants, beignets. . . . Maybe some chicory coffee? Ted, we got any of that chicory coffee left?"

"Just made us a fresh carafe," Ted announced loudly, opening the steaming lid of his rickshaw. Ted was heavily armed.

"What do you think?" said the driver to his wife.

"Beignets always get powdered sugar over everything," the Texan woman said indistinctly.

"How much for, uhm, four croissants and two coffees? With cream?"

The lieutenant muttered a canned spiel about "voluntary contributions." The driver retrieved his wallet and silently passed over a debit card. The lieutenant swiftly slotted the card through a cellular reader, relieving the couple of a hefty sum. Then she passed the food through their window. "Y'all take care now," she said, waving them on.

The couple drove away, accelerating rapidly once their car had cleared the line of fire. The lieutenant consulted a handheld readout, and waved through the next three cars, which all bore Louisiana plates. Then she pounced on another tourist.

Fontenot and Oscar edged past the blazing glare of the chopper and made their way toward the commandeered hospitality post. Chest-high tanglewire surrounded the building in a mesh of bright featherweight razors. Sheets of foil and duct tape blacked the building's windows. Military satellite antennas the size of monster birdbaths had been punched through the roof. An armed guard stood at the door.

The guard stopped them. The kid's military-police uniform was oddly rumpled—apparently dug from the bottom of a mildewed duffel bag. The kid looked them over: a well-dressed politico accompanied by his krewe bodyguard. Certainly nothing unusual there. The young soldier scanned them with a detector wand, failing to notice Oscar's all-plastic spraygun, and then addressed himself to Oscar. "ID, sir?"

Oscar passed over a gleaming dossier chip embossed with a federal Senate seal.

Four minutes later, they were ushered inside the building. There were two dozen armed men and women inside the hospitality suite. The intruders had shoved the furniture against the walls, and staked out the doors and windows. Muffled thuds, scrapes, and crunches emanated from the ceiling, as if the attic were infested with giant, armed raccoons.

The original staffers from the Louisiana tourist office were still inside the building. The hospitality krewe were well-dressed middle-aged Southern ladies, with done hair and ribbons, and nice skirts and flats. The ladies had not been arrested or formally detained, but they had been crowded together into a dismal corner of their foil-darkened office, and they looked understandably distressed.

The commanding Air Force officer was dead drunk. Oscar and Fontenot were greeted by the public relations officer. The PR man was also plastered.

The central office was crammed with portable military command-post gear, an overjammed closet full of stencils, khaki, and flickering screens. The place reeked of spilled whiskey; the commanding officer, still in full dress uniform including his spit-polished shoes, was sprawled on a khaki cot. His visored and braided hat half concealed his face.

The PR officer, a chunky, uniformed veteran with

graying hair and seamed cheeks, was busy at a set of consoles. The pegboard counters trailed fat tangles of military fiber-optic cable.

"How may I help you gentlemen?" the PR officer said.

"I need to move a bus through," said Oscar. "A campaign bus."

The officer blinked, his eyelids rising at two different instants. His voice was steady, but he was very drunk. "Can't you fellas just buy a little something from our nice little Air Force bake sale?"

"I'd like to oblige you there, but under the circumstances, it would look . . ." Oscar mulled it over. "Insensitive."

The PR officer lightly tapped Oscar's gleaming dossier card on the edge of his console bench. "Well, maybe you should think that over, mister. It's a long way back to Boston."

Fontenot spoke up. Fontenot was good-copping it, being very sane and reasonable. "If you just suspended your operations for half an hour or so, the traffic backlog would clear right up. Our vehicle would slip right through."

"I suppose that's an option," the officer said. One of his screens stopped churning, and uttered a little triumphant burst of martial brass. The PR man examined the results. "Whoa. . . . You're the son of Logan Valparaiso!"

Oscar nodded, restraining a sigh. A good netsearch program was guaranteed to puncture your privacy, but you could never predict its angle of attack beforehand.

"I knew your dad!" the PR officer declared. "I interviewed him when he starred in the remake of *El Mariachi*."

"You don't say." The computer had spewed up a bit of common ground for them. It was a cheap stunt, a party trick, but like a lot of psychological operations techniques, it worked pretty well. The three of them were no longer strangers.

"How is your ol' dad these days?"

"Unfortunately, Logan Valparaiso died back in '42. A heart attack."

"That's a shame." The officer snapped his pudgy fingers in regret. "He sure made some great action films."

"Dad took a lower profile in his later life," Oscar said. "He went into real estate." They were both lying. The films, though hugely popular, had been very bad. The later real-estate deals had been money-laundering cover for his father's Hollywood backers: émigré Colombian mafiosi.

"Could you temporarily relocate those barricades for us?" Fontenot asked gently.

"I'll let you fellas in on something," the man said. His screens were still churning away, but the three of them were all cozy now. They were swapping net-gossip, trading little confidences. You didn't shoot someone when you knew that his dad was a movie star. "We're almost done with this deployment anyhow."

Oscar lifted his brows. "Really. That's good news."

"I'm just running a few battlespace awareness scans. . . . Y'know, the problem with infowar isn't getting *into* the systems. It's getting *out of them* without collateral damage. So if you'll just be patient, we'll be packing up and lifting off before you know it."

The commander groaned in drunken nausea, and thrashed on his cot. The public relations officer hurried to his superior's side, tenderly adjusting his rough blanket and inflatable pillow. He then returned, having snagged a bottle of the commander's bourbon from beneath the cot. He absently decanted an inch or so into a paper cup, studying his nearest screen.

"You were saying?" Oscar prompted.

"Battlespace awareness. That's the key to rapid deployment. We have surveillance drones over the highway, checking car licenses. We input the licenses into this database here, run credit scans and marketing profiles, pick out the people likely to make generous financial contributions without any fuss. . . ." The officer looked up. "So you might call this an alternative, decentralized, tax-base scheme."

Oscar glanced at Fontenot. "Can they do that?"

"Sure, it's doable," Fontenot said. Fontenot was ex–Secret Service. The USSS had always been very up to speed on these issues.

The PR man laughed bitterly. "That's what the Governor likes to call it. . . . Look, this is just a standard infowar operation, the stuff we used to do overseas all the time. Fly in, disrupt vital systems, low or zero casualties, achieve the mission objective. Then we just vanish, all gone, forget about it. Turn the page."

"Right," said Fontenot. "Just like Second Panama."

"Hey," the officer said proudly, "I was *in* Second Panama! That was classic netwar! We took down the local regime just by screwing with their bitstreams. No fatalities! Never a shot fired!"

"It's really good when there are no fatalities." Fontenot flexed his false leg with a squeak.

"Had to quit my TV news work after that, though. Blew my cover. Very long story really." Their host slurped at his paper cup and looked extremely sad. "You guys need a bourbon?"

"You bet we do!" Oscar said. "Thanks a lot!" He accepted a paper cup brimming with yellow booze, and pretended to sip at it. Oscar never drank alcohol. He had seen it kill people in slow and terrible ways.

"When exactly do you plan to relocate?" Fontenot said, accepting his cup with a ready Eisenhower grin.

"Oh, nineteen hundred hours. Maybe. That's what the commander had in mind this morning."

"Your commander looks a bit tired," Oscar said.

That remark made the PR man angry. He put down

his bourbon and looked at Oscar with eyes like two shucked oysters. "Yeah. That's right. My commander is tired. He broke his sworn oath of allegiance, and he's robbing U.S. citizens, the people he swore to protect. That tends to tire you out."

Oscar listened attentively.

"Y'know, the commander here was given no choice. No choice at all. It was pull this stunt, or watch his people starving in their barracks. There's no funding now. There's no fuel, no pay for the troops, no equipment, there is *nothing*. All because you silk-suit sons of bitches in Washington can't get it together to pass a budget."

"My man just got to Washington," Oscar said. "We need a chance."

"*My* man here is a decorated officer! He was in Panama Three, Iraq Two, he was in Rwanda! He's no politician—he's a goddamn national hero! Now the feds are cracking up, and the Governor's gone crazy, but the commander, he'll be the fall guy for this. When it's all over, he'll be the man who has to pay for everything. The committees will break him in half."

Oscar was calm. "That's why I have to work in Washington."

"What's your party?"

"Senator Bambakias was elected with a thirty-eight percent plurality," Oscar said. "He isn't tied to any single party doctrine. He has multipartisan appeal."

The PR man snorted. "What's your party, I said."

"Federal Democrat."

"Aw Jesus." The man ducked his head and waved one hand. "Go home, Yankee. Go get a life."

"We were just leaving," Fontenot said, putting aside his untouched bourbon. "You happen to know a good local restaurant? A Cajun place, I mean? It has to seat a dozen of us."

The young guard at the door saluted politely as they left the hospitality building. Oscar carefully slipped his federal ID back into his eelskin wallet. He waited until they were well out of earshot before he spoke. "He may be dead drunk, but that guy sure knows the local restaurants."

"Journalists always remember these things," Fontenot said wisely. "Y'know something? I *know* that guy. I met him once, at Battledore's in Georgetown. He was doing lunch with the Vice President at the time. I can't remember his name now for the life of me, but that's his face all right. He was a big-name foreign correspondent once, a big wheel on the old TV cable nets. That was before they outed him as a U.S. infowar spook."

Oscar considered this. As a political consultant, he had naturally come to know many journalists. He had also met a certain number of spooks. Journalists certainly had their uses in the power game, but spooks had always struck him as a malformed and not very bright subspecies of political consultant. "Did you happen to tape that little discussion we just had?"

"Yeah," Fontenot admitted. "I generally do that. Especially when I'm dead sure that the other guy is also taping it."

"Good man," Oscar said. "I'll be skimming the highlights of that conversation and passing them on to the Senator."

Oscar and Fontenot's relations during the campaign had always been formal and respectful. Fontenot was twice Oscar's age, canny, and paranoid, always entirely and utterly serious about assuring the physical safety of the candidate. With the campaign safely behind them, though, Fontenot had clearly been loosening. Now he seemed inspired by a sudden attack of sincerity. "Would you like a little advice? You don't have to listen, if you don't want to."

"You know I always listen to your advice, Jules."

Fontenot looked at him. "You want to be Bambakias's chief of staff in Washington."

Oscar shrugged. "Well, I never denied that. Did I ever deny it?"

"Stick with your Senate committee job, instead. You're a clever guy, and I think maybe you could accomplish something in Washington. I've seen you run those hopeless goofballs in your krewe like they were a crack army, so I just know you could handle a Senate committee. And something's just *gotta get done*." Fontenot looked at Oscar with genuine pain. "America has lost it. We can't get a grip. Goddammit, just *look at all this*! Our country's up on blocks."

"I want to help Bambakias. He has ideas."

"Bambakias can give a good speech, but he's never lived a day inside the Beltway. He doesn't even know what that means. The guy's an architect."

"He's a very clever architect."

Fontenot grunted. "He wouldn't be the first guy who mistook intelligence for political smarts."

"Well, I suppose the Senator's ultimate success depends on his handlers. The Senate krewe, the entourage. His staff." Oscar smiled. "Look, I didn't hire you, you know. *Bambakias* hired you. The man can make good staff decisions. All he needs is a chance."

Fontenot flipped up his yellow coat collar. It had begun to drizzle.

Oscar spread his manicured hands. "I'm only twenty-eight years old. I don't have the necessary track record to become a Senator's chief of staff. And besides, I'm about to have my hands full with this Texas science assignment."

"And besides," Fontenot mimicked, "there's your little personal background problem."

Oscar blinked. It always gave him an ugly moment of vertigo to hear that matter mentioned aloud. Naturally Fontenot knew all about the "personal background problem." Fontenot made knowing such things his business. "You don't hold that problem against me, I hope."

"No." Fontenot lowered his voice. "I might have. I'm an old man, I'm old-fashioned. But I've seen you at work, so I know you better now." He thumped his artificial leg against the ground. "That's not why I'm leaving you, Oscar. But I am leaving. The campaign's over, you won. You won big. I've done a lot of campaigns in my day, and I really think yours may have been the prettiest I ever saw. But now I'm back home to the bayous, and it's time for me to leave the business. Forever. I'm gonna see your convoy safely through to Buna, then I'm outta here."

"I respect that decision, I truly do," Oscar said. "But I'd prefer it if you stayed on with us—temporarily. The krewe respects your professional judgment. And the Buna situation might need your security skills." Oscar drew a breath, then started talking with more focus and intensity. "I haven't exactly broken this to our boys and girls on the bus, but I've been scoping out the Buna situation. And this delightful Texas vacation retreat that's our destination tonight—basically, it looks to me like a major crisis waiting to happen."

Fontenot shook his head. "I'm not in the market for a major crisis. I've been looking forward to retirement. I'm gonna fish, I'm gonna hunt a little. I'm gonna get myself a shack in the bayou that has a stove and a fryin' pan, and no goddamn nets or telephones, ever, ever again."

"I can make it worth your while," Oscar coaxed. "Just a month, all right? Four weeks till the Christmas holidays. You're still on salary, as long as you're with us. I can double that if I have to. Another month's pay."

Fontenot wiped rain from his hat brim. "You can do that?"

"Well, not directly, not from the campaign funds, but Pelicanos can handle it for us. He's a wizard at that sort of thing. Two months' salary for one month's work. And at Boston rates, too. That might swing the earnest money on your standard bayou shack."

Fontenot was weakening. "Well, you'll have to let me think that over."

"You can have weekends."

"Really?"

"Three-day weekends. Since you're looking for a place to live."

Fontenot sighed. "Well . . ."

"Audrey and Bob wouldn't mind doing some real-estate scanning for you. They're world-class oppo research people, and they're just killing time out here. So why should you get taken in a house deal? They can scare you up a dream home, and even a decent real-estate agent."

"Damn. I never thought of that angle. That's true, though. That could be worth a lot to me. It'd save me a lot of trouble. All right, I'll do it."

They shook hands.

They had reached their vehicles. There was no sign of Norman-the-Intern, however. Fontenot stood up on the dented hood of his hummer, his prosthetic leg squeaking with the effort, and finally spotted Norman with his binoculars.

Norman was talking with some Air Force personnel. They were clustered together under the sloping roof of a concrete picnic table, next to a wooden walkway that led into the cypress-haunted depths of the Sabine River swamp. "Should I fetch him for you?" Fontenot said.

"I'll get him," Oscar said. "I brought him. You can call Pelicanos back at the bus, and brief the krewe on the situation."

Young people were a distinct minority in contemporary America. Like most minorities, they tended to fraternize. Norman was young enough to be of military age. He was leaning against a graffiti-etched picnic roof support and haranguing the soldiers insistently.

". . . radar-transparent flying drones with X-ray lasers!" Norman concluded decisively.

"Well, maybe we have those, and maybe we don't," drawled a young man in blue.

"Look, it's common knowledge you have them. It's like those satellites that read license plates from orbit—they're yesterday's news, you've had 'em for a zillion years. So my point is: given that technical capacity, why don't you just *take care* of this Governor of Louisiana? Spot his motorcade with drone telephotos, and follow him around. When you see him wander out of the car a little ways, you just zap him."

A young woman spoke up. " 'Zap' Governor Huguelet?"

"I don't mean kill him. That would be too obvious. I mean *vaporize* him. Just *evaporate* the guy! Shoes, suit, the works! They'd think he's like . . . you know . . . off in some hotel chewing the feet of some hooker."

It took the Air Force people some time to evaluate this proposal. The concept was clearly irritating them. "You can't evaporate a whole human body with an airborne X-ray laser."

"You could if it was tunable."

"Tunable free-electron lasers aren't radar-transparent. Besides, their power demand is out the roof."

"Well, you could collate four or five separate aircraft into one overlapping fire zone. Besides, who needs clunky old free electrons when there are quantum-pitting bandgaps? Bandgaps are plenty tunable."

"Sorry to interrupt," Oscar said. "Norman, we're needed back at the bus now."

The Air Force girl stared at Oscar, slowly taking him in, from perfect hat to shiny shoes. "Who's the suit?"

"He's . . . well, he's with the U.S. Senate." Norman smiled cheerily. "Really good friend of mine."

Oscar put a gentle hand on Norman's shoulder. "We

need to move along, Norman. We've just made a group reservation at a great Cajun restaurant."

Norman tagged along obediently. "Will they let me drink there?"

"Laissez les bon temps rouler," Oscar said.

"Those were nice kids," Norman announced. "I mean, roadblockers and all, but basically, they're just really nice American kids."

"They're American military personnel who are engaging in highway robbery."

"Yeah. That's true. It's bad. It's really too bad. Y'know? They're stuck in the military, so they just don't think politically."

They crossed the Texas border in the clammy thick of the night. The krewe was glutted with hot baked shrimp and batter-fried alligator tail, topped with seemingly endless rounds of blendered hurricanes and flaming brandied coffees. The food at the Cajun casinos was epic in scope. They even boasted a convenient special rate for tour buses.

It had been a very good idea to stop and eat. Oscar could sense that the mood of his miniature public had shifted radically. The krewe had really enjoyed themselves. They'd been repeatedly informed that they were in the state of Louisiana, but now they could feel that fact in their richly clotted bloodstreams.

This wasn't Boston anymore. This was no longer the sordid tag end of the Massachusetts campaign. They were living in an interregnum, and maybe, somehow, if you only believed, in the start of something better. Oscar could not feel bad about his life. It was not a normal life and it never had been, but it offered very interesting challenges. He was rising to the next challenge. How bad could life be? At least they were all well fed.

Except for hardworking Jimmy the driver, who was paid specifically not to drink himself senseless, Oscar was the last person awake inside the bus. Oscar was almost always the last to sleep, as well as the first to wake. Oscar rarely slept at all. Since the age of six, he had customarily slept for about three hours a night.

As a small child, he would simply lay silently in darkness during those long extra hours of consciousness, quietly plotting how to manage the mad vagaries of his adoptive Hollywood parents. Surviving the Valparaiso household's maelstrom of money, drugs, and celebrity had required a lot of concentrated foresight.

In his later life, Oscar had put his night-owl hours to further good use: first, the Harvard MBA. Then the biotechnology start-up, where he'd picked up his long-time accountant and finance man, Yosh Pelicanos, and also his faithful scheduler/receptionist, Lana Ramachandran. He'd kept the two of them on through the cash-out of his first company, and on through the thriving days of venture capital on Route 128. Business strongly suited Oscar's talents and proclivities, but he had nevertheless moved on swiftly, into political party activism. A successful and innovative Boston city council campaign had brought him to the attention of Alcott Bambakias. The U.S. Senate campaign then followed. Politics had become the new career. The challenge. The cause.

So Oscar was awake in darkness, and working. He generally ended each day with a diary annotation, a summary of the options taken and important operational events. Tonight, he wrapped up his careful annotations of the audiotape with the Air Force highway bandits. He shipped the file to Alcott Bambakias, encrypted and denoted "personal and confidential." There was no way to know if this snippet of the modern chaos in Louisiana would capture his patron's mercurial attention. But it was necessary to keep up a steady flow of news and counsel across the net. To be out of the Senator's sight might be very useful in some ways, but to drift out of his mind would be a professional blunder.

Oscar composed and sent a friendly net-note to his girlfriend, Clare, who was living in his house in Boston. He studied and updated his personnel files. He examined and totaled the day's expenditures. He composed his daily diary entries. He took comfort in the strength of his routines.

He had met many passing setbacks, but he had yet to meet a challenge that could conclusively defeat him.

He shut his laptop with a sense of satisfaction, and prepared himself for sleep. He twitched, he thrashed. Finally he sat up, and opened his laptop again.

He studied the Worcester riot video for the fifty-second time.

2

The scientist wore plaid bermuda shorts, a faded yellow tank top, flip-flop sandals, and no hat. Oscar was prepared to tolerate their guide's bare and bony legs, and even his fusty beard. But it was hard to take a man entirely seriously when he lacked a proper hat.

The beast in question was dark green, very fibrous, and hairy. This was a binturong, a mammal once native to Southeast Asia, long since extinct in the wild. This specimen had been cloned on-site at the Buna National Collaboratory. They'd grown it inside the altered womb of a domestic cow.

The cloned binturong was hanging from the underside of a park bench, clinging to the wooden slats. It was licking at paint chips, with a narrow, spotted tongue. The binturong was about the size of a well-stuffed golf bag.

"Your specimen is remarkably tame," said Pelicanos politely, holding his hat in his hand.

The scientist shook his bearded head. "Oh, we never claim that we 'tame' animals here at the Collaboratory. He's been de-feralized. But he's not what you'd call friendly."

The binturong detached itself from the bench slats and trundled through the lush grass on its bearlike paws.

The beast examined Oscar's leather shoes, lifted its pointed snout in disgust, and muttered like a maladjusted kettle. At such close and intimate range, the nature of the animal became more apparent to Oscar. A binturong was akin to a weasel. A large, tree-climbing weasel. With a hairy, prehensile tail. Also, it stank.

"We seem to be in the market for a binturong," Oscar said, smiling. "Do you wrap them up in brown paper?"

"If you mean how do we get this sample specimen to your friend the Senator . . . well, we can do that through channels."

Oscar arched his brows. " 'Channels'?"

"Channels, you know . . . Senator Dougal had his people handling that sort of thing. . . ." Their guide trailed off, suddenly guilty and jittery, as if he'd drunk the last of the office coffee and neglected to change the pot. "Look, I'm just a lab guy, I don't really know much about that. You should ask the people at Spinoffs."

Oscar unfolded his laminated pocket map of the Buna National Collaboratory. "And where would 'Spinoffs' be?"

The guide tapped helpfully at Oscar's plastic map. His hands were stained with chemicals and his callused thumb was a nice dull green. "Spinoffs was the building just on your left as you drove in through the main airlock."

Oscar squinted at the map's fine print. "The Archer Parr Memorial Competitive Enhancement Facility?"

"Yeah, that's the place. Spinoffs."

Oscar gazed upward, adjusting the brim of his hat against the Texas sun. A huge nexus of interlocking struts cut the sky overhead, like the exoskeleton of a monster diatom. The distant struts were great solid stony beams, holding greenhouse panes of plastic the size of hockey rinks. The federal lab had been funded, created, and built in an age when recombinant DNA had been considered as dangerous as nuclear power plants. The dome of the Buna National Collaboratory had been designed to survive tornadoes, hurricanes, earthquakes, a saturation bombing.

"I've never been in a sealed environment so large it required its own map," Oscar said.

"You get used to it." Their guide shrugged. "You get used to the people who live in here, and even the cafeteria food. . . . The Collaboratory gets to be home, if you stay in here long enough." Their guide scratched at his furry jaw. "Except for East Texas, outside the airlocks there. A lot of people never get used to East Texas."

"We really appreciate your demo-ing the local livestock for us," said Pelicanos. "It was good of you to spare us the time from your busy research schedule."

The zoologist reached eagerly for his belt phone. "You want me to call back your little minder from Public Relations?"

"No," said Oscar suavely, "since she was kind enough to pass us on to you, I think we'll just make our own way around here from now on."

The scientist brandished his antique and clunky federal-issue phone, which was covered with smudgy green thumbprints. "Do you need a lift to Spinoffs? I could call you a buggy."

"We'll stretch our legs a bit," Pelicanos demurred.

"You've been very helpful, Dr. Parkash." Oscar never forgot a name. There was no particular reason to remember the name of Dr. Averill Parkash, among the BNC's two thousand federal researchers and their many assorted gofers, hucksters, krewepeople, and other associated hangers-on. Oscar knew, though, that he would soon accumulate the names, the faces, and the dossiers of no end of the local personnel. It was worse than a habit. He truly couldn't help himself.

Their guide sidled backward toward the Animal Management Center, clearly eager to return to his cramped and spotty little office. Oscar waved a dismissal with a cheery smile.

Parkash tried a final yelp. "There's a pretty good

wine bar nearby! Across the road from Flux NMR and Instrumentation!"

"That's great advice! We appreciate that! Thanks a lot!" Oscar turned on his heel and headed for a nearby wall of trees. Pelicanos quickly followed him.

Soon they were safely lost in the tall cover. Oscar and Pelicanos made their way along a crooked, squelchy, peat-moss path through a cut-and-paste jungle. The Collaboratory boasted huge botanical gardens—whole minor forests, really—of rare specimens. The threatened. The endangered. The all-but-technically extinct. Wildlife native to habitats long obliterated by climate change, rising seas, bulldozers, and the urban sprawl of 8.1 billion human beings.

The plants and animals were all clones. Deep in the bedrocked stronghold of the Collaboratory's National Genome Preservation Center lurked tens of thousands of genetic samples, garnered from around the planet. The precious DNA was neatly racked in gleaming flasks of liquid nitrogen, secured in a bureaucratic maze of endless machine-carved limestone vaults.

It was considered wise to thaw out a few bits from the tissue samples every once in a while, and to use these bits to produce full-grown organisms. This practice established that the genetic data was still viable. Generally, the resultant living creatures were also nicely photogenic. The clones were a useful public relations asset. Now that biotechnology had left the hermetic realm of the arcane to become standard everyday industries, the Collaboratory's makeshift zoo was its best political showpiece.

The monster underground vaults were always first on the list for the victims of local tourism, but Oscar had found their Kafkaesque density oppressive. However, he found himself quite enjoying the local jungle. Genuine wilderness generally bored him, but there was something very modern and appealing about this rational, urbanized, pocket version of nature. The housebroken global green-

ery coruscated like Christmas trees with drip taps, sap
samplers, and hormone squirters. Trees and shrubs basked
like drunken tourists in their own private growlights.

According to their handy pocket maps, Oscar and
Pelicanos were now in a mix-and-match jungle bordered
by the Animal Engineering Lab, the Atmospheric Chem-
istry Lab, the Animal Management Center, and a very
elaborate structure that was the Collaboratory's garbage
treatment plant. None of these rambling federal buildings
were visible from within the potted forest—except, of
course, for the brutal, fortresslike towers of the Contain-
ment Facility. This gigantic Hot Zone was the massive
central buttress for the Collaboratory's dome. Its glazed
cylindrical shoulders were always visible inside the dome,
gleaming like a mighty acreage of fine china.

The probability of listening devices seemed rather
low here inside the mechanical forest. They could talk in
confidence, if they kept moving.

"I thought we'd never lose that geek," Pelicanos
said.

"You have something you need to tell me, Yosh?"

Pelicanos sighed. "I want to know when we're going
home again."

Oscar smiled. "We just got here. Don't you like
these Texas folks? They sure are mighty friendly."

"Oscar, you brought twelve people in your entourage. The locals don't even have the dorm rooms to put us
up properly."

"But I need twelve people. I need all of my krewe. I
need to keep my options open here."

Pelicanos grunted in surprise as a spined and cloven-
hoofed beast—some kind of tapir, maybe?—scampered
across their path. Rare beasts from aardwolves to zebu had
the general run of the Collaboratory. They were com-
monly sighted ambling harmlessly through the streets and
gardens, like dope-stricken sacred cows.

"You arranged a few extras after the campaign,"

Pelicanos said. "Well, Bambakias can certainly afford that, and they appreciate the gesture. But political campaigners are temp workers by nature. You just don't need them anymore. You can't need twelve people to put together a Senate committee report."

"But they're useful! Don't you enjoy their services? We have a bus, a driver, our own security, we even have a masseuse! We're living in high style. Besides, they might as well be washed up here in Wonderland as washed up anywhere else."

"Those aren't real answers."

Oscar looked at him. "This isn't like you, Yosh. . . . You're missing Sandra."

"Yeah," Pelicanos admitted. "I miss my wife."

Oscar waved his hand airily. "So, then take a three-day weekend. Fly back to Beantown. You deserve that, we can afford it. Go see Sandra. See how she is."

"All right. I guess I'll do that. I'll fly out and see Sandra." And Pelicanos cheered up. Oscar saw his spirits lift; it came across the man in a little visible wave. Strange business, but Pelicanos had just become happy. Despite the stark fact that his wife was in a mental institution, and had been there for nine years.

Pelicanos was an excellent organizer, a fine accountant, a bookkeeper of near genius, and yet his personal life was an abysmal tragedy. Oscar found this intensely interesting. It appealed to the deepest element in Oscar, his ravenous curiosity about human beings and the tactics and strategies by which they could be coaxed and compelled to behave. Yosh Pelicanos made his way through his life seemingly just like any other man, and yet he always carried this secret half-ton burden on his shoulders. Pelicanos truly knew the meaning of devotion and loyalty.

Oscar himself had no particular acquaintance with either devotion or loyalty, but he'd trained himself to recognize these qualities in others. It was no accident that Pelicanos was Oscar's oldest and longest-lasting employee.

Pelicanos lowered his voice. "But before I go, Oscar, I need you to do me a little favor. I need you to tell me what you're up to. Level with me."

"You know that I always level with you, Yosh."

"Well, try it one more time."

"Very well." Oscar walked beneath a tall green arch of pink-flowered pinnate fronds. "You see: here's our situation. I enjoy politics. The game seems to suit me."

"That's not news, boss."

"You and I, we just ran our second political campaign, and we got our man elected Senator. That's a big accomplishment. A federal Senate seat is the political big time, by anybody's standard."

"Yes it is. And?"

"And for all our pains, we're back in the political wilderness again." Oscar knocked a reeking branch from his jacket shoulder. "You think Mrs. Bambakias really wants some goddamn rare animal? I get a voice call at six in the morning, from the new chief of staff. He tells me the Senator's wife is very interested in my current assignment, and she would like to have her own exotic pet animal, please. But *she* doesn't call me—and Bambakias doesn't call me—Leon Sosik calls me."

"Right."

"The guy is sandbagging me."

Pelicanos nodded sagely. "Look, Sosik knows full well that you want his job."

"Yeah. He knows that. So he's checking on me, to make sure I'm really out here doing my time in Backwater, Texas. And then he has the nerve to give me this little errand, to boot. It's a no-lose proposition for Sosik. If I refuse him a favor, I'm being a jerk. If I blow it or get in trouble, then he runs me down for that. And if I succeed, then he takes my credit."

"Sosik knows infighting. He's spent years on the Hill. Sosik's a professional."

"Yes, he is. And in his book, we're just beginners.

But we're going to win this one anyway. You know how? It's going to be just like the campaign was. First, we're going to lowball expectations, because nobody will really believe that we have a serious chance here. But then we're going to succeed on such a level—we're going to exceed expectations to such a huge extent—we're gonna bring so much firepower onto this campaign that we just blow the opposition away."

Pelicanos smiled. "That's you all over, Oscar."

Oscar lifted one finger. "Here's the plan. We find the major players here, and we find out what they want, and we cut deals. We get our people excited, and we get their people confused. And in the end, we just out-organize anyone who tries to stop us. We just outwork them, and we swarm on them from angles they would never expect, and we never, ever stop, and we just beat them into the ground!"

"Sounds like a big job."

"Yes, it is, but I've brought enough people for a big job. They've proved they can work together politically. They're creative, they're clever, and every last one of them owes me a lot of favors. So you think I can get away with this?"

"You're asking me?" Pelicanos said, spreading his hands. "Hell, Oscar, I'm always game. You know that." And he permitted himself a merry little laugh.

The Collaboratory's aging dorms offered sadly grim hospitality. Dorm space was in high demand, because the federal lab hosted endless numbers of scholastic gypsies, contractors on the make, and various exotic species of para-scientific bureaucrats. The dorms were flimsy two-story structures, with common baths and common kitchens. The rooms had basic-brown federal pasteboard furniture, some scrappy little sheets and towels. The dorm's card-swipe doorlocks ran off Collaboratory ID cards. Presumably, these smart cards and smart doorlocks compiled automatic dossiers of everyone's daily ins and outs, for the benefit of the local security creeps.

There was no weather under the great lozenge-shaped dome. The entire gigantic structure was basically a monster intensive-care ward, all mobile shutters and glaring lights and vast air-sucking zeolite filters, with a constant thrum of deeply buried generators. The Collaboratory's biotech labs were constructed like forts. The personal residences, by stark contrast, lacked serious walls, roofs, or insulation. The flimsy dorms were small, tightly packed, and noisy.

So, for the sake of peace and quiet, Donna Nunez was doing her mending and darning on the wooden benches outside the Occupational Safety building. Donna had brought her sewing basket and a selection of the krewe's clothing. Oscar had brought along his laptop. He disliked working inside his dorm room, since he felt instinctive certainty that the place was bugged.

The Occupational Safety edifice was one of nine buildings on the central ring road circling the shiny china ramparts of the Hot Zone. The Hot Zone was surrounded by large pie-wedge plots of experimental gene-spliced crops: saltwater-sucking sorghum, and rampaging rice, plus a few genetically bastardized blueberries. The circular fields were themselves surrounded by a little two-lane road. This ring road was the major traffic artery within the Collaboratory dome, so it was an excellent place to sit and observe the quaint customs of the locals.

"I really don't mind a bit about those stinking, lousy dorm rooms," Donna remarked sweetly. "It feels and smells so lovely under this big dome. We could live outside the buildings if we wanted. We could just wander around naked, like the animals."

Donna reached out and patted an animal on the head. Oscar gave the creature a long look. The specimen stared back at him fearlessly, its bulging black eyes as

blankly suggestive as a Ouija board. The de-feralization
process, a spin-off of the Collaboratory's flourishing neural research, had left all the local animals in some strangely
altered state of liquid detachment.

This particular specimen looked as eager and healthy
as a model on a cereal box; its tusks were caries-free, its
spiky fur seemed moussed. Nevertheless, Oscar felt a very
strong intuition that the animal would take enormous
pleasure in killing and eating him. This was the animal's
primary impulse in their brief relationship. Somehow, it
had lost the will to follow through.

"Do you happen to know the name of this creature?" Oscar asked her.

Donna carefully stroked the animal's long, wrinkled
snout. It grunted in ecstasy and extruded a horrid gray
tongue. "Maybe it's a pig?"

"That's not a pig."

"Well, whatever it is, I think it likes me. It's been
following me around all morning. It's cute, isn't it? It's
ugly, but it's cute-ugly. . . . The animals here never hurt
anyone. They did something weird to them. To their
brains or something."

"Oh yes." Oscar tapped a key. In rapidity and silence, his laptop collated a huge series of Collaboratory
purchase orders with five years' worth of public-domain
Texas arrest records. The results looked very intriguing.

"Are you going to get an exotic animal for Mrs.
Bambakias?"

"After the weekend. Pelicanos is back in Boston,
Fontenot is out house hunting with Bob and Audrey. . . . Right now, I'm just trying to get some of the
local records in order." Oscar shrugged.

"I liked her, you know? Mrs. Bambakias? I liked
dressing her for the campaign. She was really elegant, and
nice to me. I thought she might take me to Washington.
But I just don't fit in there."

"Why not?" Oscar deftly twitched a fingertip and

activated a search engine, which sought out a state-federal coordination center in Baton Rouge, and retrieved the records of recent pardons and grants of clemency issued by the Governor of Louisiana.

"Well . . . I'm too old, you know? I worked for a bank for twenty years. I didn't start tailoring until after the hyperinflation."

Oscar tagged four hits for further investigation. "I think you're selling yourself short. I never heard Mrs. Bambakias mention your age."

Donna shook her graying head ruefully. "Young women nowadays, they're much better at the new economy. They're really trained for personal image services. They like being in a krewe; they like dressing the principal and doing her hair and her shoes. They make a real career of service work. Lorena Bambakias will want to entertain. She'll need people who can dress her for Washington, for the Georgetown crowd."

"But you dress us. Look at the way we dress compared to these local people."

"You don't understand," Donna said patiently. "These scientists dress like slobs, because they can get away with that."

Oscar examined a passing local, riding a bike with his shirt hanging out. He wore no socks and tattered shoes. No hat. His hair was dreadful. No one could possibly dress that badly by accident.

"I take your point," Oscar said.

Donna was in a confessional mood. Oscar had sensed this. He generally made it a point to appear in the lives of his entourage whenever they were confessing. "Life is so ironic," Donna sighed, ironically. "I used to hate it when my mother taught me how to sew. I went off to college, I never imagined I'd hand-make clothes as an image consultant. When I was young, nobody wanted handmade tailoring. My ex-husband would have laughed his head off if I'd made him a suit."

"How *is* your ex-husband, Donna?"

"He still thinks real people work nine-to-five jobs. He's an idiot." She paused. "Also, he's fired, and he's broke."

Men and women in white decontamination suits had appeared amid the genetically upgraded crops. They were wielding shiny aluminum spray-wands, gleaming chromium shears, high-tech titanium hoes.

"I love it inside here," Donna said. "The Senator was so sweet to dump us in here. It's so much nicer than I thought it would be. The air smells so unusual, have you noticed that? I could live in a place like this, if there weren't so many slobs in cutoffs."

Oscar hotlinked back to the minutes of the Senate Science and Technology Committee for 2029. These sixteen-year-old volumes of committee minutes had the works on the original founding of the Buna National Collaboratory. Oscar felt quite sure that no one had closely examined these archives for ages. They were chock-full of hidden pay dirt. "It was a hard-fought campaign. It's right to relax for a while. You certainly deserve it."

"Yeah, the campaign wore me out, but it was worth it. We really worked well together; we were well organized. You know, I love political work. I'm an American female in the fifty-to-seventy demographic, so life never made any sense to me. Nothing ever turned out the way I was taught to expect. Ever since the economy crashed and the nets ate up everything . . . But inside politics, it all feels so different. I'm not just a straw in the wind. I really felt like I was changing the world, for once. Instead of the world changing me."

Oscar bent a kindly gaze upon her. "You did a good job, Donna. You're an asset. When you're in close quarters like we were, under so much stress and pressure, it's good to have a member of the team who's so even-tempered, so levelheaded. Philosophical, even." He smiled winningly.

"Why are you being so good to me, Oscar? Aren't you about to fire me now?"

"Not at all! I want you to stay on with us. At least another month. I know that isn't much to promise you, since a woman of your talents could easily find some more permanent position. But Fontenot will be staying on with us."

"He will?" She blinked. "Why?"

"And of course Pelicanos and Lana Ramachandran and I will be plugging away. . . . So there will be work for you here. Not like the campaign was, of course, nothing so intense or hectic, but proper image is still very important to us. Even here. Maybe especially here."

"I might stay on with you awhile," Donna said serenely, "but I wasn't born yesterday. So you'd better tell me something better than that."

Oscar slapped his laptop shut, and stood up. "Donna, you're right. We should talk seriously. Let's go for a little stroll."

Donna quickly closed her sewing basket and got to her feet. She'd come to know Oscar's basic routines, and was pleased to be out with him on one of his confidential walking conferences. Oscar was touched to see her being so streetwise—she kept glancing alertly over her shoulder, as if expecting to find them trailed by sinister operatives in black trench coats.

"You see, it's like this," Oscar told her soberly. "We won that election, and we won it walking away. But Alcott Bambakias is still a newcomer, a political outsider. Even after he's sworn into office, he still won't have much clout or credibility. He's just the junior Senator from Massachusetts. He has to pick and choose the issues where he can make a difference."

"Well, of course."

"He's an architect, a large-scale builder with a very innovative practice. So science and technology issues are naturals for him." Oscar paused judiciously. "And, of course, urban development. But housing's not our problem at the moment."

"This place is our problem."

Oscar nodded. "Exactly. Donna, I know that working in a giant, airtight, gene-splicing lab might seem pretty mundane. Obviously this isn't a plum Senate assignment, compared to the Dutch Cold War or those catastrophes out in the Rockies. But this is still a major federal installation. When this place started, it worked pretty well: a lot of basic advances in biotechnology, some good jump starts for American industry, especially next door in Louisiana. But those glory days were years ago, and now this place is a pork-barrel bonanza. Kickbacks, payoffs, sweetheart deals . . . I hardly know where to start."

She looked pleased. "It sounds like you've *already* started."

"Well . . . Officially, I'm here to work for the Senate Science Committee. I no longer have any formal ties to Bambakias. But the Senator has arranged that, deliberately. He knows that this place requires a serious shaking-up. So, our agenda here is to provide him with what he needs for a real reform effort. We're laying the groundwork for his first legislative success."

"I see."

Oscar took her elbow politely as they sidestepped a passing okapi. "I'm not saying that the work will be easy. It could get ugly. There are a lot of vested interests here. Hidden agendas. Much more here than meets the eye. But if this were easy work, everybody would do it. Not people with our talents."

"I'll stay on."

"Good! I'm glad."

"I'm glad that you're leveling with me, Oscar. And you know? I think I need to tell you this, right now. Your personal background problem—I just want you to know, that whole business never bothered me. Not for one minute. I mean, I just thought the issue through, and then I put it right out of my mind."

It seemed unlikely that anybody would be doing anything ambitious with the telephones in the children's playground. So Fontenot had arranged for Oscar to take the Senator's voice call there. Oscar watched a ragged pack of scientists' children screaming like apes on the jungle gym.

Fontenot carefully hooked a Secret Service–approved encryptor to the wallphone's candy-colored mouthpiece.

"You'll notice a time lag," Fontenot warned Oscar. "They're doing traffic analysis countermeasures back in Boston."

"What about the locals? Are they a monitoring threat?"

"Have you *been* to the police offices here?"

"Not yet, no."

"I have. Maybe ten years ago they were still taking security seriously. Now you could knock this place over with a broomstick." Fontenot hung the brightly colored handset in its plastic cradle, then turned and studied the capering children. Like their parents, they were bareheaded and shaggy and wore geekish, ill-fitting clothes. "Nice-looking kids."

"Mmmmh."

"Never had the proper time for little ones. . . ." Fontenot's hooded eyes were full of obscure distress.

The phone rang. Oscar answered it at once. "Yes?"

"Oscar."

Oscar straightened a little. "Yes, Senator."

"Good to hear from you," Bambakias announced. "Good to hear your voice. I sent you a few files a while ago, but that's never the same, is it."

"No, sir."

"I want to thank you for bringing that Louisiana

matter to my attention. Those tapes you sent."
Bambakias's resonant voice glided upward into its podium
pitch. "That roadblock. The Air Force. Amazing, Oscar.
Outrageous!"

"Yes sir."

"It's a complete scandal! It beggars belief! Those are
citizens serving in the uniform of the United States! Our
own armed forces!" Bambakias drew a swift breath, and
grew yet more intense and sonorous. "How on earth can
we expect to command the loyalties of the men and
women who are sworn to defend our country, when we
cynically use them as pawns in a cheap, sordid power
struggle? We've literally abandoned them to starve to
death, freezing in the dark!"

Fontenot had joined the children at the teeter-totter.
Fontenot had shed his vest and hat and was cordially helping a squirming three-year-old onto the end of the board.
"Senator, nobody starves nowadays. With food as cheap as
it is, that's almost impossible. And they're not likely to
freeze here in the Deep South, either."

"You're evading my point. That base has no funding.
It's lost its legal standing. If you believe the Emergency
budget committee, that Air Force base no longer even
exists! They've simply been written out of the record.
They've been turned into political nonpersons by a stroke
of a bureaucrat's pen!"

"Well, that's certainly true."

"Oscar, there is a major issue here. America's had
her ups and downs, nobody denies that, but we're still a
great power. No great power can treat its soldiers this way.
I can't recognize any extenuating circumstances for this.
It's absurd, it's rank folly. What if this behavior spreads?
Do we want the Army, the Navy, and the Marines shaking down the citizens—the *voters*—just so they can scratch
up enough cash to live? That's mutiny! It's open banditry!
It's close to treason!"

Oscar turned from the shrieking children and cra-

dled the phone at his ear. Oscar knew full well that roadblocks were a very common business. On any particular
day, hordes of people blocked roads and streets all over the
USA. Roadblocking was no longer considered "highway
robbery," it had become a generally tolerated form of civil
disobedience. Roadblocking was just a real-world analog
for the native troubles that had always existed on information highways: jamming, spamming, and denial of service.
To have the Air Force getting into the act was just a
somewhat exotic extension of a very common practice.

But on the other hand, Bambakias's rhetoric clearly
had merit. It sounded very strong and punchy. It was
clear, it was quotable. It was a bit farfetched, but it was
very patriotic. One of the great beauties of politics as an
art form was its lack of restriction to merely standard
forms of realism.

"Senator, there's a great deal to what you say."

"Thank you," Bambakias said. "Of course, there's
nothing much we can do about this scandal, legislatively
speaking. Since I'm not yet officially in office and won't
be sworn in until mid-January."

"No?"

"No. So, I believe a moral gesture is necessary."

"Aha."

"At least—at the *very* least—I can demonstrate personal solidarity with the plight of our soldiers."

"Yes?"

"Tomorrow morning, I'm holding a net conference
here in Cambridge. Lorena and I are declaring a hunger
strike. Until the United States Congress agrees to feed our
men and women in uniform, my wife and I will go hungry as well."

"A *hunger strike?*" Oscar said. "That's a very radical
move for an elected federal official."

"I hope you don't expect me to lead any hunger
strikes *after* I take office," Bambakias said reasonably. He
lowered his voice. "Listen, we think this is doable. We've

discussed it at the Washington office and the Cambridge HQ. Lorena says that we're both fat as hogs from six months of those campaign dinners. If this gambit is going to work at all, it might very well work right now."

"Is it"—Oscar chose his words—"is it fully consonant with the dignity of the office?"

"Look, I never promised the voters dignity. I promised them results. Washington's lost its grip, and everything they try just makes it worse. If I don't seize the initiative from these sons of bitches on the Emergency committees, then I might as well declare myself a decorative bookend. That's not why I wanted the job."

"Yes sir," Oscar said. "I know that."

"There *is* a fallback option. . . . If a hunger strike doesn't get results, then we can start a convoy and lead our own rescue mission. We'll ride down to Louisiana and feed that air base ourselves."

"You mean," Oscar said, "something like our campaign construction rallies."

"Yes, except nationwide this time. Put the word out through the party apparatus and the net, organize our activists, and rally in Louisiana. Nationwide, Oscar. Rapid construction teams, disaster relief people, the grass-roots charities, pickets, marchers, full coverage. The works."

"I like that," Oscar said. "I like it a lot. It's visionary."

"I knew you'd appreciate that aspect. So you think it's a credible fallback threat?"

"Oh yes," Oscar said at once. "Sure. They know you can afford to do it. Of course a giant protest march is credible. A pro-military protest, that sounds great. But I do have a word of advice, if you'd like to hear it."

"Naturally."

"The hunger strike is very dangerous. Dramatic moral gestures are very strong meat. They really bring out the sharks."

"I realize that, and I'm not afraid of it."

"Let me put it this way, Senator. You and your wife had better really starve."

"That's all right," Bambakias said. "That's doable. We've been hungry for years."

———————————

Like most elements of modern American government, the Buna National Collaboratory was run by a committee. The source of local authority was a ten-person board, chaired by the Collaboratory's Director, Dr. Arno Felzian. The members of the board were the heads of the Collaboratory's nine administrative divisions.

Sunshine laws required the board's weekly meetings to take place publicly. The modern legal meaning of "public" meant camera coverage on a net-accessible address. The older tradition of a public meeting still held true in Buna, though. Collaboratory workers often showed up in person for board meetings, especially if they expected to see some personal ox gored.

Oscar had chosen to physically attend all of the Collaboratory board meetings. He had no plans to formally announce himself, or to take any part in the committee's business. He was attending strictly in order to be seen. To make sure that his ominous presence fully registered, he brought with him his net administrator, Bob Argow, and his oppo researcher, Audrey Avizienis.

The board's public studio was on the second floor of the Collaboratory's media center, across an open-air flywalk from the central administration building. The studio had been designed for public meetings back in 2030, with slanted racks of seats, decent acoustics, and nicely placed camera coverage.

But the Collaboratory's local government had had a checkered history. The net-center had been looted and partially burned during the lab's violent internal brawls of 2031. The damaged studio had naturally been somewhat neglected during the ensuing federal witch-hunts and the economic warfare scandals. It had crawled some distance back toward respectable order and repair in 2037, when the Collaboratory had shored up its perennially crisis-stricken finances. Repair contractors had papered over the burn marks and spruced the place up somewhat. The place was a miniature jungle of attractive potted plants.

The board's stage was fully functional, with sound baffles, overhead lighting, standard federal-issue table and chairs. The automatic cameras were in order. The board members were gamely plowing through the week's agenda. The issue currently at hand was replacing the ailing plumbing system in one of the Collaboratory cafeterias. The head of the Contracts & Procurements Division had the floor. He was mournfully reading a list of repair charges from a spreadsheet.

"I can't believe it's this bad," Argow muttered.

Oscar deftly adjusted the screen of his laptop. "Bob, there's something I need to show you."

"This is just so impossibly awful." Argow was ignoring him. "Before I came here, I never really understood the damage we've done. The human race, I mean. The terrible harm we've done to our planet. Once you really think about it, it's absolutely horrifying. Do you realize how many species have been killed off in the past fifty years? It's just a total, epic catastrophe."

Audrey leaned in over Oscar's shoulder. "You promised you'd stop drinking, Bob."

"I'm sober as a judge, you little shrew! While you've been sitting in the dorm with your nose in your screen, I've been touring the gardens here. With the giraffes. And the golden marmosets. All wiped out in a holocaust! We've poisoned the ocean, we've burned down and plowed the jungles, and we even screwed up the weather. All for the sake of modern life, right? Eight billion psychotic media-freaks!"

"Well," sniffed Audrey, "you're a fine one to talk on that score."

Argow flinched theatrically. "That's right! Rub it in! Look, I know full well that I'm part of the problem. I've wasted my life running networks, while the planet was destroyed all around me. Well, so have you, Audrey. We're both guilty, but the difference is that I can recognize the truth now. The truth has really touched me. It's touched me in here." Argow pounded his bulky chest.

Audrey's grainy voice grew silkier. "Well, I wouldn't fret too much, Bob. You're not good enough at your work to be any real menace."

"Take it easy, Audrey," Oscar said mildly.

Audrey Avizienis was a professional opposition researcher. Once roused, her critical faculties were lethal. "Look, we all came down here, and I'm doing my damn job. But laughing boy here is being a big, holier-than-thou, depressive bringdown. What, he thinks I can't appreciate nature just because I spend a lot of time on the net? I know plenty about the birds and the bees, and the butterflies, and the cabbages, and all the rest of that stuff."

"What I know," Argow muttered, "is that the planet is coming apart, and we're sitting in this stupid building with these hopeless bureaucratic morons dithering on and on about their sewage problems."

"Bob," Oscar said calmly, "you're missing something."

"What's that?"

"It's every bit as bad as you say. It's *worse* than you say. *Much* worse. But this is the biggest bio-research center in the world. These people in front of us—these are the people who are in charge of this place. So you're at the front lines now. You're guilty all right, but you're nowhere near as guilty as you will be, if you don't shape up. Because we are in power and you are the responsible party now."

"Oh," Argow said.

"So get a grip." Oscar flipped back his laptop screen.

"Now, take a look at this. You too, Audrey. You're systems professionals, and I need your input here."

Argow examined Oscar's laptop screen, his owlish eyes glowing. A lime-green plane with lumpy reddish mountains. "Uhm . . . yeah, I've seen those before. That's a, uhm . . ."

"It's an algorithmic landscape," Audrey said intently. "A visualization map."

"I just received this program from Leon Sosik," Oscar said. "This is Sosik's simulation map for current public issues. These mountains and valleys, they're supposed to model current political trends. Press coverage, the feedback from constituents, the movement of lobbying funds, dozens of factors that Sosik fed into his simulator. . . . But now watch this. See, I'm moving these close-up crosshairs. . . . See that big yellow amoeba sitting on that purple blur? That is the current public position of Senator-elect Alcott Bambakias."

"What," Argow said skeptically, "he's way down that slope?"

"No he's not, not anymore. He's actually moving *up* the slope. . . ." Oscar double-clicked. "See, this huge khaki mountain range represents military affairs. . . . Now I'll kick the simulation back a week, and run it back up to the Bambakias press conference this morning. . . . See the way he kind of oozes up to the issue, and then suddenly *jets* across the landscape?"

"Wow!" Audrey said. "I've always loved old-fashioned hotshot computer graphics."

"It's garbage," Argow grumbled. "Just because you have a cute simulation doesn't mean you're actually connecting to political reality. Or to any kind of reality."

"Okay, so it's not real. I know it's not real, that's obvious. But what if it works?"

"Well," Argow mused, "even *that* doesn't help much. It's just like stock-market analysis. Even if you get some technique that *does* work, that's strictly temporary.

Pretty soon everyone else gets the same analytical tools, and then your advantage disappears. You're right back where you started. Except for one thing. From then on, everything becomes much, much more complicated."

"Thanks for that technical insight, Bob. I'll try to keep that in mind." Oscar paused. "Audrey, why do you suppose Leon Sosik sent me this program?"

"I guess he appreciates the way you airmailed him that binturong," Audrey said.

"Maybe he thought you'd be impressed by this," Argow said. "Or maybe he's so old and out-of-it that he really thinks this stuff is new."

Oscar looked up from his laptop screen. The nine people on the soundstage had suddenly fallen silent. They were looking at him.

The Collaboratory's Director and his nine functionaries seemed oddly spellbound for a moment. They formed a little Rembrandtesque tableau under their media lighting. Oscar knew all their names—Oscar never forgot names—but for the moment he had mentally labeled the nine local functionaries as "Administrative Support," "Computing & Communications," "Contracts & Procurement," "Financial Services," "Human Resources," "Information Genetics," "Instrumentation," "Biomedicine," and last but not least, the ditzy crew-cut thug from "Safety & Security." They had noticed him and— Oscar realized this suddenly—they were all afraid of him.

They knew that he had the power to do them harm. He had infiltrated their ivory tower and was judging their work. He was very new to them, he owed them nothing at all, and they were all guilty.

The stares of strangers never bothered Oscar. He had grown up in a celebrity childhood. Human attention fed something in Oscar, a deep dark psychic entity that thrived and grew with the feeding. He wasn't cruel by nature—but he knew that there were moments in the game that required direct and primal acts of intimidation.

One of those moments had just arrived. Oscar flicked his gaze upward from his laptop screen and he gave the people on the board his best—his lethal—I Know All look.

The Director flinched. He grappled for his agenda, and moved on to the pressing subject of quality assessment in the technology transfer office.

"Oscar," Audrey whispered.

Oscar leaned over casually. "Yes?"

"What's going on? Why is Greta Penninger staring at you like that?"

Oscar glanced back up at the soundstage. He hadn't noticed that "Instrumentation" was staring at him, and yet she clearly was. All of them had been staring at him, but Greta Penninger hadn't stopped. Her pale and narrow face had an absent, intent cast, like a woman watching a wasp on a windowpane.

Oscar gazed back solemnly at Dr. Greta Penninger. Their eyes met. Dr. Penninger was chewing meditatively at the end of a pencil, gripping the yellow wood with her blue-knuckled, spidery, surgical fingers. She seemed to look right through him and five miles beyond. After a very long moment, she tucked the pencil in the dark ponytailed hair behind her ear, and returned her limpid gaze to her big paper notepad.

"Greta Penninger," Oscar said thoughtfully.

"She's really bored," Argow offered.

"You think so?"

"Yeah. Because she's a genuine scientist. She's famous. This administrative crap is boring her to death. It's boring *me* to death, and I don't even work here."

Audrey swiftly conjured Greta Penninger's dossier onto her laptop. "I think she likes you."

"Why do you say that?" Oscar said.

"She keeps looking your way and twisting her hair on her finger. I think I saw her lick her lips once."

Oscar laughed quietly.

"Look, I'm not being funny. She's not married, and

you're the new guy in town. Why shouldn't she be interested? I know I would be." Audrey paged a little deeper into her file of oppo data. "She's only thirty-six, you know. She doesn't look that bad."

"She *does* look bad," Argow assured her. "Worse than you think."

"No, she could look okay if she tried. Her face is kind of lopsided, and she doesn't do her hair," Audrey noted clinically. "But she's tall and she's thin. She could carry clothes. Donna could make her look good."

"I don't think Donna wants to work that hard," Argow objected.

"I have a girlfriend already, thank you," Oscar said. "But since you've got your screen up: what exactly does Dr. Penninger do?"

"She's a neurologist. A systemic zoo-neurologist. She won a big award once for something called 'Radioligand Pharmacokinetics.' "

"So she's still a working researcher?" said Oscar. "How long has she been in administration?"

"I'll check," Audrey said readily, tapping keys. "She's been here in Buna for six years. . . . Six *years* working inside this place, can you imagine that? No wonder she looks so fidgety. . . . According to this, she's been the head of the Instrumentation Division for four months."

"Then she *is* bored," Oscar said. "She's bored by her job. That's very interesting. Make a note of that, Audrey."

"Yeah?"

"Yeah. Let's have her for dinner."

Oscar had arranged a bus outing, a picnic for part of his krewe. It helped to maintain the thin fiction of "vacation," and it got them away from the fog of mechanical surveillance, and best of all, it offered some relief from the psychic oppression of the Collaboratory dome.

They took the campaign bus to a roadside stop near a bedraggled state park called Big Thicket. This Thicket was a surprisingly large area of Texas that had somehow escaped farming and settlement. It didn't seem entirely right to call the place an "unspoiled wilderness," since climate change had battered it considerably; but for people from Massachusetts the Texas-sized mess was a pleasing novelty.

The day was overcast and damp, even a little raw, but it was pleasant to encounter weather of any sort. The gusting wind through the Thicket park wasn't "fresh air" exactly—the air of East Texas was considerably less fresh than the manicured air inside the Collaboratory—but it had a wide-screen smell, the reek of a world that possessed horizons. Besides, the picnickers had Fontenot's big portable gas stove to keep them warm. Fontenot had just bought the stove, well used, from the proprietor of a Cajun boucherie in Mamou. The stove was made of disassembled oil barrels, heat-scorched tin sheeting, and brass-nozzled propane burners. It looked as if it had been welded into shape by Mardi Gras drunks.

It was good to chat and make a few unsupervised phone calls, well outside of the Collaboratory. Bugs were so cheap these days—when cellphones cost less than a six-pack of beer, covert listening devices were as cheap as confetti. But a cheap bug wouldn't be able to radiate data sixty miles back to Buna. An expensive bug would be caught by Fontenot's expensive monitors. This meant that everyone could talk.

"So, how's the new house doing, Jules?"

"Coming along, coming along," Fontenot said contentedly. "You should come see my place. We'll take out my brand-new boat. Have us a good old time."

"I'd enjoy that," Oscar lied tactfully.

Fontenot dumped chopped basil and onion into his simmering roux, then went after the sizzling mess with a wire whisk. "Y'all mind opening that ice chest?"

Oscar rose from the chest and opened its insulated lid. "What do you need?"

"Those eishters."

"The what?"

"Aishters."

"What?"

"He means the oysters," said Negi Estabrook.

"Right," said Oscar. He located an iced bag of shell-fish.

"You brang that to a rollin' boil now," Fontenot advised Negi, in his broadest and most magisterial Cajun drawl. "A little dab more of that pepper sauce. It'll forgive as it come along."

"I can make a soup, Jules," Negi announced tautly. "I have a degree in nutrition."

"Not a *Cajun* soup, girl."

"Cajun is not a difficult cuisine," said Negi patiently. Negi was sixty years old, and Fontenot was the only member of the krewe who would dare to call her "girl." "Basically, Cajun is very old-fashioned French peasant cooking. With way too much pepper. And lard. Tons of unhealthy lard."

Fontenot pulled a face. "Y'all hear that? She does that on purpose just to hurt my feelings."

Negi laughed. "As if!"

"You know," Oscar said, "I had a good idea recently."

"Do tell," said Fontenot.

"Our dorm situation inside the Collaboratory is clearly untenable. And the town of Buna can't put us up properly, either. Buna's never been a proper city: it's greenhouses, florists, seedy little motels, some run-down light industry. The town just doesn't have a proper place for us to stay; a place where we could entertain a visiting Senate committee, for instance. So, let's build our own hotel."

Fred Dillen, the krewe's laundryman/janitor, put down his beer. "Our own *hotel*?"

"Why not? We've relaxed in Buna for two whole weeks now. We have our breath back. It's time for us to reorganize and really make our mark around here. We can create a hotel. That's definitely within our means and abilities. After all, that was always our best campaign tactic. The other candidates would throw rallies and photo ops, and try to work the media. But Alcott Bambakias could bring a campaign crowd together and assemble permanent housing."

"You mean we build a hotel for profit?" Fred said.

"Well, for our own convenience mostly, but yes, for profit, of course. We can get the design plans and software from Bambakias's firm. We can certainly build the structure ourselves, and best of all, we actually have the skills it requires to successfully *run* a hotel. A traveling political campaign is basically a mobile hotel, when you think about it. But in this case, *we* stay in one place, while the crowds will come to us. And then they pay us."

"Man," Fred said. "What a weird inside-out way to think. . . ."

"I think it's doable. You can all play the same roles that you did during the campaign. Negi, you can run the kitchen. Fred, you can handle the laundry and the rooms. Corky does guest relations and works the front desk. Rebecca does physical security and the occasional massage. Everybody pitches in, and if we need them, we can take on some temp gofers locally. And we make money."

"How much money?"

"Oh, the top end of the market should be pretty generous. I've seen millionaire contractors inside the Collaboratory, crammed in right next door to postdocs and grad students. That's just not natural."

"Not nowadays," Negi admitted.

"It's a good market window. Yosh will put together our finance package. Lana will deal with local zoning and the Buna city authorities. We'll front it all through a Boston corporation to sidestep any conflict-of-interest hassles. And when we're done here, we just sell the hotel. In the meantime, we have a decent place to live and a revenue stream."

"You know," said Ando "Corky" Shoeki, "I saw that done ten times. I helped to do it, even. But I still can't get used to the concept. I mean, that big crowds of unskilled people can construct permanent housing."

"I agree, distributed instantiation still has some shock value. It's made Bambakias very rich, but it's still a novelty down here. I like the idea of doing that work in East Texas. It'll show these local yokels what we're made of."

"Y'know," Fred said slowly, "I'm trying really hard, but I can't think of any good reason not to do what Oscar says."

"You're all clever people," Oscar said. "Find me some reason why it can't be done." He ducked back into the bus, to let them argue about it. Spelling it all out for them in black and white would only spoil their fun.

He hung his hat inside the bus. "So, Moira," he said, "how's the cause célèbre coming?"

"Oh, it's great," said Moira, spinning in her chair. Moira had been looking much better since the Senator's hunger strike had started. Moira's soul waxed and waned with the tides of media exposure. "The Senator's positives are through the roof. Seventy percent, seventy-five. And the rest is real mushy, mostly undecideds!"

"Phenomenal."

"Putting Alcott's blood sugar levels onto the net—that was brilliant. People are logging on around the clock just to watch him starve! Lorena, too. Lorena has massive female positives. She's been on ten glamour sites since Wednesday. They love her bread and water diet, they just can't get enough of her!"

"How about the situation on the ground? The

Emergency committees, have they done anything useful about that Air Force base yet?"

"Oh," Moira said, "I haven't quite gotten around to that part. . . . I, uh, thought Audrey was gonna handle that."

Oscar grunted. "Okay."

Moira touched her fingertips to her powdered chin. "Alcott . . . he's just so *special*. I've seen him give so many speeches, but that stand-up he just did with the hospital pajamas and the apple juice . . . It was just ninety seconds, but it was drama, it's real confrontation, it's just pure gold. The standard site coverage wasn't so hot at first, but the chat swaps and the downloads have been huge. Alcott's coming up *way* behind ideological lines. He *never* used to get positives out of the Right Tradition Bloc, but even they are coming around now. You know, if Wyoming weren't on fire right now, I really think this would be *the* political story. For this week, anyway."

"How is that Wyoming thing shaping up, by the way?"

"Oh, the fire's a lot worse now. The President's there."

"The old guy, or Two Feathers?"

"Two Feathers of course. Nobody cares about the old guy anymore, he's finished, he's just the duck now. I know Two Feathers hasn't been sworn in yet, but people depreciate the post-election hang-time. People want in ahead of the curve."

"Right," said Oscar shortly. She was telling him the obvious.

"Oscar . . ." Moira looked at him with naked appeal. "Should I ask him to take me to Washington?"

Oscar silently spread his hands.

"He needs me. He'll need someone to speak for him."

"That's not my decision, Moira. You need to take it up with his chief of staff."

"Can you put in a good word for me with Leon Sosik? Sosik seems to like you so much."

"Let me get back to you on that," Oscar said.

The bus door banged open. Norman-the-Intern stuck his tousled head inside and yelled, "We're eating!"

"Oh, great!" said Moira, leaping from her chair. "Weird Cajun seafood, good good good!"

Oscar put on his hat and jacket and followed her outside. With a flourish, Fontenot was spooning great ladles of swimming brown murk. Oscar brought up the end of the line. He accepted a quilt-paper bowl and a biodegradable spoon.

Oscar gazed at his hot oily gumbo and thought mournfully of Bambakias. The Cambridge PR team had certainly done a thorough job surveilling the fasting Senator: blood pressure, heartbeat, temperature, calorie consumption, borborygmus, bile production—there was no possible doubt about the raw authenticity of his hunger strike. The man's entire corpus had become public domain. Whenever Bambakias had a sip of his famine apple juice, a forest of monitors twitched and heaved across the country.

Oscar followed them to a picnic table and sat down next to Negi. He examined his brimming spoon. He had seriously considered not eating this evening. That would be a very decent gesture. Well, let someone else make it.

"Angioplasty in a bowl," Negi said blissfully.

Oscar sipped from his spoon. "Well worth dying for," he nodded.

"I'm so old," Negi mourned, blowing on her soup. "Back when I had tatts and piercings, people got on your case if you ate fats and drank yourself stupid. Of course, that was before they found out the full awful truth about pseudo-estrogen poisoning."

"Well," Oscar said companionably, "at least those massive pesticide disasters got us off the hook with that diet and exercise nonsense."

"Pass the bread, Norman," Rebecca said. "Is that real butter? Real old-fashioned tub butter? Wow!"

A light aircraft flew overhead. Its tiny engine puttered energetically, like fingernails tapping a snare drum. The aircraft seemed appallingly flimsy. With its eerie, computer-designed lifting surfaces, it resembled a child's paper toy: something made with pinking shears, popsicle sticks, and tape. The wing edges trailed off into feathery ribbons and long tattered kite tails. It seemed to be staying aloft through sheer force of will.

Then three similar aircraft appeared, skidding and puttering just above the treetops. They flew like fishing lures tempting a trout. Their pilots were gloved and goggled and bulky, so wrapped in their padding that they resembled human bales of burlap.

One of the pilots detached himself from formation, settled down like a falling leaf, and gently circled the roadside bus. It was like being buzzed by a hay bale. Everyone looked up from their food and waved politely. The pilot waved back, mimicked eating with one gauntlet, and headed east.

"Airborne nomads," Fontenot said, squinting.

"They're heading east," Oscar noted.

"Green Huey's very tight with the leisure unions." Fontenot shoved his bowl aside, rose deliberately, and went into the bus to see to his machines. He had the face he wore when he meant business.

Oscar's krewe returned to their food. They ate silently now and with more purpose. No one had to remark on the obvious: that there would soon be more nomads arriving.

Fontenot emerged from the bus, where he had been checking road reports. "We may have to move soon," Fontenot said. "The Regulators have been rallying at the Alabama-Coushatta reservation, and their rally is coming through now. These local proles, they aren't tame."

"Well, we're strangers here too, you know," Negi

said. Negi had spent time on the road, back in the old days
when homeless people didn't have cellphones and laptops.

Two nomad scouts arrived ten minutes later, in a
motorcycle and sidecar. They were dressed for winter.
They wore wraparound kilts, striped ponchos, and huge
coarse cloaks beautifully embroidered with old twentieth-
century corporate logos. Their skin gleamed with a thick
layer of wind-resistant, insulating grease. They had dipped
their legs up to mid-calf in a plastic bootlike substance
with the look and sheen of vinyl.

The scouts pulled over, dismounted, and walked
over. They were silent and proud, and carrying cellular
videocams. The driver was chewing on a large square
chunk of artificial food, like a green butter stick of compressed alfalfa.

Oscar beckoned them over. It transpired that these
nomads were not, in fact, the legendary Regulators. These
were Texan road drifters, far less advanced in their peculiar
ways than the proles of Louisiana. These people spoke
only Spanish. Oscar's childhood Spanish was worse than
rusty, and Donna Nunez wasn't around, but Rebecca
Pataki had a smattering.

The nomads politely complimented them on their
bus. They offered square sticks of veggie greenery. Oscar
and Rebecca politely declined the nomad silage and
counteroffered some oyster gumbo. The nomads carefully
gulped down the last of the hot stew, commenting at
length on the flavor. As the animal fats hit their bloodstreams, they became less suspicious. They inquired non-
chalantly about the possible availability of scrap metal:
nails, metal, copper? Corky Shoeki, who was the camp
majordomo and recycling expert, obliged with some
empty cans from the bus.

Oscar was deeply bothered by their nomad laptops.
They were using nonstandard keyboards, boards where
QWERTYUIOP had been junked and the letters rede-
signed for efficient typing. The wretches didn't even type

like normal people. Somehow this bothered him far more than the fact that these particular nomads were Mexican illegals.

Moving as if they had all the time in the world, because they did, the two men drove off. Suddenly there was very little traffic on the highway. People had gotten wind of the oncoming movement of the Regulator horde, and were already avoiding the roads. Two police cars passed, lights flashing silently. The nomad tribes weren't afraid of local police. There were far too many of them to safely arrest, and in any case, the proles had their own police.

The first fringe of the Regulator convoy arrived. Plastic trucks and buses cruising by at maybe thirty miles an hour, sipping fuel and saving wear on their engines. Then came the core of the operation, the nomad technical base. Flatbed trucks and tankers, loaded with harvesting equipment, pillers, crushers, welders, rollers, fermenting pans, pipes, and valves. They lived on grass, they lived off roadside weeds and cultured yeast. Women wearing skirts, shawls, veils. Swarms of young children, their vibrant little bodies saturated with multicolored beads and handmade quillwork.

Oscar was entranced by the spectacle. These weren't the low-key dropouts of the Northeast, people who managed on cheap food and public assistance. These were people who had rallied in a horde and marched right off the map. They had tired of a system that offered them nothing, so they had simply invented their own.

The krewe cleaned up their picnic. Fontenot set to work, finding a route back to the Collaboratory that would avoid the migrating swarm. Fontenot would escort them there, towing his battered Cajun stove behind his electric hummer. Even when engulfed by a horde of Regulators, they should be safe enough, locked in the metal shell of their campaign bus. Though the situation was unlikely, they would probably simply blend in.

Oscar's phone suddenly emitted a personal ring. "Oh, Oscar," Rebecca teased him. "There's that sparky phone again."

"I've been expecting this call," said Oscar. "Excuse me." He stepped around the back of the bus as the others continued to pack.

It was his girlfriend, Clare, back in Boston. "How are you, Oscar?"

"Fine. It's going pretty well down here, all things considered. Very interesting. How's life at the homestead? I miss you."

"Your house is fine," Clare said. Too quickly.

A hairline fracture shot through him. Don't get anxious, he thought. Don't think too fast. This isn't one of the other ones, this is Clare. This is Clare, this is doable.

Oscar wanted direly to confront the source of trouble. That would be very stupid. Work around it. Let her open up first. Be funny, be charming. Make some light conversation. Find a neutral topic. For the life of him, he couldn't think of one.

"We've been having a picnic," he blurted.

"That sounds lovely. I wish I were there."

"I wish you were, too," he said. Inspiration struck him. "How about it? Can you fly down? We have some plans here, you'd be interested."

"I can't go to Texas now."

"You've heard about the Louisiana air base situation, right? The Senator's hunger strike. I've got very good sources here. It's a solid story, you could fly down, you could cover the local angle."

"I think your friend Sosik's got that story sewn up already," Clare said. "I'm not doing Boston politics. Not anymore."

"What?" He was stunned. "Why not?"

"The net's reassigned me. They want me to go to Holland."

"Holland? What did you tell them?"

"Oscar, I'm a political journalist. How could I not do The Hague? It's the Cold War, it's a dream gig. This is a big break for me, my biggest career break ever."

"Well, how long is your assignment overseas?"

"Well, that depends on how well I do at the job."

Oscar's brain began to hum. "I can appreciate that. Of course you want to do well. But still . . . the diplomatic situation . . . the Dutch are so provocative. They're very radical."

"Of course they're radical, Oscar. Their country is drowning. We'd be extremists too, if most of America was below sea level. The Dutch have got so much to lose, they've really got their backs against the dikes. That's why they're so interesting now."

"You don't even speak Dutch."

"They all speak English there, you know."

"The Dutch are militant. They're dangerous. They make crazy demands from Americans, they really resent us."

"I'm a reporter, Oscar. I'm not supposed to scare easily."

"So you're really going to do it," Oscar concluded leadenly. "You're going to leave me, aren't you?"

"I don't want to put it that way. . . ."

Oscar gazed emptily at the back of the bus. The blank shell of the bus suddenly struck him as an alien and horrible thing. It had stolen him from his home and the woman in his bedroom. The campaign bus had kidnapped him. He turned his back on the bus and began walking with his phone, randomly, toward the tangled Texan woods. "No," he said. "I know. It's the work. It's our careers. I did it first. I took on a big job, and I left you. Didn't I? I left you alone, and I'm still gone. I'm far away, and I don't know when I'll come back."

"Well," she said, "you said it, not me. But that's very true."

"So I really have no business finding fault with you. If I did, I'd be a hypocrite, wouldn't I? We both knew this might happen. It was never a commitment."

"That's right."

"It was a relationship."

"I *liked* the relationship."

"It was good, wasn't it? It was very good, for what it was."

Clare sighed. "No, Oscar, I can't let you say that. Don't say that, it wouldn't be fair. It was better than good. It was great, it was totally ideal. I mean, you were such a great source for me. You never tried to spin my stories, and you hardly ever lied. You let me live in your house. You introduced me to all your rich and influential friends. You supported my career. You never yelled at me. You were a real gentleman. Brilliant. A dream boyfriend."

"You're being so sweet." He could feel himself hemorrhage.

"I'm really sorry that I was never able to . . . you know . . . quite get over your personal background thing."

"No," Oscar said bitterly, "I'm very used to that."

"It's just—it's just one of those permanent tragedies. Like, you know, my own troubled minority background."

Oscar sighed. "Clare, I don't think anybody really holds it against you that you're a white Anglo-Saxon."

"No, life is hard in a racial minority. It just is. I mean, you of all people ought to have some feeling for what that really means. I know you can't help the way you were born, but still . . . I mean, that's one of the real reasons I want to do this Dutch assignment. There's been so much white flight from America back into Europe. . . . My people are there, you know? My roots are there. I think it might help me, somehow."

Oscar was finding it hard to breathe.

"I feel bad about this, sweetheart, like I've really let you down."

"No, this is better," Oscar said. "It hurts a lot, but it hurts less than dragging it on and keeping up a false pretense. Let's part as friends."

"I might be back, you know. You don't have to be all hasty like that. You don't have to turn on a dime. Because it's just me, your pal Clare, you know? It's not like an executive decision."

"Let's have a clean break," he said firmly. "It's best for us. For both of us."

"All right. If you're sure, then I guess I understand. Good-bye, Oscar."

"It's over, Clare. Good-bye." He hung up. Then he threw the phone into the trees.

"Nothing works," he told the red dirt and gray sky. "I can't ever make anything work!"

3

Oscar peeled a strip of tape from a yellow spool and wrapped the tape around a cinder block. He swept a hand-scanner over the block, activating the tape. It was close to one in the morning. The wind out of the tall black pines was damp and nasty, but he was working hard and the weather felt bleakly appropriate.

"I'm a cornerstone," the cinder block announced.

"Good for you," Oscar grunted.

"I'm a cornerstone. Carry me five steps to your left."

Oscar ignored this demand, and swiftly taped six more blocks. He whipped the scanner across each of them, then pulled the last block aside to get at the next level in the stack.

As he set his gloved hands to it, the last block warned him, "Don't install me yet. Install that cornerstone first."

"Sure," Oscar told it. The construction system was smart enough to manage a limited and specific vocabulary. Unfortunately, the system simply didn't hear very well. The tiny microphones embedded in the talking tape were much less effective than the tape's thumbnail-sized speakers. Still, it was hard not to reply to a concrete block when it spoke up with such grace and authority. The concrete blocks all sounded like Franklin Roosevelt.

Bambakias had created this construction system. Like all of the architect's brainchildren, his system was very functional, yet rife with idiosyncratic grace-notes. Oscar had full confidence in the system, a pragmatic faith won from much hands-on experience. Oscar had labored like a mule in many Bambakias construction sites. No one ever won the trust of Alcott Bambakias, or joined his inner circle, without a great deal of merciless grunt work.

Heavy labor was the heart and soul of the Bambakias intellectual salon. W. Alcott Bambakias had quite a number of unorthodox beliefs, but chief among them was his deep conviction that sycophants and rip-off artists always tired easily. Bambakias, like many members of the modern overclass, was always ready with an openhearted gesture, a highly public flinging of golden ducats. His largesse naturally attracted parasites, but he rid himself of "the summer soldiers and the sunshine patriots," as he insisted on calling them, by demanding frequent stints of brute physical work. "It'll be fun," Bambakias would announce, rolling up his tailored sleeves and grinning fiercely. "We'll get results."

Bambakias was no day laborer. He was a wealthy sophisticate, and his wife was a noted art collector. It was for exactly those reasons that the couple took such perverse pleasure in publicly raising blisters, straining tendons, and sweating like hogs. The architect's ruggedly handsome face would light up with hundred-watt noblesse oblige as he chugged away in his faux blue-collar overalls and back brace. His elegant wife took clear masochistic pleasure in hauling construction equipment, her chiseled features set with the grim commitment of a supermodel pumping iron.

Oscar himself had grown up in Hollywood. He'd never minded the poseur elements in the Bambakias couple. The trademark hat-and-cape ensemble, the hand-tailored couture gowns, the glam-struck Boston charity events—Oscar found this sort of thing reassuringly homey. In any case, the construction system made it all worthwhile. There was no pretense to the system—no question that it worked. Any number could play. It was a system that could find a working role for anyone. It was both a network and a way of life, flowing from its basis in digital communication and design into the rock-hard emergent reality of walls and floors. There was a genuine comfort in working within a system like this one, because it always kept its promises, it always brought results.

This Texan hotel, for instance, was an entirely virtual construction, ones and zeros embedded in a set of chips. And yet, the hotel direly wanted to exist. It would become very beautiful, and it was already very smart. It could sweet-talk itself into physical existence from random piles of raw material. It would be a good hotel. It would brighten the neighborhood and enhance the city. It would keep the wind and rain off. People would dwell in it.

Oscar lugged the self-declared cornerstone to the corner of the southern wall. "I belong here," the cornerstone declared. "Put mortar on me."

Oscar picked up a trowel. "I'm the tool for the mortar," the little trowel squeaked cheerfully. Oscar put the trowel to use and slathered up a grainy wedge of thick gray paste. This polymer goo was not actually "mortar," but it was just as cheap as traditional mortar, and it worked much better, so it had naturally stolen the word from the original substance.

Oscar hefted the cinder block to the top of the hip-high wall. "To the right," urged the block. "To the right, to the right, to the right. . . . To the left. . . . Move me backward. . . . Twist me, twist me, twist me. . . . Good! Now scan me."

Oscar lifted the scanner on its lanyard and played it across the block. The scanner logged and correlated the block's exact locale, and beeped with satisfaction.

Oscar had been installing blocks for two solid hours. He had simply walked onto the site in the middle of the night, logged on, booted the system, and started off where the krewe had stopped with darkness.

This particular wall could not rise much higher. All too soon it would be time to work on the plumbing. Oscar hated the plumbing, always the most troublesome construction element. Plumbing was a very old technology, not so plug-and-play, never so slick and easy as the flow of computation. Plumbing mistakes were permanent and ugly. When the plumbing's time had come, the Bambakias construction system would wisely balk. All higher function ceased until people came to terms with the pipes.

Oscar removed his hard hat and pressed his chilly ears with his work-gloved hands. His spine and shoulders told him that he would regret this in the morning. At least it would be a new set of regrets.

Oscar stepped under a paraboloid construction light, to search for the shipping boxes full of plumbing supplies. The nearest light smartly rotated on its tall pole to follow Oscar's footsteps. Oscar stepped up onto a monster spool of cable for an overview.

The cone of light rose with him and flew across the trampled winter grass. Oscar suddenly caught sight of a stranger, wrapped in a baggy jacket and a woolen hat. The stranger was lurking outside the plastic orange safety fence, standing on the broken sidewalk, under a pine.

Bambakias construction sites always attracted gawkers. But very few construction gawkers would lurk in cold and darkness at one in the morning. Still, even little Buna had a nightlife. Presumably the guy was just drunk.

Oscar cupped his gloved hands to his mouth. "Would you like to help?" This was a standard invitation at any Bambakias site. It was very much part of the game. It was surprising just how many selfless, energetic volunteers had been permanently lured into the Bambakias krewe through this gambit.

The stranger stepped awkwardly through a gap in the orange netting, walking into Oscar's arc-light.

"Welcome to the site of our future hotel! Have you been to our site before?"

Silent shake of the woolly head.

Oscar climbed down from the spool. He retrieved a box of vacuum-wrapped gloves and carried it over. "Try these."

The stranger—a woman—pulled bare, spidery hands from the pockets of her coat. Oscar, startled, looked up from her fingers to her shadowed face. "Dr. Penninger! Good morning."

"Mr. Valparaiso."

Oscar fetched out a pair of ductile extra-large, their floppy plastic fingers studded with grip-dots. He hadn't expected any company on the site tonight, much less a ranking member of the Collaboratory's board. He was taken aback to encounter Greta Penninger under these circumstances, but there was no sense in hesitating now. "Please try these gloves on, Doctor. . . . You see that yellow ridge of tape across the knuckles? Those are embedded locators, so our construction system will always know the position of your hands."

Dr. Penninger tugged the gloves on, twisting her narrow wrists like a surgeon washing up.

"You'll need a hard hat, a back brace, and some shoe caps. Knee guards are a good idea, too. I'll log you into our system now, if that's all right."

Searching through the krewe's piled supplies in the gloom, Oscar dug up a spare hard hat and some velcro-strapped toe-protectors. Greta Penninger strapped on her construction gear without a word.

"That's good," Oscar said. He handed her a pencil-shaped hand-scanner on its plastic lanyard. "Now, Doctor, let me acquaint you with our design philosophy here. You see, at heart, our system's very flexible and simple. The computer always knows the location of every component that's been tagged and initialized. The system also has complete algorithms for assembling the building from simple component parts. There are millions of possible ways of getting from start to finish, so it's just a question of coordinating all the efforts, and always keeping track. Thanks to distributed, parallel, assembly processing . . ."

"Never mind, I get all that. I was watching you."

"Oh." Oscar jammed his spiel back into its can. He tipped up his plastic hard-hat brim and looked her over. She wasn't kidding. "Well, you do the mortar, and I'll carry blocks. Can you do mortar?"

"I can do mortar."

Dr. Penninger began carefully lathering goo with the garrulous trowel. The components chattered on cheerfully, Dr. Penninger said nothing at all, and the pace of Oscar's work more than doubled. Dr. Penninger was really going after it. It was the middle of the night, it was lonely, desolate, windy, and near freezing, and this scientist really meant business. She worked like a horse. Like a demon.

Curiosity got the best of him. "Why did you come here at this time of night?"

Dr. Penninger straightened, her trowel clutched in her dotted glove. "This is my only free time. I'm always in my lab till midnight."

"I see. Well, I really appreciate your visit. You're a very good worker. Thanks for the help."

"You're welcome." She glanced at him searchingly across the airy pool of glare. It might have been a piquant glance if he had found her attractive.

"You should visit us in daylight, when we have the full krewe at work. It's the coordination of elements, the teamwork, that's the key to distributed instantiation. The structure simply flies up all at once sometimes, as if it were crystallizing. That's well worth watching."

She touched her gloved hand to her chin and examined the block wall. "Shouldn't we do some plumbing now?"

Oscar was surprised. "How long have you been watching me?"

Her shoulders lifted briefly within the baggy jacket. "The plumbing is obvious." Oscar realized that he had disappointed her. She had hoped that he was smarter than that.

"Time for a break," he announced. Oscar knew that he lacked the searingly high IQ of Greta Penninger. He'd examined her career stats—of course—and Dr. Greta Penninger had always been a compulsive, overachieving, first-in-her-class techie swot. Still, there was more than one kind of smarts in the world. He felt quite sure he could distract her if he simply kept changing the subject.

He walked inside the jagged circuit of raw cinderblock walls, where a fire burned in an old iron barrel under a spread of plastic awning. His back hurt like a toothache. He had really overdone it. "Cajun beef jerky? The krewe really dotes on this stuff."

"Sure. Why not."

Oscar handed over a strip of lethally spiced meat, and ripped into another blackened chunk with his teeth. He waved one hand. "The site looks very chaotic now, but try to imagine this all assembled and complete."

"Yes, I can visualize that. . . . I never realized your hotel was going to be so elegant. I thought it was prefabricated."

"Oh, it *is* prefabricated. But the plans are always adjusted by the system to fit the exact specifics of the site. So the final structure is always an original. That pile of cantilevers there, those will go over the porte cochere. . . . The patio will be here where we're standing, and just beyond that entrance loggia is the pergola. . . . Those long dual wings have the guest rooms and the diner, while the upper floor has our library, the various balconies, and the conservatory." Oscar smiled. "So, when we're all finished, I hope you'll visit us here. Rent a suite. Stay awhile. Have a nice dinner."

"I doubt I can afford that." Clouded and moody.

What on earth was the woman up to? In the blue-lit

gloom, Dr. Penninger's wide-set, chocolate-drop eyes seemed to be two different sizes . . . but surely that was just some weird illusion, something about her unplucked brows, and the visible tension wrinkling her eyelids. She had a big squarish chin, a protruding, oddly dimpled, and elaborate upper lip. No lipstick. Small, slanted, nibbling teeth. A long, cartilaginous neck, and the look of a woman who had not witnessed real sunlight in six years. She looked really and genuinely peculiar, a sui generis personage. A close examination didn't make the woman any less odd. It made her more so.

"But you'll be my personal guest," he told her. "Because I'm inviting you now."

That worked. Something clicked over in Dr. Penninger's wool-hatted head. Suddenly he had her entire and focused attention. "Why did you send me those flowers?"

"Buna's a city for flowers. After sitting through those committee meetings, I knew you must need a bouquet." Red poppies, parsley, and mistletoe—he presumed she knew the flower code. Perhaps she was so hopelessly detached from mainstream society that she couldn't even *read* a flower code. Well, if she didn't, no great harm done. It had been a very witty message, but maybe it was just as well if it were lost on her.

"Why do you send me those mail notes with all those questions?" Dr. Penninger persisted gamely.

Oscar put aside his peppered stub of jerky and spread his gloved hands. "I needed some answers. I've been studying you, during those long board meetings. I've really come to appreciate you. You're the only member of that board who can stick to the point."

She examined the dead grass at her feet. "They're really incredibly boring meetings, aren't they?"

"Well, yes, they are." He smiled gamely. "Present company excepted."

"They're bad meetings. They're really bad. They're awful. I hate administration. I hate everything about it."

She looked up, her odd face congealing with distaste. "I sit there listening to them drone, and I can feel my life just ticking away."

"Mmmhmm!" Oscar deftly poured two cups from a battered cooler. "Here, let's enjoy this sports-performance pseudo-lemon concoction." He dragged a folded tarp near to the fire barrel, careful not to scorch himself. He sat.

Dr. Penninger collapsed heedlessly to earth in a sharp sprawl of kneecaps. "I can't even *think* properly anymore. They don't *let me* think. I try to stay alert during those meetings, but it's just impossible. They won't let me get anything accomplished." She sipped cautiously at the yellow swill in her biodegradable cup, then put the cup on the grass. "Lord knows I've tried."

"Why did they put you into administration in the first place?"

"Oh," she groaned, "a slot opened up on the board. The guy running Instrumentation had to resign, after Senator Dougal cracked up. . . . The board asked for me by name because of the Nobel award nonsense, and the neuro krewe told me I should take the post. We do need the labware. They nickel and dime us to death on equipment, they just don't understand our requirements. They don't even *want* to understand us."

"Somehow, that doesn't surprise me. I've noticed that the bookkeeping at the Collaboratory is not in standard federal formats. There seem to have been some irregularities in supply."

"Oh, that's not the half of it," she said.

"No?"

"No."

Oscar leaned forward slowly on his folded tarp. "What *is* the half of it?"

"I just can't tell you," she said, morosely hugging her shins. "Because I don't know why you want to know that. Or what you'd do about it, if you knew."

"All right," Oscar said, sitting back deliberately. "That answer makes sense. You're being very cautious and proper. I'm sure I'd feel much the same about it, if I were in your position." He stood up.

The plumbing pipes were made of a laminated polyvinyl the color of dried kelp. They had been computed and built in Boston to specifically fit this structure, and they were of a Chinese-jigsaw complexity that only a dedicated subroutine could fully understand.

"You have real talent with the mortar, but this plumbing is serious work," Oscar said. "I wouldn't blame you if you gave up and left now."

"Oh, I don't mind. I don't have to hit the lab until seven AM."

"Don't you ever sleep?"

"No, I just don't sleep much. Maybe three hours a night."

"How odd. I never sleep much, either." He knelt at the side of the plumbing case. She alertly handed him a nearby pair of snips, slapping them into his gloved hand, handle first.

"Thank you." He snapped through three black plastic packing bands. "I'm glad you came here tonight. I was rather wasting my time working alone on a group project like this. But it's therapeutic for me." He pried up the lid of the case and threw it aside. "You see, I've always had a rather difficult professional life."

"That's not what your record shows." She was hugging her jacketed arms. The wool hat had slipped down on her forehead.

"Oh, I suppose you've run some searches on me, then."

"I'm very inquisitive." She paused.

"That's all right, everybody does that sort of thing nowadays. I've been a celebrity since I was a little kid. I'm well documented, I'm used to it." He smiled sourly.

"Though you can't get the full flavor of my delightful personality from some casual scan of the net."

"If I were casual about this, I wouldn't be here now."

Oscar looked up in surprise. She stared back boldly. She'd done all this on purpose. She had her own agenda. She'd plotted it all out on graph paper, beforehand.

"Do you know why *I'm* out here in the middle of the night tonight, Dr. Penninger? It's because my girlfriend just left me."

She pondered this. Wheels spun in her head so quickly that he could almost hear them sizzle. "Really," she said slowly. "That's a shame."

"She's left our house in Boston, she's walked out on me. She's gone to Holland."

Her brows rose under the rim of the woolly hat. "Your girlfriend has defected to the Dutch?"

"No, not defected! She left on assignment, she's a political journalist. But she's gone anyway." He gazed at the elaborate nest of convoluted plumbing. "It's been a blow, it's really upset me."

The sight of all that joinery and tubing, complex and gleaming in its tatty plastic straw, filled Oscar with a sudden evil rush of authentic Sartrean nausea. He climbed to his feet. "You know something? It was all my fault. I can admit that. I neglected her. We had two separate careers. . . . She was fine on that East Coast glitterati circuit; we made a good couple while we had some common interests. . . ." He stopped and gauged her reaction. "Should I be burdening you with any of this?"

"Why not? I can understand that. Sometimes these things just don't work out. Romance in the sciences . . . 'The odds are good, but the goods are odd.' " She shook her head.

"I know that you're not married. You're not seeing anyone?"

"Nothing steady. I'm a workaholic."

Oscar found this encouraging news. He felt instinctive camaraderie for any ambitious obsessive. "Tell me something, Greta. Do I seem like a frightening person to you?" He touched his chest. "Am I scary? Be frank."

"You really *want* me to be frank?"

"Yes."

"People always tell me that I'm much too frank."

"Go ahead, I can take it."

She lifted her chin. "Yes, you're very scary. People are extremely suspicious of you. No one knows what you really want from us, or what you're doing in our lab. We all expect the very worst."

He nodded sagely. "You see, that's a perception problem. I do turn up for your board meetings, and I've brought a little entourage with me, so rumors start. But in reality, I shouldn't be scary—because I'm just not very significant. I'm only a Senate staffer."

"I've been to Senate hearings. And I've heard about others. Senate hearings can be pretty rough."

He edged closer to her. "All right—sure, there might be some hard questions asked in Washington someday. But it won't be *me* asking those questions. I just write briefing papers."

She was entirely unconvinced. "What about that big Air Force scandal in Louisiana? Didn't you have a lot to do with all that?"

"What, that? That's just politics! People claim that I influence the Senator-elect—but the influence goes all the other way, really. Until I met Alcott Bambakias, I was just a city council activist. The Senator's the man with the ideas and the message. I was just his campaign technician."

"Hmmm. I know a lot of technicians. I don't know many technicians who are multimillionaires, like you are."

"Oh, well, *that.* . . . Yes, I'm well-to-do, but compared to what my father made in his heyday, or the Senator's fortune . . . I do have money, but I wouldn't call that serious money. I know people with serious money, and I'm just not in their league." Oscar hefted a long green tube from the packing case, examined its crooks and angles mournfully, and set it back down. "The wind's picking up. . . . I don't have the heart for this anymore. I think I'll walk back to the dome. Maybe somebody's still up in the dorm. We'll play some poker."

"I have a car," she said.

"Really."

"You get a car, when you're on the Collaboratory board. So I drove here. I can give you a ride back to the lab."

"That would be lovely. Just let me stow the gear and shut down the system." He took off his hard hat and kneepads. He shed his padded construction jacket, and stood there hatless in a long-sleeved shirt; the cold wind ripped into the damp at his armpits. When he was done, he set the alarms and they left the site together.

He stopped at the sidewalk. "Wait a moment."

"What is it?"

"We seem to be chatting along pretty well here. But your car may be bugged."

She brushed her windblown hair back, skeptically. "Why would anyone bug me?"

"Because it's so cheap and easy. So tell me something just now, before we get into your car. Tell me something very frankly. Do you know about my personal background problem?"

"Your *background*? I know that your father was a movie star. . . ."

"I'm sorry. I shouldn't have brought that matter up. Really, I'm being completely impossible tonight. It was really good of you to visit the site tonight, but I've gotten off on the wrong foot here. I shouldn't bother you with any of this. You're on the board of directors, and I'm a federal official. . . . Listen, if our personal circumstances were different . . . And if either of us really *had time* for our personal problems . . ."

She stood there shivering. She was tall and thin and no longer used to real weather; she had worked hard in the dark and cold, and she was freezing. The night wind rose harshly and tore at his sleeves. He felt strangely drawn to her now. She was too tall, she was too thin, she had bad clothes, an odd face, and poor posture, she was eight years older than he was. They had nothing in common as people, any relationship they might establish was clearly doomed from the outset. Relating to her was like coaxing some rare animal on the other side of a woven-wire fence. Maybe that was why he felt such a compelling urge to touch her. "Doctor, I appreciate your company tonight, but I think you'd better go on ahead in your car now. We'll be in touch later about the board meetings. I still have a lot to learn."

"I hope you don't expect me to just drive off alone after *that*. Now I *have* to know. Get in the car."

She opened the door and they jammed themselves together. It was a meager little car, a Collaboratory car, and naturally it had no heater. Their chilling breath began to smear the windows.

"I really don't think you want to know about this. It's a rather strange story. It's bad. Worse than you expect."

She adjusted her woolen hat, and blew on her bare fingers. "They never put heaters in these things. Because you're never supposed to drive them outside the dome. It'll warm up in a minute. Why don't you just tell me whatever you think you can tell me. Then *I'll* decide if I want to know more."

"All right." He hesitated. "Well, to begin with, I'm an adopted child. Logan Valparaiso was not my biological father."

"No?"

"No, he didn't adopt me until I was almost three. You see, at the time, Logan was working on an international thriller movie about evil adoption farms. Adoption mills. They were a big scandal during that period. The full scale of the hormone pesticide disasters was becoming common knowledge. There were major male-infertility problems. So, the adoption market really boomed. Infertility clinics too, obviously. The demand-pull was suddenly huge, so a lot of unsavory people, quacks, exploiters, health-fad people, they all rushed in to exploit it. . . ."

"I can remember that time."

"Suddenly there was a lot of offshore baby-farming, embryo-farming. People were taking extreme measures. It made a pretty good topic for an action film. So, my dad cast himself as a vigilante law-and-order guerrilla. He played the role of a two-fisted Chicano abortion-clinic bomber, who gets turned by the feds, and becomes a secret-agent embryo-farm demolisher. . . ."

Whenever he told this story, he could hear his voice shift into a hateful, high-pitched whine. And it was happening now, even as the car's windows began to steam. He was sliding helplessly from his standard fast-talk into something much more extreme, a kind of chronic gabbling jabber. He would really have to watch that. He *was* watching it, he was watching it as well as he could, but he just couldn't help himself. "I don't mean to go on and on about the movie, but I did have to watch that film about four hundred times as a kid. . . . Plus all the rushes and the outtakes. . . . Anyway, Logan was Method acting deep into the role, and he and wife number three had a solid relationship at the time, as Logan's marriages went, that is. So he decided that as a kind of combination personal-growth move and film-related publicity stunt, he was going to adopt a real victim child from a real embryo mill."

She listened silently.

"Well, that kid was me. My original egg cell was a product sold on the infertility black market, and it ended up in a Colombian embryo mill. It was a mafia operation, so they were buying or stealing human eggs, fertilizing them, and offering them at a black-market rate for implantation. But there were quality problems. With resultant health problems for the female buyers. Not to mention the lawsuits and ethics hassles if somebody ratted them out. So the crooks started developing the product inside hired wombs, for a somewhat more standard, post-birth adoption. . . . But that business plan didn't work out either. The rent-a-womb thing was just too slow a process, and they had too many local women involved who might rat them out, or shake them down, or get upset about surrendering the product after term. So then they decided they would try to grow the embryos to term in vitro. They got a bunch of support vats together, but they weren't very good at it, because by this point, they'd already lost most of their working capital. Still, they got their hands on enough mammal-cloning data to give the artificial-womb thing a serious try with human beings. So I was never actually born, per se."

"I see." She straightened in her seat, placed her hands on the steering wheel, and drew a breath. "Please do go on, this is truly enormously interesting."

"Well, they were trying to sell me and their other products, but the overhead was just too high, and their failure rate was huge, and worse yet the market crashed when it turned out there was a cheaper medical workaround for sperm damage. Once they had the testicular syndrome fixed, it kicked the bottom right out of the baby market. So I was less than a year old when somebody ratted them out to the world health people, and then the blue-helmet brigade busted in from Europe and shut the whole place down. They confiscated all of us. I ended up in Denmark. Those are my earliest memories, this little orphanage in Denmark. . . . An orphanage and health clinic."

He had forced himself to tell this story many times, far more times than he had ever wanted to tell it to anyone. He had a prepared spiel of sorts, but he had never fully steeled himself to the dread it caused him to talk about it, the paralyzing stage fright. "Most of the product just didn't make it. They'd really screwed with us trying to get us tank-worthy. I had a full genetic scan done in Copenhagen, and it turned out that they'd simply lopped off most of the introns from the zygote DNA. See, they somehow figured that if they could prune away some junk DNA from the human genome, then the product would be hardier in the tank and would run more efficiently. . . . Their lab guys were all med-school dropouts, or downsizees from bankrupt HMOs. Also, they spent a lot of time high on synthetic cocaine, which was always the standard collateral industry with South American genetic black-marketeering. . . ."

He cleared his throat and tried to slow down. "Anyway, to get back to the point of my personal history, they had this blue-helmet Danish commando type who had led the raid in Colombia, and he ended up as the expert technical adviser on my dad's movie. This Danish commando and my dad got to be drinking buddies on the set, so when my dad came up with this adoption notion, the Danish guy naturally thought, 'Well, why not one of the kids from my own operation?' and he pulled some strings in Copenhagen. And that's how I ended up in Hollywood."

"Are you really telling me the truth?"

"Yes, I am."

"Could I drive you back to the lab and take a tissue sample?"

"Look, the tissue's just tissue. To hell with my tissue. The truth is a much bigger thing than my tissue. The truth is that people have a prejudice against persons like me. I can take their point, too, frankly. I can run a political campaign and I can get away with that, but I don't think I'd ever actually vote for me. Because I'm not sure that I can really trust me. I'm really *different*. There are big chunks in my DNA that probably aren't even of human origin."

He spread his hands. "Let me tell you how different I am. I don't sleep. I run a permanent mild fever. I grew up really fast—and not just because I spent my childhood in the L.A. fast lane. I'm twenty-eight now, but most people assume I'm in my mid-thirties. I'm sterile—I'll never have kids of my own—and I've had three bouts of liver cancer. Luckily, that kind of cancer treats pretty easily nowadays, but I'm still on angiogenesis inhibitors, plus growth-factor blockers, and I have to take antitumor maintenance pills three times a month. The other eight kids from that raid— five of them died young of major organ cancers, and the other three . . . well, they're Danes. They are three identical Danish women with—let me just put it this way —with extremely troubled personal lives."

"Are you sure you're not making this up? It's such a compelling story. Do you really have an elevated body-core temperature? Have you ever had a PET-scan done?"

He looked at her meditatively. "You know, you're really taking this very well. I mean, most people who hear this story have to go through a certain shock period. . . ."

"I'm not a medical doctor, and genetic expression isn't really my field. But I'm not shocked by that story. I'm astonished by it, of course, and I'd really like to confirm some details in my lab, but . . ." She considered it, then found the word. "Mostly, I'm very intrigued."

"Really?"

"That was truly a profound abdication of scientific ethics. It violated the Declaration of Helsinki, plus at least eight standards of conduct with human subjects. You're obviously a very brave and capable man, to have overcome that childhood tragedy, and achieved the success that you have."

Oscar said nothing. Suddenly, his eyes were stinging. He'd seen a wide variety of reactions to his personal background confession. Mostly, reactions from women—because he rarely had to confess it at all, except to women. A business relationship could be begun and concluded without outing himself; a sexual relationship, never. He'd seen a full gamut of reactions. Shock, horror, amusement, sympathy; even a shrug and shake of the head. Indifference. Almost always, the truth gnawed at them over the long term.

But he'd never seen a reaction like Greta Penninger's.

Oscar and his secretary Lana Ramachandran were walking through the garden behind the sloping white walls of the Genetic Fragmentation Clinic. The garden bordered one of the staff housing sections, so there were children around. The constant piercing screams of young children meant that this was a good place to talk privately.

"Stop sending the flowers to her dorm residence," Oscar told her. "She never goes there. Basically, she never sleeps."

"Where should I have them delivered, then?"

"Into her laboratory. That's more or less where she lives. And let's turn up the heat on those bouquets—move off the pansies and zinnias, and right into tuberoses."

Lana was shocked. "Not tuberoses already!"

"Well, you know what I mean. Also, we're going to start feeding her soon. She doesn't eat properly—I can tell that. And later, we'll style her and dress her. But we'll have to work our way up to that."

"How are we even supposed to *reach* her? Dr. Penninger works inside the Hot Zone," Lana said. "That's a full-scale Code 4 biohazard facility. It's got its own airlocks, and the walls are eight feet thick."

He shrugged. "Dip the flowers into liquid nitrogen. Get 'em sealed in plastic. Whatever."

His secretary groaned. "Oscar, what *is it* with you?

Have you lost your mind? You can't really be making a play for that woman. I know your type really well by now, and she's definitely not your type. In fact, I've asked around some—and Dr. Penninger is not *anybody's* type. You're gonna do yourself an injury."

"Okay, maybe I have a sudden aberrant sweet tooth."

Lana was genuinely pained. She wanted the best for him. She was quite humorless, but she was very efficient. "You shouldn't act like this. It's just not smart. She's on the board of directors, she's someone who's officially in charge around here. And you're a staffer for her Senate oversight committee. That's a definite conflict of interest."

"I don't care."

Lana was in despair. "You're always doing this. Why? I can't believe you got away with shacking up with that journalist. She was covering the campaign! Somebody could have made a huge ethics stink about that. And before that, there was that crazy architecture girl . . . and before that, there was that worthless Boston city management girl. . . . You can't keep getting away with this, cutting things close this way. It's like some kind of compulsion."

"Look, Lana, you knew my romantic life was a problem as soon as you met me. I do have ethics. I draw the line at having an affair with anyone in my own krewe. All right? That would be bad, that would be workplace harassment, it's like incest. But here I am, and what's past is past. Greta Penninger has made her career here, she's someone who really understands this facility. Plus, she's very bored, and I know that I can get to her. So we have commonalities. I think we can help each other out."

"I give up! I'll never figure out men. You don't even *know* what you want, do you? You wouldn't know what to do with happiness if it was standing right in front of you, begging you to notice."

Lana had gone too far now. Oscar assembled and aimed a scowl at her. "Look, Lana, when you find me some happiness that you know will really suit me—*me,* in particular—then write me a memo about it. All right? In the meantime, can you get off the dime with the flowers effort?"

"All right, I'll try," she said. "I'll do my best." Lana was angry with him now, so she stalked off into the gardens. He couldn't help that. Lana would come around. Lana always did. Dealing with him took her mind off her own troubles. Oscar strolled on, whistling a bit, examining the fretted dome of the sky, an evil winter skein of gray scudding harmlessly above the sweet federal bubble of warm and fragrant air. He tossed his hat in his hand, catching it by its sharp and perfect brim. Life was definitely looking up for him. He skirted a blooming mass of rare azaleas in order to miss a drowsing antelope.

He'd chosen these Collaboratory gardens as his confidential offices lately. He'd given up using the Bambakias tour bus, since the bus seemed to attract so many determined bugging efforts. They would have to return the bus to Boston soon, anyway. That seemed just as well—high time, really. There was no use in remaining dependent on loaned equipment. Scratch the old bus, inhabit the brandnew hotel. Just keep the krewe together, keep up the core competencies. Keep the herd moving. It was progress, it was doable.

Fontenot emerged from the flowering brush and discovered him. To Oscar's mild surprise, Fontenot was exactly on schedule. Apparently the roadblock situation was easing in Louisiana.

The security man was wearing a straw hat, vest, jeans, and black gum boots. Fontenot had been getting a lot of sun lately. He looked more pleased with himself than Oscar had ever seen him.

They shook hands, checked by habit for tails and eavesdroppers, and fell into pace together.

"You're getting a lot of credit for this Air Force base debacle," Fontenot told him. "Somehow, it's staying news. If the pressure keeps building, something's bound to crack."

"Oh, giving me the credit for that is all Sosik's idea. It's a fallback position for the Senator. If the situation blows a valve, then the experienced chief of staff can always make a fall guy out of the rash young campaign adviser."

Fontenot looked at him skeptically. "Well, I didn't see 'em twisting your arm when you did those two major interviews. . . . I don't know how you found the time to get so fully briefed on power blackouts and Louisiana politics."

"Power blackouts are a very interesting topic. The Boston media are important. I'm very sentimental about the Boston media." Oscar laced his hands behind his back. "I admit, it wasn't tactful to publicly call Louisiana 'the Weird Sister of American States.' But it's a truism."

Fontenot couldn't be bothered to deny this. "Oscar, I've been pretty busy getting my new house set up properly. But proper security isn't a part-time job. You're still paying me a salary, but I've been letting you down."

"If that bothers you, why not put in a little work on the hotel site for us? It's a big hit locally. These Buna people love us for it."

"No, listen. Since we'll soon be parting company for good—and I really mean that, this time—I thought I'd run some full-scale security scans for you, across the board. And I've got some results for you. You have a security problem."

"Yes?"

"You've offended the Governor of Louisiana."

Oscar shook his head rapidly. "Look, the hunger strike isn't about Governor Huguelet. Huguelet has never been the issue. The issue is the starving air base and the federal Emergency committees. We've scarcely said a word in public about Green Huey."

"The Senator hasn't. But *you* sure have. Repeatedly."

Oscar shrugged. "Okay, obviously we haven't much use for the Governor. The guy's a crooked demagogue. But we're not pushing that. As far as the scandal goes, if anything, we're Huey's tactical allies at the moment."

"Don't be naive. Green Huey doesn't think the way you guys think. He's not some go-along get-along pol, who makes tactical deals with the opposition. Huey is always the center of Huey's universe. So you're for him, or you're agin him."

"Why would Huey make unnecessary enemies? That's just not smart politics."

"Huey does make enemies. He enjoys it. It's part of his game. It always has been. Huey's a smart pol all right, but he can be a one-man goon squad. He learned that when he worked in Texas for Senator Dougal."

Oscar frowned. "Look, Dougal's out of the picture now. He's finished, history. If Dougal wasn't in the dry-out clinic, he'd probably be in jail."

Fontenot glanced around them with reflexive suspicion. "You shouldn't talk like an attack ad when you're standing inside a place that Dougal built. This lab was always Dougal's favorite project. And as for Huey, he used to work in here. You're walking in Huey's footsteps. When he was the Senator's chief of staff, he twisted arms around here hard enough to break a few."

"They built this place all right, but they built it crooked."

"Other politicians are crooked too, and they don't build a goddamn thing. East Texas and South Louisiana— they finally got their heads together and cut a big piece of the pie for themselves. But things have always run crooked in this part of the country, *always*. They wouldn't know what to do with clean government. Old Dougal fell down pretty hard in the long run, but that's just Texas. Texas is ornery, Texans like to chew their good old boys up a little bit before they bury them. But Huey learned plenty from Dougal, and he doesn't make Dougal's mistakes. Huey is the Governor of Louisiana now, he's the big cheese, the boss, the kahuna. Huey's got himself two handpicked federal Senators, just to shine his shoes. You're bad-mouthing Huey up in Boston—but Huey is sitting just over yonder in Baton Rouge. And you're getting in Huey's face."

"All right. I take the point. Go on."

"Oscar, I've seen you do some very clever things with nets, you're a young guy and you grew up using them. But you haven't seen everything that I've seen, so let me spell this out for you nice and careful."

They turned around a riotous bougainvillea. Fontenot assembled his thoughts. "Okay. Let's imagine you're a net-based bad guy, netwar militia maybe. And you have a search engine, and it keeps track of all the public mentions of your idol, Governor Etienne-Gaspard Huguelet. Every once in a while, someone appears in public life who cramps the style of your boy. So the offender's name is noticed, and it's logged, and it's assigned a cumulative rating. After someone's name reaches a certain level of annoyance, your program triggers automatic responses." Fontenot adjusted his straw hat. "The response is to send out automatic messages, urging people to kill this guy."

Oscar laughed. "That's a new one. That's really crazy."

"Well, yeah. Craziness is the linchpin of the whole deal. You see, there have always been a lot of extremists, paranoiacs, and antisocial losers, all very active on the nets. . . . In the Secret Service, we found out a long time ago that the nets are a major intelligence asset for us. Demented, violent people tend to leave some kind of hint, or track, or signal, well before they strike. We compiled a hell of a lot of psychological profiles over the years, and we discovered some commonalities. So, if you know the evidence to look for, you can actually sniff some of these guys out, just from the nature of their net activities."

"Sure. User profiles. Demographic analysis. Stochastic indexing. Do it all the time."

"We built those profile sniffers quite a while back, and they turned out pretty useful. But then the State Department made the mistake of kinda lending that software to some undependable allies. . . ." Fontenot stopped short as a spotted jaguarundi emerged from under a bush, stretched, yawned, and ambled past them. "The problem came when our profile sniffers fell into the wrong hands. . . . See, there's a different application for that protective software. Bad people can use it to compile large mailing lists of dangerous lunatics. Finding the crazies with net analysis, that's the easy part. Convincing them to take action, that part is a little harder. But if you've got ten or twelve thousand of them, you've got a lotta fish, and somebody's bound to bite. If you can somehow put it into their heads that some particular guy deserves to be attacked, that guy might very well come to harm."

"So you're saying that Governor Huguelet has put me on an enemies list?"

"No, not Huey. Not personally. He ain't that dumb. I'm saying that somebody, somewhere, built some software years ago that *automatically* puts Green Huey's enemies onto hit lists."

Oscar removed his hat and carefully adjusted his hair. "I'm rather surprised I haven't heard about this practice."

"We Secret Service people don't like it publicized. We do what we can to fight back—we wiped out a whole nest of those evil things during Third Panama . . . but we can't monitor every offshore netserver in the world. About the best we can do is to monitor our own informants. We always check 'em, to see if they're getting email urging them to kill somebody. So have a look at this printout."

They found a graceful wooden garden bench. A

small child in a pinafore was sitting on it, patiently petting an exotic stoat, but she didn't seem to mind adult company. Oscar silently read through the text, twice, carefully.

The text was nowhere near so sinister and sophisticated as he had somehow imagined it. In fact, the text was crude and banal. He found it deeply embarrassing to discover his own name inserted into a murderous rant so blatant and so badly composed. He nodded, slipped the paper back to Fontenot. The two of them smiled, tipped their hats to the little girl, and went back to walking.

"It's pathetic!" Oscar said, once they were out of earshot. "That's spam from a junk mailbot. I've seen some junkbots that are pretty sophisticated, they can generate a halfway decent ad spiel. But that stuff is pure chain-mail ware. It can't even punctuate!"

"Well, your core-target violent paranoiac, he might not notice the misspellings."

Oscar thought this over. "How many of those messages were mailed out, do you suppose?"

"Maybe a couple of thousand? The USSS protective-interest files list over three hundred thousand people. A clever program wouldn't hit up every possible lunatic every single time, of course."

"Of course." Oscar nodded thoughtfully. "And what about Bambakias? Is he in danger too?"

"I briefed the Senator about this situation. They'll step up his security in Cambridge and Washington. But I figure you're in much more trouble than he is. You're closer, you're louder, and you're a lot easier."

"Hmmm. I see. Thank you for bringing this to my attention, Jules. You're making very good sense, as always. So what would you advise?"

"I advise better security. The commonsense things. Break up your daily routine. Go to places where you can't be expected. Keep a safe house ready, in case of trouble. Watch out for strangers, for anybody who might be stalk-ing you, or workin' up the nerve. Avoid crowds whenever possible. And you do need a bodyguard."

"I don't have time for all that, though. There's too much work for me here."

Fontenot sighed. "That's exactly what people always tell us. . . . Oscar, I was in the Secret Service for twenty-two years. It's a career, we have a real job of work. You don't hear a lot in public about the Secret Service, but the Secret Service is a very busy outfit. They shut down the old CIA, they broke up the FBI years ago, but the USSS has been around almost two hundred years now. We never go away. Because the threat never goes away. People in public life get death threats. They get 'em all the time. I've seen hundreds of death threats. They're very common things for famous people. I never saw a real-life attempted assassination, though. Spent my whole career carefully watchin' and waitin' for one, and it never, ever happened. Until one fine day, that car bomb happened. Then I lost my leg."

"I understand."

"You need to come to terms with this. It's reality. It's real, and you have to adjust to it, but at the same time, you can't let it stop you."

Oscar said nothing.

"The sky is a different color when you know that you might get shot at. Things taste different. It can get to you, make you wonder if a public life's worthwhile. But you know, despite stuff like this, this is not an evil or violent society." Fontenot shrugged. "Really, it isn't. Not anymore. Back when I was a young agent, America was truly violent then. Huge crime rates, crazy drug gangs, automatic weapons very cheap and easy. Miserable, angry, pitiful people. People with grudges, people with a lot of hate inside. But nowadays, this just isn't a violent time anymore. It's just a very weird time. People don't fight real hard for anything in particular, when they know their whole lives could be turned inside out in a week flat.

People's lives don't make sense anymore, but most people in America, the poor people especially, they're a lot *happier* than they used to be. They might be profoundly lost, like your Senator likes to say, but they're not all crushed and desperate. They're just . . . wandering around. Drifting. Hanging loose. They're at very loose ends."

"Maybe."

"If you lie low awhile, this business will pass right over you. You'll move on to Boston or Washington, on to other issues, out of Huey's hair. Automated hit lists are like barbed wire, they're nasty but they're very stupid. They don't even understand what they read. Once you're yesterday's news, the machines will just forget you."

"I don't intend to become yesterday's news for quite a while, Jules."

"Then you'd better learn how famous people go on living."

———————

Oscar was determined not to have his morale affected by Fontenot's security alarm. He went back to work on the hotel. The hotel was coming along with the usual fairytale rapidity of a Bambakias structure. The whole krewe was pitching in; they had all been infected by the Bambakias ideology, so they all protested stoutly to one another that they wouldn't miss the fun of construction for anything.

Strangely enough, the work really did become fun, in its own way; there was a rich sense of schadenfreude in fully sharing the sufferings of others. The system logged the movements of everyone's hands, cruelly eliminating any easy method of deceiving your friends while you yourself slacked off work. Distributed instantiation was fun in the way that hard-core team sports were fun. Balconies flew up, archways and pillars rose, random jumbles crystallized into spacious sense and reason. It was like lashing your way up a mountainside in cables and crampons, only to notice, all sudden and gratuitous, a fine and lovely view.

There were certain set-piece construction activities guaranteed to attract an admiring crowd: the tightening of tensegrity cables, for instance, that turned a loose skein of blocks into a solidly locked-together parapet, good for the next three hundred years. Bambakias krewes took elaborate pleasure in these theatrical effects. The krewe would vigorously play to the crowd when they were doing the boring stuff, they would ham it up. But during these emergent moments when the system worked serious magic, they would kick back all loose and indifferent, with the heavy-lidded cool of twentieth-century jazz musicians.

Oscar was a political consultant. He made it his business to appreciate a crowd. He felt about a good crowd the way he imagined dirt farmers feeling about a thriving field of watermelons. However, he had a hard time conjuring up his usual warm appreciation when one of the watermelons might have come there to shoot him.

Of course he was familiar with security; during the campaign, everyone had known that there might be incidents, that the candidate might be hurt. The candidate was mixing with The People, and some few of The People were just naturally evil or insane. There had indeed been a few bad moments on the Massachusetts campaign trail: nasty hecklers, nutty protesters, vomiting drunks, pickpockets, fainting spells, shoving matches. The unpleasant business that made good campaign security the functional equivalent of seat belts or fire extinguishers. Security was an empty trouble and expense, ninety-nine times in a hundred. On the hundredth instance you were very glad you had been so sensible.

The modern rich always maintained their private security. Bodyguards were basic staff for the overclass, just like majordomos, cooks, secretaries, sysadmins, and image consultants. A well-organized personal krewe, including proper security, was simply expected of modern wealthy people; without a krewe, no one would take you seriously. All of this made perfect sense.

And yet none of it had much to do with the stark notion of having one's flesh pierced by a bullet.

It wasn't the idea of dying that bothered him. Oscar could easily imagine dying. It was the ugly sense of meaningless disruption that repelled him. His game board kicked over by a psychotic loner, a rule-breaker who couldn't even comprehend the stakes.

Defeat in the game, he could understand. Oscar could easily imagine himself, for instance, swept up in a major political scandal. Crapped out. Busted. Cast into the wilderness. Broken from the ranks. Disgraced. Shunned, forgotten. A nonperson. A political hulk. Oscar could very well imagine that eventuality. It definitely gave the game a spice. After all, if victory was guaranteed, that wouldn't be victory at all.

But he didn't want to be shot. So Oscar gave up working on the building project. It was a sad sacrifice, because he truly enjoyed the process, and the many glorious opportunities it offered for shattering the preconceptions of backward East Texans. But it tired him to envision the eager and curious crowds as a miasma of enemies. Where were the crosshairs centered? Constant morbid speculation on the subject of murder was enough to convince Oscar that he himself would have made an excellent assassin—clever, patient, disciplined, resolute, and sleepless. This painful discovery rather harmed his self-image.

He warned his krewe of the developments. Heartwarmingly, they seemed far more worried about his safety than he was himself.

He retreated back inside the Collaboratory, where he knew he was much more secure. In the event of any violent crime, Collaboratory security would flip a switch on their Escaped Animal Vector alarms, and every orifice in the dome would lock as tight as a bank vault.

Oscar was much safer under glass—but he could feel

himself curtailed, under pressure, his life delimited by un-
seen hands. However, he still had one major field of coun-
terattack. Oscar dived aggressively into his laptop. He,
Pelicanos, Bob Argow, and Audrey Avizienis had all been
collaborating on the chains of evidence.

Senator Dougal and his Texan/Cajun mafia of pork-
devouring good old boys had been very dutiful at first.
Their relatively modest graft vanished at once, slipping
methodically over Texas state lines into the vast money
laundries of the Louisiana casinos. The funds oozed back
later as generous campaign contributions and unexplained
second homes in the names of wives and nephews.

But the years had gone on, and the country's financial situation had become stormy and chaotic. With
hyperinflation raging and major industries vanishing like
pricked balloons, it was hard to keep up pretenses. Covering their tracks had become boring and tiresome. The
Senator's patronage of the Collaboratory was staunch and
tireless, and the long-honored causes of advancing science
and sheltering endangered species still gave most Americans a warm, generous, deeply uncritical feeling. The
Collaboratory's work struggled on—while the rot crept
on in its shadow, spreading into parts scams, bid rigging, a
minor galaxy of kickbacks and hush money. There was
featherbedding on jobs, with small-time political allies
slotted into dull yet lucrative posts, such as parking and
plumbing and laundry. Embezzlement was like alcoholism. It was very hard to step back, and if no one ever called
you out on it, then the little red veins began to show.

Oscar felt he was making excellent progress. His options for action were multiplying steadily.

Then the first homicidal lunatic attacked.

With this occurrence, Oscar was approached by Collaboratory security. Security took the form of a middle-
aged female officer, who belonged to a tiny federal police
agency known as the "Buna National Collaboratory Security Authority." This woman informed Oscar that a man

had just arrived from Muskogee, Oklahoma, banging fruitlessly at the southern airlock and brandishing a foil-wrapped cardboard box that he insisted was a "Super Reflexo-Grenade."

Oscar visited the suspect in his cell. His would-be assassin was disheveled and wretched, utterly lost, with the awful cosmic dislocation of the seriously mentally ill. Oscar felt a sudden unexpected pang of terrible pity. It was very clear to him that this man had no focused malice. The poor wretch had simply been hammered into his clumsy evildoing through a ceaseless wicked pelting of deceptive net-based spam. Oscar found himself so shocked by this that he blurted out his instinctive wish that the man might be set free.

The local cops were wisely having none of that, however. They had called the Secret Service office in Austin. Special agents would be arriving presently to thoroughly interrogate Mr. Spencer, and discreetly take him elsewhere.

The very next day, another lethal crank showed up. This gentleman, Mr. Bell, was cleverer. He had attempted to hide himself inside a truck shipment of electrical transformers. The truck driver had noticed the lunatic darting out from beneath a tarp, and had called security. A frantic chase ensued, and the stowaway was finally found burrowing desperately into a tussock of rare marsh grass, still gamely clutching a homemade black-powder pistol.

The advent of the third man, Mr. Anderson, was the worst by far. When caught lurking inside a dumpster, Anderson screamed loudly about flying saucers and the fate of the Confederacy, while slashing at his arms with a razor. This bloodshed was very shocking, and it made Oscar's position difficult.

It was clear that he needed a safe house. And the safest area inside the Collaboratory was, of course, the Hot Zone.

The interior of the Hot Zone was rather less impres-

sive than its towering china-white shell. The Zone was a
very odd environment, since every item inside the structure had been designed to withstand high-pressure cleansing with superheated steam. The interior decor consisted
of poreless plastics, acid-resistant white ceramic benchtops,
bent-tubing metal chairs, and grainy nonslip floors. The
Hot Zone was simultaneously deeply strange and profoundly mundane. After all, it wasn't a fairyland or a
spacecraft, it was simply a set of facilities where people
carried out certain highly specific activities under closely
defined and extremely clean circumstances. People had
been working in the place for fifteen years.

Inside the dressing room—cum-airlock, Oscar was required to shed his street clothes. He outfitted himself in a
disposable paper labcoat, gloves, a bouffant cap, a mask,
and sockless ankle-wrapping clean-room booties. Greta
Penninger, swiftly appointing herself his unofficial hostess,
sent a male lab gofer to take him in hand.

Dr. Penninger possessed a large suite of laboratory
offices within a brightly lit warren known as Neurocomputational Studies. A plastic door identified her as GRETA V.
PENNINGER, PRINCIPAL INVESTIGATOR, and behind that door
was a brightly lit surgical theater. Yards of white tabletop.
Safety treading. Drying racks. Safety film. Detergents. Bal-
ances, fume hoods, graduated beakers. Hand pipettes.
Centrifuges. Chromatographs. And a great many square
white devices of utterly unknown function.

Oscar was met by Greta's krewe majordomo, Dr.
Albert Gazzaniga. Gazzaniga was the exemplar of what
Oscar had come to recognize as "the Collaboratory look,"
intense and yet strangely diffuse, like a racquetball player in
Lotusland. Gazzaniga spent his working life in clean-room
gear, and relaxed outside in rotting sneakers and khaki
shorts. Gazzaniga had an eager, honest, backpack-wearing
look about him. He was one of the few people in the
Collaboratory who identified himself as a Federal Democrat. Most politically active Collaboratory people tended

to be tedious, fuzzy Left Tradition Bloc types, party members of the Social Democrats or the Communists. It was rare to find one with enough grit and energy to take a solidly Reformist stance.

"So, what's become of Dr. Penninger?"

"Oh, you mustn't be offended, but she's running a procedure now. She'll be here when she's good and done. Believe me, when Greta wants to concentrate, it's always best to let her be."

"That's all right. I quite understand."

"It's not that she doesn't take you seriously, you know. She's very sympathetic to your situation. We've had troubles of our own with extremists. Animal rights people, vivisection nuts. . . . I know we scientists lead very sheltered lives compared to you politicians, but we're not entirely out-of-it here."

"I would never think that, Albert."

"I feel personally very sorry that you should be subject to this kind of harassment. It's an honor to help you, really."

Oscar nodded. "I appreciate that sentiment. It's good of you to take me in. I'll try not to get in the way of your labwork."

Dr. Gazzaniga led him down an aisle past seven bunny-suited workers probing at their jello dishes. "I hope you don't have the impression that Greta's lab is a biohazard zone. We never work on anything hot in this lab. We wear this clean-gear strictly to protect our cultures from contamination."

"I see."

Gazzaniga shrugged beneath his lint-free labcoat. "That whole gene-technology scare tactic—the giant towers, the catacombs, the airlocks, the huge sealed dome —I guess that made a lot of political sense in the old days, but it was always a naive idea basically, and now it's very old-fashioned. Except for a few classified military apps, the Collaboratory gave up on survivable bugs ages ago.

There's nothing growing inside the Hot Zone that could hurt you. Genetic engineering is a very stable field of practice now, it's fifty years old. In terms of bugs, we use only thermo extremophiles. Germs native to volcanic environments. Very efficient, high metabolism, and good industrial turnover, and of course they're very safe. Their metabolism doesn't function at all, under 90° C. They live off sulfur and hydrogen, which you'd never find inside any human bloodstream. Plus, all our stocks are double knockouts. So even if you literally bathed in those bugs—well, you might well get scalded, but you'd never risk infection or genetic bleed-over."

"That sounds very reassuring."

"Greta's a professional. She's a stickler for good lab procedure. No, more than that—the lab is where she really shines personally. She's very strong in neurocomputational math, don't get me wrong there—but Greta's one of the great hands-on lab fiends. She can do stuff with STM probes like nobody else in the world. And if we could just get her hands on some decent thixotropic centrifuges instead of this Stone Age rotor crap, we'd be really kicking ass in here."

Gazzaniga was on a roll now. He was visibly trembling with passionate commitment. "In publishable papers per man-hour, this is the most productive lab in Buna. We've got the talent, and Greta's lab krewe is second to none. If we could only get proper resources, there's no telling what we could accomplish here. Neuroscience is really breaking open right now, the same way genetics did forty years ago, or computers forty years before that. The sky's the limit, really."

"What is it, exactly, that you're doing in here?"

"Well, in layman's terms . . ."

"Never mind that, Albert. Just tell me about your work."

"Well, basically, we're still following up her Nobel Prize results. That was all about glial neurochemical gradients evoking attentional modulation. It was the biggest neurocognitive breakthrough in years, so there's a lot of open field for us to run in now. Karen there is working on phasic modulation and spiking frequency. Yung-Nien is our token cognition wizard in the krewe, she does stochastic resonance and rate-response modeling. And Serge over yonder is your basic receptor-mechanic, he's working on dendritic transformer uptakes. The rest of these people are basically postdoc support staff, but you never know, when you work with Greta Penninger. This is a world-famous lab. It's a magnet. It's got the right stuff. By the time she's fifty or sixty, even her junior co-authors will be running neuro labs."

"And what is Dr. Penninger working on?"

"Well, you can ask her that yourself!" Greta had arrived. Gazzaniga tactfully absented himself.

Oscar apologized for having interrupted her work.

"No, that's all right," Greta said serenely. "I'm going to make the time for you. I think it's worth it."

"That's very broad-minded of you."

"Yes," she said simply.

Oscar gazed about her laboratory. "It's odd that we should meet inside a place like this. . . . I can tell that this locale suits you perfectly, but for me, this has such a strong personal resonance. . . . Can we talk privately here?"

"My lab is not bugged. Every surface in here is sterilized twice a week. Nothing as large as a listening device could possibly survive in here." She noticed his skeptical reaction, and changed her mind. She reached out and turned a switch on a homogenizer, which began to make a comforting racket.

Oscar felt much better. They were still in plain sight, but at least the noise would drown audio eavesdropping. "Do you know how I define 'politics,' Greta?"

She looked at him. "I know that politics means a lot of trouble for scientists."

"Politics is the art of reconciling human aspirations."
She considered this. "Okay. So?"

"Greta, I need you to level with me. I need to find
some reasonable people who can testify in the upcoming
Senate hearing. The standard talking heads from senior
management just won't do anymore. I need people with
some street-level awareness of what's really going on at this
facility."

"Why ask me? Why don't you ask Cyril Morello or
Warren Titche? Those guys have tons of time for political
activism."

Oscar was already very aware of Morello and Titche.
They were two of Collaboratory's grass-roots community
leaders, though as yet they were quite unaware of that fact.
Cyril Morello was the assistant head of the Human Resources Department, a man who through his consistently
self-defeating, anti-careerist actions had won the trust of
the Collaboratory rank and file. Warren Titche was the
lab's vociferous token radical, a ragged-elbowed zealot
who fought for bike racks and cafeteria menus as if failure
meant nuclear holocaust.

"I'm not asking you for a list of specific gripes. I
have a long list of those already. What I need is, well, how
shall I put this. . . . The spin, the big picture. The pitch.
The Message. You see, the new Congress has three brand-
new Senators on the Science Committee. They lack the
in-depth experience of the Committee's very, *very* long-
serving former chairman, Senator Dougal of Texas. It's
really an entirely new game in Washington now."

Greta glanced surreptitiously at her watch. "Do you
really think this is going to help anything?"

"I'll cut to the chase. Let me put a simple question to
you. Let's assume you have absolute power over federal
science policy, and can have anything you please. Give me
the blue-sky version. What do you want?"

"Oh! Well!" She was interested now. "Well, I guess
. . . I'd want American science to be just like it was in

the Golden Age. That would be in the Communist Period, during Cold War One. You see, back in those days, if you had a strong proposal, and you were ready to work, you could almost always swing decent, long-term federal funding."

"As opposed to the nightmare you have now," Oscar prompted. "Endless paperwork, bad accounting, senseless ethics hassles . . ."

Greta nodded reflexively. "It's hard to believe how far we've fallen. Science funding used to be allocated by peer review from within the science community. It wasn't doled out by Congress in pork-barrel grants for domestic political advantage. Nowadays, scientists spend forty percent of their working time mooching around for funds. Life in science was very direct, in the good old days. The very same person who swung the grant would do her own benchwork and write up her own results. Science was a handicraft, really. You'd have scientific papers written by three, four co-authors—never huge krewes of sixty or eighty, like we've got now."

"So it's economics, basically," Oscar coaxed.

She leaned forward tautly. "No, it's much deeper than that. Twentieth-century science had an entirely different arrangement. There was understanding between the government and the science community. It was a frontier mentality. Those were the gold-rush days. National Science Foundation. NIH. NASA. ARPA. . . . And the science agencies held up their end of the deal. Miracle drugs, plastics, whole new industries . . . people literally flew to the moon!"

Oscar nodded. "Producing miracles," he said. "That sounds like a steady line of work."

"Sure, there was job security back then," Greta said. "Tenure was nice, in particular. Have you ever heard of that old term 'tenure'?"

"No," Oscar said.

"It was all too good to last," Greta said. "National

government controlled the budgets, but scientific knowledge is global. Take the Internet—that was a specialized
science network at first, but it exploded. Now tribesmen
in the Serengeti can log on directly over Chinese satellites."

"So the Golden Age stopped when the First Cold
War ended?" Oscar said.

She nodded. "Once we'd won, Congress wanted to
redesign American science for national competitiveness,
for global economic warfare. But that never suited us at all.
We never had a chance."

"Why not?" Oscar said.

"Well, basic research gets you two economic bene-
fits: intellectual property and patents. To recoup the investment in R&D, you need a gentlemen's agreement that
inventors get exclusive rights to their own discoveries. But
the Chinese never liked 'intellectual property.' We never
stopped pressuring them about the issue, and finally a major trade war broke out, and the Chinese just called our
bluff. They made all English-language intellectual property freely available on their satellite networks to anybody
in the world. They gave away our store for nothing, and it
bankrupted us. So now, thanks to the Chinese, basic science has lost its economic underpinnings. We have to live
on pure prestige now, and that's a very thin way to live."

"China bashing's out of style this year," Oscar said.
"How about bashing the Dutch?"

"Yeah, Dutch appropriate-technology. . . . The
Dutch have been going to every island, every seashore,
every low-lying area in the world, making billions building dikes. They've built an alliance against us of islands and
low-lying states, they get in our face in every international
arena. . . . They want to reshape global scientific research for purposes of ecological survival. They don't want
to waste time and money on things like neutrinos or
spacecraft. The Dutch are very troublesome."

"Cold War Two isn't on the agenda of the Senate

Science Committee," Oscar said. "But it certainly could be, if we could build a national security case."

"Why would that help?" Greta shrugged. "Bright people will make huge sacrifices, if you'll just let them work on the things that really interest them. But if you have to spend your life grinding out results for the military, you're just another cubicle monkey."

"This is good!" Oscar said. "This is just what I was hoping for—a frank and open exchange of views."

Her eyes narrowed. "You want me to be *really* frank, Oscar?"

"Try me."

"What did the Golden Age get us? The public couldn't handle the miracles. We had an Atomic Age, but that was dangerous and poisonous. Then we had a Space Age, but that burned out in short order. Next we had an Information Age, but it turned out that the real killer apps for computer networks are social disruption and software piracy. Just lately, American science led the Biotech Age, but it turned out the killer app there was making free food for nomads! And now we've got a Cognition Age waiting."

"And what will that bring us—your brand-new Cognition Age?"

"Nobody knows. If we knew what the outcome would be in advance, then it wouldn't be basic research."

Oscar blinked. "Let me get this straight. You're dedicating your life to neural research, but you can't tell us what it will do to us?"

"I *can't* know. There's no way to judge. Society is too complex a phenomenon, even science is too complex. We've just learned so incredibly much in the past hundred years. . . . Knowledge gets fragmented and ultraspecialized, scientists know more and more about less and less. . . . You can't make informed decisions about the social results of scientific advances. We scientists don't even really know what we know anymore."

"That's pretty frank, all right. You're frankly abandoning the field, and leaving science policy decisions to the random guesses of bureaucrats."

"Random guesses don't work either."

Oscar rubbed his chin. "That sounds bad. Really bad. It sounds hopeless."

"Then maybe I'm painting too dark a picture. There's a lot of life in science—we've made some major historic discoveries, even in the past ten years."

"Name some for me," Oscar said.

"Well, we now know that eighty percent of the earth's biomass is subterranean."

Oscar shrugged. "Okay."

"We know there's bacterial life in interstellar space," Greta said. "You have to admit that was big."

"Sure."

"There have been huge medical advances in this century. We've defeated most cancers. We cured AIDS. We can treat pseudo-estrogen damage," Greta said. "We have one-shot cures for cocaine and heroin addiction."

"Too bad about alcoholism, though."

"We can regenerate damaged nerves. We've got lab rats smarter than dogs now."

"Oh, and of course there's cosmological torque," Oscar said. They both laughed. It seemed impossible that they could have overlooked cosmological torque, even for an instant.

"Let me switch perspectives," Oscar said. "Tell me about the Collaboratory. What's your core competency here in Buna—what does this facility do for America that is unique and irreplaceable?"

"Well, there's our genetic archives, of course. That's what we're world-famous for."

"Hmmm," Oscar said. "I recognize that gathering all those specimens from all around the world was very difficult and expensive. But with modern techniques, couldn't you duplicate those genes and store them almost anywhere?"

"But this is the logical place for them. We have the genetic safety vaults. And the giant safety dome."

"Do you really *need* a safety dome? Genetic engineering is safe and simple nowadays."

"Well, sure, but if America ever needs a Class IV biowar facility, we've got one right here." Greta stopped. "And we have first-class agricultural facilities. A lot of crop research goes on here. Overclass people still eat crops. They love our rare animals, too."

"Rich people eat *natural* crops," Oscar said.

"Our biotech research has built whole new industries," Greta insisted. "Look at what we've done to transform Louisiana."

"Yeah," Oscar said. "Do you think I should emphasize that in the Senate hearings?"

Greta looked glum.

Oscar nodded. "Let me level with you, Greta, just like you did with me. Let me tell you about the reception you might expect in today's Congress. The country's broke, and your administrative costs are through the roof. You have well over two thousand people on the federal payroll here. You don't generate any revenue yourselves— outside of winning the favor of passing celebrities with nice gifts of fluffy rare animals. You have no major military or national security interests. The biotech revolution is a long-established fact now, it's not cutting edge anymore, it's become a standard industry. So what have you done for us lately?"

"We're protecting and securing the planet's natural heritage," Greta said. "We're conservationists."

"Come on. You're genetic engineers, you have nothing to do with 'nature.'"

"Senator Dougal never seemed to mind a steady flow of federal funds into Texas. We always have state support from the Texas delegation."

"Dougal is history," Oscar said. "You know how many cyclotrons the U.S. used to have?"

" 'Cyclotrons'?" Greta said.

"Particle accelerator, a kind of primitive, giant klystron," Oscar said. "They were huge, expensive, prestigious federal laboratories, and they're all long gone. I'd like to fight for this place, but we need compelling reasons. We need sound bites that the layman can understand."

"What can I tell you? We're not PR experts. We're only mere, lowly scientists."

"You've got to give me *something,* Greta. You can't expect to survive on sheer bureaucratic inertia. You have to make a public case."

She thought about it seriously. "Knowledge is inherently precious even if you can't sell it," Greta said. "Even if you can't *use* it. Knowledge is an absolute good. The search for truth is vital. It's central to civilization. You need knowledge even when your economy and government are absolutely shot to hell."

Oscar thought it over. " 'Knowledge will get you through times of no money better than money will get you through times of no knowledge.' You know, there might be something to that. I like the sound of it. That's very contemporary rhetoric."

"The feds *have* to support us, because if they don't, Huey will! Green Huey understands this place, he knows what we do here. Huey will get us by default."

"I appreciate that point too," Oscar said.

"At least *we* earn a living out of this mess," Greta said. "You can always call it a job-creation effort. Maybe you could declare us all insane and say that labwork is our group therapy. Maybe you could declare the place a national park!"

"Now you're really brainstorming," Oscar said, pleased. "That's very good."

"What's in this for *you*?" Greta said suddenly.

"That's a fair question." Oscar smiled winningly. "Let's just say that since meeting you I've been won over."

Greta stared. "Surely you don't expect us to believe that you plan to save our bacon, just because you're flirting with me. Not that I mind all the flirting. But if I'm supposed to vamp my way into saving a multimillion-dollar federal facility, the country's in worse shape than I thought."

Oscar smiled. "I can flirt and work at the same time. I'm learning a lot by this discussion, it's very useful. For instance, the way you stroked your hair behind your left ear when you said, 'Maybe you could declare us all insane and say that labwork is our group therapy.' That was a very beautiful moment—a little spark of personal fire in the middle of a very dry policy discussion. That would have looked lovely on-camera."

She stared at him. "Is that what you think about me? Is that how you look at me? It is, isn't it? You're actually being sincere."

"Of course I am. I need to know you better. I want to understand you. I'm learning a lot. You see, I'm from your government, and I'm here to help you."

"Well, I want to know you better. So you're not leaving this lab before I get some blood samples. And I'd like to do some PET-scans and reaction tests."

"See, we do have real commonalities."

"Except I still don't understand why you're doing this."

"I can tell you right now where my loyalties lie," Oscar said. "I'm a patriot."

She looked at him nonplussed.

"I wasn't born in America. In point of fact, I wasn't even *born*. But I work for our government because I believe in America. I happen to believe that this is a unique society. We have a unique role in the world."

Oscar whacked the lab table with an open hand. "We *invented the future*! We *built* it! And if they could design or market it a little better than we could, then we just invented something else more amazing yet. If it took imagination, we always had that. If it took enterprise, we always had it. If it took daring and even *ruthlessness*, we had it—we not only built the atomic bomb, we *used it*! We're not some crowd of pious, sniveling, red-green Europeans trying to make the world safe for boutiques! We're not some swarm of Confucian social engineers who would love to watch the masses chop cotton for the next two millennia! We are a nation of hands-on cosmic mechanics!"

"And yet we're broke," Greta said.

"Why should I care if you clowns don't make any money? I'm from the government! We *print* the money. Let's get something straight right now. You people face a stark choice here. You can sit on your hands like prima donnas, and everything you've built will go down the tubes. Or you can stop being afraid, you can stop kneeling. You can get on your feet as a community, you can take some pride in yourselves. You can seize control of your own future, and make this place what you know it ought to be. You can organize."

4

Oscar was physically safe from assault inside the Collaboratory's Hot Zone. But harassment by random maniacs had made his life politically impossible. Rumor flashed over the local community as swiftly as fire in a spacecraft. People were avoiding him; he was trouble; he was under a curse. Under these difficult circumstances, Oscar thought it wisest to tactfully absent himself. He devised a scheme to cover his retreat.

Oscar took the Bambakias tour bus into the Collaboratory's vehicle repair shed. He had the bus repainted as a Hazardous Materials emergency response vehicle. This had been Fontenot's suggestion, for the wily ex-fed was a master of disguise. Fontenot pointed out that very few people, even roadblockers, would knowingly interfere with the ominous bulk of a vivid yellow Haz-Mat bus. The local Collaboratory cops were delighted to see Oscar leaving their jurisdiction, so they were only too eager to supply the necessary biohazard paint and decals.

Oscar departed before dawn in the repainted campaign bus, easing through an airlock gate without announcement or fanfare. He was fleeing practically alone. He took only an absolutely necessary skeleton retinue: Jimmy de Paulo, his driver; Donna Nunez, his stylist; Lana Ramachandran, his secretary; and, as cargo, Moira Matarazzo.

Moira was the first in his krewe to quit. Moira was a

media spokesperson by trade; she was sadly visual and verbal. Moira had never quite understood the transcendent pleasures of building hotels by hand. Moira was also deeply repelled by the hermetic world of the Collaboratory, a world whose peculiar inhabitants found her interests irrelevant. Moira had decided to resign and go home to Boston.

Oscar made no real effort to persuade Moira to stay on with his krewe. He'd thought the matter over carefully, and he couldn't accept the risk of keeping her around. Moira had grown fatally bored. He knew he could no longer trust her. Bored people were just too vulnerable.

Oscar's trip had been designed to achieve his political goals, while simultaneously throwing off pursuit and assault by armed lunatics. He would circuit, disguised and unannounced, through Louisiana, Washington, DC, and back home to Boston in time for Christmas—all the while maintaining constant net-contact with his krewe in Buna.

Oscar's first planned stop was Holly Beach, Louisiana. Holly Beach was a seaside collection of rickety stilt housing on the Gulf Coast, a hurricane-wracked region rashly billing itself as "The Cajun Riviera." Fontenot had made arrangements for Oscar's visit, scoping out the little town and renting a beach house under cover ID. According to Fontenot, who was waiting there to join them, the ramshackle tourist burg was perfect for clandestine events. Holly Beach was so battered and primitive that it lacked net-wiring of any kind; it lived on cellphones, sat dishes, and methane generators. In mid-December—it was now December 19—the seaside village was almost deserted. The likelihood of being taped by paparazzi or jumped by insane assassins was very low in Holly Beach.

Oscar had arranged a quiet rendezvous there with Dr. Greta Penninger.

After this beach idyll, Oscar would forge on to Washington, where he was overdue for face-time with his fellow staffers on the Senate Science Committee. After making the necessary obeisances to the Hill rats, Oscar would take the tour bus north to Cambridge, and finally deliver it to the Massachusetts Federal Democrat party HQ. Bambakias would donate his campaign bus to the party. The Senator, always a stalwart party financial patron, would at last be free to write off his investment.

Once in Boston, Oscar would renew his ties to the Senator. He would also have a welcome chance to return home and reorder his domestic affairs. Oscar was very worried about his house. Clare had deserted the place and left for Europe, and it wasn't right or safe to have his home sitting empty. Oscar imagined that Moira might house-sit his place while she looked for another job in Boston. Oscar was far from happy about either the house or Moira, but the house and Moira were two of the loosest ends that he had. It struck him as handy to knit them.

Time passed smoothly on the trip's first leg, to southwest Louisiana. Oscar had Jimmy turn up the music, and while Moira sulked in her bunk with a romance novel, Oscar, Lana, and Donna passed their time debating the many potentials of Greta Penninger.

Oscar wasn't shy about this subject. There wasn't much sense in that. It was useless to attempt to hide his love affairs from his own krewe. Certainly they had all known about Clare from the beginning. They might not be entirely thrilled about the advent of Greta, but it was spectator sport.

And their discussion had a political point. Greta Penninger was the leading dark-horse candidate for the Collaboratory Director's post. Strangely, the Collaboratory scientists seemed oblivious to the stark fact that their Director's post was at risk. The scientists weren't fully cognizant of their own situation, somehow—they would refer to their power structure as "collegial assessment," or maybe the "succession process"—anything but "politics." But it was politics, all right. The Collaboratory seethed with a form of politics that dared not speak its own name.

This was not to say that science itself was politics. Scientific knowledge was profoundly different from political ideology. Science was an intellectual system producing objective data about the nature of the universe. Science involved falsifiable hypotheses, reproducible results, and rigorous experimental verification. Scientific knowledge itself wasn't a political construct, any more than element 79 in the periodic table was a political construct.

But the things people did with science were every bit as political as the things people did with gold. Oscar had devoted many fascinated hours to study of the scientific community and its weirdly orthogonal power structure. The genuine work of science struck him as sadly geekish and tedious, but he was always charmed by an arcane political arrangement.

A scientist with many citations and discoveries had political power. He had scholarly repute, he had academic coattails, he had clout. He could dependably make his voice heard within the science community. He could set agendas, staff conference panels, arrange promotions and travel junkets, take consultation work. He could stay comfortably ahead of the research curve by receiving works before their official publication. A scientist on this inside track had no army, police, or slush fund; but in that quiet yet deadly scientific fashion, he was in firm control of his society's basic resources. He could shunt the flow of opportunity at will, among the lesser beings. He was a player.

Money per se was of secondary importance in science. Scientists who relied too openly on hunting earmarked funds or kissing up for major grants acquired a taint, like politicians slyly playing the race card.

This was clearly a workable system. It was very old, and it had many quirks. Those quirks could be exploited. And the Collaboratory had never enjoyed the prolonged attentions of a crack team of political campaigners.

The current Director, Dr. Arno Felzian, was in hopeless straits. Felzian had once enjoyed a modestly successful career in genetic research, but he had won his exalted post in the Collaboratory through assiduous attention to Senator Dougal's commands. Puppet regimes might thrive as long as the empire held out, but once the alien oppressors were gone, their local allies would soon be despised as collaborators. Senator Dougal, the Collaboratory's longtime patron and official puppetmaster, had gone down in flames. Felzian, abandoned, no longer knew what to do with himself. He was a jumpy, twitching yes-man with no one left to say yes to.

Dumping the current Director was a natural first step. But this would make little sense without a solid succession plan. In the little world of the Collaboratory, the Director's departure would create a power vacuum hard enough to suck up everything not nailed down. Who would take the Director's place? The senior members of the board were natural candidates for promotion, but they were payoff-tainted timeservers, just like their Director. At least, they could easily be portrayed that way by anyone willing to work at the job.

Oscar and his krewe advisers agreed that there was one central fracture line in the current power structure: Greta Penninger. She was on the board already, which gave her legitimacy, and a power base of sorts. And she had an untapped constituency—the Collaboratory's actual scientists. These were the long-oppressed working researchers, who did their best to generate authentic lab results while cordially ignoring the real world. The scientists had been cowering in the woodwork for years, while official corruption slowly ate away at their morale, their honor, and their livelihood. But if there was to be any chance of genuine reform inside the Collaboratory, it would have to come from the scientists themselves.

Oscar was optimistic. He was a Federal Democrat, a reform party with a reform agenda, and he felt that reform could work. As a class, the scientists were untouched and untapped; they oozed raw political potential. They were a very strange lot, but there were far more of these people inside the Collaboratory than he would ever have guessed. There were swarms of them. It was as if science had sucked up everyone on the planet who was too bright to be practical. Their selfless dedication to their work was truly a marvel to him.

Oscar had swiftly recovered from his initial wonder and astonishment. After a month of close study, Oscar realized that the situation made perfect sense. There wasn't enough money in the world to pay merely normal people to work as hard as scientists worked. Without this vital-izing element of cranky idealism from a demographic fringe group, the scientific enterprise would have col-lapsed centuries ago.

He'd expected federal scientists to behave more or less like other federal bureaucrats. Instead he'd discovered a lost world, a high-tech Easter Island where a race of gentle misfits created huge and slightly pointless intellec-tual statuary.

Greta Penninger was one of these little people, the Collaboratory's high-IQ head-in-the-clouds proletariat. Unfortunately, she talked and dressed just like one of them, too. However, Greta had real promise. There was basically nothing wrong with the woman that couldn't be set straight with a total makeover, power dressing, im-proved debate skills, an issue, an agenda, some talking points, and a clever set of offstage handlers.

Such was the mature consensus of Oscar's krewe. As they discussed their situation, Oscar, Lana, and Donna were also playing poker. Poker was truly Oscar's game. He rarely failed to lose at poker. It never seemed to occur to his opponents that since he was quite wealthy he could lose money with impunity. Oscar would deliberately play just well enough to put up a fight. Then he would over-reach himself, lose crushingly, and feign deep distress. The others would delightedly rake up their winnings and look at him with Olympian pity. They'd be so pleased with themselves, and so thoroughly convinced of his touching lack of cleverness and deceit, that they would forgive him anything.

"There's just one problem though," Donna said, expertly shuffling the deck.

"What's that?" said Lana, munching a pistachio.

"The campaign manager should never sleep with the candidate."

"She's not really a candidate," Lana said.

"I'm not really sleeping with her," Oscar offered.

"He will, though," Donna said wisely.

"Deal," Oscar insisted.

Donna dealt the cards. "Maybe it's all right. It's just a fling. He can't stay there, and she can't ever leave. So it's Romeo and Juliet without that ugly bother of dying."

Oscar ignored her. "You're shy, Lana." Lana threw in half a Euro. The krewe always played poker with European cash. There was American cash around, flimsy plastic stuff, but most people wouldn't take American cash anymore. It was hard to take American cash seriously when it was no longer convertible outside U.S. borders. Besides, all the bigger bills were bugged.

———————

Corky, Fred, Rebecca Pataki, and Fontenot were already waiting in Holly Beach. Backed by the krewe with their on-line catalogs, they had made a touching effort with the rented beach house. They'd had ninety-six hours to put the wretched place in order. From the outside it was unchanged: a ramshackle mess of creaking stairs, tarry wooden stilts, salt-eaten slatted porches. A flat-roofed yellow cheesebox.

Inside, though, the desolate wooden shack now featured hooked rugs, tasteful curtains, cozy oil-flow heaters, real pillows, and flowered sheets. There was a cloud of little road amenities: shower caps, soap, towels, roses, bathrobes, house slippers. It wouldn't have fooled Lorena

Bambakias, but his krewe still had the skills; they'd pried
the place loose from squalor.

Oscar climbed into the bed and slept for five hours, a
long time for him. He woke feeling refreshed and full of
pleasantly untapped potential. At dawn he ate an apple
from the tiny fridge and went for a long walk on the
beach.

It was gusty and cold, but the sun was rising over the
steel-gray Gulf of Mexico and casting the world into win-
try clarity. This local beach wasn't much to brag about.
Since the ocean had risen two feet in the past fifty years,
the rippled brown shoreline had a gimcrack, unhappy
look. The original site of the Holly Beach settlement was
now many meters out to sea. The relocated buildings had
been moved upslope into a former cow pasture, leaving a
network of old cracked pavement diving forlornly into the
surf.

Needless to say, many such structures on the rim of
the continent had not been so fortunate. It was a common
matter to find boardwalks, large chunks of piering, even
entire homes washing up onto American beaches.

Oscar strolled past a glittering shoal of smashed aluminum. The plethora of drift junk filled him with a pleasant melancholy. Every beach he'd ever known had
boasted its share of rusted bicycles, waterlogged couches,
picturesque sand-etched medical waste. In his opinion,
zealots like the Dutch complained far too much about the
inconveniences of rising seas. Like all Europeans, the
Dutch were stuck in the past, unable to come to pragmatic, workable terms with new global realities.

Unfortunately, many of the same charges could be
leveled at his own United States. Oscar brooded over his
ambiguous feelings as he carefully skirted the foamy surf in
his polished shoes. Oscar genuinely considered himself an
American patriot. Deep in his cold and silent heart of
hearts, he was as devoted to the American polity as his profession and his colleagues would allow him to be. Oscar

genuinely respected and savored the archaic courtliness of the United States Senate. The Senate's gentlemen's-club aspect strongly appealed to him. Those leisurely debates, the cloakrooms, the rules of order, that personalized, pre-industrial sense of dignity and gravitas. . . . It seemed to him that a perfect world would have worked much like the U.S. Senate. A solid realm of ancient flags and dark wood paneling, where responsible, intelligent debate could take place within a fortress of shared values. Oscar recognized the United States Senate as a strong and graceful structure built to last by political architects committed to their work. It was a system that he would have been delighted to exploit, under better circumstances.

But Oscar was a child of his own time, and he knew he didn't have that luxury. He knew it was his duty to confront and master modern political reality. Political reality in modern America was the stark fact that electronic networks had eaten the guts out of the old order, while never finding any native order of their own. The horrific speed of digital communication, the consonant flattening of hierarchies, the rise of net-based civil society, and the decline of the industrial base had simply been too much for the American government to cope with and successfully legitimize.

There were sixteen major political parties now, divided into warring blocs and ceaseless internecine purges, defections, and counterpurges. There were privately owned cities with millions of "clients" where the standard rule of law was cordially ignored. There were price-fixing mafias, money laundries, outlaw stock markets. There were black, gray, and green superbarter nets. There were health maintenance organizations staffed by crazed organ-sharing cliques, where advanced medical techniques were in the grip of any quack able to download a surgery program. Wiretapping net-militias flourished, freed of any physical locale. There were breakaway counties in the

American West where whole towns had sold out to tribes of nomads, and simply dropped off the map.

There were town meetings in New England with more computational power than the entire U.S. government had once possessed. Congressional staffs exploded into independent fiefdoms. The executive branch bogged down in endless turf wars in an acronym soup of agencies, every one of them exquisitely informed and eager to network, and hence completely unable to set a realistic agenda and concentrate on its own duties. The nation was poll-crazy, with cynical manipulation at an all-time toxic high—the least little things produced tooth-gritting single-issue coalitions and blizzards of automated lawsuits. The net-addled tax code, having lost all connection to fiscal reality, was routinely evaded by electronic commerce and wearily endured by the citizenry.

With domestic consensus fragmenting, the lost economic war with China had allowed the Emergency congressional committees to create havoc of an entirely higher order. With the official declaration of Emergency, Congress had signed over its birthright to a superstructure of supposedly faster-moving executive committees. This desperate act had merely layered another operating system on top of the old one. The country now had two national governments, the original, halting, never-quite-superseded legal government, and the spasmodic, increasingly shrill declarations of the State-of-Emergency cliques.

Oscar had his own private reservations about certain policies of the Federal Democrats, but he felt that his party's programs were basically sound. First, the Emergency committees had to be reined in and dismantled. They had no real constitutional legitimacy; they had no direct mandate from the voters; they violated basic principles of separation of powers; they were not properly accountable; and worst of all, they had all been swiftly riddled with corruption. The Emergency committees were simply failing to govern successfully. They were

sometimes rather popular, thanks to their assiduous culti-
vation of single-issue groups, but the longer the Emergency lasted, the closer they came to a slow-motion coup
and outright usurpation of the Republic.

With the committees defanged and the State of
Emergency repealed, it would be time to reform the state-
federal relationship. Decentralization of powers had simply
gone too far. A policy once meant to be fluid and responsive had turned into blinding, boiling confusion. It would
be necessary to have a constitutional convention and abolish the outdated, merely territorial approach to citizen
representation. There would have to be a new fourth
branch of government made up of nongeographical nets.

With these major acts of reform, the stage would
finally be set to attack the nation's real problems. This had
to be done without malice, without frenzy, and without
repellent attacks of partisan histrionics. Oscar felt that this
could be done. It looked bad . . . it looked very bad
. . . to the outside observer, it looked well nigh hopeless.
Yet the American polity still had great reserves of creativity
—if the country could be rallied and led in the right
direction. Yes, it was true that the nation was broke, but
other countries had seen their currencies annihilated and
their major industries rendered irrelevant. This condition
was humiliating, but it was temporary, it was survivable.
When you came down to it, America's abject defeat in
economic warfare was a very mild business compared to,
say, twentieth-century carpet bombing and armed invasion.

The American people would just have to get over
the fact that software no longer had any economic value. It
wasn't fair, it wasn't just, but it was a fait accompli. In
many ways, Oscar had to give the Chinese credit for their
cleverness in making all English-language intellectual
property available on their nets at no charge. The Chinese
hadn't even needed to leave their own borders in order to
kick the blocks out from under the American economy.

In some ways, this brutal collision with Chinese analog reality could be seen as a blessing. As far as Oscar had it figured, America hadn't really been suited for its long and tiresome role as the Last Superpower, the World's Policeman. As a patriotic American, Oscar was quite content to watch other people's military coming home in boxes for a while. The American national character really wasn't suited for global police duties. It never had been. Tidy and meticulous people such as the Swiss and Swedes were the types who made good cops. America was far better suited to be the World's Movie Star. The world's tequila-addled pro-league bowler. The world's acerbic, bipolar stand-up comedian. Anything but a somber and tedious nation of socially responsible centurions.

Oscar turned on the brown ribbed sands of the beach and began retracing his steps. He was enjoying being out of touch like this; he'd abandoned his laptop back in the krewe bus, he'd even left all the phones out of his sleeves and pockets. He felt that he should do this more often. It was important for a professional political operative to step back periodically, to take the time necessary to put his thoughts and intuitions into order and perspective. Oscar rarely created these vital little moments for himself —he'd somehow dimly intuited that he'd have plenty of time to develop his personal philosophy if he ever ended up behind bars. But he was giving himself some time for thought now, in this forgotten world of sand and wind and waves and chilly sunlight, and he could feel that it was doing him a lot of good.

An internal pressure had been building. He'd learned a great deal in the past thirty days, devouring whole reams of alien data in order to get up to speed, but hadn't yet put it into an organized perspective. His data-stuffed head had become a disassembled mass of jumbled blocks. He was keyed up, tense, distracted, getting a little snappish.

Maybe it was just that long drought between women.

They were expecting Greta before noon. Negi had prepared a lovely seafood lunch for her. But Greta was late. The krewe ate lavishly inside the bus, popping corks and keeping up appearances, even joking about the no-show. But when Oscar left them, his mood had grown much darker.

He went into the beach house to wait for Greta, but the rooms that had once seemed louche yet charming now revealed themselves to him as merely sordid. Why was he fooling himself, taking such pains to imitate a love nest? Genuine love nests were places full of real meaning for lovers, full of things conveying some authentic emotional resonance. Little things, silly mementos maybe, a feather, a seashell, a garter, framed photos, a ring. Not these hired curtains, that hired bedspread, that set of fatally new anti-septic toothbrushes.

He sat on the creaking brass bed and gazed about the room, and the world turned inside out for him suddenly. He had been prepared to be charming and witty, he had been so looking forward to it, but she was not coming. She had wised up. She was too smart to come. He was alone in this small ugly building, marinating in his own juices.

A slow hour passed, and he was glad she hadn't come. He was glad for himself of course, because it had been stupid to imagine a liaison with that woman, but he was also glad for her. He didn't feel crushed by her rejection, but he could see himself more realistically now. He was a predator, he was seductive and cold. He was a creature of trembling web lines and shiny bright chitinous surfaces. Wise gray moth, to stay inside her home.

His course seemed very clear now. He would go back to Washington, file a committee report, and stay there at his proper job. No one would really expect much from his very first Senate assignment. He had more than enough material for a devastating exposé of the Collaboratory's internal workings. If that wasn't in the cards, he could play up the Collaboratory's positive aspects: the profound effect of biotech spinoffs on the regional economy, for instance. He could trumpet the futuristic glamour of the next big federal breakthrough: high-tech industrial neuroscience. Whatever they wanted to hear.

He could become a career Hill rat, a policy wonk. They were a large and thriving tribe. He could invest ever more elaborate amounts of energy on ever more arcane and tiresome subjects. He'd never run another political campaign, and he'd certainly never win political power in his own right, but if he didn't burn out as a policy cog, he might well flourish. There might be something pleasant at the end, maybe a cabinet post, a guest professorship somewhere in his final declining days. . . .

He left the beach house, unable to bear himself. The door was open in the tour bus, but he couldn't face his krewe. He went to Holly Beach's single grocery store, a cheerfully ramshackle place, its floors unpainted and its raftered ceiling hung with old fishing nets. It had an entire towering wall of shiny floor-to-ceiling booze. Souvenir fishing hats. Fish line and plastic lures. Desiccated alligator heads, eerie knickknacks carved from Spanish moss and coconut. Tatty, half-bootlegged music cassettes—he found it intensely annoying that Dutch music was so popular now. How on earth could a drowning country with a miniscule, aging population have better pop music than the United States?

He picked up a pair of cheap beach sandals, a deeply unnecessary impulse buy. There was a dark-haired teenage girl waiting behind the counter, a Louisiana local. She was bored and lonely in the cold and quiet grocery, and she gave him a dazzling smile, a hello-handsome-stranger smile. She was wearing a bad nubby sweater and a flowered shift of cheap gene-spliced cotton, but she was good-tempered and pretty. Sexual fantasy, crushed and derailed by the day's disappointments, flashed back into life, on a strange parallel track. *Yes, young woman of the bayous, I am indeed a handsome stranger. I am clever, rich, and powerful. Trust me, I can take you far away from all this. I can open your eyes to the great wide world, carry you away to gilded corridors of luxury and power. I can dress you, I can teach you, remold you to my will, I can transform you utterly. All you have to do for me is* . . . There was nothing she could do for him. His interest faded.

He left the grocery with his purchased sandals in a paper bag, and began walking the sandy streets of Holly Beach. There was something so naively crass and seedy about the town that it had a strange decadent charm, a kind of driftwood Gothic. He could imagine Holly Beach as queerly interesting in the summer: straw-hatted families chatting in Acadian French, tattooed guys firing up their barbecue smokers, offshore oil workers on holiday, dredging up something leathery and boneless in a seine. A spotted dog was following him, sniffing at his heels. It was very odd to encounter a dog after weeks in an environment infested with kinkajous and caribou. Maybe it was finally time for him to break down and acquire his own personal exotic animal. That would be very fashionable, a nice memento of his stay. His own personal genetic toy. Something very quick and carnivorous. Something with big dark spots.

He came across the oldest house in town. The shack was so old that it had never been moved; it had been sitting in the same place for decades as the seas rose. The shack had once been a long and lonely distance from the beach, though now it was quite near the water. The building looked queerly haphazard, as if it had been banged together over a set of weekends by somebody's brother-in-law.

Storms, sand, and pitiless Southern sun had stripped off a weary succession of cheap layered paints, but the shack was still inhabited. It wasn't rented, either. Someone was living in it full-time. There was a dented postbox and a sandblasted mesh sat-dish on the metal roof, trailing a severed cable. There were three wooden steps up to the rust-hinged door, steps thick and grained and splintery, half buried in damp sand, with a lintel of sandblasted wood that might have been sixty years old and looked six hundred.

In the winter light of late afternoon there was a look to that smoky woodgrain that enchanted him. Ancient brown nail holes. White seagull droppings. He had a strong intuition that someone very old was living here. Old, blind, feeble, no one left to love them, family gone away now, story all over.

He placed his bare palm tenderly against the sunwarmed wood. Awareness flowed up his arm, and he tasted a sudden premonition of his own death. It would be exactly like this moment: alone and sere. Broken steps too tall for him to ever climb again. Mortality's swift scythe would slash clean through him and leave nothing but empty clothes.

Shaken, he walked quickly back to the rented beach house. Greta was waiting there. She was wearing a hooded gray jacket and carrying a carpetbag.

Oscar hurried up. "Hi! Sorry! Did you catch me out?"

"I just got here. There were roadblocks. I couldn't call ahead."

"That's all right! Come on upstairs, it's warm."

He ushered her up the stairs and into the beach house. Once inside, she looked about herself skeptically. "It's hot in here."

"I'm so glad you've come." He was appallingly glad to see her. So much so that he felt close to tears. He retreated into the hideous kitchenette and quickly poured himself a glass of rusty tap water. He sipped it, and steadied himself. "Can I get you something?"

"I just wanted . . ." Greta sighed and sat down unerringly in the room's ugliest piece of furniture, a ghastly thirdhand fabric armchair. "Never mind."

"You missed lunch. Can I take your coat?"

"I didn't want to come at all. But I want to be honest. . . ."

Oscar sat on the rug near the heater, and pulled off one shoe. "I can see you're upset." He pulled off the other shoe and crossed his legs on the rug. "That's all right, I understand that perfectly. It was a long trip, it's difficult, our situation's very difficult. I'm just glad that you've come, that's all. I'm happy to see you. Very happy. I'm touched."

She said nothing, but looked warily attentive.

"Greta, you know that I'm fond of you. Don't you? I mean that. We have a rapport, you and I. I don't quite know why, but I *want* to know. I want you to be glad that you came here. We're alone at last, that's a rare privilege for us, isn't it? Let's talk it out, let's put it all on the table now, let's be good friends."

She was wearing perfume. She had brought an overnight bag. She was clearly having an attack of cold feet, but the underlying indicators looked solid.

"I want to understand you, Greta. I *can* understand, you know. I think I do understand you a little. You're a very bright woman, much brighter than most people, but you have insight, you're sensitive. You've done great things with your life, great accomplishments, but there's no one on your side. I know that's the truth. And it's sad. I could be on your side, if you'd let me." He lowered his voice. "I can't make any conventional promises, because we're just not conventional people. But the two of us could be great friends. We could even be lovers. Why can't we? The odds are against us, but that doesn't make it hopeless."

It was very quiet. He should have thought to put on some music.

"I think that you need someone. You need someone who can understand your interests, someone to be your champion. People don't appreciate you for what you are.

People are using you for their own small-minded little ends. You're very brave and dedicated, but you have to break out of your shell, you can't go on retreating and being polite, you can't go on accommodating those goons, they'll drive you crazy, they're not fit to touch the hem of your shoe. Your gown. The, what the hell, your lab coat." He paused and drew a shaky breath. "Look, just tell me what you need."

"I was wrong about you," she said. "I thought you were going to grab me."

"No, of course I'm not going to grab you." He smiled.

"Stop smiling. You think I'm very innocent, don't you. I'm not innocent. Listen to me. I have a body, I have hormones, I have a limbic system. I'm a sexual person. Look, I've been sitting up there under those cameras bored to death, restless, going crazy, and then *you* show up. You show up, and you're coming on to me."

She stood up. "I'll tell you what I need, since you want to know so badly. I need a guy who's kind of cold-blooded and disposable, who won't kick up a big fuss. He has to want me in this completely shallow, obvious way. But you're not the kind of guy I want, are you. Not really."

There was a ringing silence.

"I should have found some way to tell you all that, before you came down here, and took all this trouble. I almost didn't come at all, but . . ." She sat back down wearily. "Well, it was more honest to be here face-to-face, and have it all out, all at once."

Oscar cleared his throat. "Do you know the game of go? Go-bang? *Wei-chi,* in Chinese."

"I've heard of it."

Oscar got up and fetched his travel set. "Senator Bambakias taught me how to play go. It's a core metaphor for his krewe, it's how we think. So if you want to mix with modern politicians and accomplish something, then you need to learn this game right away."

"You're really a strange man."

He opened and set out the square-lined board, with its two cups of black and white stones. "Sit down on the rug here with me, Greta. We're going to have this out right now, Eastern style."

She sat down cross-legged near the oil heater. "I don't gamble."

"Go isn't a gambling game. Let me take your jacket now. Good. This isn't chess, either. This isn't a Western-style, mechanized, head-to-head battle. Those just don't happen anymore. Go is all about networks and territories. You play the net—you place your stones where the lines cross. You can capture the stones if you totally surround them, but killing them is just a collateral effect. You don't want to kill the stones, that's not the point. You want the blankness. You want the empty spaces in the net."

"I want the potential."

"Exactly."

"When the game ends, the player with the most potential wins."

"You *have* played go before."

"No, I haven't. But that much is obvious."

"You'll play black," he said. He set a group of black stones on the board, crisply clicking them down. "Now I'll demo the game a bit, before we start. You place your stones down like this, one at a time. The groups of stones gain strength from their links, from the network that they form. And the groups have to have eyes, blank eyes inside the network. That's a crucial point." He placed a blocking chain of white stones around the black group. "A single eye isn't enough, because I could blind that eye with one move, and capture your whole group. I could surround the whole group, drop into the middle, blind your eye, and just remove the whole group, like this. But with two eyes—like this?—the group becomes a permanent feature on the board. It lives forever."

"Even if you totally surround me."

"Exactly."

She hunched her shoulders and stared at the board. "I can see why your friend likes this game."

"Yes, it's very architectural. . . . All right, we'll try a practice game." He swept the board clean of stones. "You're the beginner, so you get nine free stones on these nine crucial spots."

"That's a lot of free stones."

"That's not a problem, because I'm going to beat you anyway." He clicked down his first white stone with two fingertips.

They played for a while. *"Atari,"* he repeated.

"You can stop saying that word now, I can see that my group's in check."

"It's just a customary courtesy."

They played more. Oscar was starting to sweat. He stood up and turned down the heaters.

He sat down again. All the tension had left their situation. The two of them were totally rapt. "You're going to beat me," she announced. "You know all those foul little tricks in the corners."

"Yes, I do."

She looked up and met his eyes. "But I can learn those little tricks, and then you're going to have a hard time with me."

"I can appreciate a hard time. A hard time is good to find."

He beat her by thirty points. "You're learning fast. Let's try a serious game."

"Don't clear the board yet," she said. She studied her defeat with deep appreciation. "These patterns are so elegant."

"Yes. And they're always different. Every game has its own character."

"These stones are a lot like neurons."

He smiled at her.

They started a second game. Oscar was very serious about go. He played poker for social reasons, but he never threw a game of go. He was too good at it. He was a gifted player, clever, patient, and profoundly deceptive, but Greta's game play was all over the map. She was making beginner's mistakes, but she never repeated them, and her mental grasp of the game was incredibly strong.

He beat her by nineteen points, but only because he was ruthless.

"This is a really good game," she said. "It's so contemporary."

"It's three thousand years old."

"Really?" She stood up and stretched, her kneecaps cracking loudly. "That calls for a drink."

"Go ahead."

She found her carpetbag and retrieved a square bottle of blue Dutch gin.

Oscar went to the kitchen and fetched two brandnew bistro glasses from their sanitary wrap. "You want some orange juice with that stuff?"

"No thank you."

He poured himself an orange juice and brought her an empty glass. He watched in vague astonishment as she decanted three fingers of straight gin, with a chemist's painstaking care.

"Some ice? We do have ice."

"That's all right."

"Look, Greta, you can't drink straight gin. That's the road to blue ruin."

"Vodka gives me headaches. Tequila tastes nasty." She placed her pointed upper lip on the rim of her bistro glass and had a long meditative sip. Then she shuddered. "Yum! You don't drink at all, do you?"

"No. And you should take it a little easier. Straight gin kills neurons by the handful."

"I kill neurons for a living, Oscar. Let's play."

They had a third game. The booze had melted something inside her head and she was playing hard. He fought as if his life depended on it. He was barely holding his own.

"Nine free stones are way too many for you," he said. "We should cut you back to six."

"You're going to win again, aren't you?"

"Maybe twenty points."

"Fifteen. But we don't have to finish this one now."

"No." He was holding a white stone between two fingertips. "We don't have to finish."

He reached out across the board. He touched his two fingers to the underside of her chin very gently. She looked up in surprise, and he drew a caress along the line of her jaw. Then he leaned in slowly, until their lips met.

A throwaway kiss. Barely there, like eiderdown. He slipped his hand to the nape of her neck and leaned in seriously. The bright taste of gin parched his tongue.

"Let's get in bed," he said.

"That really isn't smart."

"I know it isn't, but let's do it anyway."

They levered themselves from the floor. They crossed the room and climbed into the square brass bed.

It was the worst sex he had ever had. It was halting, jittery, analytical sex. Sex devoid of any warm animal rapport. All the simple, liberating pleasure of the act was somehow discounted in advance, while postcoital remorse and regret loomed by their bedside like a pair of drooling voyeurs. They didn't so much finish it, as negotiate a way to stop.

"This bed's very rickety," she said politely. "It really squeaks."

"I should have bought a new one."

"You can't buy an entire new bed just for one night."

"I can't help the one night; I leave for Washington tomorrow."

She levered herself up in the shiny sheets. Her china-white shoulders had a fine network of little blue veins. "What are you going to tell them in Washington?"

"What do you want me to tell them in Washington?"

"Tell them the truth."

"You always tell me that you want the truth, Greta. But do you know what it means when you get it?"

"Of course I want the truth. I always want the truth. No matter what."

"All right, then I'll give you some truth." He laced his hands behind his head, drew a breath, and stared at the ceiling. "Your laboratory was built by a politician who was deeply corrupt. Texas lost the space program when it shut down. They never quite made the big time in digital. So they tried very hard to move into biotech. But East Texas was the stupidest place in the world to build a genetics lab. They could have built it in Stanford, they could have built it in Raleigh, they could have built it on Route 128. But Dougal convinced them to build it miles from nowhere, in the deep piney woods. He used the worst kind of Luddite panic tactics. He convinced Congress to fund a giant airtight biohazard dome, with every possible fail-safe device, just so he could line the pockets of a big gang of military contractors who'd fallen off their gravy train and needed the federal contracts. And the locals loved him for that. They voted him in again and again, even though they had no idea what biotechnology was or what it really meant. The people of East Texas were simply too backward to build a genetic industry base, even with a massive pork-barrel jump start. So all the spin-offs moved over the state border, and they ended up in the pockets of Dougal's very best pal and disciple, a ruthless demagogue from Cajun country. Green Huey is a populist of the worst sort. He really thinks that genetic engineering belongs by right in the hands of semiliterate swamp-dwellers."

He glanced at her. She was listening.

"So Huey deliberately—and this took a weird kind of genius, I'll admit this—he deliberately boiled down your lab's best research discoveries into plug-and-play recipes that any twelve-year-old child could use. He took over a bunch of defunct Louisiana oil refineries, and he turned those dead refineries into giant bubbling cauldrons of genetic voodoo. Huey declared all of Louisiana a free-fire zone for unlicensed DNA gumbo. And you know something? Louisianans are extremely good at the work. They took to gene-splicing like muskrats to water. They have a real native gift for the industry. They love it! They love Huey for giving it to them. Huey gave them a new future, and they made him a king. Now he's power-mad, he basically rules the state by decree. Nobody dares to question him."

She had gone very pale.

"The Texans never voted Dougal out of office. Texans would never do that. They don't care how much he stole, he's their patron, the alcalde, the godfather, he stole it all for Texas, so that's good enough for them. No, the damn guy just drank himself stupid. He kept boozing till he blew out his liver, and couldn't make a quorum call anymore. So now Dougal's finally out of the picture for good. So do you know what that means to you?"

"What?" she said flatly.

"It means your party's almost over. It costs a fortune to run that giant cucumber-frame, much more than the place is really worth to anybody, and the country is broke. If you're going to do genetic research nowadays, you can do it very cheaply, in very simple buildings. In somebody else's constituency."

"But there's the animals," she said. "The genetic facilities."

"That's the truly tragic part. You can't save an en-

dangered species by cloning animals. I admit, it's better
than having them completely exterminated and lost forever. But they're curios now, they walk around looking
pretty, they've become collector's items for the ultra-rich.
A living species isn't just the DNA code, it's the whole
spread of genetic variety in a big wild population, plus
their learned behaviors, and their prey and their predators,
all inside a natural environment. But there *aren't* any natural environments anymore. Because the climate has
changed."

He sat up, the bedsprings crunching loudly. "The
climate's in flux now. You can't shelter whole environments under airtight domes. Only two kinds of plants
really thrive in today's world: genetically altered crops, and
really fast-moving weeds. So our world is all bamboo and
kudzu now, it has nothing to do with the endangered
foxglove lady's slipper and its precious niche on some forgotten mountain. Politically, we hate admitting this to
ourselves, because it means admitting the full extent of our
horrible crimes against nature, but that's ecological reality
now. That's the truth you asked me for. That is reality.
Paying tons of money to preserve bits of Humpty
Dumpty's shell is strictly a pious gesture."

"And that's what you're going to tell your Senators."

"No, no, I never said that." Oscar sighed. "I just
wanted to tell you the truth."

"What do you want to tell your Senators?"

"What do I want? I want you. I want you to be on
my side. I want to reform your situation, and I want you
to help me and counsel me."

"I have my own krewe, thank you."

"No, you don't have anything. You have a very expensive facility that is on a short-term loan. And you're
dealing with people in Washington who can misplace an
air base and laugh about it. No, when I look at your game
from your position, I see that you have two realistic options. Number one, get out now, before the purge. Take

another post, academia maybe, even Europe. If you angle it right, you can probably take some of your favorite grad students and bottle-washers with you."

She scowled. "What's option number two?"

"Take power. A preemptive strike. Just take the place over, and root out every one of those crooked sons of bitches. Come clean about everything, get ahead of the curve, and blow the place wide open." Oscar levered himself up on one elbow. "If you leak it at just the right time, through just the right sources, and in just the right order, with just the right spin, you can get rid of the featherbedders and save most of the people who are doing actual research. That's a very risky gambit, and it probably won't succeed, and it will make you stacks of bitter enemies for life. But there is one saving grace there: if you're turning the place upside down yourself, Congress will be so amazed that they won't get around to shutting you down. If you get good press, and if they like your style, they might even back you."

She sank back, crushed, against the pillow. "Look, I just want to work in my lab."

"That's not an option."

"It's very important work."

"I know it is, but that's just not an option."

"You don't really believe in anything, do you?"

"Yes I do," he said passionately. "I believe that smart people working together can make a difference in this world. I know you're very smart, and if we work together, then maybe I can help you. If you're not with me, then you're on your own."

"I'm not helpless. I have friends and colleagues who trust me."

"Well, that's lovely. You can all be helpless together."

"No, it's not lovely. Because you're sleeping with me. And you're telling me you're going to destroy everything I work for."

"Look, it's the truth! Would it be better if I slept with you and didn't tell you what was going on? Because the possibility distinctly occurred to me. But I don't have the heart."

"You have the wrong person for this. I hate administration. I can't take power. I'm no good at it."

"Greta, look at me. I could *make* you good at it. Don't you understand that? I run political campaigns, I'm an expert. That's my job."

"What a horrible thing to say."

"We could do it, all right. Especially if you weighed in with us, if you'd let us advise you and help you. My krewe and I, we took an architect who had five percent approval ratings and we made him Senator from Massachusetts. Your sad little fishbowl has never seen people like us."

"Well . . ." She sighed. "I'll have to think about it."

"Good. You do that. I'll be gone for a while. Washington, Boston. . . . Give the subject some serious thought." His stomach rumbled. "After all that ranting, I'm not a bit sleepy. Are you sleepy?"

"God, no."

"I'm starving. Let's go get something to eat. You brought a car, right?"

"It's a junker car. Internal combustion."

"It'll get us into a real town. I'll take you out tonight. We'll go out somewhere, we'll paint the town together."

"Are you nuts? You can't do that. Crazy people are trying to kill you."

He waved a hand. "Oh, who cares? We can't live that way. What's the use? Anyway, the risk is minimal here. It would take a major-league intelligence operation to track us down here in this dump. I'm much safer at some random restaurant than I'll be in Washington or Boston. This is our only night together. Let's be brave. Let's find the nerve to be happy."

They dressed, left the beach house, got into the car. Greta started it with a metal key. The engine growled in ugly piston-popping fashion. Then Greta's phone rang.

"Don't answer it," Oscar said.

She ignored him. "Yes?" She paused, then handed it over. "It's for you."

It was Fontenot. "What the hell do you think you're doing?"

"Are you still awake? We're going out for dinner."

"Of course I'm awake! I was up as soon as you left the safe house. You can't leave Holly Beach, Oscar."

"Look, it's the middle of the night, nobody knows we're here, we're in a rented car with no history, and we're picking a town at random."

"You want to eat? We'll bring you in some food. What if you get pulled over by a parish sheriff? They'll punch you into the state police net. You think that'll be a fun experience for a Yankee who's crossed Green Huey? Think otherwise, pal."

"Should that happen, I'll lodge a complaint with the American embassy."

"Very funny. Stop being stupid, okay? I finessed the Holly Beach thing for you, and that wasn't easy. If you depart from the itinerary, I can't be responsible."

"Keep driving," Oscar told Greta. "Jules, I appreciate your professionalism, I really do, but we need to do this, and there's no time to argue about it."

"All right," Fontenot groaned. "Take the highway east and I'll get back to you."

Oscar hung up and gave Greta her phone. "Did you ever have a bodyguard?" he said.

She nodded. "Once. After the Nobel announcement. It was me and Danny Yearwood. After the big news broke, Danny started getting all these threats from the animal rights people. . . . Nobody ever threatened *me* about it, and that was so typical. They just went after Danny. We shared the Nobel, but I was the one doing all the labwork. . . . We had some security during the press coverage, but the stalkers just waited them out. Later they jumped poor Danny outside his hotel and broke both his arms."

"Really."

"I always figured it was the fetal-tissue people who were the real anti-science crazies. The righters mostly just broke into labs and stole animals."

She peered carefully into the moving pool of head-lights, grasping the wheel with her narrow hands. "Danny was so good about the credit. He put my name first on the paper—it was my hypothesis, I did the labwork, so that was very ethical, but he was just such an angel about it. He just fought for me and fought for me, he never let them overlook me. He gave me every credit that he could, and then they stalked him and beat him up, and they completely ignored me. His wife really hated my guts."

"How is Dr. Yearwood, these days? How could I get in touch with him?"

"Oh, he's out. He left science, he's in banking now."

"You're kidding. Banking? He won the Nobel Prize for medicine."

"Oh, the Nobel doesn't count so much, since those Swedish bribery scandals. . . . A lot of people said that was why we got the Prize in the first place, a woman still in her twenties, they were trying some kind of clean-slate approach. I don't care, I just enjoy the labwork. I like framing the hypothesis. I like the procedures, I like proper form. I like the rigor, the integrity. I like publishing, seeing it all there in black and white, all very tight and straight. It's knowledge then. It's forever."

"You really love your work, Greta. I respect that."

"It's very hard. If you get famous, they just won't let you work anymore. They bump you up in the hierarchy, they promote you out of the lab, there's a million stupid distractions. Then it's not about science anymore. It's all about feeding your postdoc's children. The whole modern system of science is just a shadow of what it was in the Golden Age—the First Cold War. But . . ." She sighed. "I don't know. I did all right personally. Other people have had it so much worse."

"Such as?"

"There was this woman once. Rita Levi-Montalcini. You know about her?"

"I'll know if you tell me."

"She was another Nobelist. She was Jewish, in the 1930s, in Italy. A neuro-embryologist. The Fascists were trying to round her up, and she was hiding in this village in a shack. She made dissection tools out of wire and she got these hen's eggs. . . . She had no money, and she couldn't show her face, and the government was literally trying to kill her, but she got her lab results anyway, major results. . . . She survived the war and she got away. She ran to America, and they gave her a really great lab job, and she ended up as this ninety-year-old famous world-class neuro person. She's exactly what it's all about, Rita was."

"You want me to drive a little now?"

"I'm sorry that I'm crying."

"That's all right. Just pull over."

They stepped out in the darkness and switched positions in the car. He drove off with a loud crunch of roadside oyster shells. It had been a long time since he'd done any of his own driving. He tried to pay a lot of attention, as he was anxious not to kill them. Things were becoming so interesting. The sex had been a debacle, but sex was only part of it anyway. He was getting through to her now. Getting through was what counted.

"You shouldn't let them destroy my lab, Oscar. I know the place never lived up to its hype, but it's a very special place, it shouldn't be destroyed."

"That's an easy thing to say. It might even be doable. But how hard are you willing to fight for what you want? What will you give? What will you sacrifice?"

Her phone rang again. She answered it. "It's your friend again," she said, "he wants us to go to some place called Buzzy's. He's called ahead for us."

"My friend is really a very fine man."

They drove into the town of Cameron, and they found the restaurant. Buzzy's was a music spot of some pretension, it was open late and the tourist crowd was good. The band was playing classical string quartets. Typical Anglo ethnic music. It was amazing how many Anglos had gone into the booming classical music scene. Anglos seemed to have some innate talent for rigid, linear music that less troubled ethnic groups couldn't match.

Fontenot had phoned them in a reservation as Mr. and Mrs. Garcia. They got a decent table not far from the kitchen, and a healthy distance from the bar, where a group of Texan tourists in evening dress were loudly drinking themselves stupid amid the brass and the mirrors. There were cloth napkins, decent silverware, attentive waiters, menus in English and French. It was cozy, and became cozier yet when Fontenot himself arrived and took a table near the door. It felt very warm and relaxing to have a bodyguard awake, sober, and checking all the arrivals.

"I need seafood," Oscar announced, studying his menu. "Lobster would be nice. Haven't had a decent lobster since I left Boston."

"Ecrevisse," Greta said.

"What's that?"

"Top of page two. A famous local specialty, you should try it."

"Sounds great." He signaled a waiter and ordered. Greta asked for chicken salad.

Greta began to spin the narrow stem of her wine-glass, which he had filled with mineral water in order to forestall more gin. "Oscar, how are we going to work this? I mean us."

"Oh, our liaison is technically unethical, but it doesn't quite count when you're unethical away from the action. You'll be going back to your work, and I'm going to the East Coast. But I'll be back later, and we can arrange something discreet."

"That's how this works, in your circles?"

"When it works. . . . It's accepted. Like, say, the President and his mistress."

Her eyebrows rose. "Leonard Two Feathers has a mistress?"

"No, no, not him! I mean the old guy, the man who's still officially President. He had this girlfriend—Pamela something, you don't need to know her last name. . . . She'll wait till he's safely out of office. Then she'll license the tell-all book, the fragrance, the lingerie, the various ancillary rights. . . . It's her cash-out money."

"What does the First Lady think of all that?"

"I imagine she thinks what First Ladies always think. She thought she'd be an instant co-President, and then she had to watch for four long years while the Emergency committees staked her guy out in public and pithed him like a frog. That's the real tragedy of it. You know, I had no use for that guy as a politician, but I still hated watching that process. The old guy looked okay when he took office. He was eighty-two years old, but hey, everybody in the Party of American Unity is old, the whole Right Progressive Bloc has a very aged demographic. . . . The job just broke him, that's all. It just snapped his poor old bones right there in public. I guess they could have outed him on the thousand-year-old girlfriend issue, but with all the truly serious troubles the President had, trashing his sex life was overkill."

"I never knew about any of that."

"People know. Somebody always knows. The man's krewe always knows. The Secret Service knows. That doesn't mean you can get people to make a public issue of it. Nets are really peculiar. They're never smooth and uniform, they're always lumpy. There are probably creeps somewhere who have surveillance video of the President with Pamela. Maybe they're swapping it around, trading it for paparazzi shots of Hollywood stars. It doesn't matter. My dad the movie star, he used to get outed all the time, but they were always such silly things—he got outed once for punching some guy at a polo club, but he never got outed for playing footsie with mobsters. Crazy people with time on their hands can learn a lot of weird things on the net. But they're still crazy people, no matter how much they learn. They're not players, so they just don't count."

"And I'm not a player, so I just don't count."

"Don't take it badly. None of your people ever counted. Senator Dougal, he was your player. Your player is gone now, so you have nothing left on the game board. That's political reality."

"I see."

"You can vote, you know. You're a citizen. You have one vote. That's important."

"Right."

They laughed.

They had consommé. Then the waiter brought the main dish.

"Smells wonderful," Oscar said. "Got a lobster bib? Claw cracker? Hammer, maybe?" He had a closer look at the dish. "Wait a minute. What's wrong with my lobster?"

"That's your écrevisse."

"What is it, exactly?"

"Crayfish. Crawdad. A freshwater lobster."

"What's with these claws? The tail's all wrong."

"It's domestic. Natural crawdads are only three

inches long. They stitched its genetics. That's a local specialty."

Oscar stared at the boiled crustacean in its bed of
yellow rice. His dinner was a giant genetic mutant. Its
proportions seemed profoundly wrong to him. He wasn't
quite sure what to make of this. Certainly he'd eaten his
share of genetically altered crops: corncobs half the size of
his arm, UltraPlump zucchinis, tasty mottled brocco-cau-
liflowers, seedless apples, seedless everything, really. . . .
But here was an entire gene-warped animal boiled alive
and delivered in one piece. It looked fantastic, utterly un-
real. It was like a lobster-shaped child's balloon.

"Smells delicious," he said.

Greta's phone rang.

"Look, can't we eat in peace?" Oscar said.

She swallowed a forkful of vinegar-gleaming chicken
salad. "I'll shut my phone off," she said.

Oscar prodded experimentally at one of the
crawdad's many ancillary legs. The boiled limb snapped
off as cleanly as a twig, revealing a white wedge of flesh.

"Don't be shy," she told him, "this is Louisiana,
okay? Just stick the head right in your mouth and suck the
juice out."

The music from the band stopped suddenly, in mid-
quartet. Oscar looked up. The doorway was full of cops.

They were Louisiana state troopers, men in flat-
brimmed hats with headphones and holstered capture
guns. They were filtering into the restaurant. Oscar
looked hastily for Fontenot and saw the security man discreetly punching at his phone, with a look of annoyance.

"Sorry," Oscar said, "may I borrow your phone a
minute?"

He turned Greta's phone back on and engaged in
the surprisingly complex procedure of reinstalling its presence in the Louisiana net. The cops had permeated
through the now-hushed crowd, and had blocked all the
exits. There were cops in the bar, a cop with the maître d',

cops quietly vanishing into the kitchen, two pairs of cops going upstairs. Cops with laptops, cops with video. Three cops were having a private conference with the manager.

Then came the thudding racket of a helicopter, landing outside. When the rotors shut off, the entire crowd found themselves suddenly shouting. The sudden silence afterward was deeply impressive.

Two mountainous bodyguards in civilian dress entered the restaurant, followed immediately by a short, red-faced man in house shoes and purple pajamas.

The red-faced man bustled headlong into the restaurant, his furry house slippers slithering across the tiles. "HEY, Y'ALL!" he shouted, his voice booming like a kettledrum. "It's ME!" He waved both arms, pajamas flying open to reveal a hairy belly. "Sorry for the mess! Official business! Y'all relax! Ever'thing under control."

"Hello, Governor!" someone shouted. "Hey, Huey!" yelled another diner, as if it were something he'd been longing to say all his life. The diners were all grinning suddenly, exchanging happy glances, skidding their chairs back, their faces alight. They were in luck. Life and color had entered their drab little lives.

"See what the boys in the back room'll have!" screeched the Governor. "We're gonna look after you folks real good tonight! Dinner's on me, everybody! All righty? Boozoo, you see to that! Right away."

"Yessir," said Boozoo, who was one of the bodyguards.

"Gimme a COFFEE!" boomed Huey. He was short, but he had shoulders like a linebacker. "Gimme a *double* coffee! It's late, so put a shot of something in it. Gimme a demitasse. Hell, gimme a whole goddamn tasse. Somebody gonna get me two tasses? Do I have to wait all night? Goddamn, it smells good in here! You folks having a good time yet?"

There was a ragged yell of public approval.

"Y'all don't mind me now," screamed Huey, casually hitching his pajama bottoms. "Couldn't get myself a decent meal in Baton Rouge, had to fly down here to take the edge off. Gotta take a big meeting tonight." He strode unerringly into the depths of the restaurant, approaching Oscar's table like a battleship. He stopped short, looming suddenly before them, hands twitching, forehead dotted with sweat. "Clifton, gimme a chair."

"Yessir," said the remaining bodyguard. Clifton yanked a chair from a nearby table like a man picking up a breadstick, and deftly slid it beneath his boss's rump.

Suddenly the three of them were sitting face-to-face. At close range the Governor's head was like a full moon, swollen, glowing, and lightly cratered. "Hello, Etienne," Greta said.

"Hallo, *petite!*" To Oscar's intense annoyance, the two of them began speaking in rapid, idiomatic French.

Oscar glanced over to catch Fontenot's eye. There was a two-volume lesson in good sense in Fontenot's level gaze. Oscar looked away.

A waiter arrived on the trot with coffee, a tall glass, whipped cream, a shot of bourbon. "I'm starvin'," Huey announced, in a new and much less public voice. "Nice mudbug you got there, son."

Oscar nodded.

"I dote on mudbugs," Huey said. "Gimme some butter dip." He pulled his pajama sleeves up, reached out with nutcracker hands, and wrenched the tail from the carapace with a loud bursting of gristle and meat. He flexed the tail, everting a chunk of white steaming flesh. "*C'est bon,* son!" He stuffed it into his mouth, set his teeth, and tore. "That GOOD or what! Gonna BODY-SLAM them Boston lobsters! Bring me a menu. My Yankee friend the Soap Salesman here, he's gotta order hisself somethin'. Tell the chef to put some hair on his chest."

Their table was now densely crowded with waiters. They were materializing through the ranks of state cops, bringing water, cream, napkins, butter, hot bread, panniers of curdled sauce. They were thrilled to serve, jostling each other for the honor. One offered Oscar a fresh menu.

"Get this boy a jambalaya," Huey commanded, waving the menu away with a flick of his dense red fingers. "Get him two shrimp jambalayas. Big ol' shrimp. We need some jumbo shrimp here, the Child Star looks mighty peaked. Girl, you gotta eat something more than them salads. Woman can't live on chicken salad. Tell me somethin'. You. Oscar. Man's *gotta eat*, don't he?"

"Yes, Governor," Oscar said.

"This boy of yours *ain't eatin'*!" Huey crushed the crawdad's boiled red claw between his pinching thumbs. "Mr. Bombast. Mr. Architecture Boy. I cain't have a thing like that on my conscience! Thinkin' of him, and his pretty wife, just wasting away up north there on goddamn apple juice. It's got me so I cain't sleep nights!"

"I'm sorry to hear that you're troubled, Your Excellency."

"You tell your boy to stop frettin' so much. You don't see me neglectin' life and limb because the common man can't get a decent break up in Boston. We get Yankees like y'all down here all the time. They get a taste of the sweet life, and they forget all about your goddamn muddy water. Hungry Boy needs to lighten up."

"He'll eat when those soldiers eat, sir."

Huey stared at him, chewing deliberately. "Well, you can tell him from me—you tell him tonight—that I'm gonna solve his little problem. I get his point. Point taken. He can put down his goddamn cameras and the apple juice, because I'm gonna do him a favor. I am taking proactive executive measures to resolve the gentleman's infrastructural contretemps."

"I'll see to it that the Senator gets your message, sir."

"You think I'm kidding, Mr. Valparaiso? You think I'm funning with you tonight?"

"I would never think that, Your Excellency."

"That's good. That's real good. You know something? I loved your dad's movies." Huey turned to gaze over his shoulder. "WHAT'S WITH THE BAND?" he bellowed. "Are they DRUNK? Put the band on!"

The musicians rapidly reassembled and began playing a minuet. The Governor slurped a demitasse, then returned his attention to the monster crayfish and lit into it savagely. He snapped and devoured both claws, and then sucked hot spiced juice from its head with every appearance of satisfaction.

The waiters began laying out fresh platters of Cajun delicacies. Oscar examined the steaming feast. He had rarely felt less like eating.

"What about you now, darlin'?" Huey demanded suddenly. "You're not saying much tonight."

Greta shook her head.

"You gotta know what the Soap Boy here is up to, right? Dougal is out, the FedDems are in, it's s'posed to be somebody else's pork now. What do you think? Nice little lab up on Route 128? Some kind of promise, I guess."

"He doesn't make many promises," Greta murmured.

"He better not, because he can't promise Boston beans. I got two boys in the Senate who can sit on his Senator's neck from here to Sunday. I *built* that goddamn laboratory! *Me!* I know what it's worth. Up in Baton Rouge, we just put a new bill through the Ways and Means Committee. A big expansion for 'Bio Bayou.' Maybe my lab ain't as big as yours, but it don't need to be big, if you don't have to feed every pork-eatin' lawn jockey in the fifty states. I know the goddamn difference between neuroscience and them sons of bitches who are cataloging grasshoppers. You know I can tell the difference, don't you?"

"Yes, I know, Etienne."

"It's a cryin' shame, you fillin' out them federal grants in quintuplicate. A woman like you needs a *free hand*! Let's just say that you fancy workin' on . . . blocking the uptake of methylspiropedirol in extrastriatal dopamine receptors. Might sound kinda funny to the layman, but that's all the difference between sanity and total schizophrenia. I defy you to find a single elected federal official who can even pronounce them words! But that's the coming thing. Digital . . . biological . . . and now cognitive. Plain as the nose on my brain. You think we're gonna sit here in Acadiana, as the only nonnative people in America ever subjected to forced ethnic cleansing, and watch a bunch of POINTY-HEADED FAT CATS tryin' to OUTTHINK US? Out-goddamn-THINK us? In a pig's eye, sister!"

"I don't do cognition, Etienne. I'm just a neural tech."

"You won the Nobel for establishing the glial basis of attention, and you're claiming you don't do cognition?"

"I do neurons and glial cells. I do neurochemical wave propagation. But I don't do consciousness. That's not a term of art. It's metaphysics."

"You're a mile deep, darlin'. But you're an inch wide. It ain't metaphysics when it's sitting on a table in front of you with an apple in its mouth. Look, we known each other a long time. You know old Huey, don't you? You're a friend of Huey's, you can have anything you want. Anything you want!"

"I just want to work in my lab."

"You got it! Send me the specs! What do you want, airtight? We got sulfur and salt mines a mile down, holes bigger than downtown Baton Rouge. Do whatever the hell you want down there! Seal the doors behind you. Science, the endless frontier, darlin'! Can't *ask* for better than that! Never sign an impact statement again! Just get your results and publish, that's all I'm askin'! Just get your results and publish."

————————

Oscar and Greta returned to the beach house at four in the morning. They watched from the deck railings as the headlights of their six-car state police escort turned and faded into darkness.

The krewe, alerted by Fontenot, had been carefully guarding the beach house. It had not been entered or searched. That seemed like a small comfort. "I can't believe that people came up to him and kissed his hands," Oscar said.

"There were only three of them."

"They kissed his hands! They were weeping, and kissing his hands!"

"He's made a lot of difference to the local people," Greta said, yawning. "He's given them hope." She stepped into the bathroom with her overnight bag, and shut the door.

Oscar went into the kitchen. He opened the refrigerator door. His hands were shaking. Huey hadn't cracked him. Oscar hadn't lost his temper or his nerve; but he was appalled at the speed of the man's reaction and the swift price he'd had to pay for taking foolish risks in Huey's sphere of influence. He found an apple in the fridge and picked it up absently. Then he went in and sat in the hideous armchair. He stood up again, immediately. "He had that place packed with armed goons, and those people were kissing his hands!"

"The Governor needs bodyguards, he lives a very dangerous life," Greta said from behind the bathroom door. "Oscar, why did he call you the 'Soap Salesman'?"

"Oh, that. That was my first company. A biotech app. We made emulsifiers for dishwashing liquid. People don't think these things through, you know. They think biotech should be fancy and elaborate. But soap is a major consumer item. You get a five percent processing edge in a commodity market like soap, and the buyout guys will beat your doors down. . . ." His words trailed off. She was brushing her teeth, she wasn't listening.

She came out in a white flannel nightgown. It was ankle-length and had a little pastel bow at the neck. She opened her overnight bag and pulled out a compact air filter.

"Allergies?" Oscar said.

"Yes. The air outside the dome . . . well, outside air always smells funny to me." She plugged in her filter. It emitted a powerful hum.

Oscar checked the windows to make sure they were shut and curtained, then stared at her. All unknowing, his feelings about her had undergone a deep and turbulent sea change. His encounter with the Governor had roiled him inside. He was all stirred and clotted now. He was passionate. He felt aggressive and possessive. He was sick with jealousy. "Are you going to sleep in that?"

"Yes. My feet always get so cold at night."

Oscar shook his head. "You're not going to sleep in that. And we won't use the bed. This time, we'll use the floor."

She examined the floor. It had a lovely hooked rug. She looked up at him, her face flushed to the ears.

He woke just after dawn. He was asleep on the rug. Greta had stripped the bed and placed the sheet and coverlet over him. She was sitting at the bureau, scribbling in her notebook.

Oscar slowly examined the water-stained ceiling. His kneecaps were rug-burned. His back felt sore. There was a slimy damp spot congealing under his hip. He felt truly at peace with himself for the first time in weeks.

5

Without the services of Fontenot to scope out trouble and smooth his way, Oscar found travel difficult. Traffic in Alabama was snarled by manic Christian tent-revival shows, "breathing fresh life into the spirit" with two-hundred-beat-per-minute gospel raves. In Tennessee, Oscar's progress was stymied by battalions of Mexican migrant workers, battling the raging kudzu hands-on, with pick and shovel. Oscar was enjoying the relative safety of a bogus biohazard bus, but there were circumstances when even this couldn't help him.

But while Lana, Donna, and Moira grew bored in the bus and often petulant, Oscar was never idle. As long as he had his laptop and a net-link, the world was his oyster. He tended his finances. He memorized the dossiers of his fellow staffers on the Senate Science Committee. He traded mash email with Greta. Greta was particularly good with email. She mostly spoke about her work—work was the core of Greta's being—but there were entire paragraphs now in which he was actually comprehending what she said.

Political news ran constantly on the bus's back windows. Oscar made a special point of following the many ramifications of Bambakias's hunger strike.

Developments in the scandal were rapid and profound. By the time Oscar reached the outskirts of Washington, DC, the Louisiana air base had been placed under siege.

The base's electrical power supply had long since been cut off for lack of payment. The aircraft had no fuel. The desperate federal troops were bartering stolen equipment for food and booze. Desertion was rampant. The air base commander had released a sobbing video confession and had shot himself.

Green Huey had lost patience with the long-festering scandal. He was moving in for the kill. Attacking and seizing a federal air base with his loyal state militia would have been entirely too blatant and straightforward. Instead, the rogue Governor employed proxy guerrillas.

Huey had won the favor of nomad prole groups by providing them with safe havens. He allowed them to squat in Louisiana's many federally declared contamination zones. These forgotten landscapes were tainted with petrochemical effluent and hormone-warping pesticides, and were hence officially unfit for human settlement. The prole hordes had different opinions on that subject.

Proles cheerfully grouped in any locale where conventional authority had grown weak. Whenever the net-based proles were not consistently harassed by the authorities, they coalesced and grew ambitious. Though easily scattered by focused crackdowns, they regrouped as swiftly as a horde of gnats. With their reaping machines and bio-breweries, they could live off the land at the very base of the food chain. They had no stake in the established order, and they cherished a canny street-level knowledge of society's infrastructural weaknesses. They made expensive enemies.

Nomad proles didn't flourish in densely urbanized locales like Massachusetts, where video surveillance and police search engines made them relatively easy to identify and detain. But Green Huey wasn't from Massachusetts. He was totally indifferent to the standards of behavior there. Louisiana's ecologically blighted areas were ideal for proles. The disaster zones were also impromptu wildlife sanctuaries, since wild animals found chemical fouling much easier to survive than the presence of human beings. After decades of wild subtropical growth, Louisiana's toxic dumps were as impenetrable as Sherwood Forest.

Huey's favorite proles were native Louisianans, displaced by rising seas, hurricane damage, and levee-smashing floods from the rampant Mississippi. Sinking into the depths of their tattered landscape, the Louisiana hordes had become creatures of an entirely different order from the scattered dissidents of the East Coast. These Louisianans were a powerful, ambitious, thriving counter-society, with their own clothing, their own customs, their own police, economy, and media. They could rather lord it over the nation's less-organized dissies, hobos, and leisure unions. They were known as the Regulators.

Jungle war in the swamps of Louisiana gave Huey's Regulator nomads a Maoist tactical advantage. Now Huey had unleashed his dogs of netwar, and persistent low-intensity hell was breaking loose around the federal air base.

As was sadly common with American political disputes, the best and most accurate news coverage was taking place in the European media. Oscar located a European satellite feed featuring a Louisiana press conference, held by a zealot calling herself "Subcommander Ooney Bebbels of the Regulator Commando."

The guerrilla leader wore a black ski mask, mud-spattered jeans, and a dashiki. She stalked back and forth before her audience of journos, brandishing a feathered ebony swagger stick and a handheld remote control. Her propaganda conference was taking place in a large inflatable tent.

"Look at that display board," she urged the massed cameras, the picture of sweet reason in her ski mask. "Do y'all have your own copies of that document yet? Brother Lump-Lump, beam some more government files to those

nice French boys in the back! Okay! Ladies and gentlemen, this document I'm displaying is an official federal list
of American Air Force bases. You can grab that budget
document off the committee server for yourself, if you
don't believe me. Look at the official evidence. That air
base you refer to? It don't even exist."

A journalist objected. "But, ma'am, we have that air
base on live feed right now."

"Then you gotta know that's a derelict area. There's
no power, no fuel, no running water, and no food. So
that's no air base. You see any federal aircraft flying around
here? The only thing flyin' here is your press copters. And
our private, harmless, sports-hobbyist ultralights. So y'all
should can that disinformation about any so-called armed
siege. That is total media distortion. We're not armed. We
just need shelter. We're a whole lot of homeless folks, who
need a roof over our heads for the winter. That big derelict
area behind the barbed wire, that's ideal for us. So we're
just waiting here outside the gates till we get some human
rights."

"How many nomad troops do you have on the bat-
tlefield, ma'am?"

"Not 'troops,' *people*. Nineteen thousand three hundred and twelve of us. So far. We're real hopeful. Morale is
really good. We got folks coming in from all over."

A British journalist was recognized. "It's been reported that you have illegal magnetic pulse devices in your
guerrilla camps."

The subcommander shook her ski-masked head im-
patiently. "Look, we hate pulse weapons, they strip our
laptops. We strictly condemn pulse-blasting. Any pulse
attacks coming from our lines will be from provocateurs."

The British journo, nattily kitted-out in pressed
khakis, looked properly skeptical. The British had larger
investment holdings in the USA than any other national-
ity. The Anglo-American special relationship still had
deep emotional resonance, especially where the return on

investment was concerned. "What about those antiper-sonnel devices you've deployed?"

"Stop calling them that. They're our perimeter con-trols. They're for crowd safety. We got a very big crowd of people around here, so we have to take safety measures. What? Tanglewire? Yeah, of course! Spongey sticks, yeah, we always have spongey sticks. Foam barricades and the tear gas, sure, that's all over-the-counter stuff, you can buy that anywhere. What? Superglue? Hell yeah, we got a couple tanker trucks of *that* stuff. *Little kids* can make superglue."

A German correspondent took the floor. He had brought an entire media krewe with him, two bench-ranks of veteran Euro hustlers bristling with precision op-tical equipment. The Germans were the richest people on earth. They had the highly annoying habit of always sounding extremely adult and responsible. "Why are you destroying the roads?" the German inquired, adjusting his designer sunglasses. "Isn't that economically counter-productive?"

"Mister, those are *condemned* roads. They've all been condemned by the State Highway Department. Tarmac pollutes the environment. So we're cleaning up these roads as a public service. Tarmac is petroleum-based, so we can crack it for fuel. We need the fuel so our little kids don't freeze to death. Okay?"

Oscar touched his mute and the video windows in the campaign bus fell silent. He called out, "Hey, Jimmy, how are we doing for fuel?"

"We're still okay, man," Jimmy said distantly.

Oscar looked at the bunks. Lana, Donna, and Moira were fast asleep. The bus seemed painfully empty now, like a half-eaten tin of sardines. His krewe was dwindling away. He'd been forced to leave most of them in Texas, and he missed them sorely. He missed looking after his people, he missed cheering them up and cheering them on. He missed loading them and pointing them at something vulnerable.

Moira was fiercely determined to quit, and she was bitter about it. Fontenot was out of the picture for good now; he had dumped his phone and laptop in a bayou and moved into his new shack with a boat and fishing tackle. The Bambakias campaign team was the finest thing he had ever built, and now it was history, it was scattering to the winds. This realization inspired Oscar with deep, unreasoning dread.

"What do you make of all this?" he called out to Jimmy.

"Look, I'm driving," Jimmy said reasonably. "I can't watch the news and drive."

Oscar made his way up the aisle to the front of the bus, where he could lower his voice. "I meant the nomads, Jimmy. I know you've had experience with them. I just wondered what you make of this development. Regulator guerrillas, strangling a U.S. Air Force base."

"Everyone else is asleep, so now you have to talk to me, huh?"

"You know I always value your input. You have a unique perspective."

Jimmy sighed. "Look, man, I don't do 'input.' I just drive the bus. I'm your bus driver. Lemme drive."

"Go ahead, drive! I just wondered if . . . if you thought they were a serious threat."

"Some are serious. . . . Sure. I mean, just because you're a nomad, and you're on a reputation server with a big trust-rating, and you're eating grass and home-brewing all kinds of weird bio-stuff. . . . Look, that doesn't make you anything special."

"No."

"No, but some of 'em are pretty serious guys, because, well, you might bust some homeless loser someday who looks shabby and acts nuts, but it turns out he has heavy-duty netfriends from all over, and bad weird stuff starts happening to you out of thin air. . . . But hell, Oscar, you don't need me to tell you about that. You know all about power networks."

"Yeah."

"You do that kind of stuff yourself, that's how you got that guy elected."

"Mm-hmm."

"You're on the road all the time. You're a nomad yourself, just like they are. You're a suit-nomad. Most people who meet you—if they don't know you like we do —they have you figured for a really scary guy, man. You don't have to worry about your reputation. There might be some nomad netgods who are scarier guys than you are, but not many, believe me. Hell, you're *rich*."

"Money isn't everything."

"Oh, come on! Look, I'm not smart enough to talk to you, okay?" Jimmy shrugged irritably. "You should be sleeping right now. Everybody else sleeps." Jimmy checked a readout and gripped the wheel.

Oscar silently waited him out.

"I can drive eighteen hours a day, when I have to," Jimmy said at last. "I don't mind it. Hell, I like it. But I get tired out just watching *you*, man. Just watching you operate, it wears me all out. I just can't keep up with you. I'm not in your league. I'm just a normal guy, okay? I don't want to take over federal science bases. I'm just a working guy from Boston, man. I drive buses."

Jimmy checked the overhead scanner, and took a breath. "I'm gonna drive this bus back to Boston for you, and I'm gonna turn the bus in, and then I'm all done with you. Okay? I'm gonna take some time off after this. I mean, I want some real, no-kidding time off. I mean some leisure, that's what I want. I'm gonna drink a lot of beer and go bowling, and then maybe if I'm lucky, then maybe I'll get laid. But I'm not gonna hang out with politicians anymore."

"You'd really leave my krewe, Jim?" Oscar said. "Just like that?"

"You hired me to drive this bus, man! Can't you leave it at that? It's a job! I don't do crusades."

"Don't be hasty. I'm sure we could find another role for you in the organization."

"No, man. You *don't* have any role for me. Or for any guys like me. Why are there millions of nomads now? They don't have *jobs,* man! You don't care about 'em! You don't have any use for 'em! You can't *make* any use for them! They're just not necessary to you. Not at all. Okay? So, you're not necessary to them, either. Okay? They got real tired of waiting for you to give them a life. So now, they just make their own life by themselves, out of stuff they find lying around. You think the government cares? The government can't even pay their own Air Force."

"A country that was better organized would have a decent role for all its citizens."

"Man, that's the creepy part—they're a *lot* better organized than the government is. Organization is the only thing they've got! They don't have money or jobs or a place to live, but *organization,* they sure got plenty of that stuff. See, they're exactly like you are, man. You and your campaign krewe, you're a lot more organized than those dinosaur feds that are running the Collaboratory. You can take over that place anytime, right? I mean, that's exactly what you're going to do! You're gonna take that place over. Whether they like it or not. You want it, so you're just gonna take it."

Oscar said nothing.

"That's the part I'm gonna miss most, man. Watching you put your moves on people. Like that weird science chick you're recruiting. Man, that move was totally brilliant. I just didn't have the heart to leave, before I saw if you'd score with that science chick. But you nailed her, all right. You can do anything you want." Jimmy laughed.

"You're a genius! But I'm *not* a genius, okay? I'm just not up for that. It's too tiring."

"I see."

"So stop worrying so much, man. You wanna worry about something, worry about DC. We're gonna be in DC by morning, and if this bus makes it out of that town in one piece, I'm gonna be a real happy guy."

Washington, DC, enjoyed a permanent haze of aerial drones. Helicopters were also extremely common, since the authorities had basically surrendered the streets. Large sections of the nation's capital were permanently impassable. Dissidents and protesters had occupied all public areas, permanently.

Nonviolent noncooperation had reached unheard-of strategic and tactical heights in the American capital. Its functional districts were privatized and guarded by monitors and swarms of private thugs, but huge sections of the city had surrendered to the squatters. The occupying forces came in a great many ideological flavors, and while they had come to an uneasy understanding with the government per se, they violently despised one another. Dupont Circle, Adams-Morgan, and the area east of Capitol Hill boasted murder rates of almost twentieth-century proportions.

In many neighborhoods of Washington the division of streets and housing had simply dissolved. Entire city blocks had been abandoned to the protesters, who had installed their own plumbing, water systems, and power generators. Streets were permanently barricaded, swathed in camou nets and rain-streaked plastic sheeting.

The most remarkable of Washington's autonomen were the groups known as "martians." Frustrated by years of studied nonreaction to their crazy grievances, the martians had resolved to act as if the federal government simply didn't exist. The martians treated the entire structure of Washington, DC, as raw material.

Their construction techniques had originally been invented by a group of overeager would-be Mars colonizers.

These long-vanished space techies, an ingenious and fanatical group, had invented a wide variety of cheap and simple techniques by which small groups of astronauts might colonize the airless and frozen deserts of the Red Planet. Humanity had never yet reached Mars, but with the final collapse of NASA the Martian colonization plans had become public domain.

These plans fell into the eager hands of fanatical street protesters. They had dug down into the squelchy subsoil of the Potomac riverbed, squeezing water from the soil, compacting it to use as bricks, building an endless series of archways, tunnels, and kivas. The radicals found that even the sorriest patch of Earth was a cornucopia, compared to the airless deserts of Mars. Anything that might work on Mars would work a hundred times better in a deserted alley or parking lot.

Now NASA's ingenuity had borne amazing fruit, and the streets of Washington were lavishly bumped and measled with martian settlements. Slums of compacted dirt, all glue and mazy airlocks, climbed straight up the walls of buildings, where they clung like the nests of mud-daubing wasps. There were excavation hills three stories high near Union Station, and even Georgetown was subject to repeated subterranean rumblings.

Most of these martians were Anglos. In fact, sixty percent of Washington's populace were members of the troubled minority. Local DC government, a world-famous model of urban corruption, was dominated by militant Anglos. The ethnic bosses were busily exercising their traditional genius for fraud, hacking, and white-collar crime scams.

Oscar, though a stranger to Washington, knew better

than to enter the city unprepared. He abandoned his krewe inside the bus, which retreated at once to the relative safety of Alexandria. Oscar then walked two blocks on foot, through a protesters' permanent street market of flowers, medals, bracelets, bumper stickers, flags, cassettes, and Christmas toys.

He arrived at his destination, unmolested and in good order. He then discovered, without much surprise, that the federal office building had fallen into the hands of squatters.

Oscar wandered through the entry hall, passing metal detectors and a cyclops set of facial recognition units. The squat's concierge was an elderly black man with close-cropped hair and a bow tie. He gave Oscar a clip-on ID bracelet.

The system was now logging Oscar's presence and his movements, along with everything else of relevance inside the building: furniture, appliances, tools, kitchenware, clothes, shoes, pets, and of course all the squatters themselves. The locators were as small as orange pips and as rugged as tenpenny nails, so they could invisibly infest any device that anyone found of interest.

This universal tagging made the contents of the building basically theftproof. It also made communal property a rather simple proposition. It was never hard to find a tool when the locale, condition, and history of every tool was logged and displayed in real time. It was also very hard for freeloaders to anonymously steal or abuse the common goods. When it worked, this digital socialism was considerably cheaper and more convenient than private property.

However, in order to function, this technology had a major side effect: it turned people's lives inside out. There were children playing in the building's halls—in fact, to judge by the disorder, the squatters' children were *living* in the halls. The kids were bugged and safety-tagged, surrounded by a smorgasbord of the community's color-coded and positionally registered kiddie toys.

Oscar picked his way through a dense litter of tricycles and inflatable animals, then took a crowded elevator up to the third floor. This section of the building reeked powerfully of East Indian cooking—curries, papadams, maybe some chicken masala. Probably, to judge by the smell, large flocks of computer-tagged chickens.

The double doors of Room 358 opened trustingly at his touch. Oscar found himself in a sculptor's studio, a bleak, ill-smelling place reconstructed from a fire-blackened set of office cubicles. The torched federal offices had left eerie remains: a gridwork of blackened floor scars and the dripping stalagmite lumps of dead plastic workstations. The retrofitted office had been reoccupied, however. It now boasted a long makeshift workbench of bolted railway ties, amid piles of automotive scrap metal, flattened epoxy tubes, and stubby welding rods. The concrete floor echoed beneath Oscar's shoes.

Clearly he was in the wrong room.

His phone rang. He answered it. "Hello?"

"Is this really you?" It was Greta.

"It's me all right—live and in person."

"It's not a phone-sex line?"

"No. I use that phone-sex service to reroute my private calls. They have tremendous voice traffic on their lines, so it helps a lot against tracing attacks. And if anyone is running traffic analysis, they'll just assume . . . Well, never mind the technical details. The point is that we can talk safely together on an unencrypted phone."

"I guess it's okay."

"So, let's talk, Greta. Tell me how you are. Tell me everything."

"Are you safe there in Washington?"

Oscar clutched the fabric phone tenderly. It was as if he had her ear cradled in his hand. It now mattered much less to him that he was hopelessly lost and in the wrong building.

"I'm perfectly fine. This is where I make my career, after all."

"I worry about you, Oscar." Long pause. "I think . . . I think maybe I could go to Boston later. There's a neuro seminar there. Maybe I could block some time in."

"Excellent! You should come to Boston, by all means. I'll show you my house." A slow, sizzling pause.

"That sounds interesting. . . ."

"Do it. It's what we need. It's good for us."

"I have to tell you something important. . . ."

He swiftly examined his battery level and replaced the phone at his ear. "Just go ahead and tell me, Greta."

"It's so hard to explain this. . . . It's just that . . . I feel so different now and . . . I'm all inspired and it's just . . ." A lingering silence.

"Go on," he coaxed. "Get it off your chest."

Her voice dropped to a confiding whisper. "It's my amyloid fibrils. . . ."

"It's what?"

"My fibrils. There are a lot of diverse neural proteins that form amyloid fibrils in vivo. And even though they have unrelated sequences, they all polymerize into fibrils with similar ultrastructure. The conformational folding arrangements have been bothering me. A lot."

"Really? That's a shame."

"But then I was messing with my GDNF adeno carriers, yesterday, and I grafted a new amyloidogenic variant onto the carrier. I've just derived their mass with the electrospray spectrometer. And, Oscar, they're expressing. And they're all enzymatically active and they all have the correct, intact disulfide bonds."

"It's marvelous when you're expressing."

"They're going to express in vivo! And that's so much less invasive than dumb, old-fashioned gene therapy. That's been the critical limiting factor, a permanent cheap

method of delivery. And if we can do amyloids as well as
dopamine and neurotrophic factors . . . I mean, transfer
all those loads congruently into live neural tissue. . . .
Well, I don't have to tell you what *that* means."

"No, no," Oscar said deftly, "depend on it, I'm solid
on *that* issue."

"It's just that Bellotti and Hawkins are doing autoso-
mal amyloidosis, so they're right on top of this problem.
And they're doing a poster session at the Boston AMAC."

"Then you should *definitely* go to Boston," Oscar
said, "there's no way that some drone like Bellotti should
scoop you on this! I'll put it all in order for you, right
away. Never mind trying to swing the travel funding. My
krewe can book you right through to Boston. You'll have
time on the plane to assemble your presentation. We'll get
you a suite at the convention hotel and we'll have all your
meals catered, to save you time. You should seize this
opportunity, Greta. You never get proper time to think for
yourself when you're riding herd back at the lab."

She was brightening. "Well . . ."

The door of Room 358 opened, and a black woman
came through, in a creaking motorized wheelchair. She
had a shock of dirty gray hair and a load of green plastic
trash bags.

"I understand about the work," Oscar said into the
phone, while backing cautiously away from the door.
"Boston is totally doable."

"Hi there!" said the wheelchair woman, waving one
hand. Oscar slipped his fingers over the phone's mouthpiece and nodded politely.

The black woman bounded up from her wheelchair,
shut it down, and held the door open. Three Anglo men
barged into the room, in denim overalls, boots, and battered straw hats. Their hair was dyed blue, their faces were
streaked with nomad war paint, and they all wore sunglasses. One of them pushed a mighty wheelbarrow full of

wires and flatscreens, and the two others carried large khaki-colored electrical toolboxes.

"You really think that fibrils are hot enough for you to do all that for me?" Greta said plaintively.

"Fibrils are extremely hot."

The woman with the wheelchair tugged off her fright wig, revealing a neat set of cornrows. She then shrugged off her ragged caftan. Beneath it she wore a navy blue skirt, a blue vest, a silk blouse, and hose.

Her three technicians began assembling a conference network on the welder-stained workbench.

"I'm Oscar Valparaiso," Oscar announced loudly. "I'm with the committee."

"You're early," the woman told him. She fetched a power-strip and a new set of shoes from one of her trash bags.

"I enjoy a fresh start." Oscar returned to his phone. "Okay. Okay. Good. I'm glad it's working out. Lana and I will see to everything. Good-bye." He crumpled his phone and tucked it in his sleeve.

"So," he said aloud, "what's your name?"

"Chris," the new woman said, carefully straightening a seam. "I'm the committee sysop." She smiled. "Just the lowly sysop."

"And is this your krewe?"

"I don't have a krewe. I'm just a GS-Five. These guys are net subcontractors, they all live here in the squat. See, it's a little weird about this meeting room. . . . I mean, for years we met in the Dirksen Senate Building. But the President's transition team has requisitioned our old offices. So, the Senate Science Committee is kind of between permanent housing assignments right now."

"I see."

"They assigned us this room off the federal vacancy server. The trouble is, even though it's still listed in the server, in reality, this whole building's been a squat for three years. And we're not an Emergency committee, so we can't have the building cleared legally. We're too low in the chain to have anyone evicted."

"Well, at least it's a nice big room," Oscar said winningly.

"That's true!" She smiled at him.

"And the two of us are here, so that's a start. Your wheelchair bag-lady getup is extremely good, by the way."

"Well, it sure helps a lot with the local roadblocks and ID checks."

"I can see that you're a true-blue Washingtonian, Chris."

"That's me—Southern efficiency and Northern charm." Chris's eye wandered and she elbowed one of her helpers aside. "No, that's the visual outlet! It's a sixteen-pin, okay? Let me do that!" She turned to a second man. "Get the router out of the bag. A router, and a squeegee. And a divot. Two data divots. No, not that one! Get me the green one."

Oscar was charmed. "Do you do these metal sculptures, too, Chris?"

"Those are my boyfriend's. He kind of guards this space for us, because he can leave the premises on short notice." She glanced up. "It's like multitasking, see?"

"I *love* multitasking." Oscar's second phone rang. He dragged it out of his vest pocket. "What? Yeah, Lana, book her through to Boston. To the AMAC conference. No, I don't know what that acronym stands for. Just net-search it."

"Where's the mediator? Get the baffles," Chris riposted. She was watching him sidelong.

"Register her for the whole conference," Oscar said, taking a half step closer and raising his voice for effect. "Get Yosh to finesse all that. And get her some catering. She likes Thai food. Burmese? Burmese is great, but mind her allergies."

"Is it running DMAC? There's a DMAC tower right on Fourteenth. See if they're up."

"The DMAC is up," Oscar cross-posted loudly. "My phone runs on DMAC." He switched ears. "Lana, book her into the convention hotel. Be sure to get air filters. And flowers. Flowers every day."

"Did you put the compressor on the DNC?" Chris said intently, still watching Oscar with increasing interest. "You can't load the router without the CMV first. Is that the EDFA? Well, use the packet squeegee."

"Book her for a day over," Oscar said. "For two days. Yeah. No. Yeah. Okay. Thanks." He crushed the phone.

"No, wiggle it," Chris said. "It's the cable."

"It's always the cable," Oscar nodded.

The assembled screens flickered to life in a set of test patterns. "Great," Chris announced. "We're up. Where's the image groomer?"

"Got no groomer," the contractor grumbled. "You didn't say bring no groomer."

"I didn't know this new guy was gonna be here physically."

"I can manage without an image groomer," Oscar broke in. "I've brought my own makeup."

Chris favored him with a precious moment of her full attention. "You're very traditional, Mr. Valparaiso."

"Makeup is a vital part of Mr. Valparaiso's heritage." They were on the same wavelength. They were communicating beautifully on a nonverbal level. "Where's everybody else, Chris? I understood we were meeting physically."

Chris straightened warily. "Yeah, the sunshine laws do mandate open meetings, but this isn't a senatorial meeting. It's just a staff conference. No legislators present."

"I thought the staff conferences were also physical meetings."

"This is more of an informal on-line conferral, actually."

Oscar offered her a calculated frown. "My event announcement specifically stated that this is a face-to-face staff conference."

"Well, during the transition period we have to make procedural allowances. . . . Look, I know this sounds goofy. But the staff hates going into squats like this. They called this a 'conference,' so they could get the hours logged and the conference perks. But really, it's just a conferral." She smiled meekly. "I'm just the sysop, you know. This isn't my fault."

"I understand perfectly that it's not your fault, Chris. But if it's just a conferral, we're not being serious here. We won't get results."

"You can get results at a conferral."

"But I don't *want* a conferral. If we're going to shoptalk off-the-record, we could do it over dry martinis."

The door opened. Three men and a woman came in. "Here's Mr. Nakamura," Chris said with relief, "I'm sure he can help you." She retreated behind her machinery.

Nakamura stopped and read his secretary's screen for forty seconds, establishing Oscar's ID and dossier. He then moved forward briskly, hand outstretched. "Good to meet you again, Oscar! How was your trip from Texas?"

"My trip was lovely."

"Where's your krewe?" Nakamura gazed around the fire-blackened vault. "No support staff?"

"I have a secure tour bus. So I left my krewe on board there, and had them drop me off."

Nakamura glanced at his two bodyguards, who were scoping the room for bugs with small handheld sniffers. "A secure tour bus. I wish you'd called *me*. I could have hitched a ride with you, and spared myself hiring these goons."

Oscar felt very flattered to be offered such a blatant lie. "I'd have been delighted, sir."

"I'm old-fashioned," Nakamura declared. "Congress pays me, so I like to show up for duty." Nakamura was the Science Committee's longest-serving staffer. Nakamura had survived an astonishing number of purges, scandals, senatorial shake-ups—even repeated depredations and head-hunting raids from the Emergency committees.

Nakamura was a Right Tradition Bloc man, from the Economic Freedom Party. The EcFreeds pulled a twelve percent voter share, putting them well ahead of their bloc's junior partners, the Christian Democratic Union and the antifeminist Ladies' Party. Oscar considered the EcFreeds to be profoundly mistaken politically, but at least they were consistent in their errors. The EcFreeds were players.

Nakamura touched Oscar's jacket shoulder, a tender little act of political palpation. "I'm eager to hear your report on the Buna Collaboratory, Oscar. I'm sure you've been busy there."

"These are difficult times, sir."

"All the more reason to assure some stability during the new Administration's transition period."

"I fully concur," Oscar riposted at once. "Continuity, and a firm hand in the lab's administration, would be extremely helpful now. Prudence. Nothing hasty."

Nakamura nodded reflexively, then frowned. For a moment, Oscar thought he had overdone it. Nakamura had twenty years of recorded public appearances in the federal files. Oscar had taken the trouble to have the man's speech patterns analyzed, ranked, and sorted. Nakamura was especially fond of the terms "prudence" and "continuity," with "helpful" and "a firm hand" on strong upward trends lately. Verbally mimicking Nakamura was a cheap net-trick, but like most such tricks, it usually worked.

Eight more people came through the doors. These

were committee staffers Namuth and Mulnier, with their joint entourage of six krewepeople, who had brought pizza, coffee, and falafel. The aroma of fast food filled the dank, rust-smelling room with a cheering scent of human survival.

Nakamura gratefully sampled a pita sandwich. The senior staffer seemed more relaxed now that the gruesome squat had filled with familiar faces. "Namuth and Mulnier are all right," he murmured. "Staffers who take the pains to attend a mere conferral face-to-face . . . they do tend to be all right."

"Tell me, sir—is this just a conferral, or is it a conference per se?"

Nakamura looked pained as he chewed and swallowed. "Well, of course an actual *conference* would have the legislators in attendance. Or at least their leading office krewe staff, their chiefs of staff, for instance. And of course there are committee *meetings,* and then subcommittee and committee *hearings,* generally with sworn witnesses and full coverage. . . . However, in the modern legislative trend, the drafting of legislation and the budget preparation have fallen to the staff committees. Actual senatorial hearings have become highly mediated events, very formal. It follows that we staffers must have our own conferences. And then, behind those formal scenes, we do find it procedurally necessary to have these conferrals."

Nakamura examined his collapsing sandwich and tucked in a wad of sprouts with one fingertip. "We called this event a 'conference,' because that's necessary in order to get the personnel chits and travel rebates. And we do get better security service. This entire building, as you must have noticed, is sadly insecure."

Oscar, once certain that Nakamura's lips had stopped moving, leaned gently forward. "I know that we can't hold truly formal hearings until the Senate convenes. As a novice junior staffer, I'm not eager to take on that challenge until I'm much better briefed. Frankly, I look to you for some helpful guidance and continuity there."

Nakamura accepted this remark with a graceful nod. "I've been on the ground at the Collaboratory, sampling opinion. . . . Since Senator Dougal's mishaps, the rumor mills there have been grinding overtime. Morale is shaky."

" 'Shaky'?"

"The situation might stabilize, I think, if they received some reassuring gestures from Washington."

Nakamura eyed his other colleagues. Namuth and Mulnier were swilling iced coffees, tapping lackadaisically at screens, and paying them no real attention. This did not surprise Oscar, who had written off both Namuth and Mulnier after closely studying their dossiers.

Nakamura was made of sterner stuff. "What do you plan to propose?"

"I think some expression of confidence in the current Director is in order. A statement of support from this Senate committee—that might work wonders for him."

Nakamura put his sandwich aside. "Well, we can't do that."

"Why not? We need to take action. The Director's authority is visibly slipping. If the situation gets out of hand, the lab will be paralyzed."

Nakamura's face grew clouded. "Young man, you never worked with Senator Dougal. I did. The idea of our giving some blanket endorsement now to one of his krewe flunkies . . . especially first thing in a new Administration . . . No, I don't think so."

"You said that you wanted continuity in the situation."

"I didn't say that *we* should provide that continuity."

"Well, then," Oscar said, slipping with feigned disappointment into his prepared position, "maybe my notion should be scaled back. Let me ask your advice. Director Felzian has a difficult situation. What exactly can we do for the man? Without Dougal's sponsorship, his situation is dangerous. He might be denounced. He might be formally investigated. He might even be indicted."

"Indicted?" Nakamura rolled his eyes. "Not in Texas, surely!"

"He could be indicted in Louisiana. So many rare animals have vanished into the collector's market. . . . They make such photogenic evidence, rare animals. . . . The Governor of Louisiana is a highly interested party. The state courts there are completely in his pockets. This really isn't a time to show division and weakness at a federal lab."

"Young man, you've never met Governor Huguelet—"

"Oh yes, sir, I have. I had dinner with him last week."

Nakamura's face fell. "You did."

"He's a very hard presence to miss in that corner of the world. He made his intentions very clear to me."

Nakamura sighed. "Well, Huey wouldn't dare."

"Why would he draw the line at subverting a federal lab, when he's already besieging an air base?"

Nakamura's brow wrinkled in silent distress.

Oscar lowered his voice yet further. "Huey has always backed genetic and cognitive R&D. That lab has exactly what he wants and needs. It has the talent, the data, and the samples. Besides, Huey was a major force in creating that lab in the first place. He has allies all through the old guard there. His course of action is obvious."

"But he was always such a great backer of the federal presence there. It's not like we've *forgotten* the Collaboratory. We haven't misplaced it. We're not like those morons on the Emergency committee."

Oscar let the silence stretch. Then he shrugged. "Am I being unreasonable here? I'm trying to propose the *smallest* action we can take to maintain the status quo. Is it the sense of this committee that we are *unhappy* with the status quo?"

"No, of course not. Well . . . some are. Some aren't."

Oscar showed a proper skepticism. "I hope you understand that this is my very first assignment with this committee. I don't care to go out on a limb today."

"No."

"I don't grandstand in these matters. I'm a team player."

"Of course."

Oscar gently touched Nakamura's arm. "I hope you don't think I'm *enjoying* my isolation from this committee. I could have been here on the Hill, at the center of the action, instead of being marooned for six weeks inside some airtight dome. I'm going to make my interim report today, but if I'm sent back to Texas without a committee consensus and some coherent course of action, I'm going to take that very amiss. Is that unreasonable of me?"

"No. It's not unreasonable. I do appreciate your situation. Believe it or not, I was also a young staffer once."

"Sir, this is not going to be a pretty report. Especially the financial attachments. The troubles there could spin right out of control. They might even be fatal troubles. It may be that our cheapest and easiest course of action is to shut down that lab, and let Green Huey cherry-pick the wreckage."

Nakamura winced.

Oscar bored in. "But that's not my decision. And it's *certainly* not my responsibility. If my report today gets leaked, and something breaks loose, I don't want any spin from this committee suggesting that I myself have some kind of personal agenda. Or that Senator Bambakias has any untoward intentions in this matter. I've made a good-faith, objective effort here. I consider it my job to lay out the facts for the committee. But if something breaks loose, I don't want to be hung out to dry."

Oscar raised one forestalling hand, palm out. "*Not* that I'm suggesting any malice on the part of my fellow staffers! I'm just remarking on an obvious organizational truism—that it's always easiest to hang the new boy."

"Yes, it is," Nakamura told him. "You've read the situation very well. But in point of fact, you're not the only new boy on this committee."

"No?"

"No. There are three new Senators on the Science Committee, and they've all brought in krewepeople. And the two other new boys have yet to show up physically for one single goddamn conferral. They're logging in from the penthouse decks in Arlington, where they're busy kissing ass."

Oscar frowned. "That is not professional behavior."

"They're not professionals. You can't depend on them. You can depend on me, and you can depend on Mulnier. Well, Mulnier's not the man he was ten years ago —but if you're straight with me, and if you mean well, and if you're giving a hundred percent for this committee, well, you're covered. You are covered, and you have my word on that."

"That's all I ask." Oscar half stepped back. "I'm glad we've reached an understanding."

Nakamura glanced at his watch. "And before we get started today—I want you to know, Oscar, your personal background problem is not at issue here. As long as I'm chairing this committee, I will not have that matter brought up."

————————

The Bambakias town house was on New Jersey Avenue, just south of Capitol Hill. Oscar arrived just as a media krewe was leaving. New Jersey Avenue was a very well monitored area. Civil disturbances were rare in this neighborhood, and its urban infrastructure was still sound. The house itself was a historic structure, well over two hundred years old. The house was too small for the Bambakias couple and their extensive krewe, but Lorena Bambakias was an interior designer in a crowded world. She had set herself to make allowances.

As a campaign professional, Oscar made it a firm principle never to cross the person who slept with the candidate. The candidate's spouse was by necessity a major campaign player. Lorena was a player to the bone, but she was manageable, usually. She was manageable as long as her advice was always heeded with unfeigned attention and a straight face, and as long as she knew that she held big cards. Anyone who knew about Oscar's personal background problem always assumed that they possessed a killer trump against him. This was all right. He had never placed Lorena in any situation where she would feel the need to play killer trumps.

The hunger strike had made Lorena's eyes luminous, and her olive skin was so tight and smooth that it seemed almost laminated. Lorena was not an aristocrat—she was, in point of fact, the daughter of a Cambridge health-food chain-store executive—but the gauntness, and the expert video makeup, gave her the heightened, otherworldly glow of a Gainsborough portrait.

Weak with fasting, she was lounging on a scroll-armed couch of yellow silk.

"It's good of you to take the time to visit me, Oscar," Lorena told him, stirring languidly. "We rarely have the chance to really talk, you and I."

"This place looks marvelous," Oscar told her. "I can't wait to see it when you're done."

"Oh, it's just my work," Lorena told him. "I wish I could say that this was exciting—but it's just another damn design gig. I really miss the campaign."

"Do you? That's sweet of you."

"It was so exciting to be with *the people*. At least we ate well then. Now . . . well, now, we plan to entertain. We'll be the Senator and Madam Senator, and we'll be living in this sorry dump for six long years, and we plan to cut a swath through high society." She gazed about her drawing room, gazing at her newly peach-colored walls with the pensive look of an auto mechanic. "My own tastes run toward Transcendental Contemporary, but I'm doing this place entirely in Federal Period. A lot of Hepplewhite . . . black walnut . . . secretary bookcases, and shield back side chairs. . . . There was some good material in that period, if you stay away from all that tacky neoclassical."

"Very good choice."

"I need a feeling here that's responsible, and yet fully responsive. Very restrained, very American Republic, but nothing kitschy or colonial. Very Boston, you see?—but not *too* Boston. Not all identity-politics, not all Paul Revere. With an ensemble like this, something has to give. You have to make sacrifices. You can't have everything at once. Elegance is restraint."

"Yes, of course."

"I'm going to have to give up my binturong."

"Oh no," Oscar said, "not Stickley the binturong."

"I know you took a lot of trouble to obtain Stickley for me, and he really is a lovely conversation piece. But I just don't have room to showcase a rare animal here in Washington. An openwork terrarium, that would have been lovely, and I had such nice ideas for the schema. But an animal clone just clashes. He does. He's not in period. He's a distraction."

"Well, that's doable," Oscar said judiciously. "I don't think anyone has ever *returned* an animal to the Collaboratory. That would be a nice gesture."

"I might do a *small* clone. A bat, or a mole, or such. . . . Not that I don't enjoy Stickley. He's very well behaved. But you know? There's something weird about him."

"It's that neural implant they give them at the Collaboratory," Oscar said. "It's all about aggression, eating, and defecation. If you control those three behaviors, you can live in peace with wild animals. Luckily, that deep neural structure is very similar across a wide range of mammals."

"Including humans, I imagine."

"Well, of course." Oscar's phone rang. He politely turned it off without answering it.

"The neural control of eating certainly has advanced a lot," Lorena said. "I'm on appetite controllants right now. They're very neural."

"Neural is a hot technology now."

"Yes. Neural sounds very attractive."

She was telling him that she knew about Greta. Well, of course Lorena would know about Greta. Except that Lorena had also known all about Clare. Because Clare had given Lorena Bambakias some very nice press coverage. So Lorena was rather in Clare's corner. But surely Lorena must see sense there. After all, Clare had left him. . . .

Lorena's own phone rang. She answered it at once. "Yes? What? Oh dear. Oh *dear*. And how is Alcott taking the news? Oh, *poor* dear. Oh, this is very sad. You're quite sure? Really? All right. Thank you very much." Lorena paused. "Would you like to talk to Oscar Valparaiso about this? He happens to be here for tea. No? Very well, then." She hung up.

"That was Leon Sosik, our chief of staff," she announced, slipping the phone into her wide-cut sleeve. "There's been a major development in our hunger strike."

"Oh?"

"It's the air base. A fire has broken out. There's some kind of toxic spill there. They're having the whole base evacuated."

Oscar sat up in his lyre-backed mahogany chair. " 'Evacuated,' is that the story?"

"The federal troops are leaving. They're running for their lives. So of course those horrid little prole people are pouring in after them, they're swarming right over the

fences." Lorena sighed. "That means that it's over. It's
ending right now. It's finally over." She swung out her
legs, sat up on her couch, and put one slender wrist to her
forehead. "Thank God."

Oscar ran his hand over his newly coiffed hair.
"Good Lord, what next?"

"Are you kidding? Christ, I'm going to *eat*." Lorena
rang a bell on her tea trolley. A krewe member arrived—a
new person, someone Oscar had never seen before.
"Elma, bring me some tea cake. No, bring me some petit
fours, and some chocolate strawberries. Bring me . . .
oh, what's the use, bring me a jumbo roast beef sandwich." She looked up. "Would you like something, Oscar?"

"I could do with a black coffee and some media
coverage."

"Good idea." She raised her voice. "System?"

"Yes, Lorena," the house system said.

"Would you send down the screen, please."

"Yes, Lorena, right away."

"I can't employ a full-service krewe in this little
place," Lorena apologized. "So I had to install automa-
tion. It's just a baby system now, so it's still very fresh and
stupid. There's no such thing as a truly smart house, no
matter how much you train them."

A walnut television cabinet came walking down the
carpeted stairs.

"That's a lovely cabinet," Oscar said. "I've never
seen responsive furniture done in a Federal Period idiom."

The television trundled down the stairs and paused,
assessing the layout of the room. After a meditative moment, two curve-legged chairs flexed themselves like
wooden spiders, and shuffled out of its way. Lorena's
couch did a little tango and sidestep. The tea trolley rolled
aside with a jingle. The television sidled up before the two
of them, and presented itself for convenient viewing.

"My goodness, they're *all* responsive," Oscar said. "I could have sworn those were wooden legs."

"They *are* wooden. Well . . . they're flex-treated lignin." Lorena shrugged. "Period furniture is all well and good, you know, but I draw the line at living like a barbarian." She lifted one arm in its striped silk sleeve and a gilt-edged remote control leaped from the wall and flew into her hand. She tossed it to him. "Will you drive for me? Find us some decent coverage. I've never been much good at that."

"Call Sosik again, and ask what *he's* watching."

"Oh. Of course." She smiled wanly. "Never surf when you have a pilot."

Huey's rapid-response PR team was already on the job. A Louisiana environmental safety administrator was supplying the official account of the "disaster." According to him, safety procedures at the "derelict air base" had fallen into abeyance. A small fire had broken out, and it had ruptured a military stockpile of nonlethal crowd-control aerosols. These were panic-inducing disorients. Nontoxic and odorless, they were just the trick for clearing the streets of third-world cities. Cut to a med tent with young Air Force people shivering and babbling in the grip of paranoiac aerosols. Homespun local people were giving them cots, and blankets, and tranquilizers. The pathetic federal personnel were clearly getting the best of care.

Oscar sipped his coffee. "Unbelievable."

Lorena spoke around a hasty mouthful of tea cake. "I take it this spiel has no connection to reality-on-the-ground."

"Oh, there must be *some* connection. Huey's clever enough to arrange all that. He's had agents inside the base, someone to set that fire and dose the base with its own weapons. This was sabotage. Huey was impatient, so he's gone and poisoned them."

"He's deliberately gassed federal troops."

"Well, yes, but we'll never find his fingerprints."

"I can understand people who stab you in the back," Lorena said, gulping a chocolate strawberry. "What I can't understand is people so crazy that they stab you right in the front. This is medieval."

They watched with care, tagging along remotely as Sosik changed his news feeds. The Europeans had some splendid aerial footage of proles invading the base, their heads swathed in ski masks. The Regulators seemed strangely undisturbed by the aerosols.

The nomads were wasting no time. They were ushering in an endless parade of trucks—big retrofitted oil-industry tankers, by the looks of them. They were loading them up, by hand, in coordinated labor gangs. The proles were looting the air base with the decentralized efficiency of ants consuming a dead shrew.

"Let me make a little prediction for you," Oscar said. "Tomorrow, the Governor pretends to be very alarmed by all this. He sends in his state troops to 'restore order.' His militia will nail the place down for him—after the proles have stripped it all. When Washington asks what happened to the military assets, they'll be long gone, and it's all somebody else's fault."

"Why is Huey doing this crazy thing?"

"For him, it makes sense. He wanted that air base for the pork. For the local job creation, for the federal funding. But the Emergency budget people wrote off his funding. They pulled a fast one on him and screwed him out of it. Huey can't abide disrespect, so he decided to escalate. First, those highway robberies. Then, the power cutoffs. Then the proxy siege. He's methodically turned up the heat, step by step. But he still didn't get his way, so now, he just appropriates the whole air base."

"But it's not like his dirty proles can *run* a federal air base. His whole little state militia can't run a federal air base."

"That's true, but now he has the *data*. Advanced avionics, chips, software, the orders of battle and such. . . . That's a military asset of the first order. If the feds push him again, he can push back with whole new sets of options."

"Oh. I see."

"Believe me, he's thought this all through. That's the way he is."

A roast beef sandwich arrived, with mustard, a garnish, and creamed potatoes. Lorena smiled politely as her aproned krewe girl retreated toward the kitchen. She picked off a plank of crustless rye bread, examined it, and set it back down, fingers trembling. "Alcott is going to hate this. We tried so hard to stop this from happening."

"I know you did."

"We just couldn't make them pay enough attention. We pulled the biggest publicity stunt we could manage, short of rallying the party and besieging that place ourselves. Huey just moves too fast for us. Alcott's not even sworn in yet! And even after his inauguration, we'll still have the Emergency committees to deal with. Not to mention the partisan opposition. And besides, the federal government is just plain broke. . . . It's bad, Oscar. It's really bad."

"I'll be going up to Boston tomorrow. We'll think of something new. The hunger strike's over now, but I was never really pleased with that gambit. Don't worry. Just concentrate on getting your strength back. This game isn't over by a long chalk."

She looked at him gratefully. He watched more coverage as she tore into the sandwich.

Finally she put the plate aside, and leaned back on the yellow couch, her eyes glistening. "How was your first committee meeting, Oscar? I never asked. Were you brilliant?"

"Oh, heavens no. They hate it when you're brilliant. Brilliance only makes them mulish. I just recited my facts and figures until they got very bored and logged off. By then, my chairman had all their voting proxies. So I asked him for a mile, and he gave me a hundred yards. But a hundred yards was all that I wanted in the first place. So my meeting was really successful. I have a much freer hand now."

She laughed. "You're so bad!"

"It's no use being brilliant, unless it improves the situation. The Senator pulled a very brilliant stunt with this hunger strike, but now, Alcott should learn to be dull. Romantic people are brilliant, artists are brilliant. Politicians know when it's useful to be dull."

She nodded thoughtfully. "I'm sure you're right. You'll be good with Alcott, won't you? You understand him. You could always talk sense to him. You can cheer him up when he's down."

"You're not down, are you, Lorena?"

"No, I'm not down, I'm coked to the gills on diet pills. But Alcott's not like me. He's very serious. He gets depressed. I can't be with him right now. And he gets so silly about sex when he's depressed."

Oscar was silently attentive.

"Leon Sosik was silly to let Alcott talk him into a hunger strike. Alcott has a thousand ideas, but a better chief of staff would kill his silly ones. And, Oscar, if you take that little tart Moira back to Boston when I'm not around, you'll be very silly, too."

Oscar knew the city of Boston very well indeed, having meticulously canvassed every voting district for the city council races. Boston was sane, civilized, and commonsensical, compared to other American cities. Boston had so much to recommend it. A fully functional financial district. Green, quiet, showpiece parks. Real and serious museums, stocked and maintained by people with a sense of cultural continuity. Several centuries' worth of attractive public statuary. Living, commercial theater. Restaurants with dress codes. Real neighborhoods with real neighborhood bars.

Of course Boston had its less happy areas: the Combat Zone, the half-drowned waterfront . . . but being home, however briefly, gave Oscar a vital sense of grace. He had never missed the maelstrom of Los Angeles, and as for sorry old Washington, it combined the dullness of Brussels with the mania of Mexico City. East Texas, of course, was utterly absurd. The thought of ever going back there gave him a genuine pang.

"I'm going to miss that campaign bus," Oscar said. "It's pared me back, to lose that asset. It's like losing a whole group of go stones."

"Can't you buy your own bus?" Moira said, adjusting her photogenic coat collar with newly lacquered nails.

"Sure, I could afford a campaign bus, if they built them out of concrete blocks with unskilled labor," Oscar said. "But so far, that never happens. And now I've lost good old Jimmy, too."

"Some big loss that is. Jimmy's a loser. A no-neck geek from the Southside . . . the world's got a billion Jimmies."

"Yes, that's why Jimmy was important to me."

Moira jammed her bare hands in her jacket and sniffed at the freezing air. "I've spent too much time with you, Oscar. I had to live inside your pockets for months. I can't understand why I still let you make me feel guilty."

Oscar was not going to let her provoke him. They had dropped off the bus at FedDem headquarters, and they were taking a peaceful winter stroll to his town house in the Back Bay, and he was enjoying himself. "I'm not telling you to feel guilty. Am I judgmental? I was very supportive, I always looked after you. Didn't I? I never said a word about you and Bambakias."

"Yes you *did*! You kept lifting your big black eyebrows at me."

Oscar lifted his eyebrows, caught himself doing it,

put the eyebrows back in place. He hated confrontations. They always brought out the worst in him. "Look, this isn't my fault. *He* hired you, not me. I was just trying to let you know—tactfully—that you were pulling a stunt that was bound to arc out as destructive. You had to realize that."

"Yeah, I knew it."

"Well, you *had* to know it! A campaign spokes-woman, having sex with a married Senator. How on earth could that work out?"

"Well, it wasn't exactly *sex*. . . ." Moira winced. "And he wasn't a Senator then, either! When I hooked up with Alcott, he was a long-shot candidate with five per cent approval. His staff people were a bunch of weird losers, and his manager was just a young start-up guy who'd never run a federal campaign. It was a hopeless cause. But I signed on with him anyway. I just really liked him, that's all. He charmed me into it. I just thought he was this naive, brilliant, charming guy. He has a good heart. He really does. He's much too good a person to be a goddamn Senator."

"So he was supposed to lose the race, is that it?"

"Yeah. He was supposed to lose, and then that bitch would have dumped him. And I guess I figured that, somehow, I would be there waiting." Moira shuddered. "Look, *I love him,* all right? I fell in love with him. I worked really hard for him. I gave him my all. I just never realized that it would play out like this."

"I'm very sorry," Oscar said. "It really *is* all my fault, after all. I never quite made it clear to you that I actually intended to put the guy into federal office."

Moira fell silent as they forded through the pedes-trian crowd on Commercial Avenue. The trees were stark and leafless, but the Christmas shoppers were hard at it, all hats and jackets and snow boots in a mess of glittering lights.

Finally she spoke again. "This is a side of you that

people don't get to see much, isn't it. Under that suit and the hairstyle, you're a mean, sarcastic bastard."

"Moira, I have always been entirely straight with you. Right up and down. I couldn't have been any straighter. You're the one who's leaving. You're not leaving him. You never had him. You're never going to get him. He doesn't belong to you. It's *me* that you're leaving. You're leaving my krewe. You're defecting."

"What are you, a country? Get over yourself! I'm not 'defecting.' " Moira stared at him, eyes blazing. "Let me go! Let me be a normal human being! This is like a sickness with you, this controlling thing. You need help."

"Stop trying to provoke me. You're being childish."

They turned the corner onto Marlborough Street. This was his home street, it was where he lived. Time to try a fresh angle. "Look, Moira, I'm truly sorry about your feelings for the Senator. Campaigns are very intense, they make people do crazy things sometimes. But the campaign's long behind us now, and you need to reassess your position. You and I, we've been good friends, we ran a great campaign together, and we shouldn't become enemies. Be reasonable."

"I'm *not reasonable*. I'm in love."

"Think about it. I know that you're out of my krewe, I accept that, but I can still make things easy for you. I offered to let you stay at my own house, rent-free. Wasn't that the act of a friend? If you're worried about a job, we can work out something with the local FedDems. You can take a party post during the off-season. When the next campaign comes around, hey, you were the spokesperson for Bambakias! You'll have a big rep next time, you'll have some clout. All you have to do is keep your skirt on."

"I really hate you for that."

"Look, you don't mean that."

"Yes, I *do*. You're *disgusting*. You've gone too far this time. I really hate you."

"I'm telling you this for your own good! Look, *she knows*. You want to make enemies, well, you've made a big one. The wronged woman is on to you."

"So what? I know that she knows."

"She's a Senator's wife now, and she's on to you. If you cross her again, she'll crush you like a bug!"

Moira barked with laughter. "What's she supposed to do? Shoot me?"

Oscar sighed. "She'll out you on the college lesbian thing."

Moira gaped in wounded astonishment. "What is this, the twentieth century? Nobody gives a damn about that!"

"She'll leak it. She'll leak it with major-league spin. Nobody leaks like Lorena. She'll kiss up to the Capitol press at some overclass cotillion, and they'll out you like a vampire in daylight."

"Oh yeah? Well, I'm a press liaison, and if she outs me, I'll out *you*. I'll out you and your genius creep girl-friend!" She jabbed at him with a red-nailed finger. "Ha! You can't threaten me, you manipulative scumbag. I don't even *care* what happens to me! But I can kick over *your* applecart, that's for sure. You're not even *human*! You don't even have a *birthday*! I'll leak you and that creep ugly scientist, and when I'm done, she'll day the rue she . . . oh hell . . . she'll rue the day she ever met you."

"This is pathetic," Oscar said. "You've really lost it!"

"I'm strong." Moira lifted her chin. "My love has made me strong."

"What the hell are you carrying on about, anyway? You haven't even been near the guy in six weeks."

Her eyes brimmed with triumphant tears. "We trade email!"

Oscar groaned. "So that's it. Well, we'll soon put a stop to *that*. You're completely irrational! I can't have you blackmailing me, just so that you can ruin the career of the

man that I put into office. It's unconscionable! To hell
with you! Do your worst."

"I'll do it! I *will*! I'll wipe you out."

Oscar stopped short on the sidewalk. She stamped
onward, then turned on her heel, her eyes wild.

"This is my house," Oscar pointed out.

"Oh."

"Look, why don't you come inside? Let's have a cup
of coffee. I know it hurts to have a bad love affair. You can
get over that. Just concentrate on something else."

"What do you think I am, a wax dummy?" She
shoved him. "You creep."

There was a loud banging noise from across the
street. Oscar ignored it. He had one last pitch here, and he
thought it would work. If he could get her inside the
house with him, she'd sit down and cry. If she cried, she'd
confess everything. She'd pass her crisis. She'd get over it.

Another loud bang. A big chip of brick flew from his
arched doorway. "Oh hell!" he complained. "Look at my
house!"

Another bang. "Ouch," Moira remarked. Her purse
had spun off her shoulder. She picked it up and looked at
it. A hole had been punched through it. She turned and
stared across the street. "He shot me!" she realized aloud.
"He shot me in the purse!"

A gray-haired old man with a metal walker was
standing across the street. He was firing at them with a
handgun. He was extremely visible now, because the local
streetlights, attracted by the highly illegal sound of firearms, had all swiveled on their metal necks and framed
him in a torrent of glare.

Two batlike police drones detached themselves from
a utility pole. They swooped at him like sonic cutouts of
black construction paper, and as they passed him, he fell.

Oscar opened his door. He jumped through, lunged
back out, caught Moira's wrist, and dragged her inside.
He slammed the door behind them.

"Are you hurt?" he asked her.

"He shot my purse!"

She was trembling violently. Oscar looked her over carefully. Tights, skirt, hat, jacket. No holes, no blood anywhere.

Moira's knees buckled suddenly and she slumped to the floor. The street beyond the door suddenly filled with the sound of sirens.

Oscar hung his hat with care and sat down companionably, hooking his elbows over his knees. It was great to be in his own house; it was cold and dusty, but it smelled like his house, it was comforting. "It's okay, it's over now," he said. "This is a very secure street. Those police drones have got him. Let me turn on my house system, and we'll have a look outside."

Moira had gone green.

"Moira, it's okay now. I'm sure they've caught him. Don't worry, I'll stay here with you."

No answer. She was utterly terrified. There was a little bubble of spit on her lower lip.

"I'm truly sorry about this," he said. "It's that netwar harassment again. See, it's just like it was at the Collaboratory. I should have known that one of those lunatics would be staking out my home address. If I'd had Fontenot with me, this would never have happened."

Moira toppled backward, hitting the wainscoting with a thump. Oscar reached out and tapped his solid front door with his knuckles. "Bulletproof," he explained. "We're perfectly safe now, it's fine. I need a new security director, that's all. I should have hired one right away. I misplaced my priorities. Sorry. . . ."

"They tried to *kill me*. . . ."

"No, Moira, not you. *Me*. Never you, okay? Just me."

"I feel sick!" she wailed. "I'm gonna faint!"

"I'll get you something. Brandy? Some antacid?"

There was a loud, repeated knock on the door.

Moira shrank back, losing a shoe. "Oh my God! Don't! Don't open it!"

Oscar flicked on his doorbug. A lozenge of exterior video flashed on, showing a flashing police bicycle and a female Boston police officer in badge, helmet, and blue woolen jacket. Oscar thumbed the intercom. "May I help you, Officer?"

The cop examined the glowing screen of her note-pad. "Is this Mr. Valparaiso?"

"Yes it is, Officer."

"Open your door, please. Police."

"May I see some ID, please?"

The officer complied with a holographic ID card. It identified her as Sergeant Mary Elizabeth O'Reilly.

Oscar opened the door, which bumped against Moira's kneecap. Moira flinched violently and scrambled to her feet, fists clenched.

"Please come in, Sergeant O'Reilly. Thank you for being so quick in your response."

"I was in the neighborhood," the policewoman said, stepping inside. She twisted her helmeted head, methodically scanning the entrance hall with video. "Are there injuries?"

"No."

"The system has tracked those projectiles. They seem to have been aimed at you. I took the liberty of backrunning the nearest recordings. You and this female were involved in a dispute."

"Actually, that's not the case. I'm a federal Senate employee, and this was an attempted political assassination." Oscar gestured at Moira. "Our so-called dispute was strictly a private matter."

"Would you show me some identification, please."

"Certainly." Oscar reached for his wallet.

"No, not you, Mr. Valparaiso. I mean this nonresident white female."

Moira pawed by reflex at her purse. "He shot my purse. . . ."

Oscar tried some gentle coaxing. "But your ID's still in there, isn't it? This is a legal request from a public safety officer. You do need to show her some ID."

Moira stared at him with red-rimmed eyes. "You're completely insane. You're *completely* insane!"

Oscar turned to the cop. "I can vouch for her, Officer. Her name's Moira Matarazzo, she's my guest."

"You can't *act like* this!" Moira screeched. She shoved him suddenly, pushing at his shoulder. "He tried to *kill* you!"

"Well, he missed."

Moira swung up her purse, two-handed, and walloped him. "Be scared, stupid! Be scared, like me! *Act normal!*"

"Don't do that," the cop commanded. "Stop hitting him."

"Are you made out of ice? You can't act like this! Nobody thinks that fast!" She whacked him with the purse again. Oscar ducked back, raising his arms to shield his face.

"Stop that," said the cop, in a level no-nonsense tone. "Stop hitting him."

"She's hysterical," Oscar gasped. He ducked another swing.

The cop pulled her spraygun and fired. There was a hiss of high-speed mist. Moira's eyelids flicked upward like electric shutters. She collapsed to the floor.

"She was really in a state," Oscar said, rubbing his elbow. "You have to allow her some leeway."

"Mr. Valparaiso, I understand that sentiment," Officer O'Reilly said. "But I'm on live helmetcam. She disobeyed two direct orders to stop battering you. That is not acceptable. City policy is very strict regarding domestic disputes. If we have to take action to break up a physical quarrel, the offending party is gonna spend the night in the cooler. You understand me, sir? That's city policy. No ifs, ands, or buts. She's under arrest."

"She'd just been shot at. She was very upset."

"I'm very aware of that fact, but you'll have to take that up with Special Weapons and Tactics. I'm with the bicycle patrol." She paused. "Don't worry, SWAT is on their way right now. They're very rapid-response when it comes to firearm incidents."

"Oh, that's all right," Oscar said. "Please don't think I was being ungrateful. It was very brave of you to charge headlong into a shootout. That's a very commendable action."

Officer O'Reilly smiled briefly. "Oh, the drones had the perp down as soon as the shots were triangulated. He's in custody already."

"Excellent work."

The officer gazed at him thoughtfully. "Are you really sure you're all right?"

"Why do you say that?" He paused. "Oh. Yes, of course. Yes, I'm very upset by all this. It's the fourth attempt on my life in the past three weeks. I need to make my situation clear to the local authorities—but I got into town just an hour ago. I lost track of time."

Moira stirred on the floor and moaned faintly.

"Would you like a hand loading her into the paddy wagon?"

"That's all right, Mr. Valparaiso. I think we can manage."

––––––––––––

The police downtown were very polite to him. Polite, but unyielding. Once Oscar had successfully repeated his story for the third time, he relaxed.

He had been in a little mental fugue state. Not for the first time, of course—they'd been happening to him since childhood. Nothing life-threatening, but it wasn't the kind of response that formed the human standard.

Oscar sometimes liked to imagine that he was brilliant under pressure, but that was a pretense. He wasn't brilliant. He was just extremely fast. He wasn't a genius. He just burned more brightly, his internal chip-cycle ran a little faster. Now, with the fugue fading, he felt shaky—even with a solemn police promise of extra surveillance and bike patrols.

His assailant—a victim of senile paranoia—had almost managed to shoot him. But Oscar couldn't seem to connect. The facts weren't registering. He was numbed.

He went upstairs to his third-floor office. He unlocked his desk and retrieved his super-special crisis notebook. Also, a vintage Waterman pen. At times like this it always helped him to make a list. Not on a screen. With his own hands. He placed the journal down on his Eero Saarinen desktop, and began to write.

Priority A. Become Bambakias chief of staff.

*B. Reform Collaboratory. Internal coup.
Purge. Remove entire old guard. Cut
budget drastically, reform finances. Note:
with luck a success here will obviate any
need for second committee assignment.*

*C. Huey. Is deal possible? Consider full range
of countermeasures.*

*D. Augment personal krewe. Stop desertions.
Note: Buna hotel must clear profit. Note:
engage new security director at once. Must
be trusted implicitly.*

*E. Return bus to FedDems, must pay for new
paint job.*

*F. Greta. More sex, less email. Note: Boston
Visit Imminent!!! Fly krewe members in for*

conference support, prepare total makeover.
Note: use ALL extra days, insist on this.
Note: prepare groundwork within Buna
while she is OUT of lab—feigned illness
gambit. PS I think I love her.

G. *Need house-sitter.*

H. *Return stupid animal to Buna, arrange*
   good cover story. Note: avoid corruption
   entanglements.

I. *I really must stay alive and not be shot thru*
   netwar harassment. Note: this issue needs
   much higher ranking.

J. *Who the hell sent that demolition mob to*
   the bank in Worcester? Note: rational game
   strategy not possible when pieces are invisible,
   intangible, or immaterial.

K. *Emergency committees must go. They were*
   basic source of Bambakias/Huguelet
   contretemps. American political situation
   basically impossible when constitutional
   authority flouted by irresponsible usurpers.
   Note: even chief of staff position is fatally
   subject to their caprice.

L. *Sen. Bambakias—hunger strike physical*
   state depression?

Oscar gazed at his list. He had already used up half
the alphabet, and he could feel the very air around him
swarming with the unforeseen. It was all just *too much*. It
was chaos, madness, a writhing nest of eels.

It was just too complex. It was utterly unmanageable.
Unless . . . unless somehow the process was automated.
With more specific goals. Some reengineering. Critical

path analysis. Decentralization. Co-optation. Thinking outside the box. But then there were so many *other people*. They all depended on him. He had to deputize. . . .

He was stymied. He was surrounded. He was through, finished, crushed. There was no possibility of coherent accomplishment. Nothing was ever going to move.

He had to do something. Just one thing. Get one single thing accomplished, put one issue finally away.

He picked up the desk phone. Lorena's secretary fielded the call. He fought his way through.

"I'm sorry, Oscar," Lorena told him, "I have Alcott on another line. Can I call you back?"

"This won't take long. It's important."

"Yes?"

"There's news. Moira is in jail, here in Boston. I tried to reason with her about the situation. She lost control, she got violent. There happened to be a policeman handy, luckily for me. The Boston cops have nailed Moira on a domestic battery charge."

"Good Lord, Oscar."

"I don't plan to press charges against her, but I don't want to tell her that. I want *you* to handle it now. It's time for you to take over. Moira's in the slammer, I'm playing the angry heavy, and you're her forgiving guardian angel. You see? You're going to smooth it all over for her, keep it all quiet. That's how we have to play it with her, because that's how it's going to work."

"Are you kidding? Let her rot!"

"No, I'm not kidding. I'm handing you a permanent solution here. Think about it."

A long and thoughtful silence. "Yes, you're right, of course. That *is* the best way to handle it."

"I'm glad that you see it my way."

"I'll have to grit my teeth a little, but it's worth it." A meditative pause. "You're really amazing."

"Just part of the job, ma'am."

"Is there anything else?"

"No. Wait. Yes. Tell me something. Does my voice sound all right to you?"

"For an encrypted line, this is a great connection."

"No, I mean, I'm not talking really fast? Not, like, a high-pitched squeal?"

Lorena lowered her voice to a croon. "No, Oscar, you sound great. You are completely wonderful. You are handsome and charming, you are completely dependable, you are Mr. Realpolitik. I trust you completely. You have never, ever failed me, and if I had owned that goddamn lab in Colombia I would have cloned a dozen of you. You are the best in the whole wide world."

6

Greta arrived after midnight, in an unmanned cab. Oscar checked his door monitor. A Greenhouse nor'easter had come in, and fat snowflakes swirled in the conical glow of alerted streetlights. A wandering police drone zipped behind Greta's head like a black leather swallow. Oscar unlocked his door, peering with a game and cheery grin from behind its bulletproof facing.

She stamped in with a face like a thundercloud. He rapidly abandoned the notion of embracing her. "You didn't have any trouble getting here, I hope?"

"In Boston? Heavens no." She yanked her hat off and knocked snow from its brim. "Boston's so civilized."

"There was a little trouble in the street earlier." Oscar paused delicately. "Nothing too serious. Tell me all about your conference."

"I've been out with Bellotti and Hawkins. They were trying to get me drunk." She was, Oscar realized belatedly, very drunk indeed. She was plastered. He relieved her of her coat like a nurse removing a bandage. Greta was dressed in her best: knee-length woolen skirt, sensible shoes, green cotton blouse.

He hung her hat and rumpled coat inside the entrance alcove. "Bellotti and Hawkins would be the gentlemen studying fibrils," he prompted.

Her scowl faded. "Well, it's a pretty good conference. It's just a bad night. Bellotti was buying us drinks, and Hawkins was shaking me down for lab results. I don't mind talking results before publication, but those guys don't play fair. They don't want to reveal their really hot stuff." Her lips thinned with contempt. "It might have commercial potential."

"I see."

"They're industry hustlers. They're all cagey, and edgy, and streetwise. They're hopeless."

He led her through the dayroom and snapped on the kitchen lights. In the sudden cozy glow, her face looked congealed and waxy. Smudgy lipstick. Loopy-looking crisp dark hair. The unplucked eyebrows were especially unfortunate.

She closely examined the pedestal chairs, the chromed table, the ceramic rangetop island, the built-in resonators. "This is some kind of kitchen you have here," she said wonderingly. "It's so . . . *clean*. You could do labwork in this kitchen."

"Thanks."

She settled with drunken caution into the white plastic shell of a Saarinen tulip chair.

"You have every right to complain," Oscar said. "You're surrounded by exploiters and morons."

"They're not morons, they're very bright guys. It's just . . . Well, I don't do industrial work. Science is not about the money. Basic science is all about . . . Basic research, you see, it's supposed to be for . . ." She waved one hand irritably. "What the hell was it?"

"For the public good?" Oscar suggested suavely.

"Yeah, that was it! The public good! I suppose that sounds totally naive to you. But I do know one thing— I'm not supposed to be stuffing my own bank account while the taxpayers pick up my tab."

Oscar dug through the glossy sliding shelves of a Kuramata cabinet. "Would a coffee help? I've got freeze-dried."

The scowl returned, settling into her eyebrows as if tattooed there. "You can't do real science and be a businessman on your weekends. If you're serious about it, there *aren't* any weekends."

"This is a weekend, Greta."

"Oh." She gazed at him with an alcohol-fueled mélange of surprise and regret. "Well, I can't stay with you for the whole weekend. There's a hot seminar tomorrow morning at nine. 'Cytoplasm Domains.' "

"Cytoplasm sounds very compelling."

"I'm here for tonight, anyway. Let's have a little drink together." She opened her purse. "Oh no. I forgot my gin. It's in my bag." She blinked. "Oh no, Oscar, I *forgot my overnight bag*! I left it back at the hotel. . . ."

"You also forgot I don't drink," Oscar said.

She cradled her forehead on the heels of her hands.

"It's fine," Oscar said. "Just forget about work for a minute. I have a krewe. We can supply anything you need."

She was having a bad moment at the kitchen table: doubt and bitterness. "Let me show you my house," Oscar told her cheerfully. "It'll be fun."

He led her into the dayroom. It had a Piet Heim elliptical coffee table, steel-and-birchwood cantilever chairs, an inflatable vinyl divan.

"You've got modern art," she said.

"That's my Kandinsky. *Composition VIII,* from 1923." He touched the frame, adjusting it by a hair's width. "I don't know why they still call this 'modern art' when it's a hundred and twenty years old."

She carefully studied the glowing canvas, glanced at Oscar meditatively, examined the painting again. "Why do they call this stuff 'art' at all? It's just a big mess of angles and blobs."

"I know it seems that way to you, but that's because you don't have any taste." Oscar restrained a sigh. "Kandinsky knew all the big period art krewes: Blaue

Reiter group, Surrealists, Suprematists, Futurists. . . . Kandinsky was *huge*."

"Did it cost you a lot of money?" Clearly she hoped not.

"No, I picked it up for peanuts when the Guggenheim threw a fire sale. All the art between 1914 and 1989 —you know, the Communist Period, the core of the twentieth century—that's all totally out of fashion nowadays. Kandinsky is the very opposite of 'modern art' now, but you know, I find him absolutely relevant. Wassily Kandinsky really speaks to me. You know . . . if Kandinsky were alive today . . . I really think he might have understood all this."

She shook her head woozily. " 'Modern art' . . . How could they get away with all that? It's like some huge, ugly scam." She sneezed suddenly. "Sorry. My allergies are acting up."

"Come with me."

He led her to his media center. He was particularly proud of this room. It was a modern political war room done in a period idiom. Chairs of pierced aluminum were stacked against the wall, there were modular storage units, swarms of flat displays. Danish shelving, a caster-trolley, bright plastic Kartell office baskets. Handsome Milanese lamps. . . . No frills, no furbelows, no wasted motion. Everything pruned back, all very efficient and sleek.

"This looks all right," she said. "I could work in a place like this."

"I'm glad to hear you say that. I hope you'll have that chance."

She smiled. "Why not? I like it here. This place is very you."

He was touched. "That's very sweet, but I should be honest about it. . . . It's not my interior design. I mean, that Kandinsky canvas was certainly my choice, but after I sold my start-up company, I bought this house, and I brought in a professional designer. . . . I was very focused about my house then. We worked on this place for months. Giovanna was very good about it, we used to absolutely haunt the antique markets. . . ."

" 'Giovanna,' " she said. "What a lovely name. She must have been very elegant."

"She was, but it didn't work out."

Greta gazed with sudden waspish attention at the tracklights and the gleaming tower of chairs. "And then there was that other person—the journalist. She must have loved this media room."

"Clare lived here! This was her home."

"She's gone to Holland now, right?"

"Yes, she's gone. That didn't work out, either."

"Why don't they work out for you, Oscar?"

"I don't know," he said. He jammed his hands in his pockets. "That's an excellent question, isn't it?"

"Well," she said, "maybe it's an excellent question, but maybe I shouldn't have asked it."

"No, Greta, I like it when you show up drunk and confrontational."

He crossed his arms. "Let me get you fully up to speed here, all right? You see, I'm the product of unusual circumstances. I grew up in a very special milieu. Logan Valparaiso's dream home. A classic Hollywood mansion. Tennis courts. Palm trees. Monogrammed everything, zebra skins, and gold fixtures. A big playground for Logan's friends, all these maquiladora millionaires and South American dope czars. My dad had the worst taste in the world. I wanted this place to be different."

"What's different about it?"

"Nothing," he said bitterly. "I wanted my home to be genuine. But this place has never been real. Because I have no family. No one has ever lived in here who cared enough about me to stay. In fact, I'm rarely even here myself. I'm always out on the road. So this place is a fraud. It's an empty shell. I've tried my very best, but it's all been an evil fantasy, it's completely failed me." He shrugged. "So, welcome home."

She looked stricken. "Look, I didn't say any of that."

"Well, that's what you were thinking."

She shook her head. "You don't know what I'm thinking."

"I agree that I can't outthink you. Not from a dead start. But I do know how you feel."

"You don't know that, either."

"Oh yes I do. Of course I do. I know it by the way you talk. By the way you move your hands. I can see it in the way you look." He smiled. "Because I'm a politician."

She put her hand over her own mouth.

Then, without warning, she embraced him and printed a damp kiss on his upper lip. He slid his arms around her lean torso. She felt magnetic, hypnotic, absolutely compelling.

She bent backward in his tightening grip and laughed.

He pulled her toward the inflated couch. They fell together on it with a bounce and squeak. He buried his face in the sweet juncture of her neck and shoulder.

She slid her narrow hand through the open collar of his shirt. He nuzzled her jawline. Those wondrous cavities beneath her earlobes. The authentic idiosyncrasy in the tendons of her neck.

Their lips parted stickily. She pulled back half an inch. "I like feeling jealous," she said. "That's new for me."

"I could explain all that, you know."

"Stop explaining. I'd bet anything Clare's dresses are still in your bedroom closet." She laughed. "Show me, I want to see."

Once upstairs, she spun in place, swinging her purse, tottering just a little. "Now, *this* room is *amazing*. Your *closets* are bigger than my dorm room."

He set to work on his shoes. He stripped off his

socks. One, two. He started on his cuff links. Why did it always take forever to strip? Why couldn't clothes simply vanish, so people could get on with it? Clothes always vanished in movies.

"Are these walls really white suede? You have *leather* wallpaper?"

He glanced over. "You need some help undressing?"

"That's all right. You don't have to rip my clothes off more than once."

Six endless minutes later he lay gasping in a nest of sheets. She sidled off to the bathroom, her hairdo smashed and her collarbones flushed. He heard her turning on the bidet, then every faucet in the room—the shower, the tub, the white sink, the black sink. Greta was experimenting, running all the local equipment. He lay there breathing deeply and felt weirdly gratified, like a small yet brilliant child who had snatched candy from under a door with a yardstick.

She came padding from the shower, black hair lank and dripping, her eyes as bright as a weasel's. She crept into bed and embraced him, clammy, and frozen-footed, and reeking of upscale shampoo. She held him and said nothing. He fell asleep as if tumbling into a pit.

He woke later, head buzzing and muddled. Greta was standing before an open closet door, examining herself in its inset full-length mirror. She was wearing panties, and a pair of his socks, which she had jammed, inside out, onto her narrow, chilly feet.

She held a dress before herself and studied the effect. Oscar suddenly recognized the dress. He had bought Clare that sundress because she looked so lovely in yellow. Clare had hated the dress, he now realized groggily. She'd always hated the dress. Clare even hated yellow.

"What was all that noise just now?" he croaked.

"Some idiot banging the door downstairs," Greta said. She dropped the dress on the floor, in a pile of half a dozen others. "The cops arrested him." She picked out a beaded evening gown. "Go back to sleep."

Oscar turned in place, scrunched the pillow, grabbed for slumber, and missed. He gathered awareness and watched her through slitted eyes. It was half past four in the morning.

"Aren't you sleepy?" he said.

She caught his eye in the mirror, surprised to see him still awake. She turned out the closet light, crossed the room silently, in darkness, and slid into bed.

"What have you been doing all this time?" he murmured.

"I've been exploring your house."

"Any big discoveries?"

"Yes, I discovered what it means to be a rich guy's girlfriend." She sighed. "No wonder people want the job."

He laughed. "What about *my* situation? I'm the boy-toy of a Nobel Prize winner."

"I was watching you sleep," she said wistfully. "You look so sweet."

"Why do you say that?"

"You don't have an agenda while you're sleeping."

"Well, I have an agenda now." He slid his hand over her bony hip and obtained a firm, intimate grip. "I'm a hundred percent agenda. I'm going to change your life. I'm going to transform you. I'm going to empower you."

She stirred against the sheets. "How is that weird little miracle supposed to happen?"

"Tomorrow I'm taking you to meet my dear friend, Senator Bambakias."

Yosh Pelicanos, Oscar's majordomo, had a grocery delivery shipped to the house at eight AM. Yosh was not a man to be deterred by the mere fact that he was hundreds of miles from the scene. He had a keyboard and a list of

Oscar's requirements, so the electric hand of the net economy had dropped four boxes of expensive shrink-wraps at
Oscar's doorstep.

Oscar set up the new air filter in the breakfast nook.
This finessed Greta's allergy problem. Allergies were very
common among Collaboratory workers; the laundered air
was so pure that it failed to properly challenge people's
immune systems, which hence became hyperreactive.

Then Oscar tied an apron over his lounge pajamas
and put the kitchen to work. Results were gratifying. Oscar and Greta tore through lox, and bagels, and waffles,
with lashings of juice and coffee. When the ravenous edge
was blunted, they toyed with triangled rye toast and lump-
fish caviar.

Oscar gazed affectionately across the table's massive
flowered centerpiece. Things were going so well. He believed in breakfasts. Morning-after breakfasts were far
more intimate and emotionally engaging than any number
of romantic dinners. He'd been through a horrid gamut of
breakfasts: breakfasts that were hungover, shame-ridden,
full of unspoken dread or politeness stretched tighter than
a banjo string, but breakfast with Greta was a signal success. Steamed clean in a white terry bathrobe and socketed
in her Saarinen chair, she was a mutant swan in freshwater.

She smoothed a black mass of caviar across her toast
and licked a stray dab from her fingertip. "I'm gonna miss
that cytoplasm panel."

"Don't worry. I've bought you the full set of conference tapes. They'll ship in the morning set at lunch. You
can speed through all the boring parts in the media
room."

"No one goes to conferences to watch the tapes. All
the action's in the halls and the poster sessions. I need to
go back there. I need to confer with my colleagues."

"No, Greta, that's not what you need today. You
have a higher priority. You need to go to Cambridge with
me, and confer with a United States Senator. Donna is

arriving any minute; she's been shopping, and she's going to do you over."

"Who is Donna?"

"Donna Nunez is one of my krewe. She's an image consultant."

"I thought you left your krewe in Texas at the lab."

"No, I brought Donna with me. Besides, I'm in constant touch with my krewe. They haven't been abandoned, they're very busy back there—laying some groundwork. As for Donna, she's been devoting a lot of thought to this project. You'll be in very good hands."

Greta put down her toast with a resolute look. "Well, I don't do that sort of thing. I don't have time for an image."

"Rita Levi-Montalcini did."

Her eyes narrowed. "What do you know about her?"

"You once told me that this woman was very important to you. So, I put my oppo-research people on her. Now I'm an expert on your role model, Dr. Rita. Rita was a Nobelist, and a neuroscientist, and she was a major player in her country's research effort. But Dr. Rita understood how to handle her role. She dressed every day like a Milanese jewel."

"You don't do science by dressing up."

"No, you *run* science by dressing up."

"But I don't want to! I don't want to run a damned thing! I just want to work in my lab! Why can't you get that through your head? Why won't anyone let me do my work anymore? If you'd just let me do the things I'm really good at, I wouldn't have to go through any of this!"

Oscar smiled. "I bet that felt marvelous. Can we talk like adults now?"

She snorted.

"Don't think that I'm being frivolous. *You* are being frivolous. You are a national celebrity. You're not some ragged grad student who can hide out in your nice giant test tube. Rita Levi-Montalcini wore tailored lab coats, and did her hair, and had real shoes. And so will you. Relax and eat your caviar."

The door emitted a ring. Oscar patted his lips with a napkin, belted his dressing gown, stepped into his slippers.

Donna had arrived, with heaps of luggage and a set of suit bags. She had brought two winter-clad Boston high-maintenance girls in a second taxi. The three women were having an animated chat with a young Anglo man. Oscar recognized the man—he didn't know his name, but he knew the face, the cane, and the support shoes. This stranger was a local guy, a neighborhood regular.

Oscar unsealed his door. "How good of you to come. Welcome. You can take your equipment up to the prep room. We'll be sending your client in presently."

Donna ushered her charges upstairs, chatting briskly in Spanglish. Oscar found himself confronting the man with the cane. "May I help you, sir?"

"Yeah. My name's Kevin Hamilton. I manage the apartment block up the street."

"Yes, Mr. Hamilton?"

"I wonder if we could have a word together, about all these guys who've been showing up trying to kill you."

"I see. Do come in." Oscar shut the door carefully behind his new guest. "Let's talk this over in my office." He paused, noting Hamilton's cane and the clumsy orthopedic shoes. "Never mind, we can talk downstairs."

He led the limping Hamilton into the dayroom. Greta appeared suddenly, barefoot and in her bathrobe.

"All right, where do you want me?" she said resignedly.

Oscar pointed. "Upstairs, first door on your left."

Hamilton offered a gallant little salute with his cane.

"Hello," Greta told him, and trudged up the stairs.

Oscar led Hamilton into the media room and un-stacked an aluminum chair for him. Hamilton sat down with obvious relief.

"Good-looking babe," he remarked.

Oscar ignored him and sat in a second chair.

"I wouldn't have disturbed you this morning," Hamilton said, "but we don't see a lot of assassinations in this neighborhood, generally."

"No."

"Yesterday, I myself got some mail urging me to kill you."

"Really! You don't say."

Hamilton scratched at his sandy hair, which had a jutting cowlick and a part like a lightning bolt. "You know, you and I have never met before, but I used to see you around here pretty often, in and out at all hours, with various girlfriends. So when this junkbot email told me you were a child pornographer, I had to figure that was totally detached from reality."

"I think I can follow your reasoning," Oscar said. "Please go on."

"Well, I ran some backroute tracing, found the relay server in Finland, cracked that, traced it back to Turkey. . . . I was downloading the Turkish activity logs when I heard some gunfire in the street. Naturally, I checked out the local street monitors, analyzed all the movement tags on the neighborhood CCTV. . . . That was pretty late last night. But by then, I was really ticked off. So I pulled an all-nighter at the keyboard." Hamilton sighed. "And, well, I took care of it for you."

Oscar stared in astonishment. "You 'took care of it'?"

"Well, I couldn't locate the program itself, but I found its pushfeeds. It gets all its news off a service in Louisiana. So, I spoofed it. I informed the thing that I'd killed you. Then I forged a separate news release announcing your death, and I faked the headers and fed it in. It sent me a nice thank-you note. That should take care of your problem. That thing is as dumb as a brick."

Oscar mulled this over, thoughtfully. "Could I get you a little something, Kevin? Juice? An espresso, maybe?"

"Actually, I'm kind of bushed. I'm thinking I'll turn in now. I just thought I'd walk down the street and give you the news first."

"Well, that's very good news you've given me. It's excellent news. You've done me quite a favor here."

"Aw, think nothing of it," Kevin demurred. "Any good neighbor would have done the same thing. If he had any serious programming skills, that is. Which nobody much does, nowadays."

"Forgive me for asking, but how did *you* come by these programming skills?"

Hamilton nudged his chin with the handle of his cane. "Learned them from my dad, to tell the truth. Dad was a big-time coder on Route 128 before the Chinese smashed the info economy."

"Are you a professional programmer, Kevin?"

"Are you kidding? There *aren't* any professional programmers. These losers who call themselves sysadmins nowadays, they're not programmers at all! They just download point-and-click canned stuff off some pirate site, and shove it into the box."

Oscar nodded encouragement.

Hamilton waved his cane. "The art of computing hasn't advanced in ten years! It can't move anymore, 'cause there's no commercial potential left to push it. The Euros have settled all the net protocols nice and neat, and the Chinese always pirate anything you publish. . . . So the only guys who write serious code nowadays are ditzy computer scientists. And nomads—they've always got time on their hands. And, you know, various white-guy hacker crooks." Hamilton yawned. "But I have a lot of trouble with my feet, see. So coding helps me pass the time. Once you understand how to code, it's really kind of interesting work."

"Are you sure there's nothing I can do for you? I feel very much in your debt."

"Well, yeah, there is one thing. I'm chairman of the local neighborhood watch, so they're probably gonna bother me a lot about this shooting incident. It would be good if you could come over later and help me reassure my tenants."

"I'd be delighted to help you."

"Good deal, then." Hamilton stood up with a stoical wince.

"Let me see you out, sir."

After Hamilton's shuffling departure, Oscar swiftly transferred the contents of his laptop into the house system and set to immediate work. He sent notes to Audrey Avizienis and Bob Argow in Texas, urging them to run immediate oppo scans on his neighbor. It was not that he distrusted Kevin Hamilton—Oscar prided himself on his open-minded attitude toward Anglos—but news so wonderful seemed very hard put to be true.

At 11:15, Oscar and Greta took a cab to Bambakias's office in Cambridge. "You know something?" she told him. "This suit isn't as stiff as it looks. It's really very cozy."

"Donna's a true professional."

"And it fits me perfectly. How could it fit so well?"

"Oh, any smart surveillance scanner can derive body measurements. That was a military-intelligence app at first —it just took a while to work its way up to haute couture."

They sped across the Longfellow Bridge, over the Charles River basin. Yesterday's snow was already half gone to slush on the slopes of the Greenhouse dikes. Greta gazed out the taxi window at the distant pilings of the Science Park. Donna's hired girls had done the eyebrows. Sleek, arched eyebrows gave Greta's narrow face a cast of terrifying intellectual potency. The hair had real shape to it now, and some not-to-be-trifled-with gloss. Greta radiated expertise. She really looked like she counted.

"Things are so different here in Boston," she said. "Why?"

"Politics," he said. "The ultra-rich run Boston. And Boston's rich people *mean well*—that's the difference. They have civic pride. They're patricians."

"Do you want the whole country to be like this? Clean streets and total surveillance?"

"I just want my country to function. I want a system that works. That's all."

"Even if it's very elitist and shrink-wrapped?"

"You're not the one to criticize there. You live in the ultimate gated community. It's even airtight."

The office of Alcott Bambakias was in a five-story building near Inman Square. The place had once been a candy factory, then a Portuguese social club; nowadays it belonged to Bambakias's international design and construction firm.

They left the cab and entered the building. Oscar hung his hat and overcoat on a Duchampian bottle-rack tree. They waited for clearance in the first-floor reception area, which boasted six scale models of elegant Chinese skyscrapers. The Chinese were the last nation still fully alive to the rampant possibilities of skyscrapers, and Bambakias was one of the very few American architects who could design skyscrapers in a Chinese idiom. Bambakias had done extremely well for himself in the Chinese market. His reputation in Europe was similarly stellar, long preceding his rather grudging fame at home in America. He'd done swooping Italian sports arenas, stolid German dike complexes, a paranoid Swiss eco-survivalist compound. . . . He had even done a few Dutch commissions, before the Cold War had made that impossible.

Leon Sosik arrived to escort them. Sosik was a portly man in his sixties with prizefighter's shoulders, red suspenders, a silk tie. Sosik rarely wore a hat, since he proudly sported a fine head of hair—successfully treated male pattern baldness. He looked Oscar up and down. "How are tricks, Oscar?"

"Tricks are lovely. May I introduce Dr. Greta Penninger. Dr. Penninger, this is Leon Sosik, the Senator's chief of staff."

"We've heard so much about you, Doctor," said Sosik, gently gripping Greta's newly manicured fingertips. "I wish we were meeting under better circumstances."

"How is the Senator?" Oscar said.

"Al has been better," Sosik said. "Al is taking this hard. Al is taking this *very* hard."

"Well, he's eating, isn't he?"

"Not so you'd notice."

Oscar was alarmed. "Look, you *announced* he was eating. The hunger strike is *over* now. The guy should be wolfing raw horsemeat. Why the hell isn't he eating?"

"He says his stomach aches. He says . . . well, he says a lot of things. I gotta warn you, you can't take everything Al says as gospel right now." Sosik sighed heavily. "Maybe *you* can talk some sense into him. His wife says you're great at that." Sosik reached absently into his trouser pocket. "Dr. Penninger, do you mind if I debug you? Normally we'd have our new security guy doing this, but he's still in Washington."

"That's quite all right," Greta said.

Sosik swept the air around her body like a weary bishop sprinkling holy water. His device registered nothing in particular.

"Debug me too," Oscar said. "I insist."

"It's a hell of a thing," Sosik said, pursuing the ritual. "We've had Al bugged top to bottom for weeks. His nervous system's bugged, his bloodstream's bugged, his stomach is bugged, his colon is bugged. He did public MRI scans, he did PET-scans, he drank tagged apple juice—the inside of his carcass was a goddamn public circus. And when we finally got him off all the monitors, that's when he goes haywire."

"The hunger strike got great coverage, Leon. I'm giving you that."

Sosik put the scanner away. "Sure, but what is it with that crazy scumbag in Louisiana? How the hell did *that* ever get on the agenda? Al is an architect! We could have stuck with public-works issues, and done just fine."

"You let him talk you into the idea," Oscar said.

"I knew it was a goofy idea! It's just . . . Well, for Al it made sense. Al's the kind of guy who can get away with that kind of thing."

Sosik led them up a glass-and-plastic elevator. Bambakias had caused the former fifth floor to cease to exist, leaving a cavernous contemporary hangar with exposed water pipes, airducts, and elevator cabling, all tastefully done-over in tangerine, turquoise, peach, and Prussian blue.

Thirty-five people lived within the offices, Bambakias's professional krewe. It was both a communal residence and a design center. Sosik led them past ergonomic office chairs, platelike kevlar display tables, and twitching heaps of cybernetic Archiblocks. It was cold outside, so squishy little rivulets of tame steam warmed the bubbled membranes underfoot.

A corner office had been outfitted as a combination media room and medical center. The health monitors were inert now, and lined against a wall, but the screens were alive and silent, flicking methodically over their feeds.

The Senator was lying naked and facedown on a massage table, with a towel across his rump. A krewe masseur was working at his neck and shoulders.

Oscar was shocked. He'd known that the near-total hunger strike had cost Bambakias a lot of weight, but he hadn't realized what that meant to human flesh.

Bambakias seemed to have aged ten years. He was wearing his skin like a jumpsuit.

"Good to see you, Oscar," Bambakias said.

"May I introduce Dr. Penninger," Oscar said.

"Not another doctor," the Senator groaned.

"Dr. Penninger is a federal science researcher."

"Oh, of course." Bambakias sat up in bed, vaguely adjusting his towel. His hand was like a damp clump of sticks. "That's enough, Jackson. . . . Bring my friends a couple of . . . what have we got? Bring 'em some apple juice."

"We could use a good lunch," Oscar said. "I've promised Dr. Penninger some of your Boston chowder."

Bambakias blinked, his eyes sunken and rimmed with discolor. "My chef's a little out of practice lately."

"Out of practice on the *special chowder*?" Oscar chided. "How can that be? Is he dead?"

Bambakias sighed. "Jackson, see to it that my fat campaign manager gets some goddamn chowder." Bambakias glanced down at his shrunken hands, studied their trembling with deep disinterest. "What were we talking about?"

"Dr. Penninger and I are here to discuss science policy."

"Of course. Then I'll get dressed." Bambakias tottered to his bony feet and fled the room, exiting through a sliding shoji screen. They heard him call out feebly for his image consultant.

A fluted curtain shriveled upward like an eyelid, revealing a lucid gush of winter sunlight through the glass blocks. The corner office was a minor miracle of air and light; even half-empty, the space somehow felt complete and full.

A small furry robot entered the office with a pair of plastic packets in its tubular arms. It placed the packets neatly on the carpet, and left.

The abandoned packages writhed and heaved, with a

muted internal symphony of scrunches and springs. Geodesic sticks and cabling flashed like vector graphics beneath the translucent upholstery. The packets suddenly became a pair of armchairs.

Greta opened her new, executive-style purse and touched a tissue to her nose. "You know, the air is very nice in here."

Bambakias returned in gray silk trousers and undershirt, shadowed by a silent young woman, her arms laden with shoes, shirt, and suspenders. "Where's my hat?" he demanded querulously. "Where's my cape?"

"These are very interesting chairs," Greta told him. "Tell me about these chairs."

"Oh, these chairs of mine never caught on," Bambakias said, jamming one scrawny arm through the ruffled sleeve of his dress shirt. "For some reason, people just don't trust computation enough to sit on it."

"I trust computation," Greta assured him, and sat. The internal spokes and cables adjusted beneath her weight, with a rapid crescendo of tiny guitar-string shrieks She settled daintily in midair, a queen on a tensile throne of smart chopsticks and spiderweb. Oscar admired responsive tensegrity structures as much as the next man, but he sat in the second chair with considerably less brio.

"An architect gets the credit for design successes," Bambakias told her. "The failures you can cover with ivy. But weird decor schemes that just don't work out—well, those you have to keep inside the office."

A silent group of krewepeople removed the massage table and replaced it with a folding hospital bed. The Senator sat on the bed's edge, pulling up his gaunt bare feet like a giant seabird.

"I noticed another set of these armchairs on the way in," Greta said. "But they were solid."

"Not 'solid.' Rigid. Spray-on veneer."

" 'Less is more,' " Greta said.

A spark of interest lit the Senator's sagging face as his

dresser saw to his shoes and socks. "What did you say your name was?"

"Greta," she told him gently.

"And you're, what, you're a psychiatrist?"

"That's close. I'm a neuroscientist."

"That's right. You already told me that, didn't you."

Greta turned and gave Oscar a look full of grave comprehension and pity. Since her makeover, Greta's expressions had a new and shocking clarity—her flickering glance struck Oscar to the heart and lodged like a harpoon.

Oscar leaned forward on his thrumming piano-wire seat, and knotted his hands. "Alcott, Lorena tells me you're a little upset by developments."

" 'Upset'?" Bambakias said, lifting his chin as the dresser tucked in his ascot. "I wouldn't say 'upset.' I would say 'realistic.' "

"Well . . . realism is a matter of opinion."

"I've triggered a state and federal crisis. Four hundred and twelve million dollars' worth of military hardware has been looted by anarchist bandits and has vanished into the swamps. It's the worst event of its kind since Fort Sumter in 1861; what's there to be upset about?"

"But, Al, that was never your intention. You can't be blamed for those developments."

"But I was *there*," Bambakias insisted. "I was *with* those people. Yeah . . . I talked to all of them, I gave them my word of honor. . . . I have the tapes to prove it! Let's run through all the evidence just one more time. We should see this together. Where's my sysadmin? Where's Edgar?"

"Edgar's in Washington," the dresser told him quietly.

The Senator's hollow face tightened drastically. "Do I have to do everything myself?"

"I followed the siege situation," Oscar said. "I'm very up to speed on developments."

"But I was *there*!" Bambakias insisted. "I could have helped. I could have built barricades. I could have brought in generators. . . . But when that gas hit them, they lost their minds. That's when it all really hit me. This wasn't a game at all. It was no game. We weren't players. We'd all gone mad."

There was an evil silence.

"He spent a lot of time on the net with those Air Force people," the dresser told them meekly. "He really was almost there with them. Practically." Suddenly her eyes brimmed with tears. "I'll find his hat," she said, and left with her head hung low.

A lunch trolley arrived, set for two. The chowder was served.

Oscar moved his featherweight responsive chair and flicked a linen napkin ostentatiously. "This is not a defeat, Al. It's just a skirmish. There's still plenty of space on the old go board. A Senate term lasts six years."

"A lot of good that does *them*. They're in camps now! Can you believe that our government is that cynical? They've left our soldiers in the hands of the man who gassed them!" Bambakias waved a hand at the flickering screen behind him. "I've been watching him spin this. Huey. As if he'd *rescued* them. The son of a bitch is their public savior!"

"Well, it was a very ugly incident, but at least there were no fatalities. We can put that behind us now. Tomorrow's another day." Oscar lifted his gleaming soup spoon and creamed off a layer of chowder. He sipped it pretentiously. It was, as always, superb.

"Hold on," he told Greta, who had made no move to eat. "This isn't right." He sat up. "What's with your chef, Alcott? *Canned* chowder?"

Bambakias scowled. "What?"

"This is not your special chowder."

"Of course it is. Has to be."

"Try it," Oscar insisted.

Greta nodded permission, unneeded since the Senator had lunged from his bed and grabbed at her spoon. He sampled the bowl.

"Kind of a coppery undertaste," Oscar alleged, squinting.

Bambakias had two more spoonfuls. "Nonsense," he growled. "It's delicious."

The two of them ate rapidly, in rabid silence. "I'll find another chair," Greta murmured. She rose and left the room.

Bambakias settled into Greta's vacated chair and crunched half a handful of oyster crackers. His dresser arrived again, and set the Senator's hat and cape nearby. Bambakias ignored her, bending over his bowl with a painful effort. His hands were badly palsied; he could barely grip his spoon.

"I could sure do with a milk shake right now," Oscar mused. "You know, like we used to have on the campaign."

"Good idea," Bambakias said absently. He lifted his chin, gestured with two fingertips, and spoke into apparently empty air. "Vince, two campaign power milk shakes."

"Did Sosik show you the latest polls, Al? You've done a lot better by this episode than you seem to think."

"No, that's where you are both *totally wrong*. I've ruined everything. I provoked a major crisis before I was even sworn into office. And now that I'm a stinking criminal just like the rest of them, I'll have no choice—from now on I'll have to play the game just the way they like it. And the Senate is a sucker's game."

"Why do you say that?" Oscar said.

Bambakias swallowed painfully and raised one bony finger. "There are sixteen political parties in this country. You can't govern with a political culture that fragmented. And the parties are just the graphic interface for the real chaos underneath. Our education system has collapsed.

Our health system is so bad that we have organ-sharing cliques. We're in a State of Emergency."

"You're not telling me anything new here," Oscar chided. He leaned over and stared enviously into Bambakias's chowder. "Are you going to finish that?"

Bambakias hunched over his bowl with a wolfish glare.

"Okay, no problem." Oscar raised his voice to address the hidden microphones. "Vincent, hurry up with those shakes! Bring us more chowder. Bring dinner rolls."

"I don't want any damn dinner rolls," Bambakias muttered. His eyes were watering and his face was flushed. "Our wealth disparities are insane," he mumbled into his soup. "We have a closed currency and a shattered economy. We have major weather disasters. Toxic pollution. Plunging birth rates. Soaring death rates. It's bad. It's really bad. It's totally hopeless, it's all over."

"Vincent, bring us something serious. Quick. Bring us teriyaki. Bring us some dim sum."

"What are you rambling on about?" Bambakias said.

"Alcott, you're embarrassing me. I promised Dr. Penninger some good food here, and you've gone and eaten her lunch!"

Bambakias stared at the dregs of chowder. "Oh my God . . ."

"Alcott, let me handle this. The least you can do is sit here with us and see that your guest is properly fed."

"God, I'm sorry!" Bambakias moaned. "God, I've been so wrong about everything. You handle it, Oscar! You handle it."

Two milk shakes arrived in fluted glasses, their bases caked with frost. The chef himself brought them in, on a cork-lined salver. He gazed at Oscar with a look of dazed gratitude and backed hastily out of the office.

Bambakias's lean Adam's apple glugged methodically. "Let me tell you something really awful," he said, wiping his mouth on his shirtsleeve. "This whole business has been a tragic error from day one. The Emergency committee never *meant* to drop that air base. Their management and budget software was buggy. Nobody ever double-checked, because everything the stupid bastards do is an official emergency! So when the screwup became obvious, everybody just assumed it had been done deliberately—because it was such a clever, sneaky way to screw with Huey. They're dying to screw him, because Huey's the only politician in America who knows what he wants and can stick with it. But when I went looking for the silent genius who was running this brilliant conspiracy, there was nobody there."

"They gave you that line of guff? I hope you didn't believe that," Oscar said, silently switching Bambakias's empty glass for his own. "These Emergency creeps are geniuses at sleight of hand."

"Yeah? Then tell me who has been trying to get you shot!" Bambakias belched. "Same issue, same controversy —you could have been *killed* because of this! But whose fault is it? Nobody's fault. You hunt for the man responsible, and it's some nasty piece of software half a light-year out of the chain of command."

"That's not political thinking, Alcott."

"Politics don't work anymore! We can't make politics work, because the system's so complex that its behavior is basically random. Nobody trusts the system anymore, so nobody ever, ever plays it straight. There are sixteen parties, and a hundred bright ideas, and a million ticking bleeping gizmos, but nobody can follow through, execute, and deliver the goods on time and within specs. So our politics has become absurd. The country's reduced to chaos. We've given up on the Republic. We've abandoned democracy. I'm not a Senator! I'm a robber baron, a feudal lord. All I can do is build a personality cult."

Five of Bambakias's krewepeople arrived in force. They were thrilled to see the man eating. The room became an instant bedlam of kevlar picnic tables, flying silverware, packs of appetizers and aperitifs.

"I *know* that it's chaos," Oscar insisted, raising his voice above the racket. "Everybody knows that the system is out of control. That's a truism. The only answer to chaos is political organization."

"No, it's too late for that. We're so intelligent now that we're too smart to survive. We're so well informed that we've lost all sense of meaning. We know the price of everything, but we've lost all sense of value. We have everyone under surveillance, but we've lost all sense of shame." The sudden wave of nourishment was hitting Bambakias hard. His face was beet-red and he was having trouble breathing. And he had apparently stopped thinking, for he was quoting his campaign stump speech by rote.

Greta reappeared at the doorway, dodging the hospital bed as two krewemen wheeled it out. She entered and sat demurely in a newly structured chair.

"So you might as well just grab whatever you can," Bambakias concluded.

"Thank you, Senator," Greta said, deftly seizing a skewer of teriyaki chicken. "I enjoy these little office brunches."

"See, it all moves too fast and in too complex a fashion for any human brain to keep up."

"I suppose that's why we can sit on it!" Greta said.

"What?" Oscar said.

"This furniture thinks much faster than a human brain. That's why this fragile net of sticks and ribbons can become a functional chair." She examined their stunned expressions. "Aren't we still discussing furniture design? I'm sorry."

"Don't apologize, Doctor," Bambakias told her. "That's my worst regret. I should have stayed in architecture, where I was needed. I was getting things accomplished there, you see? A truly modern sense of structure

. . . that could have been my monument. I might have done wonderful things. . . . Doctor, that old glass dome of yours in Texas, it's twenty years behind the times. Nowadays we could create a dome ten times that size out of straw and pocket money! We could make your sad little museum really live and bloom—we could make that experiment into everyday reality. We could integrate the natural world right into the substance of our cities. If we knew how to use our power properly, we could guide herds of American bison right through our own streets. We could live in an Eden at peace with packs of wolves. All it would take is enough sense and vision to know who we are, and what we want."

"That sounds wonderful, Senator. Why don't you do it?"

"Because we're a pack of thieves! We went straight from wilderness to decadence, without ever creating an authentic American civilization. Now we're beaten, and now we sulk. The Chinese kicked our ass in economic warfare. The Europeans have sensible, workable policies about population and the weather crisis. But we're a nation of dilettantes who live on cheap hacks of a dead system. We're all on the take! We're all self-seeking crooks!"

Oscar spoke up. "You're not a criminal, Alcott. Look at the polls. The people are with you. You've won them over now. They trust your intentions, they sympathize."

Bambakias slumped violently into his chair, which thrummed alertly. "Then tell me something," he growled. "What about Moira?"

"Why is that subject on the agenda?" Oscar said.

"Moira's in jail, Oscar. Tell me about that. Do you want to tell us all about that?"

Oscar chewed with polite deliberation on a dinner roll. The room had gone lethally silent. Against the glass block a mobile mosaic had established itself, gently altering the daylight. A maze of dainty lozenges, creeping like adhesive dominoes, flapping neatly across the glass.

Oscar pointed to a netfeed. "Could we have a look at that coverage, please? Turn the sound up."

One of Bambakias's krewe spoke up. "It's in French."

"Dr. Penninger speaks French. Help me with this coverage, Doctor."

Greta turned to the screen. "It's defection coverage," she translated. "Something about a French aircraft carrier."

Bambakias groaned.

"There's been a statement from the French foreign office," Greta said tentatively, "something about American military officers . . . Electronic warfare jets . . . Two American Air Force pilots have flown jets to a French aircraft carrier, offshore in the Gulf of Mexico. They're asking for political asylum."

"I knew it!" Oscar announced, throwing his napkin on the table. "I knew Huey had people on the inside. See, now the other shoe drops. This is big, this is a major twist."

"Oh, that's bad," Bambakias groaned. He was ashen. "This is the final indignity. The final disgrace. This is the very end." He swallowed noisily. "I'm going to be sick."

"Help the Senator," Oscar commanded, jumping to his feet. "And get Sosik in here, right away."

Bambakias vanished in a cluster of panicked retainers. The room emptied as suddenly as a Tokyo subway car. Oscar and Greta found themselves suddenly alone.

Oscar watched the screen. One of the American defectors had just appeared on-camera. The man looked very familiar, utterly cynical, and extremely drunk. Oscar recognized him as an acquaintance: he was the public relations officer for the Louisiana air base. He was wearily delivering a prepared statement, with French subtitles. "What a genius move! Huey's dumped his Trojan horse people into the hands of French spooks. The French will hide those rogue airboys in some bank vault in Paris. We'll never hear from them again. They've sold out their country, and now the crooked sons of bitches will live like kings."

"What a convenient interruption that was," Greta told him. She was still eating lunch, pincering her chopsticks with surgical skill. "The Senator had you pinned down and right on the spot. I can't believe you had the nerve to pull that trick."

"Actually, I was keeping a weather eye on that screen all along, just in case I needed a nice distracting gambit."

She sampled the dim sum and smiled skeptically. "No you weren't. Nobody can do that."

"Actually, yes, I *can* do that sort of thing. I do it every day."

"Well, you're not distracting *me*. What was it about this Moira person? It must be something pretty awful. I could tell that much."

"Moira is not your problem, Greta."

"Ha! Nobody around here is addressing *my* problems." She frowned, then poured a little more soy. "Really good food here, though. Amazing food."

"I'm going to *get* to your problems. I haven't forgotten them. I just had to shelve those issues for a minute while I was getting the poor man to eat."

"Too bad you couldn't get him to keep it down." Greta sighed. "This has certainly been eye-opening. I had no real idea what to expect from your Senator. Somehow, I imagined he'd be just like you."

"Meaning what, exactly?"

"Oh . . . a Machiavellian, showboating, ultra-wealthy political hack. But Alcott's not like that at all! Alcott's a real idealist. He's a patriot! It's a tragedy that he's clinically depressed."

"You really think that the Senator is clinically depressed?"

"Of course he is! It's obvious! He's crashed from starvation stress. And that myoclonic tremor in his hands —that's an overdose of neural appetite suppressants."

"He's supposed to be long off all those pills."

"Then he must have been hoarding them, and eating them secretly. Typical behavior in the syndrome. Those repeated presentations about his so-called criminality— those far-fetched guilt obsessions. . . . He's very depressed. Then when you tricked him into eating, he turned manic. His affect is all over the map! You need to test him for cognitive deficits."

"Well . . . he was just faint from hunger. Normally, he'd see right through a childish gambit like that chowder stunt."

Greta put down her chopsticks and lowered her voice. "Tell me something. Tell me the truth. Did you ever notice that he's enormously outspoken and energetic in public, but then he always retreats and cocoons himself? For, say, two or three days?"

Oscar nodded slowly. "Yes."

"First, he's very expressive and charming, working twenty-hour days, throwing off a lot of sparks. Then, he's just gone. He claims he's thinking things over, or that he needs his privacy—but basically, he's dug himself a hole and pulled it over him. That's not uncommon with creative personalities. Your Senator has bipolarity. I imagine he's always been bipolar."

"He's 'in the back of the bus.' " Oscar sighed. "That's what we used to call it, when he pulled that routine on the campaign."

"In the back of the bus, with Moira."

"Yeah. Exactly. Moira was very good at getting next to him when his guard was down."

Greta narrowed her eyes. "You did something awful to Moira, didn't you?"

"Look, the man is a U.S. Senator. I put him into office, I have to look after his interests. He had an indiscretion during the campaign. So what? Who am I to judge about that?" He paused. "And who are you, for that matter?"

"Well, I came here so that I could judge the Senator," she said. "I hoped he could really help me. We could have used an honest, decent Senator to back the lab, for once. Obviously, Alcott's someone who could really understand us. But now he's been destroyed, because he went head-to-head against Huey—a man who just chews up people like him. Politics always chews up people like him." Her face grew long and grim. "Look what he's done with this hopeless old building, look at this beautiful work he's done. He must be some kind of genius, and now they've just crushed him. This really makes me sick at heart. What a loss. He's lost his mind. It's a national tragedy."

"Well, I admit that it's a setback."

"No, it's over. He's not going to come around just because you force-fed him. Because he is demented. He can't help you anymore—and that means that you can't help me. So it's all over, and it's time for me to give this thing up."

"We're not going to give up."

"Oscar, let me go back to my lab now. Let me work. It's the reasonable thing."

"Sure it is, but I'm not a reasonable person, and these aren't reasonable times."

Leon Sosik came into the office. "Bit of a debacle there." His face was gray.

"Can you believe the audacity of that guy?" Oscar said. "Huey had a French aircraft carrier waiting offshore. The guy's a traitor! He's in league with a foreign power!"

Sosik shook his head. "That's not what I'm talking about."

"We can't acquiesce in a naked power grab like this.

We've got to nail Huey's feet to the Senate floor and beat him like a drum."

Sosik stared at him. "You're serious, aren't you?"

"Of course I'm serious! Our man has flushed Huey out of the canebrake, and now he's revealed his true colors. He's a clear and present menace to national security. We've got to take him out."

Sosik turned to Greta with courtly concern. "Dr. Penninger, I wonder if you'd allow me to speak to Mr. Valparaiso privately for a moment."

"Oh, of course." Greta rose reluctantly, setting down her chopsticks.

"I could get our chef to put together a little takeout box for you," Sosik said considerately.

"Oh no, I do need to be going. . . . If you could just get me a cab. There's a conference in town. I have work to do."

"I'll have our chauffeur take you to your meeting, Doctor."

"That would be perfect. Thank you very much." She gathered her purse and left.

Oscar watched her reluctantly, then spotted a screen remote and plucked it up. "I wish you hadn't done that," he told Sosik. "She has an agenda, you know. We could have gotten to her a little later."

"They told me you were like this," Sosik said soberly. "They told me you were exactly like this, and I couldn't believe it. Would you put down that remote control, please?"

Oscar squeezed his way through a set of feeds. "This is a breaking development, Leon. We've got to spin this quick, and nail the guy before he launches his next cover story."

Sosik gently plucked the remote from Oscar's hand. He put his hand over Oscar's shoulder. "Kid," he said, "let's go for a walk. Let's do some serious face-time together."

"We don't have a lot of time to kill right now."

"Kid, I'm the chief of staff. I don't think I'll be wasting your time. All right?"

A krewewoman handed them their hats and coats. They took an elevator down to the street.

"Let's walk toward Somerville," Sosik said. "The audio surveillance is a lot less tight there."

"Is that a problem? We could walk apart and talk things over on encrypted phones."

Sosik sighed. "Would you slow down to human speed for a minute? I'm an old man."

Oscar said nothing. He followed Sosik north up Prospect Street, hunching his shoulders against the chill. Bare trees, straggling Christmas shoppers, the occasional Caribbean storefront.

"I can't stand it in that office just now," Sosik said. "He's throwing up, he's shaking like a leaf. And the people in there, they all worship the ground the man walks on. They've had to watch him come apart at the seams."

"Yeah, and our walking out on them isn't likely to help their morale much."

"Shut up," Sosik explained. "I've been in this business thirty years. I've seen a lot of politicians come to bad ends. I've seen them go drunk, I've seen them go crooked, sex scandals, money scandals. . . . But this is the first guy I ever saw who cracked up completely before he even made it to Washington."

"Alcott's always ahead of the curve," Oscar nodded. "He's a visionary."

Sosik shot him a nettled glance. "Why'd you pick on this poor guy? He's not any kind of normal pol. Was it the wife? Did she have something on you? Was it the personal background thing?"

"Normal pols aren't getting the job done, Leon. These aren't normal times. America's not a normal country. We've used up all our normality. There isn't any left."

"*You're* not normal. What are *you* doing in politics?"

Oscar shrugged. "Someone has to deal with your thirty-year legacy of solid professional achievement, Leon."

Sosik grimaced. "Well, he gave it his best shot. And now he's toast."

"He's not toast. He's just crazy."

"Crazy is toast. Okay?"

"No, it isn't. It's true—he's had a mental breakdown. That's a problem. It's an image problem. When you get a problem that big, you can't stonewall it. You have to shine a light on it. This is the problem: he starved himself half to death in a sincere protest, and now he's lost his mind. But our keyword here isn't 'crazy.' Our keywords are 'sincere' and 'protest.' "

Sosik turned up his coat collar. "Look, you can't possibly play it that way and get away with it."

"Yes, Leon, I could. The question here is whether *you* could."

"We can't have a Senator who's non compos mentis! How the hell could he ever get a bill passed?"

"Alcott was never cut out to be a legislative technician. We've had enough of those nitpickers. Alcott's a charismatic, he's a moral leader. He can wake the people up, he can guide them and show them the mountaintop. What he needs is a way to compel their attention and make them believe in him. And now, he's finally got it."

Sosik considered this. "Kid, if you did that and it really worked, it would mean that the whole country's gone crazy."

Oscar said nothing.

"How exactly would you angle it?" Sosik said at last.

"We have to demonize Huey on the patriotism issue, while we come clean on the medical problem. Constant bedside reports whenever Al is lucid. Winston Churchill was bipolar. Abraham Lincoln was a depressive. We call in all our chits from the FedDems, we get the party to stay with him. We fly the wife in, she's a fighter, she's standing by him loyally. Grass-roots sympathy mail, we're spooling it in by the ton. I think it's doable."

"If *that's* doable, then I've lost touch. That's not the America I know. I don't have the stomach for that. I'd have to resign. You'd have to be chief of staff."

"No, Leon, *you've* got to be chief of staff. You're the seasoned professional, you've got Beltway credibility, and I'm . . . Well, I can't be in the picture at all. With my personal background, I can't possibly front a big medical-publicity spin."

"I know you want my job."

"I've got my hands full already."

Sosik snorted. "Don't give me that."

"All right," Oscar said. "I admit that I'd like to have your job, but I have my own agenda to look after now. You see, it's Greta."

"Who?"

"The scientist, damn it! Dr. Penninger."

Sosik was astonished. "What? Her? She's pushing forty and she's got a face like a hatchet! What is it with you, kid? Not two months ago you had your pants around your ankles for some campaign journalist. You were lucky as hell not to be outed on that. And now *her?*"

"Yeah. That's right. Her."

Sosik rubbed his chin. "I forgot how hard up a young guy can get. . . . Can it possibly be that good?"

"No, it's not that good," Oscar told him. "It's no good at all, it's bad. It's real bad. It's worse than you could imagine, it's terrible. If we're ever caught, we get outed. She's a fanatic workaholic—science is the only thing in the world that doesn't bore her to death. Huey adores her and wants to recruit her for some kind of mad-genius brain lab he's building in a salt mine. . . . She drinks too much. She has allergies. She's eight years older than me. . . . And oh, she's also Jewish. Though for some reason the Jewish thing hasn't come up much."

Sosik sighed, his breath steaming in the air. "So that's your situation, huh?"

"That's almost it. Except for one more thing. She's truly a genius. She's a unique, brilliant, wonderful thing."

———————————————

Kevin Hamilton was visiting Oscar's house for a neighborly chat. Kevin, a man of deeply irregular schedules, had brought a peanut butter and jelly sandwich and a bag of dried banana chips.

"Politics are irrelevant now," Kevin informed him airily.

"I'm not asking you to become a political activist, Kevin. I'm just asking you to join my krewe and run my security."

Kevin munched a handful of banana chips and had a swig of chocolate milk. "Well, you being the guy you are, I guess you've got the money for that sort of thing. . . ."

Oscar adjusted his laptop on the conference table. "There's not a lot of time for idle chitchat here, so let's put our cards on the table. I know you're a rather special guy, but you're not the only guy in the world who can do net research. So can I. You've got a civil disobedience record as long as my arm. You spent ten years with no visible means of support. Your dad is a convicted computer criminal on electronic parole. You're a police informant and a surveillance freak. I really think I need a guy like you in my outfit."

"Nice of you not to mention my dicey ethnic background," Kevin said. He set his sandwich aside and produced his own laptop from a battered valise. The ancient machine was pasted together with tension straps and travel decals.

"I never, ever mention that sort of thing," Oscar said.

"Not that you would. You're not an 'ethnic' guy."

Kevin consulted his own screen. "As far as I can figure out, you're some kind of lab product."

"Guilty as charged."

"My dad went bad after his business crashed—but *your* dad was a genuine gangster. Good thing for you that the feds don't like to bust movie stars."

"Yeah, and his films were criminal acts, too."

"You must be really hard up, man. I don't do body-guard work. I've got it together to run a successful neighborhood watch. It's a good gig for a guy who was a big-time nomad—I get to sit still now, and I've got a roof over my head. But you're a dodgy politician with some major-league enemies. I could get killed working for a guy like you."

"The plan here is that I don't get killed, and you get paid for that."

"I dunno why I'm even listening to you, man. But you know—I gotta admit that I kinda like your proposal. I like a guy who knows what he wants and just goes right after it. There's something about you that . . . I dunno . . . it just inspires confidence."

Time to play the next card. "Look, I understand about your father, Kevin. A lot of decent people suffered when intellectual property crashed. Friends of mine in the Senator's office could talk to the Governor about a grant of clemency. I believe I could do something for you here."

"Now, that would be great. You know, my dad really got a raw deal. He was never your typical racist white-power bomber. The feds just brought up that ter-ror-and-conspiracy indictment, so he would plead out on the embezzlement and wiretapping charges."

"He must have had a good lawyer."

"Sorta . . . his lawyer had the good sense to defect to Europe when the real heat came down." Kevin sighed. "I almost went to Europe myself, and then I thought . . .

what the hell? You can drop out as a road prole and it's almost the same as leaving the country."

"You don't mind traveling to Texas? You don't mind missing Christmas? We'll be flying there right away."

"I don't care. Not as long as I can still log on to my own servers."

The door chimed. Moments later, Donna arrived with an airmailed packet.

"Is that for me?" Kevin said brightly. He eviscerated the package with a massive Swiss Army knife. "Mayonnaise," he announced unconvincingly, producing a sealed jar of unlabeled white goo. "This stuff could be really handy." He stuffed the jar into his accordion-sided valise.

"She's arrived," Donna whispered.

"I have to see another guest," Oscar told Kevin.

"Another 'guest'?" Kevin winked. "What happened to the cute one in the bathrobe?"

"Can you get back to me in the morning with your decision?"

"No, man, I've made up my mind. I'm gonna do it."

"You're sure?"

"Yeah, it sounds like a nice change of pace. I'll get right on the job. Clear it with your sysadmin, and I'll see what I can do about shoring up your net."

7

Life in the Collaboratory lacked the many attractive facilities of the Back Bay in Boston.

Oscar and Greta met in a broken car in the dark parking lot behind the Vehicle Repair Facility. This assignation spot was Kevin Hamilton's idea. Kevin was very big on secure meetings inside anonymous cars. Kevin was no Secret Service agent, but he brimmed over with rule-of-thumb street smarts.

"I'm afraid," Greta confessed.

Oscar adjusted his jacket, tugging for elbow room. The car was so small that they were almost sitting in each other's laps. "How could you have stage fright over such a simple thing? You gave a Nobel Prize speech in Stockholm once."

"But then I was talking about my own work. I can always do that. This is different. You want me to stand up in front of the board of directors and tell them off to their face. In front of a big crowd of my friends and colleagues. I'm not cut out for that."

"Actually, you *are* cut out for it, Greta. You're absolutely perfect for the role. I knew it from the moment I saw you."

Greta examined her laptop screen. It was the only light inside the dead vehicle, and it underlit their faces with a gentle glow. They were meeting at two in the morning. "If it's really this bad here—as bad as you claim it is—then it's really no use fighting, is it? I should just resign."

"No, you don't have to resign. The point of this speech is that *they* have to resign." Oscar touched her hand. "You don't have to say anything you don't know to be true."

"Well, I know *some* of these things are true, because I leaked them to you myself. But I would never have *said them out loud*. And I wouldn't have said them *this way*. This speech, or this rant, or whatever it is—it's a violent political attack! It's not scholarly. It's not objective."

"Then let's talk about how you should say it. After all, you're the speaker—you're the one who has to reach the audience, not me. Let's go over your talking points."

She scrolled up and down fitfully, and sighed. "All right. I guess this is the worst part, right here. This business about scientists being an oppressed class. 'A group whose exploitation should be recognized and ended.' Scientists rising up in solidarity to demand justice—good Lord, I can't say that! It's too radical, it sounds crazy!"

"But you *are* an oppressed class. It's the truth, it's the central burning truth of your existence. Science took the wrong road somewhere, the whole enterprise has been shot to hell. You've lost your proper niche in society. You've lost prestige, and your self-respect, and the high esteem that scientists once held in the eyes of the public. Demands are being made of you that you'll never be able to fulfill. You don't have intellectual freedom anymore. You live in intellectual bondage."

"That doesn't make us some kind of 'oppressed class.' We're an elite cadre of highly educated experts."

"So what? Your situation stinks! You have no power to make your own decisions about your own research. You don't control the purse strings. You don't have tenure or job security. You've been robbed of your peer review traditions. Your traditional high culture has been crushed underfoot by ignoramuses and fast-buck artists. You're the technical intelligentsia all right, but you're being played for suckers and patsies by corrupt pols who line their pockets at your expense."

"How can you say that? Look at this amazing place we live in!"

"You just *think* that this is the ivory tower, sweetheart. In reality, you're slum tenants."

"But *nobody* thinks that way!"

"That's because you've been fooling yourselves for years now. You're smart, Greta. You have eyes and ears. Think about what you've been through. Think about how your colleagues really have to live now. Think a little harder."

She was silent.

"Go ahead," he said. "Take your time, think it through."

"It *is* true. It's the truth, and it's awful, and I'm very ashamed of it, and I hate it. But it's politics. There's nothing anyone can do about it."

"We'll see about that," he said. "Let's move on into the speech."

"Okay." She wiped her eyes. "Well, this is the really sick and painful part. Senator Dougal. I know that man, I've met him a lot of times. He drinks too much, but we all do that nowadays. He's not as bad as all this."

"People can't unite against abstractions. You have to put a face on your troubles. That's how you rally people politically. You have to pick your target, freeze it, personalize it, and polarize it. Dougal's not your only enemy, but you don't have to worry about *that*. The rest of them will come running out of the woodwork as soon as you nail him to the wall."

"But he built everything here, he built this whole laboratory!"

"He's a crook. We've got chapter and verse on him now. Nobody dared to cross him while he was in power. But now that he's shipping water and going down fast, they'll all rat him out. The kickbacks, the money launder-ing. . . . You're in charge of Instrumentation. Dougal and his cronies have been skimming your cream for years. You've got a legal and moral obligation to jump on him. And best of all, jumping on Dougal is a free ride politi-cally. He can't do a thing about it. Dougal is the easy part." Oscar paused. "It's Huey that I'm really worried about."

"I don't see why I have to be so nasty."

"You need an issue, and there's no such thing as a noncontroversial issue. And ridicule is the radical's best weapon. The powers that be can stand anything but being laughed at."

"It's just not me."

"Give it a chance first. Try the experiment. Launch one or two of those zingers, and see how your audience responds."

She sniffed. "They're scientists. They're not going to respond to partisan abuse."

"Of course they are. Scientists fight like crazed weasels. Look at your own history here at the lab! When Dougal got this place built, he had to cash in a lot of favors. He needed the Christian fundie vote before he could build a giant gene-splicing lab in the East Texas Bible Belt. That's why the Collaboratory used to have its own Creation Science department. That setup lasted six weeks! There were fistfights, riots, and arson! They had to call in the Texas Rangers to restore order."

"Oh, the creation-science problem wasn't all that bad."

"Yes it *was*! Your little society has blocked out that memory because it was so embarrassing. That wasn't the half of it. Next year they had a major brawl with the Buna residents, regular town-gown riots. . . . And it really hit the fan during the economic war. There were federal witch-hunts for foreign science spies, there was hyperin-flation and lab guys living on bread crusts. . . . See, I'm not a scientist like you. I don't have to take it on faith that science is always a noble endeavor. I actually look these things up."

"Well, I'm not a politician like you. So I don't have to spend my life digging up ugly scandals."

"Darling, we'll have a little chat sometime about your twentieth-century Golden Age—Lysenkoism, atom spies, Nazi doctors, and radiation experiments. In the meantime, though, we need to stick to your speech."

She gazed at her laptop. "It just gets worse and worse. You want me to cut our budget and get people fired."

"The budget has to be cut. Cut drastically. People have to be fired. Fired by the truckload. The lab's sixteen years old, it's full of bureaucratic deadwood. Get the deadwood out of here. Fire the Spinoffs department, they're all Dougal's cronies and they're all on the take. Fire the lab procurement drones and put the budgets back into the hands of researchers. And, especially, fire the police."

"I can't possibly fire the police. That's crazy."

"The police have to go as soon as possible. Hire your own police. If you don't control your own police, you live on sufferance. The police are the core of *any* society, and if you don't have them on your side, you can't hold power. Huey knows that. That's why Huey owns the cops in here. They may be feds officially, but they're all in his pockets."

The car jostled with a thump and a creak. Oscar yelped. A shapeless black beast was bumping and clawing at the hood.

"It's a lemur," Greta said. "They're nocturnal."

The lemur stared through the windshield with yellow eyes the size and shape of golf balls. Pressed flat against the glass, its eldritch protohuman mitts gave him a serious turn. "I've had it with these animals!" Oscar shouted. "They're like Banquo's ghost, they never let us alone!

Whose bright idea was this anyway? Wild animals loose in a science lab? It doesn't make any sense!"

"They *are* ghosts," Greta said. "We raised them from the dead. It's something we learned how to do here." She opened her door and stepped half out, waving one arm. "Go on. Shoo."

The lemur sidled off reluctantly.

Oscar had broken into a cold sweat. His hair was standing on end and his hands were shaking. He could actually smell his own fear: a sharp pheromonal reek. He crossed his arms and shivered violently. His reaction was all out of whack, but he couldn't help it: he was very inspired tonight. "Give me a minute. . . . Sorry. . . . Where were we?"

"I can't stand up in public and start screaming for people to be fired."

"Don't prejudge the evidence. Try it out first. Just suggest that a few of these creeps should be fired, and see what the public response is." He drew a breath. "Remember the climax—you do have a final ace to play."

"Where I say that I refuse my own salary."

"Yeah, I thought voluntarily cutting it in half might be good—I'd like to see the Collaboratory's budget cut about in half—but it's a better and stronger gesture if you just refuse your pay altogether. You refuse to take government pay until the lab is put back in order. That's a great conclusion, it shows you're really serious and it gets you out with a punch, and a nice hot sound bite. Then you sit back and watch the fireworks."

"I sit back, and the Director fires me on the spot."

"No, he won't. He won't dare. He's never been his own man, and he's just not bright enough to react that quickly. He'll stall for time, and he's all out of time. Getting the Director out of office is not a problem. The next big step is getting you in as Director. And the real challenge will be keeping you in office—long enough for you to push some real reforms through."

She sighed. "And then, finally, when that's all over, do I get to go back and do my labwork?"

"Probably." He paused. "No, sure, of course. If that's what you really want."

"How am I supposed to eat with no salary?"

"You've got your Nobel Prize money, Greta. You've got big piles of Swedish kronor that you've never even touched."

She frowned. "I kept thinking I would buy new equipment with it, but the lab procurement people wouldn't let me do all the paperwork."

"Okay, that's your problem in a nutshell. Fire all those sorry bastards first thing."

She shut her laptop. "This is serious. When I do this, it will make a terrible stink. Something will happen."

"We *want* things to happen. That's why we're doing all this."

She turned in her seat, anxiously poking him with a kneecap. "I just want to be truthful. Not political. Truthful."

"This is an honest political speech! Everything there can be documented."

"It's honest about everything but you and me."

Oscar exhaled slowly. He'd been expecting this development. "Well, that's where we have to pay the price. After tomorrow, you're on campaign. Even with the best will and intention, we won't have any time for ourselves anymore. When we had our stolen moments, we could meet in Boston or Louisiana, and that was lovely, and we could get away with that. But we lose that privilege from now on. This is the last time that you and I can meet privately. I won't even be in the audience when you speak tomorrow. It mustn't look like I'm prompting you."

"But people know about us. A lot of people know. I *want* people to know."

"All political leaders lead double lives. Public, and private. That's not hypocrisy. That's just reality."

"What if we're outed?"

"Well, there's two ways to play that development. We could stonewall. That's simplest and easiest—just deny everything, and let them try to prove it. Or, we could be very coy and provocative, and say that we're flattered by their matchmaking. We could lead them on a little, we could be sexy and glamorous. You know, play it the good old Hollywood way. That's a dangerous game, but I know that game pretty well, and I like that one better, myself."

She was silent for a moment. "Won't you miss me?"

"How can I miss you? I'm *managing* you. You're the very center of my life now. You're my candidate."

———————————

Oscar and Yosh Pelicanos were enjoying a healthful stroll around the china tower of the Hot Zone. Pelicanos wore a billed hat, khaki walking shorts, and a sleeveless pullover. Two months inside the dome had caused almost all of Oscar's krewe to go native. Oscar, by stark contrast, wore his nattiest suit and a sharp new steam-blocked hat. Oscar rarely felt the need of serious exercise, since his metabolic rate was eight percent higher than that of a normal human.

Their walk was a deliberate and public promenade. The Collaboratory's board was meeting, Greta was about to speak, and Oscar was very conspicuously nowhere near the scene. Oscar was especially hard to miss when publicly trailed by his bodyguard: the spectral Kevin Hamilton, parading in his motorized wheelchair.

"What is it with this Hamilton guy?" Pelicanos grumbled, glancing over his shoulder. "Why on earth did you have to hire some Anglo hustler? His only credential is that he limps even worse than Fontenot."

"Kevin's very gifted. He got that netwar program off my back. Besides, he works cheap."

"He dresses like a loan shark. The guy gets eighteen package deliveries a day. And that headphone and the scanning gear—he's sleeping in it! He's getting on our nerves."

"Kevin will grow on you. I know he's not the standard team player. Be tolerant."

"I'm nervous," Pelicanos admitted.

"No need for that. We've laid all the groundwork perfectly," Oscar said. "I've got to hand it to the krewe, you've really done me proud here." Oscar's mood was radiant. Unbearable personal tension, stress, and agonizing suspense always brought out his boyish, endearing side. "Yosh, you did first-class work on those audits. And the push-polling was superb, you handled that beautifully. A few dozen loaded questions on the Science Committee letterhead, and the locals are hopping like puppets, they're gun-shy now, they're ready for anything. It's been a tour de force all around. Even the hotel's making money! Especially now that we lured in all those expense-account headhunters from out of state."

"Yeah, you've got us all working like mules—you don't have to tell me that. The question is, is it enough?"

"Well, nothing's ever *enough*. . . . Politics isn't precision machinery, it's a performance art. It's stage magic. It's a brand-new year, and now the curtain's going up. We've got our plants primed in the audience, we've got scarves and ribbons up our sleeve, we've saturated the playing field with extra hats and rabbits. . . ."

"There's *way too many* hats and rabbits."

"No there aren't! Can't have too many! We'll just use the ones that we need, as we need them. That's the beauty of multitasking. It's that fractal aspect, the self-similarity across multiple political layers. . . ."

Pelicanos snorted. "Stop talking like Bambakias. That highbrow net-jive gets you nowhere with me."

"But it works! If the feds somehow fail us, we've got leaks in at the Texas comptroller's office. The Buna city council loves us! I know they're not worth much politically, but hey, we've paid more attention to them in the past six weeks than the Collaboratory has paid them in fifteen years."

"So you're keeping all your options open."

"Exactly."

"You always say that you hate doing that."

"What? I never said that. You're just being morose. I feel very upbeat about this, Yosh—we've had a few little setbacks, but taking this assignment was a wise decision. It's been a broadening professional experience."

They paused to let a yak cross the road. "You know what I really like about this campaign?" Oscar said. "It's so *tiny*. Two thousand political illiterates, sealed inside a dome. We have complete voter profiles and interest-group dossiers on every single person in the Collaboratory! It's so sealed off and detached—politically speaking, there's something perfect and magical about a setup like this."

"I'm glad you're enjoying yourself."

"I'm determined to enjoy this, Yosh. We might be crushed here, or we might soar to glory, but we'll never have the chance to do something quite like this again."

A supply truck lumbered past them, laden with mutant seedlings. "You know something?" Pelicanos said. "I've been so busy playing the angles that I never got the chance to understand what they actually do in here."

"I think you understand it a lot better than they do."

"Not their finances, I mean the actual science. I can understand commercial biotech well enough—we were in that business together, in Boston. But the real cutting edge here, those brain people, the cognition people . . . I know I'm missing something important there."

"Yeah? Personally, I've been trying to get up to speed on 'amyloid fibrils.' Greta really dotes on those things."

"It's not just that their field is technically difficult to grasp. It is, but I also have a feeling they're hiding something."

"Sure. That's science in its decadence. They can't

patent or copyright their findings anymore, so sometimes
they try for trade secrets." Oscar laughed. "As if that could
really work nowadays."

"Maybe there's something going on in this place that
could help Sandra."

Oscar was touched. His friend's dark mood was clear
to him now, it had opened up before him like an origami
trick. "Where there's life, there's hope, Yosh."

"If I had more time to figure it out, if there weren't
so many distractions. . . . *Everything* is hats and rabbits
now. Nothing's predictable, nothing makes sense anymore, it's all rockets and potholes. There's no foundation
left in our society. There's no place left for us to take a
stand. There's a very dark momentum going, Oscar.
Sometimes I really think the country's going mad."

"Why do you say that?"

"Well, just look at us. I mean, look what we've been
dealing with." Pelicanos hunched his head and began
counting off on his fingers. "My wife is a schizophrenic.
Bambakias has major depression. Poor Moira finally
cracked in public, and pitched a fit. Dougal is an alcoholic.
Green Huey is a megalomaniac. And those sick lunatics
trying to kill you—there was an *endless supply* of those
people."

Oscar walked on silently.

"Am I reading too much into this? Or is there a
genuine trend here?"

"I'd call it a groundswell," Oscar said thoughtfully.
"That accounts for those sky-high poll ratings ever since
Bambakias's breakdown. He's a classic political charismatic. So even his personal negatives boost his political
positives. People just sense his authenticity, they recognize
that he's truly a man of our time. He represents the American people. He's a born leader."

"Does he have it together to take action for us in
Washington?"

"Well, he's still a name for us to conjure with. . . .

But practically speaking, no. I've got good backchannel from Lorena, and frankly, he's really delusionary now. He's got some weird fixation about the President, something about hot-war with Europe. . . . He sees Dutch agents hiding under every bed. . . . They're trying him out with different flavors of antidepressant."

"Will that work? Can they stabilize him?"

"Well, the treatments make great media copy. There's a huge Bambakias medical fandom happening, ever since his hunger strike, really. . . . They've got their own sites and feeds. . . . Lots of get-well email, home mental-health remedies, oddsmaking on the death-watch. . . . It's a classic grass-roots phenomenon. You know, T-shirts, yard signs, coffee mugs, fridge magnets. . . . I dunno, it's getting kind of out of hand."

Pelicanos rubbed his chin. "Kind of a tabloid vulture pop-star momentum there."

"*Exactly*. Perfect coinage, you've hit the nail on the head."

"How bad should we feel about this, Oscar? I mean, basically, this *is* all our fault, isn't it?"

"You really think so?" Oscar said, surprised. "You know, I'm so close to it I can't really judge anymore."

A bicycle messenger stopped them. "I've got a packet delivery for a Mr. Hamilton."

"You want that guy in the wheelchair," Oscar said.

The messenger examined his handheld satellite readout. "Oh yeah. Right. Thanks." He pedaled off.

"Well, you were never his chief of staff," Pelicanos said.

"Yeah, that's true. That's a comfort." Oscar watched as the bike messenger engaged in the transaction with his security chief. Kevin signed for two shrink-wrapped bundles. He examined the return addresses and began talking into his head-mounted mouthpiece.

"You know that he eats out of those packages?"

Pelicanos said. "Big white sticks of stuff, like straw and chalk. He chews 'em all the time. He kind of grazes."

"At least he eats," Oscar said. His phone rang. He plucked it from his sleeve and answered it. "Hello?"

There was a distant, acid-scratched voice. "It's me, Kevin, over."

Oscar turned and confronted Kevin, who was rolling along in his chair ten strides behind them. "Yes, Kevin? What's on your mind?"

"I think we have a situation coming. Somebody just pulled a fire alarm inside the Collaboratory, over."

"Is that a problem?"

Oscar watched Kevin's mouth move. Kevin's voice arrived at his ear a good ten seconds later. "Well, this is a sealed, airtight dome. The locals get pretty serious about fires inside here, over."

Oscar examined the towering gridwork overhead. It was a blue and lucid winter afternoon. "I don't see any smoke. Kevin, what's wrong with your telephone?"

"Traffic analysis countermeasures—I routed this call around the world about eight times, over."

"But we're only ten meters apart. Why don't you just roll up over here and do some face-time with me?"

"We need to cool it, Oscar. Stop looking at me, and just go on walking. Don't look now, but there are cops tailing us. A cab in front and a cab behind, and I think they have shotgun mikes. Over."

Oscar turned and threw a companionable arm over Pelicanos's shoulder, urging him along. There were, in point of fact, some laboratory cops within sight. Normally the cops employed their "Buna National Collaboratory Security Authority" trucks, macho vehicles with comic-opera official seals on the doors, but these officers had commandeered a pair of the Collaboratory's little phone-dispatched cabs. The cops were trying to be inconspicuous.

"Kevin says the cops are tailing us," Oscar told Pelicanos.

"Delighted to hear it," Pelicanos said mildly. "There were three attempts on your life in here. You must be the most excitement that these local cops have had in years."

"He also says there's been a fire alarm."

"How would he know that?"

A bright yellow fire truck emerged from the bowels of the Occupational Safety building. It set its lights flashing, opened up with a klaxon blare, and headed south, off the ring road.

Oscar felt an odd skin-creeping feeling, then a violent huff of atmospheric pressure. An invisible door slammed shut in his head. The Collaboratory had just fully sealed its airlocks. The entire massive structure had gone tight as a drum.

"Jesus, it *is* a fire!" Pelicanos said. Acting on instinct, he turned and began jogging after the fire truck.

Oscar thought it more sensible to stay with his bodyguard. He tucked his phone in his sleeve and walked over to join Kevin.

"So, Kevin, what's in those delivery packets?"

"Heavy-duty sunblock," Kevin lied, yawning to clear his ears. "It's an Anglo thing."

Oscar and Kevin left the ring road, heading south past the Computation Center. Their police escorts were still dutifully trailing them, but the little cabs were soon lost in a curious pedestrian crowd emerging from their buildings.

The fire truck stopped outside the Collaboratory's media center. This building was the site of Greta's public board meeting. Oscar's carefully drummed-up capacity crowd was pouring from the exits, loudly milling in confusion.

A fistfight had broken out on the steps at the eastern exit. A gray-haired man with a bloody nose was cowering under the metal handrails, and a young tough with a cowboy hat and shorts was struggling to kick him. Four men were grappling reluctantly at the young man's arms and shoulders, trying to restrain him.

Kevin stopped his wheelchair. Oscar waited at Kevin's elbow and examined his watch. If all had gone as planned—which it clearly hadn't—then Greta should have finished her speech by now. He looked up again to see the cowboy lose his hat. To his deep astonishment he recognized the assailant as his krewe gofer, Norman-the-Intern.

"Come with me, Kevin. Nothing that we want to see here." Oscar turned hastily on his heel and walked back the way he'd come. He glanced over his shoulder, once. His police escort had abandoned him. They had dashed forward with gusto, and were busy arresting young Norman.

Oscar waited until he received official notification from the police about Norman's arrest. He then went to police headquarters, in the east central side of the dome. The Collaboratory's police HQ was part of a squat fortress complex, housing the fire department, the power generators, the phone service, and the internal water supply.

Oscar was quite familiar with the internal routines of the local police headquarters, since he'd visited three of his would-be assailants in custody there. He presented himself to the desk officer. He was informed that young Norman had been charged with battery and disturbing the peace.

Norman was wearing orange coveralls and a wrist cuff. Norman looked surprisingly spiffy in his spotless prison gear—he was rather better dressed than most Collaboratory personnel. The cuff was a locked-on shatterproof bracelet studded with tiny mikes and surveillance lenses.

"You should have brought a lawyer," Norman said from behind the cardboard briefing table. "They never turn off this cuff unless there's attorney-client privilege."

"I know that," Oscar said. He opened his laptop and set it on the table.

"I never knew how awful this was," Norman mourned, rubbing at his monster cuff. "I mean, I used to see guys on parole wearing these things, and I'd always wonder, you know, what's with this evil scumbag. . . . But now that I've got one myself . . . They're really *demeaning*."

"I'm sorry to hear that," Oscar said blandly. He began typing.

"I knew this kid at school once who got into trouble, and I used to hear him spoofing his cuff. . . . You know, he'd sit there in math class muttering 'crime drugs robbery murder assault. . . .' Because the cops run voice recognition scans. That's how these cuffs surveil you. We thought he was totally nuts. But now I get why he did that."

Oscar turned his laptop screen to face Norman, showing a dimly legible set of 36-point capitals. WE'LL KEEP UP THE SMALL TALK AND I'LL LEVEL WITH YOU ON THIS.

"You don't have to worry about the local law enforcement people. We can talk freely here," Oscar said aloud. "That device is meant for your own protection as well as the safety of others." JUST KEEP YOUR ARM DOWN IN YOUR LAP SO THE CAMERAS CAN'T READ THIS SCREEN. He erased the screen with a keystroke.

"Am I in big trouble, Oscar?"

"Yes you are." NO YOU'RE NOT. "Just tell me what happened." TELL ME WHAT YOU TOLD THE POLICE.

"Well, she was giving one heck of a speech," Norman said. "I mean, you could barely hear her at first, she was so nervous, but once the crowd started yelling, she really got pretty worked up. Everybody got really excited. . . . Look, Oscar, when the cops arrested me, I lost my head. I told them a lot. Pretty much everything. I'm sorry."

"Really," Oscar said.

"Yeah, like, I told them why you sent me there. Because we knew from the profiles who was likely to make trouble, and that it would probably be this guy Skopelitis. So that's who I was casing. I was sitting right behind him in the fifth row. . . . So every time he got all ready to stand up and really give it to her, I ran a preemption. I asked him to explain a term for me, I got him to take off his hat, I asked him where the rest room was. . . ."

"All perfectly legal behavior," Oscar said.

"Finally he screamed at me to shut up."

"Did you stop conversing with Dr. Skopelitis when you were asked to stop?"

"Well, I started eating my bag of potato chips. Nice and crunchy." Norman smiled wanly. "He sort of lost his head then, he was trying to find cues in his laptop. And I was shoulder-surfing him, and you know, he had a whole list of prepared statements there. He went in there loaded. But she was really tearing through her material by then, and they were applauding, and cheering, even . . . lots of major laugh lines. They couldn't believe how *funny* she was. He finally jumped up and yelled something totally stupid about how dare she this, and how dare she that, and the place just went ape. They just shouted him down. So he walked out of the meeting in a major huff. And I followed him."

"Why did you do that?"

"Mostly just to distract him some more. I was really enjoying myself."

"Oh."

"Yeah, I'm a college student, and he's just like this professor I had once, a guy I really couldn't stand. I just wanted him to know that I had his number. But once he was outside the briefing room, he took off running. So then I knew he was up to something bad. So I followed him, and I saw him trip a fire alarm."

Oscar removed his hat and set it on the table. "You say you actually witnessed this?"

"Heck yeah! So I had it out with him. I ran up to him and I said, 'Look, Skopelitis, you can't pull a dirty stunt like that! It's not professional.' "

"And?"

"And he denied it to my face. I said, 'Look, *I saw you do it.*' He panics and takes off. I run after him. People are pouring into the halls because of the fire alarm. It gets really exciting. I'm trying to apprehend him. We get into a fight. I'm a lot stronger than him, so I punch his lights out. I'm running down the hall after him, jumping down the steps, he's got a bloody nose, people are yelling at us to stop. I pretty much lost my temper."

Oscar sighed. "Norman, you're fired."

Norman nodded sadly. "I am?"

"That's not acceptable behavior, Norman. The people in my krewe are political operatives. You're not a vigilante. You can't beat people up."

"What was I supposed to do, then?"

"You should have informed the police that you saw Dr. Skopelitis committing a crime." HE'S FINISHED! GOOD WORK! TOO BAD I HAVE TO FIRE YOU NOW.

"You're really going to fire me, Oscar?"

"Yes, Norman, you are fired. I'll go to the clinic, I'll apologize to Dr. Skopelitis personally. I hope I can persuade him to dismiss the charges against you. Then I'm sending you home to Cambridge."

———

Oscar went to visit Skopelitis in the Collaboratory clinic. He brought flowers: a lushly symbolic bouquet of yellow carnations and lettuce. Skopelitis had a private room, and with Oscar's sudden arrival, he had hastily returned to his

bed. He had a black eye and his nose was heavily bandaged.

"I hope you're not taking this too badly, Dr. Skopelitis. Let me ring the nurse for a vase."

"I don't think that will be necessary," Skopelitis said
nasally.

"Oh, but I insist," Oscar said. He went through the
agonizing ritual, shuttling the nurse in, accepting her
compliments on the flowers, small-talking about water and
sunshine, carefully judging the patient's growing discom-
fort. This shaded into open horror as Skopelitis glimpsed
Kevin in his wheelchair, stationed outside in the hall.

"Is there anything we can do to assist in your conva-
lescence? A little light reading matter, maybe?"

"Stop it," Skopelitis said. "Stop being so polite, I
can't stand it."

"I beg your pardon?"

"Look, I know exactly why you're here. Let's cut to
the chase. You want me to get the kid off. Right? He
assaulted me. Well, I'll do that on one condition: he has to
stop telling those lies about me."

"What lies are those?"

"Look, don't play your games with me. I know the
score. You had your dirty tricks team in there. You set up
that whole thing from the very beginning, you wrote that
speech for her, those slanders against the Senator, you
planned it all. You waltzed into my lab with your big
campaign machine, muckraking all the tired old stories,
trying to wreck people's careers, trying to destroy people's
lives. . . . You make me sick! So I'm giving you one
chance, straight across: you shut him up, and I'll drop the
charges. That's my best offer. So take it or leave it."

"Oh dear," Oscar said. "I'm afraid you've been mis-
informed. We don't want the charges dropped. We intend
to contest them in court."

"What?"

"You're going to twist in the wind for weeks. We're

going to have a show-trial here. We're going to squeeze
the truth out of you under oath, drop, by drop, by drop.
You have no bargaining position with me. You're sunk.
You can't pull a stunt like that on an impulse! You left
DNA traces on the switch. You left your *fingerprints* on it.
There's an embedded vidcam inside the thing! Didn't
Huey warn you that the lab's alarms are bugged?"

"Huey has nothing to do with this."

"I could have guessed *that*. He wanted you to disrupt
the speech, he didn't want you to fly totally off the handle
and send the whole population into the streets. This is a
science lab, not a ninja academy. You dropped your pants
like a circus clown."

Skopelitis had gone a light shade of green. "I want a
lawyer."

"Then get one. But you're not talking to a cop here.
You're just having a friendly bedside chat with a U.S.
Senate staffer. Of course, once you're questioned by the
U.S. Senate, you'll surely need a lawyer then. A very ex-
pensive lawyer. Conspiracy, obstruction of justice . . .
it'll be juicy."

"It was just a false alarm! A false alarm. They happen
all the time."

"You've been reading too many sabotage manuals.
Proles can get away with urban netwar, because they don't
mind doing jail time. Proles have nothing much to lose—
but you do. You came in there to shout her down and
cover your own ass, but you lost your temper and destroyed your own career. You just lost twenty years of
work in the blink of an eye. And you've got the nerve to
dictate terms to me? You dumb bastard, I'm gonna *crucify*
you. You just pulled the bonehead move of your life. I'm
going to make you a public laughingstock, from sea to
shining sea."

"Look. Don't do that."

"What's that?"

"Don't do that to me. Don't ruin me. Please. He

broke my nose, okay? He broke my nose! Look, I lost my head." Skopelitis wiped tears from his blackened eye. "She *never* acted like that before, she's *turned* on us, it was like she'd gone crazy! I had to *do something,* it was just . . . it just . . ." He broke into sobs. "Jesus . . ."

"Well, I can see I'm distressing you," Oscar said, rising. "I've enjoyed our little confab, but time presses. I'll be on my way."

"Look, you just can't do this to me! I only did one little thing."

"Listen." Oscar sat back down and pointed. "You've got a laptop there. You want off the hook? Write me some mail. Tell me all about it. Tell me every little thing. Just between the two of us, privately. And if you're straight with me . . . well, what the hell. He did break your nose. I apologize for that. That was very wrong."

Oscar was studying the minutes from the latest Senate Science Committee meeting when Kevin walked into the room.

"Don't you ever sleep?" Kevin said, yawning.

"No, not particularly."

"I'm kind of gathering that." Kevin dropped his cane and sat down in a sling chair. Oscar had a rather spartan room at the hotel. He was forced to move daily for security reasons, and besides, the best suites were all taken by paying customers.

Oscar shut his laptop. It was quite an intriguing report—a federal lab in Davis, California, was sorely infested with hyperintelligent lab mice, provoking a lawsuit-slinging panic from the outraged locals—but he found Kevin very worthwhile.

"So," Kevin said, "what happens next?"

"What do *you* think happens next, Kevin?"

"Well," Kevin said, "that would be cheating. Because I've seen this sort of thing before."

"You don't say."

"Yeah. Here's the situation. You've got a group of people here who are about to all lose their jobs. So you're gonna organize them and fight back politically. You'll get a lot of excitement and solidarity for about six weeks, and then they'll all get fired. They'll shut the whole place down and lock the gates in your face. Then you'll all turn into proles."

"You really think so?"

"Well, maybe not. Maybe basic research scientists are somehow smarter than computer programmers, or stock traders, or assembly-line workers, or traditional farmers. . . . You know, all those other people who lost their professions and got pushed off the edge of the earth. But that's what everybody always thinks in these situations. 'Yeah, *their* jobs are obsolete now, but people will always need *us.*' "

Oscar drummed his fingers on his laptop. "It's good of you to take such a lively interest, Kevin. I appreciate your input. Believe it or not, what you're saying isn't exactly news to me. I'm very aware that huge numbers of people have been forced out of the conventional economy and become organized network mobs. I mean, they don't *vote,* so they rarely command my professional attention, but over the years they're getting better and better at ruining life for the rest of us."

"Oscar, the proles *are* 'the rest of us.' It's people like you who *aren't* 'the rest of us.' "

"I've never been the rest of anybody," Oscar said. "Even people like me are never people like *me.* You want a coffee?"

"Okay."

Oscar poured two cups. Kevin reached companionably into his back pocket and pulled out a square white baton of compressed vegetable protein. "Have a chew?"

"Sure." Oscar gnawed thoughtfully on a snapped-off chunk. It tasted like carrots and foam.

"You know," Oscar ruminated, "I have my share of prejudices—who doesn't, really?—but I've never had it in for proles, per se. I'm just tired of living in a society permanently broken into fragments. I've always hoped and planned for federal, democratic, national reform. So we can have a system with a decent role for everyone."

"But the economy's out of control. Money just doesn't need human beings anymore. Most of us only get in the way."

"Well, money isn't everything, but just try living without it."

Kevin shrugged. "People lived before money was invented. Money's not a law of nature. Money's a medium. You *can* live without money, if you replace it with the right kind of computation. The proles know that. They've tried a million weird stunts to get by, roadblocks, shakedowns, smuggling, scrap metal, road shows. . . . Heaven knows they never had much to work with. But the proles are almost there now. You know how reputation servers work, right?"

"Of course I know about them, but I also know they don't really work."

"I used to live off reputation servers. Let's say you're in the Regulators—they're a mob that's very big around here. You show up at a Regulator camp with a trust rep in the high nineties, people will make it their business to look after you. Because they know for a fact that you're a good guy to have around. You're polite, you don't rob stuff, they can trust you with their kids, their cars, whatever they got. You're a certifiable good neighbor. You always pitch in. You always do people favors. You never sell out the gang. It's a network gift economy."

"It's gangster socialism. It's a nutty scheme, it's unrealistic. And it's fragile. You can always bribe people to boost your ratings, and then money breaks into your little pie-in-the-sky setup. Then you're right back where you started."

"It can work all right. The problem is that the organized-crime feds are on to the proles, so they netwar their systems and deliberately break them down. They *prefer* the proles chaotic, because they're a threat to the status quo. Living without money is just not the American way. But most of Africa lives outside the money economy now— they're all eating leaf protein out of Dutch machines. Polynesia is like that now. In Europe they've got guaranteed annual incomes, they've got zero-work people in their Parliaments. Gift networks have always been big in Japan. Russians still think property is theft—those poor guys could *never* make a money economy work. So if it's so impractical, then how come everybody else is doing it? With Green Huey in power, they've finally got a whole American state."

"Green Huey is a pocket Stalin. He's a personality cultist."

"I agree he's a son of a bitch, but he's a *giant* son of a bitch. His state government runs Regulator servers now. And they didn't overrun that air base by any accident. Huey's nomads really have what it takes now—no more of this penny-ante roadblock and wire-clipper nonsense. Now they've got U.S. Air Force equipment that's knocked over national governments. It's a silent coup in progress, pal. They're gonna eat the country right out from under you."

"Kevin, stop frightening me. I'm way ahead of you here. I know that the proles are a threat. I've known it since that May Day riot in Worcester, back in '42. Maybe you didn't care to notice that ugly business, but I have tapes of all that—I've watched it a hundred times. People in my own home state tore a bank apart with their hands. It was absolute madness. Craziest thing I ever saw."

Kevin munched his stick and swallowed. "I didn't have to tape it. I was there."

"You were?" Oscar leaned forward gently. "Who ordered all that?"

"Nobody. Nobody ever orders it. That was a fed bank, they were running cointelpro out of it. The word bubbled up from below, some heavy activists accreted, they wasp-swarmed the place. And once they'd trashed it, they all ducked and scattered. You'd never find any 'orders,' or anyone responsible. You'd never even find the software. That thing is a major-league hit-server. It's so far underground that it doesn't need eyes anymore."

"Why did you do that, Kevin? Why would you risk doing a crazy thing like that?"

"I did it for the trust ratings. And because, well, they stank." Kevin's eyes glittered. "Because the people who rule us are spooks, they lie and they cheat and they spy. The sons of bitches are rich, they're in power. They hold all the cards over us, but they *still* have to screw people over the sneaky way. They had it coming. I'd do it again, if my feet were a little better."

Oscar felt himself trembling on the edge of revelation. This was almost making sense. Kevin had just outed himself, and the facts were finally falling into place. The situation was both a lot clearer and rather more dangerous than he had imagined.

Oscar knew now that he had been absolutely right to follow his instincts and hire this man. Kevin was the kind of political creature who was much safer inside the tent than outside it. There had to be some way to win him over, permanently. Something that mattered to him. "Tell me more about your feet, Kevin."

"I'm an Anglo. Funny things happen to Anglos nowadays." Kevin smiled wearily. "Especially when four cops with batons catch you screwing with traffic lights. . . . So now, I'm a dropout's dropout. I had to go straight, I couldn't keep up on the road. I got myself a crap security gig in a tony part of Beantown. I put most of the old life behind me. . . . Hey, I even voted once! I voted for Bambakias."

"That's extremely interesting. Why did you do that?"

"Because he builds houses for us, man! He builds 'em with his own hands and he never asks for a cent. And I'm not sorry I voted for him either, because you know, the man is for real! I know that he blew it, but *that's* for real—the whole country has blown it. He's rich, and an intellectual, and an art collector, and all that crap, but at least he's not a hypocrite like Huey. Huey claims he's the future of America, but he cuts backroom deals with the Europeans."

"He sold out our country, didn't he?" Oscar nodded. "That's just too much to forgive."

"Yup. Just like the President."

"*Now* what? What's the problem with Two Feathers?"

"Actually, the President's not a bad guy in his own way. He's done some good refugee work out in the West. It's really different out there now; since the giant fires and relocations, they've got nomad posses taking over whole towns and counties. . . . But that doesn't cut much ice with me, Two Feathers is a Dutch agent."

Oscar smiled. "You lost me there. The *President* is a Dutch agent?"

"Yeah, the Dutch have been backing him for years. Dutch spooks are very big on disaffected ethnic groups. Anglos, Native Americans. . . . America's a big country. It's your basic divide-and-conquer hack."

"Look, we're not talking Geronimo here. The President is a billionaire timber baron who was Governor of Colorado."

"We *are* talking Geronimo, Oscar. Take away America's money, and you've got a country of tribes."

Once the charges were dismissed against Norman-the-Intern, Oscar's krewe held a nice going-away party for him. It was very well attended. The hotel was crowded with Collaboratory supporters, who professed heartfelt admiration for Norman and deeply appreciated the free drinks and food.

"This is such a beautiful hotel," said Albert Gazzaniga. Greta's majordomo had arrived in the company of Warren Titche and Cyril Morello—two of the Collaboratory's permanently disaffected activists. Titche fought for perks and cafeteria fare like a radical wolverine, while Morello was the only man in the Human Resources Department who could be described as honest. Oscar was delighted to see the three of them spontaneously coalescing. It was a sure sign that trends were going his way.

Gazzaniga was clutching a hurricane glass with a little paper parasol. "Great little restaurant here, too. I'd eat here every day if I didn't have to breathe all this filthy outside air."

"It's a shame about your allergy problems, Albert."

"We've all got allergies in there. But I just had a good idea—why don't you roof over a street between here and the dome?"

Oscar laughed. "Why settle for half measures? Let's roof over the whole damn town."

Gazzaniga squinted. "Are you serious? I can never tell when you're serious."

Norman tugged at Oscar's sleeve. His face was scarlet and his eyes were wet with sentimental tears. "I'm leaving now, Oscar. I guess this is my last good-bye."

"What?" Oscar said. He took Norman's suit-jacketed elbow and steered him away from the crowd. "You have to stay after the party. We'll play some poker."

"So you can send me back to Boston with a nice cash present, and it won't have to show on the books?"

Oscar stared at him. "Kid, you're the first guy on my krewe who's ever said a word about that sad little habit of mine. You're a big boy now, okay? You need to learn to be tactful."

"No I don't," said Norman, who was very drunk. "I can be as rude as I want, now that you've fired me."

Oscar patted Norman's back. "That was strictly for your own good. You pulled a major coup, so you're all used up now. From now on, they'd sandbag you every time."

"I just wanted to tell you, no hard feelings. I have no regrets about any of this. I really learned a lot about politics. Also, I got to punch out a professor, and I got away with it. Heck, that was worth it all by itself."

"You're a good kid, Norman. Good luck in engineering school. Try and take it a little easy with the X-ray laser gambit."

"I've got a car waiting," Norman said, shuffling from foot to foot. "My dad and mom will be real glad to see me. . . . It's okay that I'm leaving. I hate to go, but I know it's for the best. I just wanted to clear one last thing with you before I left. Because I never really leveled with you about the, uh . . . well, you know."

"The 'personal background problem,' " Oscar said.

"I never got used to that. Lord knows I tried. But I never got used to you. Nobody *ever* gets used to you. Not even your own krewepeople. You're just too weird, you're just a very, very weird guy. You think weird. You act weird. You don't even sleep. You're not exactly human."

He sighed, and swayed a little where he stood. "But you know something? Things really *happen* around you, Oscar. You're a mover and shaker, you *matter*. The country *needs* you. Please don't let us down, man. Don't sell us out. People trust you, we trust you. I trust you, I trust your judgment. I'm young, and I need a real future. Fight the good fight for us. Please."

———————————

Oscar had time to examine the Director's outer office as Dr. Arno Felzian kept him waiting. Kevin passed the time feeding bits of protein to Stickley the binturong, who had just arrived from Boston by air shipment. Stickley wore a radio-tracking collar; his claws were clipped, his fangs were polished, and he was groomed and perfumed like a prize poodle. Stickley scarcely smelled at all now.

Someone—some kreweman of Senator Dougal's, presumably—had seen fit to decorate the Director's federal offices in high Texas drag. There were wall-mounted rifles, steer heads, lariats, cowhide seats, a host of shiny commemorative plaques.

Felzian's secretary announced him. Oscar hung his hat on a towering antler rack inside the door. Felzian was sitting behind his inlaid oak-and-cedar desk, looking as unhappy as politeness would allow. The Director wore bifocal glasses. The metal-and-glass prosthetic gave Felzian a touchingly twentieth-century look. Felzian was a short, slender man in his sixties. He might have been bald and fat in a crueler century.

Oscar shook the Director's hand and took a brindled leather chair. "Good to see you again, Dr. Felzian. I appreciate your taking the time to meet me today."

Felzian was wearily patient. "I'm sure that's quite all right."

"On behalf of Senator and Mrs. Alcott Bambakias, I want to present you with this laboratory specimen. You see, Mrs. Bambakias takes a lively personal interest in animal welfare issues. So she had this specimen thoroughly examined in Boston, and she discovered that he has an excellent bill of health. Mrs. Bambakias congratulates the Collaboratory on its sound animal rights practices. She also grew very fond of the animal personally, so although she's returning him to you now, she's also sending along this personal contribution to help assure his future welfare."

Felzian examined the document Oscar proffered. "Is that really a signed, paper bank check?"

"Mrs. Bambakias likes a traditional, personal touch," Oscar said. "She's very sentimental about her friend Stickley here." He smiled, and produced a camera. "I hope you don't mind if I take a few farewell photos now, for her family scrapbook."

Felzian sighed. "Mr. Valparaiso, I know you didn't come here to dump a stray animal in my lap. Nobody ever returns our animals. Never. Basically, they're party favors. So if your Senator is returning a specimen to us, that can only mean he plans to do us real harm "

Oscar was surprised to hear Felzian speaking so grimly. Given that this was the Director's office, he'd naturally assumed that they were being taped. And bugged. Maybe Felzian had just given up on discretion. He accepted surveillance as a chronic disease—like smog, like asthma. "Not at all, sir! Senator Bambakias is deeply impressed by this facility. He strongly supports the federal research effort. He plans to make science policy a mainstay of his legislative agenda."

"Then I can't understand what you're up to." Felzian reached into a desk drawer and removed a sheaf of printout. "Look at these resignations. These are veteran scientists! Their morale has been crushed, they're leaving us."

"That would be Moulin, Lambert, Dulac, and Dayan?"

"They're four of my very best people!"

"Yes, I agree that they're very bright and determined. Unfortunately, they're also Dougal loyalists."

"So that's it. So they're very much in your way?"

"Yes, certainly. But you know, they're not suffering by this. They're moving out well ahead of the curve. They've all been snapped up by offers from private industry."

Felzian leafed delicately through his papers. "How on earth do you arrange things like this? You've scattered them all over the country. It's amazing."

"Thank you. It's a difficult project, but with modern techniques, it's doable. Let's just take Dr. Moulin, for instance. Her husband's from Vermont, and her son's in school there. Her specialty is endocrinology. So, we input the relevant parameters, and the optimal result was a small genetics firm in Nashua. The firm wasn't eager to take her on a placement-service cold-call, but I had the Senator's office call them, and talk about their domestic competition in Louisiana. The company was very willing to see reason then. And so was Dr. Moulin, once we queried her on those eccentricities in her lab's expense accounts."

"So you deliberately targeted her for elimination."

"It's *attrition*. It's distraction. It looks perfectly natural. Those four are influential people, they're local opinion leaders. They're smart enough to create real trouble for us —if they had a mind to try it. But since they are, in fact, *very* smart people, we don't have to beat them over the head with the obvious. We just point out the reality of their situation, and we offer them a golden parachute. Then they see sense. And they leave."

"This is truly monstrous. You're ripping the heart and soul out of my facility, and nobody will know— nobody will even see it."

"No, sir, it's not monstrous. It's very humane. It's good politics."

"I can understand that you have the ability to do this. I don't understand why you think you have the right."

"Dr. Felzian . . . it's not a question of rights. I'm a professional political operative. That's my job. Nobody ever elected people like me. We're not mentioned in the Constitution. We're not accountable to the public. But nobody can get elected without a campaign professional. I admit it: we're an odd class of people. I agree with you, it's very peculiar that we somehow have so much power. But I didn't invent that situation. It's a modern fact of life."

"I see."

"I'm doing what this situation requires, that's all. I'm a Federal Democrat from the Reform Party Bloc, and this place needs serious reform. This lab requires a new

broom. It's full of cobwebs, like, let me think . . . well,
like that casino yacht in Lake Charles that was purchased
out of the irrigation funds."

"I had nothing to do with that matter."

"I know you didn't, not personally. But you turned
a blind eye to it, because Senator Dougal went to Congress every session, and he brought you back your bacon. I
respect the effort that it takes to run this facility. But
Senator Dougal was chair of the Senate Science Committee for sixteen years. You never dared to cross him. You're
probably lucky you didn't—he'd have crushed you. But
the guy didn't steal just a little bit—he ended up stealing
truckloads, and the country just can't afford that anymore."

Felzian leaned back in his chair. Oscar could see that
he was beyond mere horror now—he was finding a peculiar gratification in all this. "Why are you telling me these
things?"

"Because I know you're a decent man, Mr. Director.
I know that this lab has been your life's work. You've been
involved in some contretemps, but they were meant to
protect your position, to protect this facility, under very
trying conditions. I respect the efforts you've undertaken.
I have no personal malice against you. But the fact of the
matter is that you're no longer politically expedient. The
time has come for you to do the decent thing."

"And what would that be, exactly?"

"Well, I have useful contacts in the University of
Texas system. Let's say, a post in the Galveston Health
Science Center. That's a nice town, Galveston—there's
not a lot left to the island since the seas have risen, but
they've rebuilt their famous Seawall and there's some
lovely old housing there. I could show you some very nice
brochures."

Felzian laughed. "You can't outplace every last one
of us."

"No, but I don't have to. I only have to remove key

opinion leaders, and the opposition will collapse. And if I can win *your* cooperation, we can get this all over with in short order. With dignity, maintaining all the proprieties. That's in the best interests of the science community."

Felzian crossed his arms triumphantly. "You're sweet-talking me like this because you don't really have anything on me."

"Why should I resort to threats? You're a reasonable man."

"You've got nothing! And I'm supposed to collaborate with you, resign my Directorship, and quietly fall on my sword? You've got a lot of nerve."

"But I'm telling you the truth."

"The only problem I see here is *you*. And your problem is that you can't do me any harm."

Oscar sighed. "Yes, I can, actually. I've read your lab reports."

"What are you talking about? I'm in administration! I haven't published a paper in ten years."

"Well, I've read your papers, Mr. Director. Of course, I'm not a trained geneticist, so, sad to say, I didn't understand them. But I did audit them. They all received full-scale, nitpicking scans from an oppositional research team. You published seventy-five papers in your scientific career, every one of them jam-packed with numerical tables. Your numbers add up beautifully. Too beautifully, because six of them have the same sets of data."

"What do you mean by that?"

"I mean that someone got lazy at the lab bench, and skipped the boring gruntwork."

Felzian turned red. "What? You can't prove that."

"Unfortunately for you, yes, I can prove it. Because it's all there in black and white. Back in your publish-or-perish days, you were in a big hurry, you had to cut some corners. And that's bad. It's very bad. For a scientist, it's professionally fatal. Once we out you as a scientific fraud, you won't have a friend left to your name. Your colleagues will break your sword and tear off your epaulets."

Felzian said nothing.

Oscar shrugged. "As I said before, I'm not a scientist. I don't take scientific fraud with the lethal seriousness that you scientists do. Personally, I don't see how your fraud did any great harm, since no one was paying attention to those papers anyway. You were just a fair-to-middling talent in a very competitive field, trying to pad out your résumé."

"I was completely unaware of this so-called problem. It must have been my grad students."

Oscar chuckled. "Look, we both know that can't get you off the hook. Sure, you can hide behind buck-passing when it comes to mere financial fraud. But this isn't mere money. These are your lab results, your contribution to science. You cooked the books. If I out you on that, we both know you're through. So why discuss this any further? Let's get to the real agenda."

"What is it you want from me?"

"I want you to resign, and I need your help in establishing the new Director."

"Greta Penninger."

"No," Oscar said at once, "we both know that's just not doable. Greta Penninger has been tactically useful to me, but I have another candidate that will be much more to your liking. In fact, he's an old colleague of yours— Professor John Feduccia, the former president of Boston University."

Felzian was astonished. "John Feduccia? How did he get onto the A-list?"

"Feduccia's the ideal candidate! He's very seasoned in administration, and he had an early career at the University of Texas, so that gives him the necessary local appeal. Plus, Feduccia is a personal friend of Senator Bambakias. Best of all, Feduccia is politically sound. He's a Federal Democrat."

Felzian stared at him in amazement. "Do you mean to tell me that you've been leading on poor Greta Penninger, while all this time you've been planning to bring in some Yankee who's a personal crony of your boss?"

Oscar frowned. "Look, don't be uncharitable. Of course I admire Greta Penninger. She was perfectly suited for the role that she's already played here. She's created a groundswell for change, but she can't possibly run this facility. She doesn't understand Washington. We need a responsible adult for that job, a seasoned hand from outside, someone who understands political reality. Feduccia's a pro. Greta's naive, she's too easily swayed. She'd be a disaster."

"Actually, I think she might do very well."

"No, she'll do much better where she belongs— back behind her lab bench. We can ease her off the board now, and back to her proper role as a working researcher, and everything will fall neatly into place."

"So that you can continue having an affair with her, and nobody will bother to notice it."

Oscar said nothing.

"Whereas, if she became Director, she'd be right in the public spotlight. So your sordid little dalliance becomes impossible."

Oscar stirred in his seat. "I really didn't expect this of you. This is truly beneath you. It's not the act of a gentleman and scholar."

"You didn't think I knew anything about that business, did you? Well, I'm not quite the helpless buffoon that you take me for! Penninger is the next Director. You and your scurvy krewe can sneak back to Washington. I'm leaving this office—no, not because you're forcing me out, but because I'm *sick to death of this job!*"

Felzian banged his desk. "It's *very* bad here now. Since we lost our support in the Senate, it's impossible. It's a farce now, it's untenable! I'm washing my hands of you, and Washington, and everything that you stand for. And keep one thing in mind, young man. With Penninger in office here, if you out me, I can out you. You might embarrass me—even humiliate me. But if you ever try it, I'll out you and the new Director. I'll break you both in public, like a pair of matchsticks."

The abrupt departure of Dr. Felzian gave Oscar a vital window of opportunity. With the loss of his patron Bambakias, he had very little to fall back on. He had to seize the initiative. Their numbers were small, their resources narrow, their budget nonexistent. The order of the day was sheer audacity.

During Greta's first day as Director, her followers formed a Strike Committee and physically occupied the Hot Zone. Strikers commandeered the airlocks overnight, overriding all the police-installed safety locks and replacing them with brand-new strikers' pass-cards. Seizing the Hot Zone made excellent strategic sense, since the giant ceramic tower dominated the facility. The Hot Zone was a natural fortress.

Given this physical safe haven, the second order of business in Oscar's internal coup was to attack and seize the means of information. The Hot Zone's computers received a long-postponed security overhaul. This revealed an appalling number of police back doors, unregistered users, and whole forests of snooping crackerware. These freeloaders were all swiftly purged.

The lab's internal phone system was still under the control of the Collaboratory police. The lab's tiny corps of police were something of a comic-opera outfit, but they had been suborned by Huey long ago. They represented the greatest local threat to Greta's fledgling administration.

The lab's phone system was riddled with taps, and beyond secure repair.

So, the strikers simply abandoned the phone system entirely, and replaced it with a homemade network of dirt-cheap nomad cellphones. These semi-licit gizmos ran off relay stakes, hammered into walls, ceilings, roofs, and (in a particularly daring midnight maneuver) all across the underside of the dome.

Greta's first official act as Director was to abolish the Public Relations department. She accomplished this through the lethally effective tactic of zeroing-out the PR budget. She then returned the funds to Congress. Given the ongoing federal budget crisis, this was a very difficult move to parry politically.

Within the lab itself, abolishing the PR department was a hugely popular decision. At long last, the tedious jabber of the obnoxious pop-science pep squad ceased to irritate the local populace. There was no more chummy propaganda from on high, no more elbow-grabbing official email, no more obligatory training videos, nothing but blissful quiet and time to think and work.

The Collaboratory's official PR was replaced by Oscar's revolutionary poster campaign. A Strike, of course, needed effective propaganda even more than did the dead Establishment, and Oscar was just the man to supply this. The giant cyclopean walls inside the dome were absolutely perfect for political poster work. Oscar had never run a campaign among people with such extremely high levels of literacy. He took real pleasure in the antique handicrafts involved.

Greta's postindustrial action was a highly unorthodox "strike," because the strikers were not refusing to do their work. They were refusing to do anything *except* their work. The general tenor of the Strike strategy was highly public noncooperation, combined with passive-aggressive cost-cutting.

The scientists were continuing their investigations,

but they were refusing to fill out the federal paperwork. They refused to ask for grants, refused to pay rent on their barracks rooms, refused to pay for their food, refused to pay their power bills. They were refusing everything except for new instrumentation, a deeply embedded vice that simply could not be denied to scientists.

All the Strike Committee's central members were also refusing their salaries. This was a deeply polarizing maneuver. Reasonable people simply couldn't bring themselves to hold their breath and leap into the unknown in this way. Most of the lab's "reasonable people" had long since made their peace with the Collaboratory's institutional corruption. Therefore, they were all on the take. It followed that they were personally compromised, at war with themselves, riddled with guilt. Greta's stalwart core of dissidents were made of sterner stuff.

So, through this swift and unpredictable seizure of the tactical initiative, the Strike won a series of heartening little moral victories. Oscar had arranged this situation deliberately, in order to build community self-confidence. The rent strike seemed very dramatic, but a rent strike was an unbeatable gambit. There was no internal competition for the rents in the Collaboratory. If the strikers were somehow thrown out of their lodgings, the buildings would simply stay empty.

The power strike succeeded in a very similar way, because there was no effective method to shut off the electricity for nonpayment. By its very nature as a sealed environment, the Collaboratory dome always required uninterrupted power, supplied by its own internal generators. There simply wasn't any way to shut it off. It had never occurred to the original designers that the dome's inhabitants might someday rebel and refuse to pay.

Each successful step away from the status quo won Greta more adherents. The long-oppressed scientists had always had many galling problems. But since they lacked a political awareness of their plight, they had never had any burning issues—they'd simply endured a bad scene. Now, organization and action had shattered their apathy. Aches and pains they'd long accepted as parts of the natural order were searingly revealed to them as oppression by evil know-nothings. A new power structure was aborning, with new methods, new goals, brave new opportunities for change. The Hot Zone had become a beehive of militant activism.

Within a week, the dome's internal atmosphere was charged like a Leyden jar; it crackled with political potential. Greta's unflinching radicalism had whipped the place into a frenzy.

Having built up a manic pressure for change, Greta took action to shore up her official legal situation. The Directorship had never been a strong executive post, but Greta engineered the forced resignations of all her fellow board members. The original board was, of course, deeply unwilling to leave power, but the sudden resignation and departure of Dr. Felzian had left them stunned. Outmaneuvered and discredited, they were soon replaced by Greta's zealous fellow-travelers, who trusted her implicitly and granted her a free hand.

The Collaboratory's party of the status quo had been decimated before they could organize any resistance. Years without serious challenge or controversy had made them fat and slow. They'd been crushed before they could even recognize the threat. Greta still held the initiative. She had excellent operational intelligence, thanks to Oscar's oppositional research and his plethora of demographic profiles. The forced confession of Dr. Skopelitis had also been very useful, since Skopelitis had spilled his guts in a torrent of email and fingered his fellow conspirators.

Behind these vibrant, stage-managed scenes of unleashed popular discontent, the transition of actual day-to-day power had gone remarkably smoothly. Felzian had always run the lab like a high school vice principal; the real power decisions in the Collaboratory had always rested in the distant hands of Dougal and his Senate krewe.

Now Dougal and his cronies were finished. However, the power vacuum was brief. Oscar's own krewe was a group of political operatives who could easily have become a Senate staff. With a little bending and jamming, they slotted very nicely into place, and quietly usurped the entire operation.

Oscar himself served as Greta's (very unofficial) chief of staff. Pelicanos oversaw lab finances. Bob Argow and Audrey Avizienis were handling constituency services and counterintelligence. Lana Ramachandran dealt with scheduling, office equipment, and press relations. "Corky" Shoeki, formerly in charge of the Bambakias campaign's road camps and rallies, was handling the scramble for office space inside the Hot Zone. Kevin Hamilton was doing bravura work on security.

Greta was acting as her own press spokeswoman. That would have to change eventually, but it made excellent sense during the Strike crisis. Greta became the only official source of Strike news, and her solo public role made her seem to be handling matters all by herself. This gave her heroic charisma.

In point of fact, Greta and her zealous idealists had no real idea how to run a modern executive staff. They'd never held power before, so they were anxious to have glamorous jobs with titles and prestige, rather than the gruntwork jobs by which the acts of government were actually accomplished. This charade suited Oscar perfectly. He knew now that if he could simply keep the lab alive, solvent, and out of Huey's hands, he would have accomplished the greatest feat of his career.

So Oscar took a deeply shadowed backseat, well behind the throne. The new year ground on. Many scientists found the Strike to be an ideal opportunity to quietly resign and leave, but that left the remaining hard-core scientists saturated with revolutionary fervor. Like revolutionaries everywhere, they were discovering that every tri-fling matter was a moral and intellectual crisis. Every aspect of their former lives and careers seemed to require a radical reformulation. These formerly downtrodden wretches spent most of their free hours raising one another's consciousnesses.

And it all suited Oscar very well. His political instincts had never been sharper and his krewe, frenetic neurotics to the last man and woman, always shone in a crisis.

At this particular moment—January 8, 2045—Greta and her kitchen cabinet were engaged in particularly intense debate. The scientists were anxiously weighing new candidates for the board: Information Genetics and Biomedicine. Oscar, accompanied by his ever-present bodyguard Kevin, lurked behind a tower of instrumental clutter. He planned to let them talk until they got very tired. Then he would ask a few pointed Socratic questions. After that, they would accept a solution that he had decided a week ago.

While Kevin munched a set of color-coded protein sticks, Oscar was enjoying a catered lunch. Since Oscar's krewe had taken over the Collaboratory, they'd been forced to hire a new Texan krewe to run their hotel. Given the tepid economy in Buna, finding new staff hadn't been difficult.

Kevin stopped tinkering with the microchipped innards of a phone, zipped its case shut, and passed the phone to Oscar. Oscar was soon chatting in blissful security to Leon Sosik in Washington.

"I need Russian Constructivist wall posters," he told Sosik. "Have Alcott's Boston krewe hit the art museums for me. I need everything they can get from the early Communist Period."

"Oscar, I'm glad that you're having fun at the lab, but forget the big glass snow globe. We need you here in

DC, right away. Our anti-Huey campaign just crashed and burned."

"What? Why? I don't need to go to Washington to feud with Huey. I've got Huey on the ropes right here. We've fingered all his cronies in the lab. I've got people here who are literally picketing them. Give me another week, and we'll purge all the local cops, too. Once those clowns are out of the picture, I can get to some serious work around here."

"Oscar, try to stick to the point. That lab is just a local sideshow. We have a national-security crisis here. Huey has a radar hole."

"What is that supposed to mean?"

"It means the North American radar coverage. The Air Force military radar. Part of the Southern U.S. radar boundary was run out of that Louisiana air base. Now that radar's gone, and there's a missing overlap between Texas and Georgia. The bayous have gone black. They've dropped right out of military surveillance."

Oscar put his fork down. "What the hell does that have to do with anything? I can't believe that. How is that even possible? No *radar*? A ten-year-old child can do radar!" He took a breath. "Look, surely they've still got air traffic control radar. New Orleans wouldn't last two days without air traffic. Can't the Air Force use the civilian radar?"

"You'd think so, but it just doesn't work that way. They tell me it's a programming problem. Civilian radar runs off a thousand decentralized cells. It's *distributed* radar, on packet networks. That doesn't work for the Air Force. The military has a hierarchical system architecture."

Oscar thought quickly. "Why is that a political problem? That's a technical issue. Let the Air Force handle that."

"They *can't* handle it. Because those are old federal missile-detection systems, they date back to Cold War One! They're mil-spec hardware running antique code.

That system just isn't flexible—we're lucky it still runs at all! But the point is, there's no federal radar coverage in Louisiana. And that means that enemy aircraft can invade the United States! Anywhere from Baton Rouge south!"

"Oh, for heaven's sake, Leon. It can't possibly be that bad," Oscar said. "How could the military miss a problem that size? There must be contingency plans. Who the hell was keeping track of all that?"

"No one seems to know," Sosik said mournfully. "When the Emergency committees took over the base closures, the radar issue got lost in competing jurisdictions."

Oscar grunted. "Typical."

"It *is* typical. It's totally typical. There's just too much going on. There's no clear line of authority. Huge, vital issues just fall through the cracks. We can't get anywhere at all."

Oscar was alarmed to hear Sosik sound so despondent. Clearly Sosik had been spending rather too much time at the Senator's bedside. Bambakias became ever more fluent and compelling as his grip on reality faded. "All right, Leon. I agree with that diagnosis, I concede your point. I am with you all the way there. But let's face it—nobody's going to invade the United States. Nobody invades national boundaries anymore. So what if some idiot Emergency committee misplaced some ancient radar? Let's just ignore the problem."

"We *can't* ignore it. Huey won't let us. He's making real hay out of the issue. He says this proves that his Louisiana air base was vital to national security all along. The Louisiana delegation is kicking our ass in Congress. They're demanding that we build them a whole new air base from the ground up, immediately. But that'll cost us billions, and we just don't have the funds. And even if we can swing the funding, we can't possibly launch a major federal building program inside Louisiana."

"Obviously not," Oscar said. "Roadblocks,

NIMBY suits, eminent-domain hassles . . . that's tailor-made for Huey. Once he's got federal contractors stuck knee-deep in the swamp, he could rip off a leg and bleed the whole budget to death."

"Exactly. So we're stuck. We were trashing Huey big-time on the patriotism charge, but he's turned the tables on us. He's wrapping himself in the very same flag that we stitched for him. We've played right into his hands. And we *can't* ignore his radar hole, because he's already exploiting it. Last night, French unmanned aircraft started buzzing South Louisiana. They're flying over the swamps, playing French pop music."

"French *pop music*?"

"Multichannel broadcasts off unmanned aerial drones. It's the Cajun Francophone card."

"Come on. Even Huey can't seriously believe that anybody listens to French pop music."

"The *French* believe it. They can smell Yankee blood in the water. It's your basic culture-war gambit. The French have always loved French-language confrontations. Now they can turn up their amps till we pull every burger joint out of Paris."

"Leon, calm down. You're a professional. You can't let him get you rattled like this."

"He *does* have me rattled, damn it. The son of a bitch just doesn't play by the rules! He does two contradictory things at once, and he screws us coming and going. It's like he's got two brains!"

"Get a grip," Oscar said. "It's a minor provocation. What are we supposed to do about this so-called problem? Declare war on France?"

"Well . . ." Sosik said. He lowered his voice. "I know this sounds strange. But listen. A declaration of war would dissolve the Emergency committees by immediate fiat."

"What!" Oscar shouted. "Are you *crazy*? We can't

invade France! France is a major industrial democracy! What are we, *Nazis*? That's totally out of the question!"

Oscar looked up. He confronted a looming crowd of astonished scientists. They'd left their own discussion and had gathered on the far side of the lab bench, where they were straining to overhear him.

"Listen, Oscar," Sosik continued tinnily, "nobody's suggesting that we actually *fight* a war. But the concept is getting a pretty good float in DC. A *declaration* of war is a manual override of the federal system. As a domestic maneuver, a foreign war could be a real trump card. France is much too much, I agree with that—hell, the French still have nuclear power! But we could declare war on *Holland*. Holland's a tiny, unarmed country, a bunch of radical pipsqueaks. So we throw a proper scare into the Dutch, the phony war lasts a week or so, and then the President declares victory. The Emergency is over. Then, once the dust settles, we have a fully functional Congress again."

Oscar removed the phone from his ear, stared at it with distaste, and replaced it at his ear. "Look, I gotta get back to you later, Leon. I have some serious work to accomplish here."

"The Senator's very big on this idea, Oscar. He really thinks it could fly. It's visionary."

Oscar hung up. "They're playing French pop music in Louisiana," he told his impromptu audience.

Albert Gazzaniga scratched his head. "Big deal! So what?"

The crux of the matter was, of course, the money. It had always been the money. Money was the mother's milk of politics. And although scientific politics were several steps removed from conventional politics, money was the milk of science, too.

All strikes were, at the bottom line, struggles over economic power. All strikers made a bold declaration that they were willing to outstarve their employers, and if they backed it up with enough bad press and moral pressure, they were sometimes right.

So it was lovely to declare that Greta and her cadre were ready and eager to do science for nothing, asking for nothing, and refusing to supply anything but the results they themselves found of scientific interest. It was a holy crusade. But even a holy crusade needed a revenue stream.

So Oscar, Yosh, and the omnipresent Kevin found an empty corner in the hotel kitchen to discuss finances.

"We could hit up Bambakias for a couple of million, just to tide us over," Pelicanos said. "There's no question he's got the funds."

"Forget it," Oscar said. "The Senate's a billionaire's club, but if they start running the country right out of their own pockets, that's feudalism. Feudalism is not professional."

Pelicanos nodded. "Okay. Then we'll have to raise funds ourselves. How about the standard campaign methods? Direct mail. Rubber-chicken banquets. Raffles, garage sales, charity events. Who are the core prospects here?"

"Well, if this were a normal campaign . . ." Oscar rubbed his chin thoughtfully. "We'd hit up the alumni of her alma mater, Jewish temple groups, scientific professional societies. . . . And of course the Collaboratory's business suppliers. They're plenty mad at us right now, but they'll fall out of the trough completely, if the place ever closes down. We might be able to sweet-talk them into fronting us some cash, if we threaten them with total destruction."

"Are there any rich, overclass scientists? There have got to be *some* rich scientists, right?"

"Sure there are—in Asia and Europe."

"You guys sure don't think very big," Kevin chided.

Oscar gazed at him tolerantly. He was growing rather fond of Kevin. Kevin really worked hard; he'd be-

come the heart and soul of the foulest part of the coup.
"How big are we supposed to think, Kevin?"

"You guys don't realize what you have here. You've
got a perfect nomad rally-ground inside that lab. It's like
you've roadblocked the place; you can do anything you
want with it. Why don't you ask all the scientists in America to come down here and join you?"

Oscar sighed. "Kevin, bear with us. You've got the
problem exactly backward. The point is, we're trying to
feed and supply two thousand people, even though they're
on strike. If we get a million of them, we're sunk."

"No you're not," Kevin said. "If a million scientists
showed up here and joined you, that wouldn't be just a
strike anymore. It would be a revolution. You wouldn't
just take over this one federal lab. You could take over the
whole town. Probably the whole county. Maybe a big part
of the state."

Pelicanos laughed. "How are we supposed to manage a giant horde of freeloading scientists?"

"You'd use nomads, man. Who else knows how to
run a giant horde of people with no money? You throw
open your airlocks, and you promise them shelter in there.
You give 'em propaganda tours, you show 'em all the
pretty plants and animals. You get the cops and the feds off
their backs for once, and you give them a big role to play
in your own operation. The proles would become a giant
support krewe for your egghead contingent. See, it's people power, street power. It's an occupying army, just like
Huey likes to use."

Oscar laughed. "They'd tear this place apart!"

"Sure, they *could* do that—but what if they decided
not to? Maybe they'd decide that they liked the place.
Maybe they'd look after it. Maybe they'd build it even
bigger."

Oscar hesitated. The construction angle hadn't occurred to him. He'd always done extremely well by the
construction angle. The construction angle was the best

political wild card he'd ever had. Most politicians couldn't create luxury hotels out of software and sweat equity, but those who could had an off-the-wall advantage. He was sitting inside the construction angle at this very moment, and it was working out just fine. "How *much* bigger?"

"How big would we need it?" Pelicanos said.

"Well, how many nomad proles would be joining our construction krewe?"

"You want me to load a spreadsheet?" Kevin said.

"Forget it, it's too good to be true," Pelicanos said. "Sure, maybe we could get distributed instantiation to scale-up. But we'd never be able to trust nomads. They're all in Huey's pockets."

Kevin snorted. "The Regulators are in Huey's pockets, but good Lord, fellas, Louisiana proles are not the only proles around. You guys have spent too much time in Boston. Wyoming was *on fire,* man! There are proles and dissidents all over the USA. There's *millions* of proles."

With a stern effort of will, Oscar forced himself to consider Kevin's proposal seriously. "An army of unemployed nomads, constructing giant, intelligent domes. . . . You know, that's really a compelling image. I really hate to dismiss that idea out of hand. It's so modern and photogenic and nonlinear. There's a lovely carrying-the-war-to-the-enemy momentum there."

Pelicanos narrowed his eyes. "Kevin, who's the heaviest prole mob you know?"

"Well, the Regulators are the heaviest. They have state support from Huey, and they just smashed a federal air base. So they've got to be the strongest mob around—everybody knows that by now. But, well, there's the Moderators. The Moderators are big. Plus, they hate the Regulators' guts."

"Why is that?" Oscar said, leaning forward with galvanized interest.

Kevin shrugged. "Why do mobs always hate other mobs? Somebody stole somebody's girlfriend, somebody hacked somebody's phones. They're mobs. So they have no laws. So they have to feud with each other. It's tribal. Tribes always act like that."

Pelicanos scratched his jaw. "You know, Oscar, there's no question that the Collaboratory is a much more attractive facility than some run-down federal air base."

"You're absolutely right, Yosh. That dome has real charisma. There's a definite demand-pull there."

There was a long, thoughtful silence.

"Time for a coffee," Oscar announced, rising and fetching some. "Let's run a reality check, guys. Forget all this blue-sky stuff—what's the agenda? Our agenda here is to gently embarrass the powers that be, and get them to cut some operational slack for federal researchers. At the end of the day, Congress will fund this place at about half last year's fiscal levels. But in return, we'll get more direct power into the hands of the lab people. So we'll create a workable deal. We'll keep the lab in business, but without all the pork and the graft. That's a perfectly decent accomplishment. It's something we could all be very proud of."

He sipped his coffee. "But if we let this situation spin out of control like Kevin is suggesting . . . Well, I actually suspect that it's possible. What Huey did to the Air Force, that proves that it's possible. But it's not *doable,* because there's *no brakes.* There are no brakes, because I can't control the course of events. I don't have the authority. I'm just a Senate staffer!"

"That's never stopped you so far," Kevin pointed out.

"Well, I admit that, Kevin, but . . . Well, I don't like your idea because it's bad ideology. I'm a Federal Democrat. We're a serious-minded Reform party. We're not a revolutionary vanguard, we can leave all that to self-marginalizing, violent morons. I'm operating under a lot of legal and ethical constraints here. I can't have huge mobs commandeering federal facilities."

Kevin sniffed. "Well, Huey did it."

"Huey's a Governor! Huey has a legislative branch and a judiciary. Huey was *elected by the people,* he won his last race with seventy-two percent of a ninety-percent voter turnout! I can't paralyze the country with insane stunts like that, I just don't have the power! I'm not a magician! I'm just a freshman Senate staffer. I don't get my own way just because things are theoretically possible. Hell, I can't even sleep with my own girlfriend."

Kevin looked at Pelicanos. "Yosh, can't you arrange it so this poor bastard can sleep with his girlfriend? *She'd* understand this situation. He's getting all mentally cramped now. He's losing his edge."

"Well, *that's* doable," Pelicanos said. "You could re-sign from the Senate Science Committee, and take over here as Greta's official chief of staff. I don't think anyone would mind Greta sleeping with one of her staffers. I mean, technically it's workplace sex harassment, but gee whiz."

Oscar frowned darkly. "I am *not* leaving the Senate Science Committee! You people have no understanding of what I have been through all this time, massaging those creeps backstage in Washington. It is incredibly hard doing that over a network; if you're not in the office doing face-time with the Hill rats, they always write you off and screw you. I've been wiring flowers to their goddamn sysadmin for three weeks. When I get back to Washington, I'll probably have to date her."

"Okay, then we're back to square one," Pelicanos said gloomily. "We still don't know what we're doing, and we still don't have any money."

Oscar was up at three in the morning, examining sched-ules of upcoming Senate hearings, when there was a tap at his door. He glanced over at Kevin, who was snoring peacefully in his hotel bunk. Oscar fetched his plastic spraygun, checked the squirt chamber to see that it was loaded, and sidled to the door. "Who is it?" he whispered.

"It's me." It was Greta.

Oscar opened the door. "Come in. What are you doing here? Are you crazy?"

"Yes."

Oscar sighed. "Did you check to see if your clothes are bugged? Did you watch to see if anyone was tailing you? Would you not wake up my bodyguard please? Give me a kiss."

They embraced. "I know I'm being terrible," she whispered. "But I'm still awake. I wore the rest of them out. I had one little moment to myself. And I thought, I know what I want. I want to be with Oscar."

"It's impossible," he told her, slipping his hand under her shirt. "This is risking everything, it's really foolish."

"I know we can't meet anymore," she said, leaning against the wall and closing her eyes in bliss. "They watch me every second."

"My bodyguard's right in this room with us. And he's totally trigger-happy."

"I only came here to talk," she said, pulling his shirt out of his trousers.

He led her into the bathroom, shut the door, flicked on the lights. Her lipstick was smeared and her pupils were like two saucers.

"Just to talk," she repeated. She set her purse on the sink. "I brought you something nice."

Oscar locked the bathroom door. Then he turned on the shower, for the sake of the cover noise.

"A little gift," she said. "Because we don't get to be together anymore. And I can't stand it."

"I'm going to take a cold shower," he announced, "just in case Kevin gets suspicious. We can talk, but talk quietly." He began unbuttoning his shirt.

Greta dug into her purse and removed a wrapped

and ribboned box. She set the box on the bathroom counter, then turned and looked at him thoughtfully. Oscar dropped his shirt on the cold tiles.

"Hurry up," she suggested, stepping out of her underwear.

They threw a pair of towels on the floor, and slid onto them together. He got his elbows into the backs of her knees, bent her double, and went at it like a madman. It was a forty-second mutual frenzy that ended like an oncoming train.

When he'd caught his breath, he managed a weak smile. "We'll just pretend that incident never happened. All right?"

"All right," she said, and levered herself up with trembling arms. "I sure feel better though." She climbed to her feet, pulling her skirt down. Then she fetched the box, and offered it. "Here, this is for you. Happy birthday."

"I don't have birthdays," he said.

"Yes, I know that. So I made a birthday present, just for you."

He found his pants, stepped back into them, and picked up her gift. To his vague alarm, the little ribboned box felt hot to the touch. He stripped off the gaudy paper and the plywood lid. The box was tightly packed with a gray bag of chemical heating element, surrounding a small curved device. He plucked the gift from its wedge of hot packing.

"It's a wristwatch," he said.

"Try it on!" she said with an eager smile.

He removed his classic Japanese chronometer and strapped on Greta's watch. The watch was hot and clammy, the color of boiled okra. He examined the greenish glowing numerals in the face. The watch was six minutes slow. "This thing looks like it's made out of jelly."

"It *is* made of jelly! It's a neural watch!" she told

him. "It's the only one in the world! We made it in the lab."

"Amazing."

"You bet it is! Listen. Every mammal brain has a built-in circadian clock. In the mousebrain, it's in the suprachiastic nucleus. So we cloned a chunk of suprachiastic tissue, and embedded it in support gel. Those numerals are enzyme-sensitive cells that express firefly genes! And, Oscar, we gave it three separate neural clumps inside, with a smart neural net that automatically averages out cumulative error. So even though that's a totally organic watch, it supplies accurate time! As long as it stays right at blood temperature, that is."

"Tremendous."

"Oh, and you do have to feed it. That little packet there is bovine serum. You just boil up a couple of cc's once a week, and inject it through that little duct." She paused. "Rat brains do leak some waste product, but just a drop or two."

Oscar twisted his wrist and examined the translucent strap. They'd made the tooth and buckle out of some kind of mouse bone. "This is quite a technical feat, isn't it?"

"And you can't let it get cold, or it dies. But listen: if you want to reset it, you just flip up that patch in the back and expose it to sunlight. We put retinal cells there. When retinal cells see sunlight, they release glutamate. Which binds to receptors. Which produce nitric oxide. Which activates enzymes. Which add phosphate to a nuclear protein. The protein sends a genetic message, and the genes reset the neurons in the clock!"

"So, is there, uh, documentation with this product?"

She hesitated. "Well, never mind all that. You're just a layman. You don't really have to understand how a watch works."

Oscar looked at the eerie device. It was clinging to his wrist like raw liver. "It's a homemade birthday watch," he said. "In the middle of all this trouble, you've gone and made me a watch. With your own hands."

"I'm so glad you're pleased with it."

" 'Pleased'? This is the finest birthday gift I've ever had."

Her eyebrows twitched just a bit. "You don't think it's creepy, do you?"

"Creepy? Heavens no! It's just a step or two beyond the current cutting edge, that's all. I could foresee big consumer demand for an item like this."

She laughed delightedly. "Ha! Exactly. That's just what I told my lab krewe, when we were putting it together. We've finally come up with a mass consumer product that has real market demand!"

Oscar was touched. "They've been harassing you for years about your 'pure science,' haven't they. As if they had the right to control your imagination, just because they pay your bills. Well, I'll tell you a secret, Greta. There's no such thing as 'pure science.' 'Pure science' is an evil lie, it's a killer fraud, like 'pure justice' or 'pure liberty.' Desire is never pure, and the desire for knowledge is just another kind of desire. There's never been a branch of knowledge so pure and abstract that it can't get down and dirty. If the human mind can comprehend it, then the human mind can desire it."

She sighed. "I never know what to make of you when you start talking like that. . . . I wish I could tell you everything I've been thinking lately."

"Try me."

"It's that . . . you want something, but you know it's bad for you. So you deny it, and want it, and deny it, and want it—but it's just too seductive. So you give in, and then it just happens. But when it happens, it's not as bad as you thought. It's not half bad. In fact, it's good. It's really good. It's wonderful. It makes you better. You're a better human being. You're stronger. You understand yourself. You're in touch with yourself. You're not in denial. You're not remote and pure. You're alive and you're part of the real world. You know what you want."

Oscar felt a soaring sense of absolute masculine triumph. It lasted three seconds, crested, and left him tingling with premonitory dread.

"A love affair isn't always peaches and cream," he said.

She stared at him in utter astonishment. "Oscar, sweetie, I'm not talking about the sex. That's all very nice, and I'm happy about it, but you and I could have all the sex in the world, and it wouldn't change a thing. I mean that you gave me a real and lasting gift, Oscar, because you put me in power. And now, I really know what power means. For the first time in my life, I can speak to people. When they're all there in front of me, a big crowd of my own people, I can tell them the truth. I can persuade them. I can lead them. I've become their leader. I've found my own voice. I have real power. I think I *always* wanted power, but I always resisted it, because I thought it was bad for me—but it isn't! Now I know what power is, and my God, it's really good. It's changing me completely. I just want more and more."

To end her second week as Director, Greta fired the entire Materials Processing department. This freed up a great deal of valuable lab space in the Materials Lab, which was situated on the eastern wall of the dome next to the Plant Engineering Complex. The long-impoverished botanists were overjoyed at their floor-space bonanza. Shutting down the gluttonous Materials Lab was also a financial boon for the lab itself.

It was also a considerable boon for Oscar's hotel. His hotel was now crowded with laboratory equipment scavengers, fly-by-night middlemen who'd flocked into Buna as soon as the news of a hardware sale hit their net.

Most of the materials scientists sullenly recognized

the fait accompli. But not Dr. David Chander. Chander had been an early and zealous striker, and he was also a quick study. To resist his own firing, he had taken his tactical cues from the Strike Committee. He had super-glued his equipment to the lab benches and barricaded himself inside the research facility. There he sat, in occu-pation, categorically refusing to leave.

Kevin was in favor of bringing in a hydraulic ram and blasting Chander out. The Collaboratory's federal po-lice were far too confused and sullen to do any such thing themselves. Kevin would have been delighted to play the role of strong-arm vigilante, but Oscar considered this a bad precedent for the lab's new regime. He couldn't countenance violent confrontations; they were unprofes-sional, not his style.

Instead, he decided to talk the man down.

Oscar and Kevin went up to Chander's third-floor lab, and Oscar announced himself. He waited patiently as Chander unjammed his lab doors. Then Oscar slipped in, leaving a disgruntled Kevin lurking in the hall.

Chander immediately began barricading the doors again. "Let me give you a hand with that," Oscar volun-teered. He helped Chander wedge a dismantled chair leg against a superglued door chock.

Unlike the majority of Collaboratory locals, Chander, as an industrial researcher, wore a business suit and a tie, with a serious hat. His dusky face was ashen and his eyes were puffy with stress. "I was wondering if she'd have the nerve to meet with me herself," he said, biting his plump lower lip. "I can't say I'm surprised to see *you* show up."

Oscar opened his plastic carry-case. "I brought some supplies for your sit-in," he said. "A little frozen gumbo, some tasty rice. . . ."

"You know that I'm on a hunger strike, don't you?"

"I hadn't heard that," Oscar lied.

"Get 'em to turn on my lab phones again, and you'll hear plenty about all of my problems."

"But that's why I came here personally," Oscar said cheerily. "To hear you out, man to man."

"I'm not going to put up with this," Chander announced. "She's destroying my life's work, it's completely unfair. I can wait just as long as the rest of you can. I can do anything that you can do. I've got my own friends and supporters, I've got industrial backers from out of state. I'm an honest man—but *you* don't have a leg to stand on. Once word gets out about all the stunts you've pulled around here, you'll all be indicted."

"But I'm from the Senate Science Committee," Oscar said. "Of course the Senate will take an interest in your plight. Let's have a seat, and you can fill me in on the issues."

He sat cautiously in a partially wrecked lab chair and produced a paper notebook and a classic fountain pen.

Chander dragged up a plastic lab crate and sat with a groan. "Look, Congress won't help me. Congress is hopeless, they never understand the technical issues. The point is . . . I have a *breakthrough* here. I'm not just *promising* a breakthrough. This isn't just some empty last-minute gambit to get me off the hook. I have a major technical innovation here! I've had it for two years!"

Oscar examined his notes. "Dr. Chander . . . as you know, there's been a general productivity audit here at the Collaboratory. Every department has gone through the same assessments: Genetic Fragmentation, Flux NMR . . . your department has been through five reorganizations in four years. Your production record is, frankly, abysmal."

"I'm not denying that," Chander said. "But it was sabotage."

"That's a remarkable claim."

"Look. It's a long, dismal story but . . . look, basic science and corporate sponsorship have *never* worked out.

My problems aren't scientific at all, they're all in management. Our agenda here is organic materials processing, we're looking for new biologically based solutions to traditional engineering problems. There's a lot of room to work there. Our problem was our corporate sponsorship in Detroit."

Chander sighed. "I don't know why the automobile industry got involved in sponsoring our work. That wasn't my decision. But ever since they first showed up, five years ago, they've wrecked everything we do. They keep demanding results from us, then shortening our schedules and changing our deliverables. They micromanage everything. They send in brain-damaged car executives on sabbaticals, who show up, and steal rare animals, and run goofy futurist scenarios, and talk nonsense to us. We've been through absolute hell here: reengineering, outplacement, management by objective, total customer service, you name it! Every kind of harassment imaginable."

"But industry supplied your funding. Those were your corporate sponsors. You couldn't win complete federal funding for your proposals. If you can't make your own sponsors happy, then why are you here?"

"Why am I here?" Chander said. "It's simple! It's a very simple, straightforward thing! I'm here because of power."

"You don't say."

"Electromotive power! My krewe and I were researching new power sources for the American transportation industry. And we've created a new working model. It's mitochondrial ATP power generation. With signal transduction, protein phosphorylation, membrane diffusion potentials. . . . Look, do you even know what a 'mitochondrion' is?"

"I've heard that term, I think."

"The mitochondrion is the power plant in the cell. It generates energy from adenosine triphosphate, it's the basic reason we can live and breathe. Mitochondria are microscopic. But imagine they were"——Chander spread his hands violently—"a meter across."

"So you've cloned a piece of a living cell and made it a meter across?"

"I was never any good at explaining science to the layman. . . . No, of course it's not a meter across. It's not a mitochondrion at all. It's a biomechanical device that uses the membranes and the structure of a mitochondrion. They've all been scaled up, industrially. It's a giant waffle of membranes and gelatin matrix. It's not a living thing, it's biological hardware, engineered and turned into an electrochemical battery. You could drive a car with it. You could drive a truck! And it runs on sugar."

"So you've created an automobile engine that runs on sugar."

"Now you're getting it! That's it! Sugar, water, and a few trace elements. Totally organic and totally recyclable. No combustion, no emissions, and no toxins! And it runs at room temperature."

"So this is another new automobile power plant. Sure, fine. There are plenty of those on the market already —flywheels, steam, liquid nitrogen. How is the acceleration?"

Chander punched the air. "It's like that! It's like punching my fist! Mitochondria did that! It's the technology that powers muscle! It's fast, it's clean! It really works!"

"What's the catch?"

"There isn't one! It works fine! Well, it'll work better when we get the prototype bugs worked out . . . there's some problems with osmotic pressure, and even flow-through . . . oh, and if the battery gets infected, then it rots pretty quickly. But those are just shakedown problems. The real problem is that Detroit doesn't want our product. They won't put it into production."

"So you've achieved a great success," Oscar said. "Then explain something to me. Your lab's had more private funding than any other Materials facility, but you've never shipped a product. You're the Principal Investigator here, but you've had more krewe turnover than any other lab. . . ."

"They were all *spies*!" Chander said. "They were spies and saboteurs! I didn't have any choice but to fire them."

"I've noticed that the rest of your krewe hasn't joined your personal industrial action here."

"Their morale's been destroyed. They know we've been targeted for removal. They know all their hard work will come to nothing. They're just hoping that someday the memories will fade." Chander's shoulders slumped.

"This is a remarkable story. I'll have to check this story out with your industrial liaison."

"Sure. Go ahead. His name is Ron Griego, he's a project manager for corporate R&D up in Detroit."

Oscar blinked. "Would that be Ronald K. Griego?"

"You actually *know* Ron Griego?"

"I think I do," Oscar said, frowning. "In fact, I suspect we can see this matter properly expedited in short order."

———————————

After leaving Dr. Chander, mollified at least to the point of eating, Oscar and Kevin sought shelter in the lush foliage north of the Genetic Fragmentation unit. Oscar then called Griego's krewe secretary in Detroit.

"Forgive me for cold-calling you, ma'am, but I think Mr. Griego will want to talk to me. Would you please tell Ron that it's Oscar Valparaiso, class of '37, and that it's an urgent federal matter?"

Griego was on the phone within five minutes. He and Oscar traded wary pleasantries.

"Went into the family car business after all, eh, Ron?"

"That's why Dad sent me to Harvard," Griego said. "What's with this awful phone connection?"

"Encryption and rerouting. Sorry. Look, it's about the Buna National Collaboratory."

"I hear you're shutting the place down," Griego said cheerfully. "There's a big workers' strike going on there. Well, of course that's a blow to our futuristic research effort, but I don't want you to worry. We understand labor troubles, here in the auto business. If we can lobby Congress to let us keep this fiscal year's R&D deductions, we think we can survive the loss of our Buna lab."

"Sorry, but it won't be quite that easy, Ron."

"But I'm *making* it easy for you," Griego said, wounded. "Shut the place down, fire 'em all. Zero it out, lock the doors, it's over, they're history. What could be easier than that?"

"Oh, that's easy enough for *me*—I meant to say that it wouldn't be easy for *you*."

"I might have known," Griego groaned. "Why can't it ever be easy with you, Valparaiso? What have you got against the rest of us? What is your problem?"

"Just fitting a few loose ends together. Believe me, Ron, I can sympathize. It must have been a nightmare for you—netwarring some krewe of lunatics who built a magic sugar battery."

"Oh, Christ."

"Look, Ron, relax. Remember that time I hid those two hookers from the campus police? I never outed you on anything, and I'm not planning to out you now. Just level with me. That's all that I ever ask."

There was a long uneasy silence. Then Griego burst out in a fury. "Don't get all high-and-mighty with me, Mr. Third-in-His-Class. You think it's easy running corporate R&D? It was just fine, as long as the guy didn't have anything. Jesus, nobody ever thought a goddamn sugar engine would *work*. The goddamn thing is a giant germ in a box! We build cars up here, we don't build giant germs! Then they pull this crazy stunt and . . . well, it just makes our life impossible! We're a classic, metal-bending industry! We have interlocking directorates all throughout the structure, raw materials, fuel, spare parts, the dealerships. . . . We can't get into the face of our fuel suppliers, telling them that we're replacing them with sugar water! We *own* our fuel suppliers! It'd be like sawing off our own foot!"

"I understand about interlocking directorates and mutual stock ownership, Ron. I was sitting right next to you in business school, remember? Cut to the chase—what about the battery?"

"Batteries have the highest profit margin of any automobile component. We were making money there. You can't make real money anywhere else in our business. The Koreans are building auto bodies out of *straw and paper*! We can't support an industry when cars are cheaper than grocery carts! What are we gonna tell our unions? This is a great American tradition at stake here! The car *defines* America: the assembly line, suburbs, drive-ins, hot rods, teenage sex, everything that makes America great! We can't turn ourselves inside out because some big-brained creep has built an engine out of bug guts! There wouldn't be anything left of us! The guy is a menace to society! He had to be stopped."

"Thank you for that, Ron. Now we're getting somewhere. So tell me this—why didn't you just pull his damn funding?"

"If only it were that simple! We're required by federal fiat to invest in basic R&D. It was part of our federal bailout deal. We're supposed to have trade protection, and we're supposed to catch our breath, and jump a generation ahead of our foreign competitors. But if we jump a generation ahead of the damn Koreans, our industry will vanish entirely. People will make cars the way they make pop-up toast. Proles will build cars out of bio-scrap, and compost them in the backyard. We'll all be doomed."

"So you're telling me that you've achieved a tremendous scientific R&D success, but as a collateral effect, it will eliminate your industry."

"Yeah. That's it. Exactly. And I'm sorry, but we just can't face that. We have stockholders to worry about, we have a labor force. We don't want to end up like the computer people did. Jesus, there's no sense to that. It's total madness, it's demented. We'd be cutting our own throats."

"Ron, take it easy, okay? I'm with you here, I'm following your argument. Thanks for leveling with me. I comprehend your situation now. It fits into the big picture."

Oscar drew a breath. "You see, Ron, the true core issue here is the basic interplay of commerce and science. I've been giving a lot of thought to this problem recently, and now I realize that the old-style big-science game is just no longer tenable. Only savages and Congressmen could believe that science is a natural friend of commerce. Science has never been the friend of commerce. The truth doesn't have any friends. Sometimes the interests of science and commerce can coincide for a little while, but that's not a marriage. It's a dangerous liaison. If you're a working businessman, R&D can turn on you with sudden, vicious speed."

"You got that right," Griego said fervently.

"Ron, it saddens me to see you jerked around in this way. If you don't want to finance R&D, that ought to be a decision properly left to the industry. You shouldn't be compelled to take action by distant, uncaring federal bureaucrats who don't understand the real dynamics of private enterprise. And most of all, you certainly shouldn't have to waste your time, and mine, running sabotage mind games against a federal laboratory. That's just a big, counterproductive distraction that puts you and me at unnecessary loggerheads. We're serious players, Ron. People like us ought to be talking this over as mature individuals and arriving at a modus vivendi."

Griego sighed into the phone. "Okay, Oscar. You can stop sweet-talking me now. What are you planning to do to me?"

"Well, I could out this whole ugly thing. Then we'd have investigations, and Senate hearings, and possible indictments, and the whole tiresome, unfortunate business. But suppose that never happened. Suppose that I could personally guarantee you that this guy's miracle battery drops right off the edge of the earth. And all that costs you is a mere fifty percent of your current R&D investment."

"I'd say that's much too good to be true."

"No, Ron. It's the new order, here at the Collaboratory. You just don't *need* major scientific advances in the American car industry. You've already had more of that than you can stand. You guys are a national historic treasure, like a buffalo herd or Valley Forge. You need *protection* from the menace of basic research. Instead of paying federal scientists to march your industry right off the cliff, you should be paying scientists protection money *not* to research your business. That'll ensure that your industry doesn't go anywhere."

"That sounds so beautiful," Griego said wistfully. "Is it legal?"

"Why not? Your sabotage routine can't be legal, but you've been getting away with that for years. My proposal is a major improvement on the status quo, because now we're being honest about it. As a gesture of goodwill, I'll not only overlook your sad little corporate espionage, I'll cut your R&D expenditure in half!"

"What's the catch?"

"The catch is—the Collaboratory is in a small financial bind at the moment, so you'll have to ship us an entire year's corporate R&D funding, up front. Given our understanding, can you clear that financial move with your people in Detroit?"

"Well, I'll have to talk to Dad about it."

"You have a word with the higher-ups, Ron. Tell Dad and the other board members that if they don't accept my offer pronto, I'll turn this entire lab's brainpower onto that project. And we'll be shipping sugar engines out the doors by next June. In a giant blaze of publicity." He hung up.

"Did you really mean all that?" Kevin said. He'd been eavesdropping with great interest.

"I don't know," Oscar said. "I just came into some luck there. I happened to know the buttons that work on good old Ronnie, and the whole scheme just came to me in a blaze of inspiration. It's a very weird, lateral move, but it gets us off three or four hooks at once. It wins us a nice financial breathing space. Ron's happy, we're happy, everyone but Chander is happy, and Chander was finished anyway. Because Chander got in my face by stealing my moves."

"You can't really protect the car industry from a basic scientific discovery like a new power source."

"Kevin, wake up. You need to stop thinking like a technician. Where did that habit ever get you? Don't you see what I just pulled here? For the first time ever, we're getting people to pay us *not* to do research. *That* is a genuine new power source. For the first time, federal scientists have a real economic weapon—they can carry the war right to their enemy. Who cares about another damned battery? It's probably a crock anyway. Did you ever see an atomic-powered car? Just because it's technically possible doesn't mean it's practically doable."

"People will do something with it anyway. You politicians can't control the flow of technical knowledge. They'll exploit it no matter what the government says."

"Kevin, I *know* that. I am living proof of that phenomenon. It's what made me what I am today."

At two in the morning on January 20, there came a tap on Oscar's hotel room door. It was Fred Dillen, the krewe's janitor and launderer. Fred was drunk—the krewe had been celebrating the official and long-awaited swearing-in of Senator Bambakias, while drinking many patriotic toasts to the new Administration of President Two Feathers. Fred was accompanied by a chunky Anglo woman in her thirties, who was wearing bright orange medical-emergency gear.

"Party getting out of hand?" Oscar said.

"Oscar, this lady needs to talk to you," Fred said.

"I didn't know what room you were in," the paramedic said sullenly. "Had to bust in on a whole bunch of drunks downstairs."

"I'm glad you're here. Is there a problem?" Oscar said.

"Yeah. We have an injured female, mid-thirties. She broke her ankle. But she says she doesn't want to go to our clinic. She won't even give us her name and ID. She says she wants to talk with you first."

"What clinic are you taking her to?" Oscar said.

"Well, we want to take her to the ER in Buna. She wanted to go into the Collaboratory, but we can't take her in there. They got all these giant airlocks and all this security crap and besides, we're not legally cleared to do ER services inside a federal facility."

"What happened to her? How did she have the accident?"

"Well, she says she just happened to be walkin' over here in the middle of the road, in the middle of the night, and she tripped on something." The paramedic looked at Oscar with distaste. "Listen, all this is way against regulations. Most people who break a leg are plenty happy to see an ambulance. But she wouldn't shut up about it. She begged me to find some guy named Valparaiso, so now I found you. You wanna do something about it? Because if you don't, *adiós, muchacho.*"

"No, please don't be hasty, I'll go with you. I very much want to talk to your patient." Oscar looked at the paramedic's nametag. "Thank you very much for taking the trouble to find me, Ms. Willis. I know this isn't orthodox procedure, but I can make it well worth your while."

Willis settled back onto the worn heels of her white athletic shoes. "Well then," she said, and smiled. "Then maybe it ain't so bad after all."

Oscar found a jacket, his wallet, and a pair of shoes. He glanced at the slumbering Kevin. To observe strict security, he ought to wake his bodyguard and drag him along in the wheelchair—but it was two in the morning, and the hardworking Kevin had been drinking like a pig. Oscar tucked a telephone in his pocket and stepped into the hall. He closed the door silently, then handed Willis a twenty-ecu European bill.

Willis tucked the cash into a velcro-tabbed orange pocket. *"Muchas gracias, amigo."*

"I hope Greta's all right," Fred said anxiously.

"Try not to worry," Oscar told him. Fred was not the brightest light in the krewe. But Fred was a very loyal and good-hearted sort, a man who repaid a kind word with dogged loyalty. "You can go back to the party now. We really want to keep this little business quiet. Don't tell anyone. Okay?"

"Oh," Fred said. "Right. No problem, Oscar."

Oscar and Ms. Willis went downstairs and through the lobby. Dutch party music echoed down the entrance loggia. "Sure is a nice hotel," Willis remarked.

"Thanks. Maybe you'd like to check in for the weekend."

"On my salary? I can't afford a classy place like this."

"If you're discreet about this little incident, ma'am, I'll treat you and any guest of your choice to a three-day stay with full room service."

"Gee, that's a mighty generous offer. This Gretel person must really mean a lot to you." Willis led him down the paved walkway and into the street. A limo-sized white ambulance waited under the pines, with its lights on and the driver's door open. Willis waved cheerily at the driver, who waved back in evident relief.

"She's lyin' in the back, on a stretcher," Willis said. "It's a pretty bad break. You want some good advice, *compadre*? From now on, don't make your dang girlfriends sneak around in the dark."

"I'm sure that's good advice," Oscar said. He stood up on the bumper and gazed into the ambulance. Greta was lying on a canvas stretcher in a metal rack, with her hands behind her head.

Willis slapped her hands against Oscar's rump and gave him a hefty shove. Oscar stumbled into the ambulance, and Willis immediately slammed the double doors. The vehicle went as black as a tomb.

"Hey!" Oscar blurted.

The vehicle left the curb and racketed away with a jounce of hydraulics.

"Greta," he said. No response. He crawled in darkness to her side, reached out. His questing hand landed somewhere on her rib cage. She was unconscious. But she was alive; she was breathing.

Oscar quickly produced his telephone. He was grimly unsurprised to see it fail to register a signal. But there was enough feeble glow from the dial face for him to painstakingly scope out his surroundings. He brought the faint glow of the phone to her face. She was out cold— and for good measure, they'd glued a membrane strip of adhesive over her mouth. Her hands were cuffed with thin plastic police straps. There was, of course, nothing wrong with her ankle.

The back of the vehicle resembled an ambulance, but only at first glance. It had some battered secondhand stretcher gear, but there was no life-support equipment. It was windowless. To judge by the way it took corners, the phony ambulance was sheathed in solid metal like a bank vault. They'd lured him into an armored thermos bottle, corked him up, and driven away.

By phone light, with his fingernails, he slowly peeled the gag from her mouth. He gave her silent lips a healing kiss. There was no heating inside the evil little vault. Greta felt chilled. He climbed onto the stretcher with her and embraced her. He held her tightly, pressing warmth into her body. He was appalled to discover how much he cared for her. She was so human. So far beyond his help.

They'd been disappeared. It was as simple as that. They had made a little too much trouble for someone, and they had exhausted the patience of some deeply evil player. Now they were heading for an assassin's graveyard. They were going to be tortured, humiliated, and buried with bullets in the backs of their heads. They would be gassed, rendered, and cremated. Vile and hideous people would replay the videotapes of their secret and lingering deaths.

Oscar rose from the stretcher. He lay on his back on the floor, and began stamping on the forward bulkhead. He industriously kicked his way through paint, a layer of porous plastic, and hit a wall of solid iron. The perambulating coffin now began producing a series of drumlike booms. This was progress. Oscar continued to kick, and with more enthusiasm.

A speaker crackled to life somewhere in the rear of the compartment. "Would you knock it off with the noise, please?"

"What's in it for me?" Oscar said.

"You really don't want us to get tough, *compadre,*" the speaker said. It was Willis. "You know, just 'cause you can't see *us,* doesn't mean we can't see *you.* We can see every dang move you make back there. And frankly, I wish you wouldn't feel up the merchandise while she's unconscious. It's kinda disgusting."

"You think that I'm helpless back here—but I still

have options. I could choke her to death. I could say you'd
done it."

Willis laughed. "Jesus, would you listen to this character? Listen, *vato*—you try anything stupid, and we'll just
turn on the knockout gas. Would you take it easy back
there, please? We're not your problem. We're not gonna
do anything to you. We're just your delivery service."

"I've got a lot of money," Oscar said. "I bet you'd
like some."

There was no response.

He returned his attention to Greta. He searched her
pockets, finding nothing useful for chiseling through solid
metal. He tried to ease her position. He put her feet up,
chafed her bound wrists, massaged her temples.

After half an hour, she emitted a series of groans and
woke up.

"I feel so dizzy," she said hoarsely.

"I know."

She stirred. Her wrists drew up short with a hiss of
plastic strap. "Oscar?"

"We've been kidnapped. It's an abduction."

"Oh. All right. I remember now." Greta gathered
her wits. "They told me you'd been hurt. That you
needed to see me at your hotel. So when I left the dome,
they just . . . grabbed me."

"That's my story too," Oscar said. "They used us as
bait for each other. I should have been more suspicious, I
guess. But why? How on earth could we live like that?
There's no way to outguess something like this. An abduction is completely stupid. It's such a weird gambit."

"What are they going to do to us?" Greta said.

Oscar was briskly cheerful. He'd already worked
himself through a black pit of terrified despondency, and
was properly anxious that she not share this experience
with him. "I can't really tell you, because I don't know
who they are yet. But they haven't really hurt us, so they
must want something from us. They took a lot of trouble,

with the disguise and the ambulance and so forth. This isn't my usual crowd of assassin lunatics." He lifted his voice. "Hey! Hello! Would you people care to tell us what you want from us?" There was no answer. This was much as he had expected.

"They can hear everything we say," he told her. "We're bugged, of course."

"Well, can they see everything we do? It's pitch-black in here."

"Actually, they can. I think they have infrared cameras."

Greta thought this over for some time. "I'm really thirsty," she said finally.

"Sorry."

"This is craziness," she said. "They're going to kill us, aren't they? This is such a mess."

"Greta, that's just a speculation."

"They're taking us for a gangster ride. They're going to bump us off. I'm going to die pretty soon." She sighed. "I always wondered what I'd do, if I knew I was going to die."

"Really?" Oscar said. "I never gave that issue much thought."

"You didn't?" She stirred. "How could you not think about that? It's such an interesting question. I used to think I'd react like Évariste Galois. You know, the mathematician. I'd write down all my deepest speculations in my math notebook, and hope that somebody understood someday. . . . See, if you think that problem through, there's an obvious deduction. Death is universal, but knowing when you'll die is a rare statistical privilege. So since you'll probably never know, you should take a few hours out of some random day, and prepare your final testament beforehand. Right? That's the rational conclusion, given the facts. I actually did that once—when I was eleven." She drew a breath. "Unfortunately, I've never done it since."

"That's too bad." He realized that Greta was utterly terrified. She was babbling. His own fear had vanished completely. He was overwhelmed with protective instinct. He felt elated with it, half-drunk. He would do absolutely anything for the slightest chance to save her.

"But I'm not eleven anymore. Now I know what grown-ups do in this situation. It has nothing to do with big ideas. It really, *really* makes you want to have sex."

This was a completely unexpected observation, but it landed on Oscar like a match on oil-soaked rags. It was so utterly and compellingly true that he couldn't think of a thing to say. He felt dual rushes of fear and arousal strong enough to split his brain. His ears rang and his hands began itching.

"So," she whispered hotly, "if I weren't all tied up right now . . ."

"Actually," he breathed, "I don't mind that very much. . . ."

The speaker crackled into life. "Okay. Just stop that right now. Knock it off with that. That's really disgusting."

"Hey!" a second, male voice objected. "Give 'em a break."

"Are you crazy?" Willis objected.

"Girl, you never been a combat veteran. On the last night before you go out to get killed—hell yeah, you wanna get laid! You'll hump anything in a skirt."

"Ha!" Oscar shouted. "So you don't like it? Come back here and stop us."

"Don't try me."

"What can you do to us? We have nothing left to lose now. You know that we're lovers. Sure, that's our big dark secret, but we've got nothing to hide from *you*. You're just voyeurs. You mean nothing to us. To hell with you. We can do whatever we want."

Greta laughed. "I never thought of it that way," she

said giddily. "But it's so true. We're not *making* them watch us. They *have to* watch us."

"Hell, I *wanna* watch 'em," the male kidnapper said. "I like their attitude! I'll even play 'em some music." A radio snapped on, playing a lively Cajun two-step.

"Get your hands off that thing!" Willis commanded.

"Shut up! I can drive while I watch."

"I'm gonna gas both of 'em."

"What are you, crazy? Don't do that. Hey!"

The ambulance veered wildly. There was a loud splattering of mud and the overloaded vehicle yawed and half spun. Oscar was flung from Greta's side, and thrown bruisingly against the bulkhead. The vehicle ground to a halt.

"Now you've done it," Willis said.

"Don't get in a twist," the man grumbled. "We'll make it on time."

"Not if you just broke the axle, you horny moron."

"Stop bitching, lemme think. I'll check." A door squealed open.

"I broke my arm!" Oscar yelled. "I'm bleeding to death back here!"

"Would you stop being so goddamn clever?" Willis shouted. "Jesus Christ, you're a pain! Why can't you make this easy? It doesn't have to be this hard! Just shut up and go to sleep." There was an evil hiss of gas.

Oscar woke in darkness to a violent racket of tearing metal. He was lying on his back and there was something very heavy on his chest. He was hot and dizzy and his mouth tasted like powdered aluminum.

There was a vicious screech and a sullen pop. A diamond-sharp wedge of sunlight poured in upon him. He found that he was lying at the bottom of a monster coffin, with Greta sprawling on his chest. He squirmed, and shoved her legs aside with an effort that brought lancing pain behind his eyeballs.

After a few clear breaths, Oscar grasped his situation. The two of them were still lying inside the ambulance. But the vehicle had tumbled onto its side. He was now lying flat on one narrow wall. Greta was dangling above him, still handcuffed to the stretcher stanchions, which were now part of the roof.

There was more banging and scraping. Suddenly one of the back doors broke open, and fell flat against the earth.

A crew-cut young man in overalls looked in, a crowbar in one hand. "Hey," he said. "You're alive!"

"Yeah. Who are you?"

"Hey, nobody! I mean, uhm . . . Dewey."

Oscar sat up. "What's going on, Dewey?"

"I dunno, but you're some lucky guy to be alive in there. What's with this lady? Is she okay?"

Greta was dangling limply by her wrists with her head flung back and her eyes showing rims of white. "Help us," Oscar said, and coughed. "Help us, Dewey. I can really make it worth your while."

"Sure," Dewey said. "I mean, whatever you say. C'mon out of there!"

Oscar crawled out of the back of the ambulance. Dewey caught his arm and helped him to his feet. Oscar felt a spasm of nauseated dizziness, but then his pumping heart jumped on a gout of adrenaline. The world became painfully clear.

The shattered ambulance was lying on a dirt road next to a swampy, sluggish river. It was early morning, chill and foggy.

The air stank of burned upholstery. The ambulance had taken a direct hit from some kind of explosive—maybe a mortar round. The concussion had blasted it entirely from the road, and it had tumbled onto its side in red Texas mud. The engine was a blackened mess of shredded metal and molten plastic. The cab had been sheared in half, revealing the thick, dented armor of the interior prison vault.

"What happened?" Oscar blurted.

Dewey shrugged, bright-eyed and cheery. "Hey, mister—you tell me! Somebody sure shot the hell out of somebody's ass last night. I reckon that's all I can say." Dewey was very young, maybe seventeen. He had a single-shot hunting rifle strapped across his back. An ancient, rusty pickup truck sat nearby, with Texas plates. It had a smashed motorcycle in the back.

"Is that your truck?" Oscar said.

"Yup!"

"Do you have a tool chest in there? Anything that can cut through handcuffs?"

"I got me a power saw. I got bolt cutters. I got a towing chain. Hey, back at the farm, my dad's got welding equipment!"

"You're a good man to know, Dewey. I wonder if I might borrow your tools for a moment, and saw my friend loose."

Dewey looked at him with puzzled concern. "You sure you're okay, mister? Your ear's bleeding pretty bad."

Oscar coughed. "A little water. Water would be good." Oscar touched his cheek, felt a viscous mass of clotted blood, and gazed down at the riverbank. It would feel lovely to wash his head in cold water. This was a brilliant idea. It was totally necessary, it was his new top priority.

He stumbled through thick brown reeds, sinking ankle-deep in cold mud. He found a clear patch in the algae-scummed water and bathed his head with his cupped hands. Blood cascaded from his hair. He had a large, gashed bruise above his right ear, which announced itself with a searing pang and a series of sickening throbs. He risked a few mouthfuls of the river water, crouching there doubled over, until the shock passed. Then he stood up.

Twenty meters away, he spotted another wreck, bobbing slowly in the river. Oscar took it for a half-submerged tanker truck at first, and then realized, to his profound astonishment, that it was a midget submarine. The black craft had been peppered from stern to bow with thumb-sized machine-gun holes. It was beached in the mud in a spreading rainbow scum of oil.

Oscar clambered back up the riverbank, spattered with mud to his kneecaps. On his way to the ambulance he noted that the cab's windshield had exploded, and that many of the fragments were liberally splashed with dried blood. There was no sign of anyone at all. The rain-damp dirt road was furiously torn with motorcycle tracks.

The muffled sound of Dewey's power saw echoed from inside the smashed ambulance. Oscar trudged to the back and looked inside. Dewey had given up on his attempt to saw through the handcuffs, and was sawing through the slotted metal stanchion of the stretcher frame. He bent the metal frame and slipped the cuffs through.

Oscar helped him carry Greta into daylight. Her hands were blue with constriction and her wrists were badly skinned, but her breathing was still strong.

She had been gassed unconscious—twice—and had lived through a car wreck and a firefight. Then she'd been abandoned in a locked and armored vault. Greta needed a hospital. Some nice safe hospital. A hospital would be an excellent idea for both of them.

"Dewey, how far is it to Buna from here?"

"Buna? About thirty miles as the crow flies," Dewey allowed.

"I'll give you three hundred dollars if you'll take us to Buna right now."

Dewey thought about the offer. It didn't take him long. "Y'all hop on in," he said.

Oscar's phone couldn't find a proper relay station this far from Buna. They stopped at a grocery in the tiny hamlet of Calvary, Texas, where he bought some first-aid supplies and tried a local pay phone. He couldn't get through to the lab. He couldn't even reach the hotel in Buna. He was able to restore Greta to consciousness with a cautious application of temple rubbing and canned soda, but she was headachy and nauseous. She had to lie still and groan, and the only place available for lying down was the back of Dewey's truck, next to the salvaged wreck of a motorcycle.

Oscar waited in anguished silence as the miles rolled by. He had never much liked the lurking somnolence of the East Texas landscape. Pines, marsh, creeks, more pines, more marsh, another creek; nothing had ever happened here, nothing would ever be allowed to happen here. But something important had finally happened. Now its piney hick tedium crackled with silent menace.

Four miles from Buna they encountered a lunatic in a rusted rental car. He raced past them at high speed. The car then screeched to a halt, did a U-turn, and rapidly pulled up behind them, honking furiously.

Dewey, who had been chewing steadily on a rock-like stalk of sugarcane, paused to spit yellow flinders through his wind vent. "You know this guy?" he said.

"Does that gun work?" Oscar countered.

"Heck, yeah, my rifle works, but I ain't shooting anybody for no three hundred dollars."

Their pursuer stuck his head out the window of his car and waved. It was Kevin Hamilton.

"Pull over," Oscar said at once, "he's one of mine."

Oscar left the truck. He checked briefly on Greta, who was doubled over in the truckbed, racked with car sickness. He then joined Kevin, who had thrown his door open and was beckoning wildly.

"Don't go into Buna!" Kevin yelled as he drew near. "It's hit the fan."

"It's good to see you, too, Kevin. Can you help me with Greta? Let's get her into the backseat of the car. She's all shaken up."

"Right," Kevin said. He gazed at the truck. Dewey had just decamped from the driver's seat, carrying his rifle under his arm. Kevin reached below his own seat and pulled out an enormous chromed revolver.

"Cool it!" Oscar told him. "The kid's on the payroll." He stared at the handgun in alarm. He had never suspected Kevin of possessing such a thing. Handguns were extremely illegal, and a source of endless trouble.

Kevin hid his gun without another word, then limped out of the car. They helped Greta out of the truck, across the dirt, and into the backseat of Kevin's ratty, ill-smelling rental car. Dewey stood beside his truck, chomping sugarcane and waiting patiently.

"What's with the handgun, Kevin? We've got problems enough without *that*."

"I'm on the lam," Kevin told him. "There's a counter-coup at the lab—they're trying to put us all away. I'm not staying there to get busted, thank you. I had a lifetime's worth of encounters with the properly constituted authorities."

"All right, forget the handgun. Do you have any money?"

"As a matter of fact, yeah. Lots. I kinda took the liberty of cleaning out the hotel till this morning."

"Good. Can you give this kid three hundred dollars? I promised it to him."

"Okeydoke." Kevin reached behind the driver's seat and produced a well-stuffed Yankee carpetbag. He looked at Greta, who was stirring on the backseat in a futile search for comfort. "Where are your shoes, Dr. Penninger?"

"They're in the truck," she groaned. She was very pale.

"Let me take care of this," Kevin said. "You two just aren't your usual suave selves." Kevin limped back to the pickup truck, had a few cordial words with Dewey, and presented him with a horse-choking wad of flimsy American currency. Kevin then returned with Greta's shoes, started the car, and drove away from Buna. They left Dewey standing on the weed-strewn roadside, thumbing through his cash with an unbelieving grin.

As he drove, Kevin examined a cheap Chinese navigation screen, which was stuck to the cracked dashboard with a black suction cup. Then he ceremoniously rolled down his driver's window and carefully flung both of Greta's shoes out of the car and onto the side of the road. "I guess it's time for me to explain how I found you," Kevin said. "I bugged your shoes, Dr. Penninger."

Oscar digested this information, then looked at his own feet. "Did you bug my shoes too?"

"Well, yeah, but just short-range trackers. Not the full-audio bugs like hers."

"You put listening devices into my shoes?" Greta croaked.

"Yeah. Nothing to it. And I wasn't the only guy on the job, either. Your shoes had six other bugs planted inside the heels and seams. Very nice devices too—I figured them to be planted by players a lot heavier than I am. I could have removed them all, but I figured . . . hey, *this many*? There must be some kind of gentlemen's agreement going on here. I'll do better if I just stand in line."

"I can't believe you'd do that to me," Greta said. "We're supposed to be on the same side."

"You talking to me?" Kevin said, eyes narrowing. "I'm *his* bodyguard. Nobody ever said I was *your* bodyguard. You ever pay me a salary? Did you ever *talk* to me, even? You don't even live in my universe."

"Relax, Kevin," Oscar said. He flipped down a windshield visor, examined the cracked mirror, and brushed cautiously at a huge crust of blood in his hair. "It was good of you to show so much enterprise under these difficult circumstances. It's been a rough day for the forces of reason. However, our options are multiplying now. Thanks to you, we're regaining the tactical initiative."

Kevin sighed. "It's incredible that you can still spout that crap, even with your head knocked in. You know what? We're in terrible shape, but I feel good, out on the road like this. It's homey. You know? I've spent so much of my life dodging cops in beat-up cars. The old fugitive game . . . I guess it's got its drawbacks, but it sure beats having them know your home address."

"Tell me what's been going on at the lab," Oscar said.

"Well, it didn't take me long to figure out you'd been kidnapped, what with my hotel security videos, and the fact that your phones didn't answer, and the bugs in the doctor's shoes. So I get up from my laptop screen, and I check my real-life windows. Sheriff's department on the prowl outside, three AM. Not healthy. . . . Time for Scenario B, discreet planned withdrawal."

"So you robbed the hotel and ran away?" Greta said, raising her head.

"He was accumulating capital while enhancing his freedom of action," Oscar pointed out.

"That was my best move under the circumstances," Kevin said mournfully. "Because what I just saw—that was a leadership decapitation. It's a classic cointelpro thing. A tribe that's making big trouble—they've gotta have a charismatic leader. If you're a sensible, modern cop, you don't want to butcher a crowd in the streets—that's old-fashioned, it looks bad. So you just target the big cheese. You knock that lead guy out, smear him some-how. . . . Child abuse is a pretty good rap, satanic rituals maybe. . . . Any kind of ugly-paint that'll stick a little while and really stink . . . and in a pinch, you just steal him. So then, when all the second-rankers are wondering where King Bee went, that's when you round 'em up. After that, even if Mr. Wonderful comes back, their big momentum's over. They just give up and scatter."

"They wouldn't do that to us, though," Greta said. "We're not a mob, we're scientists."

Kevin laughed. "The word's out already about you two! You're a major scandal. You eloped together last night, and oh, by the way, while you were doing that, you somehow cleaned out the lab's treasury. Terrible embarrassment for all your friends. While your krewes and your Strike Committee are scratching their heads, the Collaboratory cops are gonna round everybody up. Because there's no denying that story they planted. Because you're not around to deny it."

"Well, I'm denying it now!" Greta said, wrenching herself up with her cuffed hands. "I'll go back there and take them all on face-to-face."

"Softly, softly," Oscar said. "When the timing's right."

"So, there I was, in a bad corner," Kevin said. "I was thinking—who has the gall and the muscle to kidnap two famous people like that? And then spread all this killer disinformation about them. . . ."

"Huey," Oscar said.

"Who else? So now, it's little me versus Green Huey, right? And who's gonna help me against Huey? The lab's cops? They're all Huey's people from way back. Buna city cops? Forget it, they're way too dumb. Texas Rangers maybe? The Rangers are very scary people, but they wouldn't believe me, I'm not Texan. So then I thought of Senator Bambakias—he's an okay guy, I guess, and at least he's a real sworn-in Senator now, but he's somewhat insane at the moment. So, I'm ready to cash in my chips and head for sunny Mexico. But then, just before I go, I think—what the hell, what have I got to lose? I'll call the President."

"The President of the United States?" Greta said.

"Yeah, him. So that's what I did."

Oscar considered this fact. "When was this decision made?"

"I called the White House this morning at four AM."
Oscar nodded. "Hmmm. I see."

"Don't tell me that you actually *talked* to the President," Greta said.

"Of course I didn't talk to the President! The President's not awake at four AM! I can tell you who's up at four AM, at the White House national security desk. It's this brand-new, young, military aide from Colorado. He's a fresh new transition-team guy. It's his very first day on the job. He's working the graveyard shift. He's kinda twitchy. Nothing important has ever happened to him before. He's not real streetwise. And he's not that hard a guy to reach, either—especially if you call him on twenty or thirty phones, all at once."

"And what did you tell the President's new national security aide?" Oscar prompted gently.

Kevin examined his navigation console and took a left turn into the deeper woods. "Well, I told him that the Governor of Louisiana had just kidnapped the Director of a federal laboratory. I kinda had to spice up my story to hold his interest—Huey's gang was holding her hostage, there were French secret agents involved, you know, that sort of thing. I chucked in some juicy details. Luckily, this guy was very up to speed on the Louisiana air base problem. Real aware of the Louisiana military radar hole, and all that. See, this guy's a lieutenant colonel, and he happens to come from Colorado Springs, where they have this very massive Air Force Academy. Seems there is, like, extremely irritated Air Force sentiment in Colorado. They hate Huey's guts for making the Air Force look like weak sisters."

"So this colonel believed your story?" Oscar said.

"Hell, I dunno. But he told me he was gonna check his satellite surveillance records, and if they backed up my story, he was gonna *wake up the President*."

"Amazing," Greta said, impressed despite herself.

"They'd have never woken up the old guy for a thing like that."

Oscar said nothing. He was trying to imagine the likely consequences if the President's national security team pressed their panic buttons at four AM, on the very first day on the job. What weird entities might leap from the crannies of the American military-entertainment complex? There were so many possibilities: America's aging imperial repertoire of Delta forces, SWATs, SEALs, high-orbital, antiterrorist, rapid-deployment, pep-pill-gobbling, macho super-goons. . . . Not that these strange people would ever be *used,* in modern political reality. The military killer elite were creatures of a long-vanished era, strictly ceremonial entities. They would jog around the subterranean secret bases doing their leg lifts and push-ups, reading bad historical technothriller novels, watching their lives and careers slowly rust away. . . .

At least, that had always been the implicit understanding. But understandings could change. And after his night's experience, he found himself inhabiting a different world.

"Unless I miss my guess," Oscar said, "our kidnappers had a rendezvous at the Sabine River last night. They were planning to smuggle us across the state line, to hand us over to some crowd of Huey's militia. But they were jumped in the dark, by some kind of night-flying U.S. tiger team. Airborne armed commandos of some kind, who surprised Huey's people on the ground last night, and absolutely shot them to pieces."

"Why on earth would they do such a thing?" Greta said, shocked. "They should have used nonlethal force and arrested them."

"Airborne commandos aren't policemen. They're genuine special-forces fanatics, who still use real guns! And when they spotted that French spy submarine in the water, they must have lost their tempers. I mean, imagine their reaction. If you're a heavily armed U.S. black-helicopter ace, and you see a secret submarine sneaking up an American river . . . well, once you've pulled the trigger, you can't strafe a thing like that just once."

Greta's brows knitted. "Did you really see a submarine, Oscar?"

"Oh yes. I can't swear that it was French, but it sure wasn't one of ours. Americans don't build cute, efficient little submarines. We prefer our submarines bigger than a city block. Besides, it all makes sense that way. The French have an aircraft carrier offshore. They've got drones flying over the bayous. The French invented the frogman-spy tradition. . . . So of course it was a cute little French sub. Poor bastards."

"You know," Kevin said thoughtfully, "normally, I'm very down on law-and-order issues, but I think I *like* this Two Feathers guy. The deal is—all you have to do is call him! They wake him up at four AM, and your problem is solved before dawn! This new President is a take-charge guy! The old guy would *never* have pulled a stunt like that. This is a real change of pace for America, isn't it? It's executive authority in action, that's what it is! It's like— he's the Chief Executive, so he just *executes* 'em!"

"I don't think that a shooting war between state and federal spooks is what the President had in mind for his first day in office," Oscar said. "That's not a healthy development for American democracy."

"Oh, get over it!" Kevin scoffed. "*Kidnapping* is *terrorism!* You can't take a soft line with *terrorists*—there's no end to that crap! The bastards got exactly what was coming to them! And that's just what we need inside the Collaboratory, too. We need an *iron hand* with these scumbags. . . ." Kevin scowled mightily, gripping the peeling wheel of the car in uncontrollable excitement. "Man, it chaps my ass to think of those crooked Tinkertoy coppers in there, getting ready to bust up those eggheads. And here I am—me, Kevin Hamilton, thirty-two years old—a fugitive again, running scared. If I only had, like, twenty heavy-duty Irish Southies with some pool cues and table legs. There's only twelve lousy cops in that whole laboratory. They haven't been doing anything for ten years, except tapping phone lines and taking payoffs. We could beat those sons of bitches into bad health."

"This is a new you we're hearing from, Kevin," Oscar observed.

"Man, I never knew that I could just *talk to the President*! Y'know, I'm a prole, and a hacker, and a phone phreak. I admit all that. But when you get to be my age, you just get sick of outsmarting them all the time! You get tired of having to dodge 'em, that's all. How come I have to sneak around in the cracks in the floorboards? I tell you, Dr. Penninger—you let *me* run your security, you'd see some changes made."

"Are you telling me that you want to be the lab's security chief, Mr. Hamilton?"

"No, of course I'm not, but . . ." Kevin paused in surprise. "Well, *yeah*! Yeah, *sure*! I can do it! I'm up for the damn job! Give *me* the damned cop budget. Give *me* all the badges and the batons. Hell yeah, I can do anything you want. Make *me* the federal authorities."

"Well," she said, "I'm the lab's Director, and I'm lying down in your backseat, wearing handcuffs. I don't see anyone else volunteering to help me."

"I could do it for you, Dr. Penninger, I swear I could. I could take that whole place over, if there were more than three of us. But as it is . . ." He shrugged. "Well, I guess we just drive around at random, makin' phone calls."

"I never drive without a goal," Oscar told him.

"So, man, do you know where we're going? Where is that?"

"Where's the nearest big camp of Moderators?"

9

The Canton Market had been a Texas tradition since the 1850s. Every weekend before the first Monday of the month, traders, collectors, flea marketeers, and random gawkers gathered from hundreds of miles around for three days of hands-on commercial scrap-and-patchwork. Naturally this ancient and deeply attractive tradition had been completely co-opted by prole nomads.

Oscar, Greta, and Kevin found themselves joining a road migration heading northeast toward the makeshift city. In Kevin's rented junker, they fitted with ease into the traffic: tankers, flatbeds, gypsy buses, winter-wrapped roadside hitchhikers.

In the meantime, Oscar and Greta climbed into the backseat together, to see to one another's scrapes, welts, and bruises. Greta was still handcuffed, while Oscar's broken head had barely clotted. They sat together while Kevin munched a take-out sandwich and wiped the fog of breath from his car's cold windows.

Checking one another's injuries was a slow and intimate process. It involved much tender unbuttoning of shirts, indrawn breaths of hurt surprise, sympathetic tongue-clicking, and the ultragentle dabbing of antiseptic unguents. They'd both taken a serious pounding, in normal circumstances requiring a medical checkup and a couple of days of bed rest. Their heads swam and ached from the knockout gas, a side effect only partly curable by temple rubbing, brow smoothing, and gentle lingering kisses.

Greta was stoic. She forced him to share her personal hangover cure: six aspirin, four acetaminophen, three heaping spoonfuls of white sugar, and forty micrograms of over-the-counter lysergic acid. This mélange, she insisted authoritatively, would "pep them up."

In the late afternoon, they left the crowded highway and darted east on an obscure country dirt road. There they parked and awaited a rendezvous. Within an hour they were joined by Yosh Pelicanos, who was piloting a rental car with his own satellite locator.

Pelicanos was, as always, efficient and resourceful. He had brought them laptops, cash cards, a first-aid kit, two suitcases of clothes, plastic sprayguns, new phones, and last but far from least, a new, yard-long bolt cutter.

Kevin had the most extensive experience with police handcuffs. So he set to work on Greta's bonds with the bolt cutter, while Oscar changed clothes inside Pelicanos's spacious and shiny rental car.

"You people look like three zombies. I hope you know what you're doing," Pelicanos told him mournfully. "All hell is breaking loose back at the lab."

"How's the krewe handling the crisis?" Oscar said, tenderly shaving the hair from the ragged gash above his ear.

"Well, some of us are with the Strike Committee, some are holing up in the hotel. We can still move in and out of the lab, but that won't last. Word is that they'll seal the facility soon. The Collaboratory cops are going to break the Strike. There are Buna city cops and county sheriffs cruising all around our hotel, and Greta's committee is too scared to leave the Hot Zone. . . . We've been sucker-punched, Oscar. Our people are totally confused. Word is out that you're criminals, you've abandoned us. Morale is subterranean."

"So how's the float going on our black-propaganda rap?" Oscar said.

"Well, the elopement pitch was very hot. How could a sex angle not be hot? I mean, basically, that's the outing move that we always expected. They're circulating photo stills of you and Greta at that dump in Holly Beach."

"Those Louisiana state troopers had telephotos," Oscar sighed. "I knew it all along."

"The sex scandal didn't break in the straight press yet. I've had dozens of calls, but the journos can't get any confirmation. That's just a typical sex smear. Nobody in the Collaboratory takes that seriously. Everybody in Buna already knows that you're having sex with Greta. No, the serious attack was the embezzlement rap. That's dead serious. Because the lab's money is really gone."

"How much did he steal?" Oscar said.

"He stole the works! The lab is bankrupt. It's bad. It's worse than bad. It's beyond mere bankruptcy. It's total financial wreckage, because all the lab's budgets and all the records are trashed. I've never seen anything like it. Even the backups have been targeted and garbaged. The system can't even add, it can't update, it churns out nonsense. It's a total financial lobotomy."

"American military infowar viruses," Oscar said. "Huey's loot from the Air Force base."

"Sure, that had to be military," Pelicanos nodded. "People have brought down national governments with those things. The lab's computers never had a chance."

"How long before you can restore functionality?" Oscar said.

"Are you kidding? What am I, a miracle worker?" Pelicanos was genuinely wounded. "I'm just an accountant! I can't repair the damage from a military netwar attack! In fact, I think someone's been monitoring me, personally. Every file that I've accessed in the past two months has been specifically destroyed. I think they've even screwed with my own laptop—some kind of black-bag job. I can't trust my own personal machine anymore. I can't even trust my off-site records."

"Fine, Yosh, I take the point, it's out of your league. So whose league is this in? Who's going to help us here?"

Pelicanos thought hard about the question. "Well, first, you'd need a huge team of computer-forensics specialists to go over the damaged code line by line. . . . No, forget that. Investigating and describing the damage would take years. It would cost a fortune. Let's face it, the lab's books are a write-off, they're totaled. It would be cheaper to drop the whole system off a cliff and start all over from scratch."

"I think I understand," Oscar said. "Huey permanently trashed the lab's finances. He's ruined a federal laboratory with an interstate netwar attack, just to get his krewe off a few corruption hooks. That's appalling. It's horrifying. The man has no conscience. Well, at least we know where we stand now."

Pelicanos sighed. "No, Oscar, it's much, much worse than that. The Spinoffs people were always Huey's favorite allies. They knew they were next up on Greta's chopping block, so last night they rebelled. The Spinoffs gang have launched a counterstrike. They've sealed and barricaded the Spinoffs building, and they're having a round-the-clock shredding orgy. They're stealing all the data they can get their hands on, and they're shredding everything else. When they're done, they'll all defect to Huey's brand-new science labs in Louisiana. And they're trying to convince everyone else to go with them."

Oscar nodded, absorbing the news. "Okay. That's vandalism. Obstruction of justice. Theft and destruction of federal records. Commercial espionage. All the Spinoffs people should be arrested immediately and prosecuted to the fullest extent of the law."

Pelicanos laughed dryly. "As if," he said.

"This isn't over," Oscar said. "Because our kidnapping fell through. We have the tactical initiative again. Huey doesn't know where we are. At least we're well out of his reach."

"So—what'll it be? Where should we go now? Boston? Washington?"

"Well . . ." Oscar rubbed his chin. "Huey's next moves are obvious, right? He's going to crash the Collaboratory just like he did the Air Force base. Thanks to his infowar attack, there's no money now. Soon, there will be no supplies, no food. . . . Then he'll send in a massive crowd of proles to occupy the derelict facility, and it's all over."

"That's how it looks, all right."

"He's not superhuman, Yosh. Well, I take that back —I'm pretty sure that Huey *is* superhuman. But Huey screwed up. If Huey hadn't screwed up, Greta and I would be languishing in some private prison in a dismal swamp right now."

Greta's handcuffs parted, with a ping and snap so loud that Oscar heard it from outside the car. Greta opened the back door of Kevin's wretched car, and she climbed out, stretching her cramped back and shoulders. While Kevin stowed the bolt cutter in the trunk, Greta came to join them. She approached Pelicanos's car and looked through the driver's window, rubbing her sore wrists.

"What's the game plan?" she said.

"We have the element of surprise," Oscar said. "And we'll have to use that for all it's worth."

"When can I go back to the lab? I really want to go back to my lab."

"We'll go. But when we go, we'll have to go back very hard. We'll have to attack the Collaboratory and take it over by force."

Pelicanos stared at Oscar as if he had lost his mind. Greta rubbed her chilly arms, and looked grave and troubled.

"Now you're talking!" Kevin announced, punching the air.

"It's doable," Oscar said. He opened the car door and stepped into the cold winter wind. "I know it sounds crazy, but think it through. Greta is still the legitimate Director. The Collaboratory's cops aren't crack troops, they're just a bunch of functionaries."

"You can't ask the people in the Collaboratory to attack the police," Greta said. "They just won't do that. It's illegal, it's immoral, it's unethical, it's unprofessional . . . and, besides, it's very dangerous, isn't it?"

"Actually, Greta, I'm dead certain that your scientists would love to beat up some cops, but I take your point. It would take us far too long to talk those harmless intellectuals into clobbering anyone. My little krewe of pols aren't exactly hardened anarchist street-fighters, either. But if we can't restore order in the lab, right away, today, then your administration is doomed. And your lab is doomed. So we have to risk it. This crisis requires total resolve. We have to physically seize that facility. What we need at this juncture are some tough, revolutionary desperados." Oscar drew a breath. "So let's drive into this flea market and hire ourselves some goons."

They abandoned Pelicanos's perfectly decent car for security reasons, and piled together into Kevin's unlicensed junker. Then they drove on.

Their first challenge was a Moderator roadblock, south of Canton. The Texan prole lads manning the roadblock gave them curious stares. Oscar's hat was askew, barely hiding the bandaged gash in his head. Kevin was unshaven and twitchy. Greta had her arms crossed to hide her chafed wrists. Pelicanos looked like an undertaker.

"Come down from outta state?" the Moderator said. He was a freckle-faced Anglo kid with blue plastic hair, headphones, eight wooden beaded necklaces, a cellphone, and a fringed deerskin jacket. His legs were encased from the knees down in giant mukluks of furry plastic.

"Yo!" Kevin said, offering a wide variety of secret high signs.

The Moderator watched Kevin's antics with bemusement. "Y'all ever been to Texas before?"

'We've heard of the Canton flea market," Kevin assured him. "It's famous."

"Could I have a five-dollar parkin' fee, please?" The Moderator pocketed his plastic cash and glued a sticker to their windshield. "Y'all just follow the beeps on this sticker, it'll lead to y'all's parking lot. Have a good time at the fair!"

They drove slowly into the town. Canton was a normal East Texas burg of modest two- and three-story buildings: groceries, clinics, churches, restaurants. The streets were swarming with weirdly dressed foot traffic. The huge crowds of proles seemed extremely well organized; they were serenely ignoring the traffic lights, but they were moving in rhythmic gushes and clumps, filtering through the town in a massive folk dance.

Kevin parked below a spreading pine tree in a winter-browned cow pasture, and they left their vehicle. The sun was shining fitfully, but there was an uneasy northern breeze. They joined a small crowd and walked to the edge of the market.

The sprawling market campground was dominated by the soaring plastic spines of homemade cellular towers. Dragonfly flocks of tinkertoy aircraft buzzed the terrain. The biggest shelters were enormous polarized circus tents of odd-smelling translucent plastic on tall spindly poles.

Kevin bought four sets of earclips from a blanket vendor. "Here, put these on."

"Why?" Greta said.

"Trust me, I know my way around a place like this."

Oscar pinched the clamp onto his left ear. The device emitted a little wordless burbling hum, the sound a contented three-year-old might make. As long as he moved with the crowd, the little murmur simply sat there at his ear, an oddly reassuring presence, like a child's make-believe friend. However, if he interfered with the crowd flow—if he somehow failed to take a cue—the earcuff grew querulous. Stand in the way long enough, and it would bawl.

Somewhere a system was mapping out the flow of people, and controlling them with these gentle hints. After a few moments Oscar simply forgot about the little murmurs; he was still aware of them, but not consciously. The nonverbal nagging was so childishly insistent that accommodating it became second nature. Soon the four of them were moving to avoid the crowds, well before any approaching crowds could actually appear. Everyone was wearing the earcuffs, so computation was arranging human beings like a breeze blowing butterflies.

The fairground was densely packed with people, but the crowd was unnaturally fluid. All the snack-food stands had short, brisk lines. The toilets were never crowded. Children never got lost.

"I'll line up someone that we can talk to seriously," Kevin told them. "When I've made the arrangements, I'll call you." He turned and limped away.

"I'll help you," Oscar said, catching up with him.

Kevin turned on him, his face tight. "Look, am I your security chief, or not?"

"Of course you are."

"This is a security matter. If you want to help me, go watch your girlfriend. Make sure that nobody steals her this time."

Oscar was annoyed to find himself persona non grata in Kevin's private machinations. On the other hand, Kevin's anxiety made sense—because Oscar was the only man in this crowd of thousands who was wearing a full-scale overclass ensemble of suit, hat, and shoes. Oscar was painfully conspicuous.

He glanced over his shoulder. Greta had already vanished.

He quickly located Pelicanos, and after four increasingly anxious minutes they managed to find Greta. She had somehow wandered into a long campground aisle of tents and tables, which were packed with an astounding plethora of secondhand electronic equipment.

"Why are you wandering off on your own?" he said.

"I didn't wander! You wandered." She dipped her fingers through a shallow brass tray full of nonconductive probes.

"We need to stick together, Greta."

"I guess it's my little friend here," she said, touching her earcuff. "I'm not used to it." She wandered bright-eyed down to the next table, which bore brimming boxes of multicolored patch cables, faceplates, mounting boxes, modular adaptors.

Oscar examined a cardboard box crammed with electrical wares. Most were off-white plastic, but others were nomad work. He picked an electrical faceplate out of the box. It had been punched and molded out of mashed grass. The treated cellulose was light yet rigid, with a crunchy texture, like bad high-fiber breakfast cereal.

Greta was fascinated, and Oscar's interest was caught despite himself. He hadn't realized that nomad manufacturing had become so sophisticated. He glanced up and down the long aisle. They were entirely surrounded by the detritus of dead American computer and phone industries, impossibly worthless junk brightly labeled with long-dead commercial promos. "Brand-New In the Box: Strata VIe and XIIe!" There were long-dead business programs no sane human being would ever employ. Stacks of bubblejet cartridges for nonexistent printers. Nonergonomic mice and joysticks, guaranteed to slowly erode one's wrist tendons. . . . And fantastic amounts of software, its fictional "value" exploded by the lost economic war.

But this was not the strange part. The strange part was that brand-new nomad manufacturers were vigorously infiltrating this jungle of ancient junk. They were creating

new, functional objects that were not commercial detritus
—they were sinister mimics of commercial detritus, created through new, noncommercial methods. Where there
had once been expensive, glossy petrochemicals, there was
now chopped straw and paper. Where there had once
been employees, there were jobless fanatics with cheap
equipment, complex networks, and all the time in the
world. Devices once expensive and now commercially
worthless were being slowly and creepily replaced by near-
identical devices that were similarly noncommercial, and
yet brand-new.

A table featuring radio-frequency bugs and taps was
doing a bang-up business. A man and woman with towering headdresses and face paint were boldly retailing the
whole gamut of the covert-listening industry: bodywires,
gooseneck flashlights, wire crimpers, grounding kits, adhesive spongers, dental picks and forceps, and box after
box of fingernail-sized audio bugs. Who but nomads, the
permanently unemployed, would enjoy the leisure of patiently listening, collating, and trading juicy bits of overheard dialogue? Oscar examined a foam-filled box
jammed with hexhead cam wrenches.

"Let's try this other row," Greta urged him, eyes
bright and hair tousled. "This one's medical!"

They drifted into a collateral realm of undead commerce. Here, the market tables were crowded with hemo-
static forceps, surgical scissors, vascular clamps, resistant
heat-sealed plastic gloves from the long-vanished heyday
of AIDS. Greta pored, transfixed, over the bone screws,
absorption spears, ultracheap South Chinese magnifier
spectacles, little poptop canisters of sterile silicone grease.

"I need some cash," she told him suddenly. "Loan
me something."

"What is with you? You can't buy this junk. You
don't know where it's from."

"That's *why* I want to buy it." She frowned at him.
"Look, I was the head of the Instrumentation Depart-

ment. If they're giving away protein sequencers, I really
need to know about that."

She approached the table's owner, who was sitting at
his open laptop and chuckling over homemade cartoons.
"Hey, mister. How much for this cytometer?"

The hick looked up from his screen. "Is that what
that is?"

"Does it work?"

"I dunno. Kinda makes the right noises when you
plug it in."

Pelicanos appeared. He had bought her a secondhand jacket—a gruesome sporty disaster of indestructible
black and purple Gore-Tex.

"Thank you, Yosh," she said, and slipped into the
jacket's baggy entrails. Once she'd snapped the ghastly
thing up to her chin, Greta immediately became an inte-
gral part of the local landscape. She was passing for normal
now, just another poverty-stricken bottom-feed female
shopper.

"I wish Sandra were here," Pelicanos said quietly.
"Sandra would enjoy this place. If we weren't in so much
trouble, that is."

Oscar was too preoccupied for junk shopping. He
was worried about Kevin. He was struggling to conjure up
a contingency plan in case Kevin failed to make a useful
contact, or worse yet, if Kevin simply vanished.

But Greta was picking her way along the tables with
heartfelt enthusiasm. She'd transcended all her pains and
worries. Scratch a scientist, find a hardware junkie.

But no, it was deeper than that. Greta was in her
element. Oscar had a brief intuitive flash of what it would
mean to be married to Greta. Choosing equipment was
part of her work and work was the core of her being.
Domestic life with a dedicated scientist would be
crammed full of moments like this. He would be dutifully
tagging along to keep her company, and she would be
investing all her attention into things that he would never

understand. Her relationship with the physical world was
of an entirely different order from his own. She loved
equipment, but she had no taste. It would be hell to fur-
nish a home with a scientist. They'd be arguing over her
awful idea of window curtains. He'd be giving in on the
issue of cheap and nasty tableware.

His phone rang. It was Kevin.

Oscar followed instructions, and located the tent
where Kevin had found his man. The place was hard to
miss. It was an oblong dome of tinted parachute fabric,
sheltering a two-man light aircraft, six bicycles, and a host
of cots. Hundreds of multicolored strings of chemglow
hung from the seams of the tent, dangling to shoulder
height. A dozen proles were sitting on soft plastic carpets.
To one side, five of them were busily compiling a printed
newspaper.

Kevin was sitting and chatting with a man he introduced as "General Burningboy." Burningboy was in
his fifties, with a long salt-and-pepper beard and a filthy
cowboy hat. The nomad guru wore elaborately hand-
embroidered jeans, a baggy handwoven sweater, and ancient military lace-up boots. There were three parole cuffs
on his hairy wrists.

"Howdy," the prole General said. "Welcome to
Canton Market. Pull up a floor."

Oscar and Greta sat on the carpet. Kevin was already
sitting there, in his socks, absently massaging his sore feet.
Pelicanos was not attending the negotiations. Pelicanos
was waiting at a discreet distance. He was their emergency
backup man.

"Your friend here just paid me quite a sum, just to
buy one hour of my time," Burningboy remarked. "Some
tale he had to tell me, too. But now that I see you
two . . ." He looked thoughtfully at Oscar and Greta.
"Yeah, it makes sense. I reckon I'm buying his story. So
what can I do y'all for?"

"We're in need of assistance," Oscar said.

"Oh, I knew it had to be somethin'," the General nodded. "We never get asked for a favor by straight folks till you're on the ropes. Happens to us all the time—rich idiots, just showin' up out of the blue. Always got some fancy notion about what we can do for 'em. Some genius scheme that can only be accomplished by the proverbial scum of the earth. Like, maybe we'd like to help 'em grow heroin. . . . Maybe sell some aluminum siding."

"It's not at all like that, General. You'll understand, once you hear my proposal."

The General tucked in his boots, cross-legged. "Y'know, this may *amaze* you, Mr. Valparaiso, but in point of fact, we worthless subhumans are kinda busy with lives of our own! This is Canton First Monday. We're smack in the middle of a major jamboree here. I've gotta worry about serious matters, like . . . sewage. We got a hundred thousand people showin' up for three days. You *comprende*?" Burningboy stroked his beard. "You know who you're talking to here? I'm not a magic elf, pal. I don't come out of a genie bottle just because you need me. I'm a human being. I got my own problems. They call me 'General' now. . . . But once upon a time, I used to be a real-live mayor! I was the elected two-term mayor of Port Mansfield, Texas. Fine little beachfront community—till it washed away."

An elderly woman in a hairy robe entered the tent. She carefully tied two knots into a dangling cord of chemglow, and left without a word.

The General picked up the thread. "You see, son—and Dr. Penninger"—he nodded at Greta in courtly fashion—"we're all the heroes of our own story. You tell me you've got a big problem—hell, we've all got big problems."

"Let's discuss them," Oscar said.

"I got some excellent career advice for you overachievers. Why don't you clowns just *give up*? Just *quit*! Knock it off, hit the road! Are you enjoyin' life? Do you have a *community*? Do you even know what a real community *is*? Is there any human soul that you poor haunted wretches can really trust? Don't answer that! 'Cause I already know. You're a sorry pair of washouts, you two. You look like coyotes ate you and crapped you off a cliff. Now you got some crisis you want me to help you with. . . . Hell, people like you are *always* gonna have a crisis. You *are* the crisis. When are you gonna wake up? Your system don't work. Your economy don't work. Your politicians don't work. Nothing you ever do works. You're over."

"For the time being," Oscar said.

"Mister, you're never gonna get ahead of the game. You've had a serious wake-up call here. You're disappeared, you're *dispossessed*. You've been blown right off the edge of the earth. Well, you know something? There's a soft landing down here. Just go ahead and leave! Burn your clothes! Set fire to your damn diploma! Junk all your ID cards! You're a sickening, pitiful sight, you know that? A nice, charming, talented couple. . . . Listen, it's not too late for you two to get a life! You're derelicts right now, but you could be bon vivants, if you knew what life was for."

Greta spoke up. "But I really need to get back to my lab."

"I tried," said Burningboy, flinging up both hands. "See, if you just had the good sense to listen to me, that fine advice of mine would have solved your problems right away. You could be eatin' mulligatawny stew with us tonight, and probably getting laid. But no, don't mind old Burningboy. I'm much, much older than you, and I've seen a lot more of life than you ever have, but what do I know? I'm just some dirt-ignorant fool in funny clothes, who's gonna get arrested. Because some rich Yankee from outta town needs him to commit some terrible criminal act."

"General, let me give you the briefing," said Oscar.

He proceeded to do this. Burningboy listened with surprising patience.

"Okay," Burningboy said at last. "Let's say that we go in and strong-arm this giant glass dome full of scientists. I gotta admit, that's a very attractive idea. We're extremely nice, peaceful people in the Moderators, we're all love and sunshine. So we might do a thing like that, just to please you. But what's in it for us?"

"There's money," Oscar said.

Burningboy yawned. "Sure, like that'll help us."

"The lab is a self-sufficient structure. There's food and shelter inside," Greta offered.

"Yeah, sure—as long as it suits you to give it to us. Once that's done, then it's the run-along as usual."

"Let's be realistic," Oscar said. "You're a mob. We need to hire some mob muscle to back up our labor strike. That's a very traditional gambit, isn't it? How hard can that be?"

"They're very small, timid cops," Greta offered. "They hardly even have guns."

"Folks, we carry our own food and shelter. What we don't have is bullet holes in us. Or a bunch of angry feds on our ass."

Oscar considered his next move. He was dealing with people who had profoundly alien priorities. The Moderators were radical, dissident dropouts—but they were nevertheless people, so of course they could be reached somehow. "I can make you famous," he said.

Burningboy tipped his hat back. "Oh yeah? How?"

"I can get you major net coverage. I'm a professional and I can spin it. The Collaboratory a very famous place. Dr. Penninger here is a Nobel Prize winner. This is a major political scandal. It's very dramatic. It's part of a major developing story, it ties in with the Bambakias hunger strike, and the Regulator assault on a U.S. Air Force base. You Moderators could get excellent press by restoring order at a troubled federal facility. It would be the very opposite of the dreadful thing that the Regulators did."

Burningboy reached thoughtfully into his jacket. He removed three small bars of substances resembling colored chalk. He set them onto a small slab of polished Arkansas whetstone, drew a pocketknife, and began chopping the bars into a fine powder.

Then he sighed heavily. "I really hate having my chain pulled just because a hustler like you happens to know that we Mods have it in for the Regulators."

"Of course I know that, General. It's a fact of life, isn't it?"

"We love those Regulators like brothers and sisters. We got nothing in common with you. Except that . . . well, we're Moderators because we use a Moderator network. And the Regulators use a Regulator interface, with Regulator software and Regulator protocols. I don't think that a newbie creep like you understands just how political a problem that is."

"I understand it," Kevin said, speaking up for the first time.

"We used to get along with the Regulators. They're a civilized tribe. But those Cajun goofballs got all puffed up about their genetic skills, and their state support from Green Huey. . . . Started bossin' other people around, doing talent raids on our top people, and if you ask me, them gumbo yaya voodoo-krewes are way too fond of gas and poison. . . ."

Sensing weakness, Oscar pounced. "General, I'm not asking you to attack the Regulators. I'm only asking you to do what the Regulators themselves have done, except for much better motives, and under much better circumstances."

General Burningboy arranged his chopped powder into straight lines, and dumped them, one by one, into a small jar of yellow grease. He stirred the grease with his forefinger, and rubbed it carefully behind his ears.

Then he waited, blinking. "Okay," he said at last. "I'm putting my personal honor on the line here, on the say-so of total strangers, but what the hell. They call me 'General' because of my many hard-won years of cumulative trust ratings, but the cares of office hang kinda heavy on my hands right now, quite frankly. I might as well destroy everything I've built in one fell swoop. So, I'm gonna do you three rich creep palookas a very, very big favor. I'm going to loan you five platoons."

"Fifty Moderator toughs?" Kevin said eagerly.

"Yep. Five platoons, fifty people. Of course, I'm not sayin' our troops can hold that lab against a federal counterassault, but there's no question they can take it."

"Do these men have the discipline that it takes to maintain civil order in that facility?" Oscar said.

"They're not men, pal. They're teenage girls. We *used* to send in our young men when we wanted to get tough, but hey, young men are extremely tough guys. Young men *kill people*. We're a well-established alternative society, we can't afford to be perceived as murdering marauders. These girls keep a cooler head about urban sabotage. Plus, underage women tend to get a much lighter criminal sentencing when they get caught."

"I don't mean to seem ungrateful, General, but I'm not sure you grasp the seriousness of our situation."

"No," Greta said. "Teenage girls are perfect."

"Then I reckon I'll be introducing you to some of our chaperone field commanders. And you can talk about tactics and armament."

Oscar rode back to Buna in a phony church bus, crammed with three platoons of Moderator nomad soldiers. He might have ridden with Kevin, but he was anxious to study the troops.

It was almost impossible to look at girls between fourteen and seventeen and envision them as a paramilitary task force that could physically defeat police. But in a society infested with surveillance, militias had to take strange forms. These girls were almost invisible because they were so improbable.

The girls were very fit and quiet, with the posture of gymnasts, and they traveled in packs. Their platoons were split into operational groups of five, coordinated by elderly women. These little-old-lady platoon sergeants looked about as harmless and inoffensive as it was possible for human beings to look.

They all looked harmless because they dressed the part, deliberately. The nomad crones had given up their usual eldritch leather-and plastic road gear. They now wore little hats, orthopedic shoes, and badly fitting floral prints. The young soldiers painstakingly obscured their tattoos with skin-colored sticks of wax. They had styled and combed their hair. They wore bright, up-tempo jackets and patterned leggings, presumably shoplifted from malls in some gated community. The Moderator army resembled a girl's hockey team on a hunt for chocolate milk shakes.

Once the buses and their soldiery had successfully made it through the eastern airlock gate, the assault on the Collaboratory was a foregone conclusion. Oscar watched in numb astonishment as the first platoon ambushed and destroyed a police car.

Two cops in a car were guarding one of the airlocks into the Hot Zone, where Greta's Strike Committee was sullenly awaiting eviction. Without warning, the youngest of the five girls clapped her hands to the sides of her head, and emitted an ear-shattering scream. The police, galvanized with surprise, left their car at once and rushed over to give the girl aid. They fell into an invisible rat's nest of tripwires, which lashed their booted legs together with a stink of plastic. The moment they hit the ground, two other girls coolly shot them with sprayguns, pasting them firmly to the earth.

A second platoon of girls united and turned the tiny police truck onto its roof, and web-shot its video monitors and instrument panels.

At his own insistence, Kevin personally led the assault on the police station. Kevin's contribution consisted of fast-talking with the female desk sergeant as thirty young women walked into the building, chatting and giggling. Smiling cops who trustingly emerged to find out what was going on were webbed at point-blank range. Gagged, blinded, and unable to breathe, they were easy prey for trained squads who seized their wrists, kicked their ankles, and knocked them to the floor with stunning force. They were then swiftly cuffed.

The Moderators had seized a federal facility in forty minutes flat. A force of fifty girls was overkill. By six-thirty the coup was a fait accompli.

Still, there had been one tactical misstep. The lab's security director was not at his work, and not at his home, where a platoon had been sent to arrest him. There was no one at home but his greatly surprised wife and two children.

It turned out that the security chief was in a beer bar with his mistress, drunk. Teenage girls couldn't enter a bar without attracting attention. They tried luring him out; but, confused by bad lighting, they attacked and tackled the wrong man. The chief escaped apprehension.

Two hours later the chief was rediscovered, sealed into an impromptu riot vehicle in the basement of the Occupational Safety building. He was frantically brandishing a cellphone and a combat shotgun.

Oscar went in to negotiate with him.

Oscar stood before the rubber bumper of the squat decontamination vehicle. He waved cheerfully through the armored window, showing his empty hands, and called the police chief on one of the Collaboratory's standard phones.

"What the hell do you think you're doing?" the

chief demanded. His name, Oscar recalled flawlessly, was Mitchell S. Karnes.

"Sorry, Chief Karnes, it was an emergency. The situation's under control now. No one is going to be hurt."

"I'm the one who handles emergencies," said the chief.

"You and your men *were* the emergency. Since Director Penninger was abducted yesterday, I'm afraid you and your team have forfeited her trust. However, the lab is now back in the hands of its properly constituted authorities. So you and your staff will be relieved of duty and placed under detention until we can restore the situation to normalcy."

"What on earth are you talking about? You can't fire me. You don't have the authority."

"Well, Chief, I'm very aware of that. But that doesn't change the facts of our situation. Just look at us. I'm standing out here, trying to be reasonable, while you're holed up in an armored vehicle with a shotgun, all by yourself. We're both adults, let's be sensible men here. The crisis is over. Put the gun down and come on out."

Karnes blinked. He'd been drinking heavily earlier in the day, and the full gravity of his situation hadn't entirely registered on him. "Look, what you're saying is completely crazy. A labor strike is one thing. Computer viruses are one thing. Netwar is one thing, even. But this is an armed coup. You can't get away with attacking police officers. You'll be arrested. Everybody you know will get arrested."

"Mitch, I'm with you on this issue. In fact, I'm way ahead of you. I stand ready to surrender myself to the properly constituted authorities, just as soon as we can figure out who they are. They'll show up sooner or later; this will all shake out in the long run. But in the meantime, Mitch, *act normal,* okay? All your colleagues are down in detention. We've got the crisis handled now.

This is doable. We're having the place catered tonight, there's doughnuts, coffee, and free beer. We're playing pinochle together and swapping war stories. We're planning to set up conjugal visits."

"Oscar, you *can't arrest me*. It's against the law."

"Mitch, just relax. You play ball with Dr. Penninger, probably we can work something out! Sure, I guess you can stand on principle, if you want to get all stiff-necked about it. But if you sit in that truck with a loaded shotgun all night, what on earth will that get you? It's not going to change a thing. It's over. Come on out."

Karnes left the truck. Oscar produced a pair of hand-cuffs, looked at the plastic straps, shrugged, put them back in his pocket. "We really don't need this, do we? We're grown-ups. Let's just go."

Karnes fell into step with him. They left the base-ment, and walked out together beneath the dome. There were winter stars beyond the glass. "I never liked you," Karnes said. "I never trusted you. But somehow, you al-ways seem like such a reasonable guy."

"I *am* a reasonable guy." Oscar clapped the police-man on the back of his flak jacket. "I know things seem a little disordered now, Chief, but I still believe in the law. I just have to find out where the order is."

After seeing the former police chief safely incarcerated, Oscar conferred with Kevin and Greta in the comman-deered police station. The nomad girls had changed from their dainty infiltration gear into clothing much more their style: webbing belts, batons, and cut-down combat fatigues. "So, did you get our internal publicity statement released?"

"Of course," Kevin said. "I called up every phone in the lab at once, and Greta went on live. Your statement was a good pitch, Oscar. It sounded really . . ." He paused. "Soothing."

"Soothing is good. We'll have new posters up by morning, declaring the Strike over. People need these symbolic breathers. 'The Strike Is Over.' A declaration like that takes a lot of the heat off."

All enthusiasm, Kevin pitched from the chief's leather chair and crawled on his hands and knees to a floor-level cabinet. It was crammed with telecom equipment, a dust-clotted forest of colored fiber optics. "Really neat old phone system here! It's riddled with taps, but it's one of a kind; it has a zillion cool old-fashioned features that nobody ever used."

"Why is it so dirty and neglected?" Oscar said.

"Oh, I had to turn these boards backward to get at the wiring. I've never had such total control over a switching station. A couple of weeks down here, and I'll have this place ticking like a clock." Kevin stood up, wiping clotted grime from his fingers. "I think I'd better put on one of these local cop uniforms now. Does anybody mind if I wear a cop uniform from now on?"

"Why do you want to do that?" Oscar said.

"Well, those nomad girls have uniforms. I'm now your chief of security, right? How am I supposed to control our troops, if I don't have my own uniform? With some kind of really cool cop hat."

Oscar shook his head. "That's a moot point, Kevin. Now that they've conquered the lab for us, we really need to usher those little witches out of here just as soon as possible."

Kevin and Greta exchanged glances. "We were just discussing that issue."

"They're really good, these girls," Greta said. "We won the lab back, but nobody got killed. It's always very good when there's a coup d'état and nobody gets killed."

Kevin nodded eagerly. "We still need our troops, Oscar. We have a gang of dangerous Huey contras who are holed up in the Spinoffs building. We have to break them right where they stand! So we'll have to use heavy nonlethals—spongey whips, peppergas, ultrasonic bull-horns. . . . Man, it's gonna be juicy." Kevin rubbed his hands together.

"Greta, don't listen to him. We can't risk serious injury to those people. We're in full command of the lab now, so we need to behave responsibly. If we have trouble from Huey's loyalists, we'll behave like normal authorities do. We'll just glue their doors shut, cut their phone and computer lines, and starve them out. Overreaction would be a serious mistake. From now on, we have to worry about how this plays in Washington."

Greta's long face went bleak. "Oh, to hell with Washington! They never do anything useful. They can't protect us here. I'm sick of them and their double-talk."

"Wait a minute!" Oscar said, wounded. "*I'm* from Washington. I've been useful."

"Well, you're the one exception." She rubbed her skinned wrists angrily. "After what happened to me today, I know what I'm up against. I don't have any more illusions. We can't trust anyone but ourselves. Kevin and I are going to seize the airlocks and seal this entire facility. Oscar, I want you to resign. You'd better resign before the people in Washington fire you." She began jabbing her spidery fingers at him. "No, before they arrest you. Or indict you. Or impeach you. Or kidnap you. Or just plain kill you."

He gazed at her in alarm. She was losing it. The skin of her cheeks and forehead had the taut look of a freshly peeled onion. "Greta, let's go for a little walk in the fresh air, shall we? You're overwrought. We need to discuss our situation sensibly."

"No more talking. I'm through being played for a sucker. I won't be gassed and handcuffed again, unless they come in here with tanks."

"Darling, *nobody* uses 'tanks.' Tanks are very twenti-eth century. The authorities don't have to use violent armed force. The world is past that phase as a civilization. If they want to pry us out of here, they'll just . . ."

Oscar fell silent suddenly. He hadn't really considered the options from the point of view of the authorities. The options for the authorities didn't seem very promising. Greta Penninger—and her allies—had just seized an armored biological laboratory. The place was blast-resistant and riddled with underground catacombs. There were hundreds of highly photogenic rare species inside, forming a combination mobile food source and corps of potential hostages. The facility had its own water supply, its own power supply, even its own atmosphere. Financial threats and embargoes were meaningless, because the financial systems had already been ruined by netwar viruses.

The place was sewn up tight. Greta's pocket revolutionaries had seized the means of information. They had commandeered the means of production. They had a loyal and aroused populace in a state of profound distrust for the outside world. They had conquered a mighty fortress.

Greta returned her attention to Kevin. "When can we junk these lousy prole phones and get our regular system back?"

Kevin was all helpfulness. "Well, I'll have to make sure it's fully secure first. . . . How many programmers can you give me?"

"I'll run a personnel search for telecom talent. Can you find me my own office here in the police station? I may be spending a lot of time in here."

Kevin grinned gamely. "Hey, you're the boss, Dr. Penninger!"

"I need some time off," Oscar realized. "Maybe a nice long nap. It's really been a trying day." They cordially ignored him. They were busy with their own agenda. He left the police station.

As he tottered through the darkened gardens toward the looming bulk of the Hot Zone, weariness overcame him with an evil metabolic rush. His day's experiences suddenly struck him as being totally insane. He'd been abducted, gassed, bombed; he'd traveled hundreds of miles in cheerless, battered vehicles; he'd concluded an unsavory alliance with a powerful gang of social outcasts; he'd been libeled, accused of embezzlement and criminal flight across state boundaries. . . . He'd arrested a group of police; he'd talked an armed fugitive into surrendering. . . . And now his sometime lover and his dangerously unbalanced security director were uniting to plot behind his back.

It was bad. Impossibly bad. But it still wasn't the worst. Because tomorrow was yet another day. Tomorrow, he would have to launch into a massive public-relations offensive that would somehow justify his actions.

He realized suddenly that he wasn't going to make it. It was overwhelming. It was just too much. He'd reached a condition of psychic overload. He was black, blue, and green with wounds and bruises; he was hungry, tired, overstressed, and traumatized; his nervous system was singing with stale adrenaline. Yet in his heart of hearts, he felt *good* about the day's events.

He'd outdone himself.

True, he'd suffered the elemental blunder of being kidnapped. But after that, he had handled every situation, every developing crisis, with astonishing aplomb and unbroken success. Every move had been the proper move at the proper moment, every option had been an inspired choice. It was just that there were *too many of them*. He was like an ice-skater performing an endless series of triple axels. Something was going to snap.

He felt a sudden need for shelter. Physical shelter. Locked doors, and a long silence.

Returning to the hotel was out of the question. There would be people there, questions, trouble. The Hot Zone, then.

He trudged to a Hot Zone airlock, now manned by a pair of elderly nomad sergeants, up on the night shift.

The camou-clad grannies were amusing themselves, doing cat's-cradle string-games with homemade yoyos of chemically soaked sponge. Oscar walked by the women with a ragged salute, and entered the empty halls of the Hot Zone.

He searched for a place to hide. An obscure equipment closet would be ideal. There was just one more little matter, before he relaxed and came fully apart at the seams. He needed to have his laptop. That was a deeply comforting thought to Oscar: retreating into a locked closet with a laptop to hold. It was an instinctive reaction to unbearable crisis; it was something he had been doing since the age of six.

He had left a spare laptop in Greta's lab. He crept into the place. The former Strike headquarters, once sterile and pristine, bore the scars of political backroom maneuvers—it was filthy now, full of scattered papers, half-eaten food, memos, bottles, junk. The whole room stank of panic. Oscar found his laptop, half buried below a stack of tapes and catalogs. He pulled it out, tucked it under his arm. Thank God.

His phone rang. He answered it by reflex. "Yes?"

"Am I lucky! Got the Soap Salesman first try! How's it goin', Soapy? Everything under control?"

It was Green Huey. Oscar's heart skipped a beat as he snapped to full attention. "Yes, thank you, Governor."

How on earth was Huey inside the lab's phones? Kevin had assured him that their encryption was uncrackable.

"I hope you don't mind a late cold-call, *mon ami*."

Oscar sat slowly on the laboratory floor, bracing his back on a metal cabinet. "By no means, Your Excellency. We live to serve."

"That's mighty good of you, Soapy! Lemme tell you where I am right now. I'm riding in a goddamn helicopter above the Sabine River, and I'm lookin' at a goddamn air strike."

"You don't say, sir."

"I DO SAY!" Huey screamed. "Those sons of bitches blew my people away! Black helicopters with missiles and automatic weapons, murdering American civilians on the ground! It was a goddamn massacre!"

"Were there many casualties, Governor? I mean, besides that unfortunate French submarine?"

"HELL YES there were casualties!" Huey screeched. "How could there not be casualties? Woods on both sides of the river were crawlin' with Regulators. Total operational dysfunction! Too many spooks spoil the broth! A total screwup! Goddammit, I *never ordered* those pencilnecks to dump you and the Genius Girl inside some goddamn fake ambulance!"

"No, Your Excellency?"

"Hell no! They were supposed to wait patiently and catch you when you were sneaking out of the lab together on a hot date. In *that* context, an abduction woulda *made sense*. The problem with nomads is mighty poor impulse control. Not what I wanted, boy, not on my agenda! I just had something that I needed to show ya, that's all. Right now, you and me and the ladylove coulda been puttin' our feet up, with parasols in our drinks. We're supposed to be havin' a scientific summit over here, we're supposed to be ironing out all our difficulties."

Oscar narrowed his burning, grainy eyes. "But the abduction team had a mishap on the road. They arrived late for the rendezvous. Your reception committee became anxious. When a federal SWAT team arrived unexpectedly, a violent encounter ensued."

Huey was silent.

Oscar felt his voice rising to a high, rapid-fire gabble. "Governor, I hope you'll believe me when I say I regret this event even more than you do. I can understand that it would have been of considerable political advantage to you if your agents could have apprehended us during a scandalous rendezvous. We'd have had very little recourse then, and it would have been a very effective gambit on your part. But let's face facts. You can't simply physically abduct a lab director and a federal official. That's not how the game is played. Commando adventures are politically foolish. They rarely work out in real life."

"Huh! Well, *you* seem to have managed a commando attack pretty well, bubba."

"Governor, when I arrived here two months ago, commandeering this lab by force of arms was the furthest thing from my mind. But given the circumstances, I had no other choice. Now just look at our situation. It's critically overburdened with extraneous factors. It's no longer simply a question of you, and me, and Senator Bambakias, and the scientists on Strike, and your loyal fifth column inside the lab. That was a very complex situation! But now we have federal SWAT teams, semicompetent Regulator goons, armed teenage girls, software attacks, libelous black-propaganda operations. . . . It's *all spinning totally out of control!*" Oscar's throat constricted in a shriek. He yanked the phone from his face.

Then he deliberately placed the phone against his ear again, as if it were the muzzle of a revolver. "This is going to cost me my Senate career. I suppose it's petty of me to mention that, but I enjoyed that work. I regret that. Personally."

"Son, it's *all right.* Calm down. I know what a promising Senate career can mean to a young man like you. That's exactly how I got into politics myself, don't you see? I was Senate chief of staff for Dougal of Texas when we built that lab in the first place."

"Governor, why have we come to this? Why are you trying so hard to outsmart me? We're both very smooth operators. We're outsmarting ourselves out of all sense and reason. Why didn't you just call me in for a private conference? I would have gone to see you. I would have negotiated. I'd have been happy to."

"No you wouldn't. Your Senator wouldn't have stood for that kind of mischief."

"I wouldn't have *told him* about it. I would have gone to meet you anyway. You're a major player. I have to talk to the players, or I'll never accomplish anything."

"Then the poor bastard really *is* through," Huey sighed. "You really don't care a hang about ol' Bambakias, you're runnin' around behind his back. Poor old Bombast Boy. . . . I never had nothin' against him; hell, I *love* Yankee egghead liberals who can't park their bicycles straight! Why on God's green earth did he ever get on my case about some pissant base-finance hassle? I cain't put up with that! I cain't have some freshman Senator yankin' my chain when he's got no grip on reality. A *hunger strike,* for Christ's sake—hell, *I* didn't starve him! He's rich, he could *afford* a lunch tab. He's got no common sense at all! You're a smart boy, you musta known all o' that."

"I knew that he was an idealist."

"Why'd you even pick on him?"

"He was the only one who was willing to hire me to run a Senate campaign," Oscar said.

Huey grunted. "Well! Okay then! Now it's makin' sense to me. I mighta known it was *you* all along, because you're a boy who's got some starch and fiber. But why the hell did you wind him up and send him after *me? Who are you,* anyhow? What the hell are you doin' inside my favorite science lab? You don't even know what they're up to in there. You don't even know what they're worth!"

"I have my suspicions," Oscar said. "They've got something crucially important to you here, and it's worth plenty."

"Look, I *need* that lab. I need those people. Sure, they've got something very special going on. I wouldn't fuss so much, otherwise. I was gonna demonstrate the app for y'all. It would have changed everything."

"Governor, don't try to mystify me. I already know what you were planning for us. Greta and I would have vanished into some offshore salt mine, where you and your industrial spies have been developing neural technology. It's a big neural breakthrough that's got you so anxious, and it has something to do with mind control. It's just like the animals in here. We would have turned into well-mannered zombies. We'd have become your de-feralized pets, and we would have agreed to anything you said. That's your ultimate network attack: subverting the human nervous system."

Huey barked with astonished laughter. "*What?* Who do you take me for, Mao Zedong? I don't need any brainwashed robots! I need *smart people,* all the smart people I can get! You just don't understand!"

"So what am I missing, exactly?"

"You're missing me, boy, *me*! I love my state! I love my people! Sure, *you* despise Louisiana, Mr. Harvard Business Boy—it's corrupt, it's too hot, it's half under water, it's dirt poor, it's poisoned with years of pesticides and pollution, it's all outta gas and oil for you Yankees to burn in the winter. Half its people speak the wrong goddamn language, but goddamn you, *people are still real here*! My people got soul, they've got spirit, they're authentic real-live *people*! We're not like the rest of the USA, where people are too sick and shocked and tired and spied-on even to fight for a decent future."

Huey coughed loudly and resumed bellowing into the phone. "They call me a 'rogue Governor'—well, what else *can* I be? All them 'Emergency committees'—they're totally illegal, oppressive, and unconstitutional! Look at this new President! He's a trigger-happy killer—and that's the very best man you got! That man wants me driven out of my own statehouse—hell, the President would like to *kill me*! I'm under constant threats to my life now! I watch the skies every minute so's I don't get fried like a fritter by goddamn X-ray lasers! And *you*—you think that I wanna lobotomize Nobel Prize winners! Are you as nuts as your boss? My God Almighty, why would I do that? Where is that supposed to get me?"

"Governor, if you'd told me these things earlier, I think we could have come to an understanding."

"Why the hell am *I* supposed to tell *you* a damn thing? You don't rank! You don't count! Am I supposed to drop my pants to every pipsqueak Senate staffer in America? You are a *political nightmare,* kid—a player with no history and no power base, who comes totally out of left field! If it weren't for you, everything would have been perfect! The air base would have gone broke. The science lab would have gone broke. All the people would have left nice and peaceable. I woulda picked 'em all up for a song."

Kevin arrived in the laboratory. He was wearing an ill-fitting cop's uniform, and he looked as if his feet ached badly. "Just a moment, Governor," Oscar said. He put his hand over the mouthpiece. "Kevin, how'd you find me in here?"

"There are location trackers in those phones."

Oscar throttled the phone with his fist. "You never told me that."

"You didn't need to know." Kevin frowned. "Oscar, pay attention, man. We have to go to the media center, right away. The President of the United States is on the line."

"Oh." Oscar removed his hand from the phone's mouthpiece. "Excuse me, Governor. I can't continue our discussion now—I have to field a call from the President."

"Now?" Huey yelled. "Doesn't anybody sleep anymore?"

"Good-bye, Governor. I appreciate your call."

"Wait! Wait. Before you do something stupid, I want you to know that you can still come and talk to me. Before everything gets out of hand . . . next time, let's talk it out first."

"It's good to know that we have that option, Your Excellency."

"Kid, listen! One last thing! As Governor of Louisiana, I strongly favor genetic industries. I got *no problem at all* with your personal background problem!"

Oscar hung up. His nerves were buzzing like a shattered electrical transformer. His eyes burned and the bare walls seemed to pitch. He threw an arm over Kevin's shoulder. "How are your feet, Kevin?"

"You sure you're all right?"

"I'm really dizzy." He snorted. His heart was pounding.

"Must be allergies," Kevin said. "Everybody gets allergies when they work in the Hot Zone. Kind of an occupational hazard."

Kevin's blather was light-years away. "Uh, why do you say that, Kevin?"

"Understanding workplace hazards is a basic mandate for the security professional, man."

The event affecting Oscar didn't feel like allergy. It felt like an undiagnosed concussion. Maybe some evil side effect of military knockout gas. Maybe an oncoming case of bad flu. It was bad. Very bad. He wondered if he was going to survive it. His heart gave a sudden lurch and began beating fast and lightly in his rib cage, like a trapped moth. He stumbled and almost fell.

"I think I need a doctor."

"Sure, man, *later*. Just as soon as you talk to the President."

Oscar blinked repeatedly. His eyes were swimming with tears. "I can't even *see*."

"Take some antihistamines. Listen, man—you can't blow it now, because this is *the President*! Get it? This is the big casino. If you don't chill him out about this Sabine River shootout, I'm done for. I'll be doing a bad-whitey terrorist rap, right next to my dad. And you, you personally, and Dr. Penninger too, you're both gonna go down in major flames. Okay? You have *got* to handle this."

"Right," Oscar said, straightening his back. Kevin was absolutely correct. This moment was the crux of his career. The President was waiting. Failure at this point was unthinkable. And he was having a heart fibrillation.

Kevin led him through the Hot Zone airlock. Then he pulled a monster beltphone and called a cab, and a fleet of twelve empty cabs arrived at once. Kevin picked one, and it took them to the media center. Up an elevator. Kevin led him to the green room, where Oscar scrubbed his head in the sink. He was coming apart. There were scarlet hives on his chest and throat. His hands were palsied. His skin was taut and prickly. But still, somehow, a gush of cold water on the nape of his neck brought him to snakelike alertness.

"Is there a comb?" Oscar asked.

"You won't need a comb," Kevin said. "The President's calling on a head-mounted display."

"What?" Oscar said. "Virtual reality? You're kidding! That stuff never works."

"They had VR installed in all the federal labs. Some high-bandwidth initiative from a million years ago. There's a VR set in the White House basement."

"And do you really know how to run this gizmo?"

"Hell no! I had to roust up half the lab just to find somebody who could boot it. Now there's a huge crowd sitting in there. They all know it's the President calling. You know how long it's been since a President took any notice of this place?"

Oscar fought for breath, staring in the mirror, willing his heart to slow. Then he walked into the studio, where they produced a casque like a deep-sea diver's helmet. They bolted it over his head.

The President was enjoying a stroll through amber waves of grain below the purple majesty of Colorado's Rocky Mountains. Oscar, after a moment's disorientation, recognized the backdrop as one of Two Feathers's campaign ads. Apparently this was the best virtual backdrop that the new White House staff could produce on short notice.

Leonard Two Feathers was a creature in stark contrast to a generation of prettified American politicians. The President had huge flat cheekbones, a great prow of a nose, a bank-vault slit of a mouth. Long black-and-gray hair streamed down his shoulders, which were clad in his trademark fringed buckskin jacket. The President's black, canny eyes seemed as wide apart as a hammerhead shark's.

"Mr. Valparaiso?" the President said.

"Yes? Good evening, Mr. President."

The President gazed at him silently. Apparently, to the President's eye, Oscar was a disembodied face floating somewhere at shoulder level.

"How is the situation at your facility? You and the Director, Dr. Penninger—are you safe and well?"

"So far so good, sir. We've sealed the premises. We suffered a severe netwar attack that trashed our financial systems, so we've had to cut most of our phone and computer lines. We still have internal problems with a group of malcontents who are occupying a building here. But our situation seems stable at this hour."

The President considered this. He was buying the story. It wasn't making him happy. "Tell me something, young man. What have you gotten me into? Why did it take a French submarine and three hundred Cajun guerrillas to kidnap you and some neurologist?"

"Governor Huguelet wanted to see us. He wants this facility, Mr. President. He has a great deal of irregular manpower. He has more manpower than he can properly control."

"Well, he *can't have* that facility."

"No sir?"

"No, he can't have it—and neither can you. Because it belongs to the country, dammit! What the hell are you up to? You can't hire Moderator militia and overpower a federal lab! That is not in your job description! You are a campaign organizer who has a patronage job. You are not Davy Crockett!"

"Mr. President, I completely concur. But we had no other realistic option. Green Huey is a clear and present danger. He's in league with a foreign power. He completely dominates his own state, and now he's launching paramilitary adventures over state borders. What else could I do? My security staffer informed your national security office as soon as he could. In the meantime, I took what steps I could."

"What is your party affiliation?" the President said.

"I'm a Federal Democrat, sir."

The President pondered this. The President's party was the Social Patriotic Movement, the "Soc-Pats." The Soc-Pats were the leading faction in the Left Tradition Bloc, which also included the Social Democrats, the Communist Party, Power to the People, Working America, and the ancient and shriveled Democratic Party. The Left Tradition Bloc had been suffering less ideological disarray than usual, lately. They had been able—barely—to seize the American Presidency.

"That would mean Senator Bambakias of Massachusetts?" he said.

"Yes, sir."

"What did you ever see in him?"

"I liked him. He has imagination and he's not corrupt."

"Well," the President said, "I am not a mentally ill Senator. I happen to be your President. I am your newly sworn-in President, and I have naive, new-hire staffers who are easily fooled by fast-talking hustlers with family links to white-supremacist gangsters. Now, thanks to you, I am also a President who has had the misfortune to kill and wound several dozen people. Some of them were foreign spies. But most of them were our fellow citizens."

Despite his expressed regret, the President looked quite ready to kill again.

"Mr. Valparaiso, I want you to listen to me carefully. I have about four more weeks—maybe three weeks—of political capital to expend. Then the honeymoon is over, and my office will be broken on the rack. I will have to face all the lawsuits, constitutional challenges, palace revolutions, outings, banking scandals, and Emergency machinations that have screwed every American President in the past twenty years. I want to survive all that. But I have no money, because the country is broke. I can't trust the Congress. I certainly can't trust the Emergency committees. I can't trust my own party apparatus. I'm the nation's Commander in Chief, but I can't even trust the armed forces. That leaves me with one source of direct Presidential power. My spooks."

"Yes, Mr. President."

"My spooks are gung ho! They just shot up a bunch of people in the dark of night, but at least they're not politicians, so at least they do what they're told. And since they're spooks, they don't officially exist. So the things they do don't officially happen. So if all the relevant parties keep their mouths shut, I might not have to account for this bloody debacle last night on the Louisiana border. Are you following me?"

"Yes, sir."

"I want you to resign your Senate post, first thing tomorrow. You cannot pull a stunt like the one you just pulled and call yourself a congressional staffer. Forget the Senate, and forget your poor friend the Senator. You are a pirate. The only way you can survive this situation is if you join my National Security staff. So, that's what you'll have to do. From now on, you'll be working for your President. You will be reporting to me. Your new title will be—NSC Science Adviser."

"I understand, sir. If I may say so, that's a very good situational analysis." There was no question that he would take the job. It would mean pruning himself away from the Bambakias inner circle; it would also mean abandoning months of painstaking backstage work in the Senate Science Committee. That was like losing two lobes of his brain in an instant. But of course he would drop everything to work for the President. Because it meant an instant leap to a much higher pinnacle of power—a pinnacle where options bloomed all around him like edelweiss. "Thank you for your offer, Mr. President. I'm honored. I accept with pleasure."

"You have been a cowboy. That was bad. Very bad. However, from now on, you are *my* cowboy. And just to make sure there are no more of these untoward incidents, I'm sending in a paratroop regiment of crack U.S. Army personnel to secure the lab's perimeter. You can expect them by seventeen hundred hours, tomorrow."

"Yes, Mr. President."

"My staff will be sending along a prepared statement for your Director to read to the cameras. That'll establish who's who and what's what, from now on. Now these are your marching orders, direct from your Commander in Chief. You keep that place out of the hands of Governor Huguelet. You will keep the data away from him, you will keep the personnel away from him, you will keep that place sewn up completely, until I understand just why that little man is so desperate to have it. If you succeed, I'll bring you into the White House. Fail, and we'll both go down in flames. But you will go down first, and hardest, and hottest, because I will be landing on top of you. Are we clear?"

"Perfectly clear, Mr. President."

"Welcome to the glamorous world of the executive branch." The President vanished. The amber waves continued on, serenely.

With persistent effort, they pried Oscar's head out of the virtuality rig. He found himself the center of the transfixed attention of two hundred people.

"Well?" Kevin demanded, brandishing a leftover microphone. "What did he say?"

"He hired me," Oscar announced. "I'm on the National Security staff."

Kevin's eyes widened. *"Really?"*

Oscar nodded. "The President is backing us! He's sending troops here to protect us!"

A ragged cheer broke out. The crowd was overjoyed. There was a pronounced hysteric edge to their reaction: farce, tragedy, triumph; they were punch-drunk. It was all they could do to jostle each other and yak into their phones.

Kevin shut off the microphone and tossed it aside. "Did he say anything about me?" Kevin asked anxiously. "I mean, about my waking him up last night, and all that?"

"Yes he did, Kevin. He mentioned you specifically."

Kevin turned to the person nearest at hand, who happened to be Lana Ramachandran. Lana had been rousted from a shower and had rushed to the media center in her dressing gown and slippers. "The President noticed me!" Kevin told her loudly, rising to his full height with a look of ennobled astonishment. "He talked about me! I really count for something! I matter to the President."

"God, you are hopeless!" Lana told him, gritting her teeth. "How could you do this to poor Oscar?"

"Do what?"

"*Look* at him, stupid! He's covered with hives!"

"Those aren't hives," Kevin corrected, staring at Oscar analytically. "It's more like heat rash or something."

"What is this huge bloody lump on his head? You're supposed to be his bodyguard, you dumb bastard! You're killing him! He's only flesh and blood!"

"No he's not," Kevin said, wounded. His phone rang. He answered it. "Yes?" He listened, and his face fell.

"That big stupid cop-dressing faker," Lana growled. "Oscar, what's wrong with you? Say something to me. Let me feel your pulse." She seized his wrist. "My God! Your skin's so hot!"

The front of Lana's dressing gown fell open. Oscar examined a semicircle of puckered brown nipple. The hair stood up on his neck. He suffered a sudden, violent, crazy surge of sexual arousal. He was out of control. "I need to lie down," he said.

Lana looked at him, biting her lip. Her doelike eyes brimmed with tears. "Why can't they tell when you're coming apart? Poor Oscar! Nobody even cares."

"Maybe a little ice water," he muttered.

Lana found his hat and set it gently on his head. "I'll get you out of here."

"Oscar!" Kevin shouted. "The south gate is open! The lab is being invaded! There are hundreds of nomads!"

Oscar responded instantly, with whipcrack precision. "Are they Regulators or Moderators?" But the emerging words were gibberish. His tongue had suddenly swollen inside his head. His tongue was bloated and huge. It was as if his mouth had two tongues in it.

"What'll we do?" Kevin demanded.

"Just *get away* from him! Let him be!" Lana shrieked. "Somebody help me with him! He needs help."

Once checked into the Collaboratory clinic, Oscar got the reaction he always received from medical personnel: grave puzzlement and polite distress. He was exhibiting many symptoms of illness, but he couldn't be properly diagnosed, because his metabolism simply wasn't entirely human. His temperature was soaring, his heart was racing, his skin was erupting, his blood pressure was off the scale.

Given his unique medical background, there was no obvious course of treatment.

Nevertheless, a proper head bandage, an ice pack, and a few hours of silence did him a lot of good. He finally drifted into a healing sleep. He woke at noon, feeling weary, sore, and shaken, but back in control. He sat up in his hospital bed, sipping tomato juice and examining news on his laptop. Kevin had abandoned him. Lana had insisted that the rest of the krewe leave him alone.

At one o'clock Oscar had an impromptu gaggle of visitors. Four hairy, booted nomads burst into his private room. The first was General Burningboy. His three young toughs looked impossibly sinister—war-painted, glowering, muscular.

The General had brought him a large bouquet. Holly, yellow daffodils, and mistletoe. The floral symbolism was painfully obvious.

"Howdy," said Burningboy, appropriating a vase and dumping its previous contents. "Heard you were feelin' poorly, so me and my boys dropped by to cheer you up."

Oscar gazed thoughtfully at the invaders. He was glad to see them. It improved his morale to be back on the job so quickly. "That's very good of you, General. Do have a seat."

Burningboy sat on the foot of the clinic bed, which squealed alarmingly under his weight. His three followers, ignoring the room's two chairs, crouched sullenly on the floor. The oldest one set his back firmly against the door.

"Not 'General.' Corporal. I'm Corporal Burningboy now."

"Why the demotion, Corporal?"

"Simple matter, really. I used up all my network trust and credibility when I ordered fifty girls into this facility. Those young women have fathers, mothers, brothers, and sisters—boyfriends, even. I put those little darlings into harm's way, just on my own recognizance.

And, well, that pretty much burned out all my credibility. Years of effort, right down the drain! Now, I'm just some little jasper."

Oscar nodded. "I take it this has something to do with reputation servers and your nomad networks of trust."

"Yup. You got it."

"It seems absurd that you should be demoted, when your paramilitary operation was such a signal success."

"Well now . . ." Burningboy squinted. "I *might* recoup some of my lost prestige—if it could be shown that we Moderators were derivin' some *benefit* from all this risky activity."

"Aha."

"So far, we haven't gotten a dang thing outta any of this, except a sleepless night for the worried families of our valiant warriors."

"Corporal, you are right. I completely concur with your analysis. Your help was invaluable, and as yet, we've done nothing for you in return. I acknowledge that debt. I am a man of my word. You were there for us when we needed you. I want to see you happy, Corporal Burningboy. Just tell me what you want."

Burningboy, all beard-grizzled smiles, turned to one of his companions. "Did you hear that? Beautiful speech, wasn't it? Didya get all that down on tape?"

"Affirmative," the nomad thug growled.

Burningboy returned his attention to Oscar. "I seem to recall a lot of pretty promises about how we Moderators were going to get a lovely press spin out of this, and how we were going to be knights and paladins of federal law and order, and all about how we were going to embarrass our old rivals the Regulators. . . . And not that I doubt your sworn word for a minute, Mr. Presidential Science Adviser, sir, but I just figured that with four hundred Moderators in-house, that would be . . . how do I put this?"

"You said it was an incentive," offered thug number two.

"That's the very word. 'Incentive.' "

"Very well," Oscar said. "The facility is in your hands. Your troops took it over last night; and now you've occupied it with hundreds of squatters. That wasn't a part of our original agreement, but I can understand your motives. I hope you can also understand mine. I talked to the President of the United States last night. He told me he's sending in troops."

"He did, eh?"

"Yes. He promised that a crack brigade of armed paratroops would be flying in this very evening, actually. You might want to take that matter under advisement."

"Man, that's Two Feathers all over," Burningboy sighed. "I'm not sayin' that old Geronimo actually *lied* to you or anything, but he's kind of famous for that gambit. We Moderators go back pretty far in Colorado, and back when Two Feathers was Governor, he was always sayin' he'd roust out the National Guard and restore so-called law and order. . . . Sometimes he actually *did it,* enough to keep you off balance. But just 'cause Two Feathers is wearin' his war paint, that don't guarantee any war."

"So you're alleging that the President won't send troops?"

"No. I'm just sayin' that we don't plan to leave until these so-called troops show up. In fact, we probably won't leave, even *after* they show up. I'm not sure you grasp this situation, you being from Massachusetts and all. But we Moderators have had some dealings with the Governor of Colorado. In fact, he owes us some favors."

"That's an interesting allegation, Corporal."

"We nomads tend to stick around in times and places where nobody else can survive. That makes us pretty useful sometimes. Especially given that Wyoming was on fire recently, and all that."

"I see." Oscar paused. "Why are you telling me this?"

"Well, sir, I hate to badger a man when he's feeling poorly. . . . But frankly, you're the only man I *can* tell these things to. You seem to be pretty much *all there is* around here. I mean, we just got a very firm lecture from your so-called Director. The woman just don't *listen*. She has no idea how people live! We were explainin' to her that we hold all the cards now, and she's totally at our mercy and so on, but she's just not buyin' any of it. She just waits for my lips to stop movin', and then she launches into this nutty rant about intellectual freedom and the advancement of knowledge and Christ only knows what else. . . . She's really *weird*. She's just a weird-actin', weird-looking, weird, witchy woman. Then we tried talkin' to your so-called chief of police. . . . What is it with that guy?"

"What do you mean, Corporal?"

Burningboy became uneasy, but he was determined to see the matter through. "It's not that I have anything against Anglos! I mean, *sure* there are good, decent, law-abiding Anglo people. But—you know—look at the statistics! Anglos have white-collar crime rates right off the scale. And talk about *violent*—man, white people are the most violent ethnic group in America. All those cross burnings, and militia bombings, and gun-nut guys . . . the poor bastards just can't get a grip."

Oscar considered this. It always offended him to hear his fellow Americans discussing the vagaries of "white people." There was simply no such thing as "white people." That stereotype was an artificial construct, like the ridiculous term "Hispanic." In all the rest of the world, a Peruvian was a Peruvian and a Brazilian was a Brazilian— it was only in America that people somehow became this multilingual, multinational entity called a "Hispanic." Oscar himself passed for a "Hispanic" most of the time, though his own ethnic background was best described as "Not of Human Origin."

"You need to get to know my friend Kevin," he said. "Kevin's a diamond in the rough."

"Okay. Sure. I like a man who sticks up for his friends," Burningboy said. "But that's the real reason we're here now, Oscar. You're the only man in this place who can talk sense to us. You're the only one who even knows what's going on."

10

Oscar now worked for the President of the United States. His new position was enormously helpful in dealing with two thousand naive scientists inside a dome in East Texas. As a practical matter, however, it merely added a new layer of complexity to Oscar's life.

Oscar swiftly discovered that he was not, in fact, the National Security Council's official Science Adviser. A routine security check by the White House krewe had swiftly revealed Oscar's personal background problem. This was a serious hitch, as the President did not currently employ anyone who was a product of outlaw South American genetic engineering. Given the circumstances, hiring one seemed a bad precedent.

So, although Oscar had obediently resigned his Senate committee post, he failed to achieve an official post with the National Security Council. He was merely an "informal adviser." He had no official ranking in the government, and did not even receive a paycheck.

Despite the President's assertion, no "crack U.S. Army personnel" arrived in Buna. It seemed that a Presidential order had been issued, but the Army deployment had been indefinitely delayed due to staffing and budget problems. These "staffing and budget problems" were certainly likely enough—they were chronic in the military—but the deeper problems were, of course, political. The U.S. Army as an institution was very mulish about being ordered into potential combat against American civilians. The U.S. Army hadn't been involved in the gruesome and covert helicopter shoot-out on the banks of the Sabine River. The Army wasn't anxious to take the political heat for trigger-happy spooks from the NSC.

As a sop to propriety, Oscar was told that an NSC lieutenant colonel would soon arrive, with a crack team of very low-profile Marine aviators. But then the lieutenant colonel was also delayed, due to unexpected foreign-policy developments.

An American-owned fast-food multinational had accidentally poisoned a number of Dutch citizens with poorly sterilized hamburger meat. In retaliation, angry Dutch zealots had attacked and torched several restaurants. Given strained Dutch-American relations, this was a serious scandal and close to a casus belli. The President, faced with his first foreign-policy crisis, was blustering and demanding reparations and formal apologies. Under these circumstances, military disorder within the U.S. was not an issue that the Administration cared to emphasize.

These were all disappointments. However, Oscar bore up. He was peeved to be denied a legitimate office, but he wasn't surprised. He certainly wasn't under the illusion that the presidency worked any better than any other aspect of contemporary American government. Besides, there were distinct advantages to his questionable status. Despite the humiliations, Oscar was now far more powerful than he had ever been before. Oscar had become a spook. Spookhood was doable.

Oscar swiftly made himself a factor with the new powers lurking in the basement below the Oval Office. He studied their dossiers, memorized their names and the office flowcharts, and asserted himself in the organization by humbly demanding favors. They were small, easily granted favors, but they were carefully arranged so that a failure to grant them was sure to provoke a turf war in the White House staff. Consequently, Oscar got his way.

He resolved one nagging problem by obliterating the local police force. He had the Collaboratory's captive police flown out of Texas in an unmarked cargo helicopter. They were transferred to a federal law enforcement training facility in West Virginia. The Collaboratory's cops were not fired, much less were they tried for malfeasance and bribe-taking; but the budget of their tiny agency was zeroed-out, and the personnel simply vanished forever into the mazes of federal reassignment.

This left the Collaboratory with no working budget for a police force. But that was doable. Because at the moment, there were no budgets of any kind at the Collaboratory. Everyone was working for no pay. They were living off barter, back gardens, surplus office equipment, and various forms of left-handed pin money.

The days that followed were the most intense and productive of Oscar's political life. The lab's situation was an absolute shambles. Only organizational skill of genius could have retrieved it. Oscar didn't possess the skill of genius. However, he could successfully replace genius through the simple expedient of giving up sleep and outworking everyone else.

The first truly serious challenge was to mollify the giant invasion of Moderators. The Moderators had to be dissuaded from wrecking and sacking the facility. Oscar finessed this through the simple gambit of informing the Moderators that they now *owned* the facility. Obviously, they could wreck the place at will, but if they did so, the life-support systems would collapse, the atmosphere would sour, and all the glamorous and attractive rare animals would die. The Moderators would choke with everyone else, in an uninhabitable glass ghetto. However, if they came to working terms with the aboriginal scientists, the Moderators would possess a giant genetic Eden where they could live outdoors without tents.

Oscar's argument carried the day. There were naturally a few ugly incidents, in which proles abducted and

barbecued some especially tasty animals. But the ghastly
stench made it clear that open fires within the dome were
counterproductive for everyone. The situation failed to
explode. As days passed it began to show definite signs of
stabilizing.

A new committee was formed, to negotiate the
terms for local coexistence between the scientists and the
invading dropouts. It consisted of Greta, the board's division heads, Kevin, Oscar himself, occasional consultant
members of Oscar's krewe, and a solemn variety of gurus,
sachems, and muckety-mucks from Burningboy's contingent. This new governing body needed a name. It
couldn't be called the "Strike Committee," as that term
had already been used. It swiftly became known as the
"Emergency Committee."

Oscar regretted this coinage, as he loathed and despised all Emergency committees; but the term had one
great advantage. It didn't have to be explained to anyone.
The American populace was already used to the spectacle
of its political institutions collapsing, to be replaced by
Emergency committees. Having the Collaboratory itself
run by an "emergency committee" was an easy matter to
understand. It could even be interpreted as a prestigious
step upward; it was as if the tiny Collaboratory had collapsed as grandly as the U.S. Congress.

Oscar canceled his public relations poster campaign.
The Strike was well and truly over now, and the lab's new
regime required a new graphic look and a fresh media
treatment. After a brainstorming session with his krewe,
Oscar decided on the use of loudspeakers. The Emergency
Committee's continuing negotiations would be broadcast
live on half a dozen loudspeakers, situated in various public areas within the dome.

This proved a wise design choice. The loudspeakers
had a pleasantly makeshift, grass-rootsy feeling. People
could gently drift in and out of the flow of political agita-
tion. The antiquated technology provided a calming, pe-

ripheral media environment. People could become just as aware of the continuing crisis as they felt they needed to be.

Thanks to the use of loudspeakers, the Collaboratory personnel and their mongrelized invaders were placed on an equal informational plane. As an additional gambit, tasteful blue plastic "soapboxes" were set up here and there, where especially foolish and irate people could safely vent their discontents. Not only was this a safety valve and a useful check on popular sentiment, but it made the gimcrack Emergency Committee seem very adult and responsible by contrast.

This media campaign was especially useful in finessing the severe image problem presented by Captain (once General, once Corporal) Burningboy. In person or on video, the prole leader looked impossibly crazed and transgressive. However, he had a deep, fatherly speaking voice. Over the loudspeakers, Burningboy radiated the pious jollity of an arsonist Santa Claus.

It was a misconception to imagine that the Moderators were merely violent derelicts. The roads of America boasted a great many sadly desperate people, but the Moderators were not a mob of hobos. The Moderators were no longer even a "gang" or a "tribe." Basically, the Moderators were best understood as a nongovernmental network organization. The Moderators deliberately dressed and talked like savages, but they didn't lack sophistication. They were organized along new lines that were deeply orthogonal to those of conventional American culture.

It had never occurred to the lords of the consumer society that consumerism as a political philosophy might one day manifest the grave systemic instabilities that Communism had. But as those instabilities multiplied, the country had cracked. Civil society shriveled in the pitiless reign of cash. As the last public spaces were privatized, it became harder and harder for American culture to breathe. Not only were people broke, but they were

taunted to madness by commercials, and pitilessly sur-
veilled by privacy-invading hucksters. An ever more aggressive consumer-outreach apparatus caused large
numbers of people to simply abandon their official identi-
ties.

It was no longer any fun to be an American citizen.
Bankruptcies multiplied beyond all reason, becoming a
kind of commercial apostasy. Tax dodging became a spectator sport. The American people simply ceased to behave. They gathered to publicly burn their licenses, chop
up their charge cards, and hit the road. The proles considered themselves the only free Americans.

Nomadism had once been the linchpin of human
existence; it was settled life that formed the technological
novelty. Now technology had changed its nonexistent
mind. Nomads were an entire alternate society for whom
life by old-fashioned political and economic standards was
simply no longer possible.

Or so Oscar reasoned. As a wealthy New Englander,
he had never had much political reason to concern himself
with proles. They rarely voted. But he had no prejudice
against proles as a social group. They were certainly no
stranger or more foreign to his sensibilities than scientists
were. Now it was clear to him that the proles were a
source of real power, and as far as he knew, there was only
one American politician who had made a deliberate effort
to recruit and sustain them. That politician was Green
Huey.

Having pacified the Moderators, Oscar's second order of business was reconciling the Collaboratory's scientists to their presence. Oscar's key talking point here was
their stark lack of choice in the matter.

The Collaboratory's scientists had always had firm
federal backing; they had never required any alternate
means of support. Now there was no federal largesse left.
That was bad, but the underlying reality was much, much
worse. The lab's bookkeeping had been ruined by a

netwar attack. The Collaboratory was not only broke, its inhabitants were fiscally unable even to assess how broke they were. They couldn't even accurately describe the circumstances under which they might be bailed out.

Morale at the lab had soared on the news that the President had taken notice of their plight. The President had even gone so far as to send a prepared speech for the lab's Director, which was duly recited by Greta. However, the speech had a very conspicuous omission: money. The press release was basically a long grateful paean to the President's talent for restoring law and order. Financing the Collaboratory was not the President's problem. The Congress was in charge of the nation's purse strings, and despite frenzied effort, the Congress had still not managed to pass a budget.

For a federal science facility, this was a disaster of epic magnitude, but for proles, it was business as usual.

So—as Oscar explained to the Emergency Committee—it was a question of symbiosis. And symbiosis was doable. Having boldly cut its ties to the conventional rules of political reality, the Collaboratory's new hybrid population could float indefinitely within their glass bubble. They had no money, but they had warmth, power, air, food, shelter; they could all mind the business of living. They could wait out the turbulence beyond their borders, and since they were also ignoring federal oversight, they could all concentrate on their favorite pet projects. They could get some genuine scientific work accomplished, for once. This was a formidable achievement, a Shangri-la almost, and it was there within their grasp. All they had to do was come to terms with their own contradictions.

There was a long silence after Oscar's presentation. The Emergency Committee gazed at him in utter wonderment. At the moment, the Committee's quorum consisted of Greta, her chief confidant and backer Albert Gazzaniga, Oscar himself, Yosh Pelicanos, Captain Burningboy, and a representative Moderator thug—a kid named Ombahway Tuddy Flagboy.

"Oscar, you're amazing," Greta said. "You have such talent for making impossible things sound plausible."

"What's so impossible about it?"

"Everything. This is a federal facility! These Moderator people invaded it by force. They're occupying it. They are here illegally. We can't aid and abet that! Once the President sends in troops, we'll all be outed for collaboration. We'll be arrested. We'll be fired. No, it's worse than that. We'll be purged."

"That never happened in Louisiana," Oscar said. "Why should it happen here?"

Gazzaniga spoke up. "That's because Congress and the Emergency committees never really wanted that air base in Louisiana in the first place. They never cared enough about it to take action."

"They don't care about you, either," Oscar assured him. "It's true that the President expressed an interest, but hey, it's been a long week now. A week is forever during a military crisis. There aren't any federal troops here. Because there isn't any military crisis here. The President's military crisis is in Holland, not East Texas. He's not going to deploy troops domestically when the Dutch Cold War is heating up. If we had better sense, we'd realize that the Moderators *are* our troops. They're *better* than federal troops. Real troops can't *feed us*."

"We can't afford thousands of nonpaying guests," Pelicanos said.

"Yosh, just forget the red ink for a minute. We don't have to 'afford them.' They are affording *us*. They can feed and clothe us, and all we have to do is share our shelter and give them a political cover. That's the real beauty of this Emergency, you see? We can go on here indefinitely! This is the apotheosis of the Strike. During the Strike, we were all refusing to do anything except work on science. Now that we have an Emergency, the scientists can continue their science, while the Moderators will assume the role of a supportive, sympathetic, civil population. We'll just *ignore* everyone else! Everything that annoyed us in the past simply falls off our radar. All those senseless commercial demands, and governmental oversight, and the crooked contractors . . . they're all just gone. They no longer have any relevance."

"But nomads don't understand science," Gazzaniga said. "Why would they support scientists, when they could just loot the place and leave?"

"Hey," said Burningboy. "I can understand science, fella! Wernher von Braun! Perfect example. Dr. von Braun lucked into a big ugly swarm of the surplus flesh, just like you have! They're heading for Dachau anyway if he don't use 'em, so he might as well grind some use out of 'em, assembling his V-2 engines."

"What the hell is he talking about?" Gazzaniga demanded. "Why does he always talk like that?"

"That's what science is!" Burningboy said. "I can define it. Science is about proving a mathematical relationship between phenomenon A and phenomenon B. Was that so hard? You really think that's beyond my mental grasp? I'll tell you something *way* beyond *your* mental grasp, son—surviving in prison. You fair-haired folks might have, like, a bruising collision with nonquantum reality if somebody drove a handmade shiv right through your physics book."

"This just isn't going to work," Greta said. "We don't even speak the same language. We have nothing in common." She pointed dramatically. "Just look at that laptop he's carrying! It's *made out of straw*."

"Why am I the only one who sees the obvious here?" Oscar said. "You people have amazing commonalities. Look at all that nomad equipment—those leaf grinders, and digesters, and catalytic cracking units. They're using biotechnology. And computer networks, too. They live off those things, for heaven's sake."

Greta's face hardened. "Yes but . . . not *scientifically*."

"But they live exactly like you live—by their reputations. You are America's two most profoundly noncommercial societies. Your societies are both based on reputation, respect, and prestige."

Gazzaniga frowned. "What is this, a sociology class? Sociology's not a hard science."

"But it's true! You scientists want to become the Most Frequently Cited and win all the honors and awards. While Moderators, like the Captain here, want to be streetwise netgod gurus. As a further plus, neither of you have any idea how to dress! Furthermore, even though you are both directly responsible for the catastrophe that our society is undergoing, you are both incredibly adept at casting yourselves as permanent, misunderstood victims. You both whine and moan endlessly about how nobody else is cool enough or smart enough to understand you. And you both never clean up your own messes. And you both never take responsibility for yourselves. And that's why you're both treated like children by the people who actually run this country!"

They stared at him, appalled.

"I am talking sense to you here," Oscar insisted, his voice rising to an angry buzz. "I am *not ranting*. I possess a perspective here that you people, who are locked in the ivory basements of your own subcultures, simply do not possess. It is no use my soft-pedaling the truth to you. You are in a crisis. This is a crux. You have both severed your lifelines to the rest of society. You need to overcome your stupid prejudice, and unite as a powerful coalition. And if you could only do this, the world would be yours!"

Oscar leaned forward. Inspiration blazed within him like Platonic daylight. "We can survive this Emergency. We could even prevail. We could grow. If we handled it right, this could catch on!"

"All right," Greta said. "Calm down. I have one

question. They're *nomads*, aren't they? What happens after they leave us?"

"You think that we'll run away," Burningboy said.

Greta looked at him, sad at having given offense. "Don't you always run away? I thought that was how you people survived."

"No, *you're* the gutless ones!" Burningboy shouted. "You're supposed to be intellectuals! You're supposed to be our visionaries! You're supposed to be giving people a grasp of the truth, something to look up to, the power, the knowledge, *higher reality*. But what are you people really? You're not titans of intellect. You're a bunch of cheap geeks, in funny clothes that your mom bought you. You're just another crowd of sniveling hangers-on who are dying for a government handout. You're whining to me about how dirty morons like us can't appreciate you—well, what the hell have you done for us lately? What do you want out of life, besides a chance to hang out in your lab and look down on the rest of us? Quit being such a pack of sorry weasels—do something *big,* you losers! Take a chance, for Christ's sake. Act like you matter!"

"He's really lost it," Gazzaniga said, goggling in wounded amazement. "This guy has no grasp of real life."

Flagboy's phone rang. He spoke briefly, then handed the phone to his leader.

Burningboy listened. "I gotta go," he announced abruptly. "There's been a new development. The boys have brought in a prisoner."

"What?" Kevin demanded. As the new police chief, Kevin was instantly suspicious. "We already agreed that you have no authority to take prisoners."

Burningboy wrinkled his large and fleshy nose. "They captured him in the piney woods east of town, Mr. Police Chief, sir. Several kilometers outside your jurisdiction."

"So then's he's a Regulator," Oscar said. "He's a spy."

Burningboy put his notes and laptop in order, and nodded at Oscar reluctantly. "Yup."

"What are you going to do to this captured person?" Greta said.

Burningboy shrugged, his face grim.

"I think this Committee needs to see the prisoner," Oscar said.

"Oscar's right," said Kevin sternly. "Burningboy, I can't have you manhandling suspects inside this facility, just on your own recognizance. Let's interrogate him ourselves!"

"What are we, the Star Chamber?" Gazzaniga said, aghast. "We can't start interrogating people!"

Kevin sneered. "Okay, fine! Albert, you're excused. Go out for an ice cream cone. In the meantime, us grownups need to confront this terrorist guerrilla."

Greta declared a five-minute break. Alerted by the live coverage over the loudspeakers, several more Committee members showed up. The break stretched into half an hour. The meeting was considerably enlivened by an impromptu demonstration of the prisoner's captured possessions.

The apprehended Regulator had been posing as a poacher. He had a pulley-festooned compound bow that would have baffled William Tell. The bow's graphite arrows contained self-rifling gyroscopic fletching and global-positioning-system locator units. The scout also owned boot-spike crampons and a climber's lap-belt, ideal for extensive lurking in the tops of trees. He carried a ceramic bowie knife.

These deadly gizmos might have passed muster on a standard hunter, but the other evidence cinched the case against him: he had a hammer and a pack of sabotage tree-spikes. Tree-spikes, which ruined saw blades, were common enough for radical Greens; but these spikes contained audio bugs and cellphone repeaters. They could be hammered deep into trees, and they would stay there forever, and they would listen, and they would even take phone calls. They had bizarre little pores in them so that they could drink sap for their batteries.

The Committee passed the devices from hand to hand, studying them with grave attention, much as if they captured saboteurs every day. Producing a pocket multitool, Gazzaniga managed to pry one of the spikes open. "Wait a minute," he said. "This thing's got a mitochondrial battery."

"Nobody has mitochondrial batteries," objected the new head of the Instrumentation division. "*We* don't even have mitochondrial batteries, and the damned things were invented here."

"Then I want you to explain to me how a telephone runs on wet jelly," Gazzaniga said. "You know something? These spikes sure look a lot like our vegetation monitors."

"It was *all* invented here," Oscar said. "This is all Collaboratory equipment. You've just never seen it repackaged and repurposed."

Gazzaniga put the spike down. Then he picked up a dented tin egg. "Now this thing here—see, this is the sort of thing you associate with nomad technology. Scrap metal, all crimped together, obviously homemade. . . . So what is this thing?" He shook it near his ear. "It rattles."

"It's a piss bomb," Burningboy told him.

"What?"

"See those holes in the side? That's the timer. It's genetically engineered corn kernels. Once they're in hot water, the seeds swell up. They rupture a membrane inside, and then the charge ignites."

Oscar examined one of the crude arson bombs. It had been created by hand: by a craftsman with a hole punch, a ball peen hammer, and an enormous store of focused resentment. The bomb was a dumb and pig-simple incendiary device with no moving parts, but it could easily incinerate a building. The seeds of genetically engineered maize were dirt-cheap and totally consistent. Corn like that was so uniform in its properties that it could even be used as a timepiece. It was a bad, bad gizmo. It was bad enough as a work of military technology. As a work of primitive art, the piss bomb was stunningly effective. Oscar could feel sincere contempt and hatred radiating from it as he held it in his hand.

The prisoner now arrived, handcuffed, and with an escort of four Moderators. The prisoner wore a full-length hunter's suit of gray and brown bark-and-leaf camou, including a billed cap. His lace-up boots were clogged with red mud. He had a square nose, large hairy ears, heavy brows, black shiny eyes. He was a squat and heavy man in his thirties, with hands like callused bear paws. He'd suffered a swollen scrape along his unshaven jaw and had a massive bruise on his neck.

"What happened to him? Why is he injured?" Greta said.

"He fell off his bicycle," Burningboy offered flatly.

The prisoner was silent. It was immediately and embarrassingly obvious to all concerned that he was not going to tell them a thing. He stood solidly in the midst of their boardroom, reeking of woodsmoke and sweat, radiating complete contempt for them, everything they stood for, and everything they knew. Oscar examined the Regulator with deep professional interest. This man was astoundingly out of place. It was as if a rock-hard cypress log had been hauled from the bat-haunted depths of the swamp and dumped on the carpet before them.

"You really think you're a tough customer, don't you?" Kevin said shrilly.

The Regulator signally failed to notice him.

"We can make you talk," Kevin growled. "Wait'll I load up my anarchy philes on improvising interrogation! We'll do hideous and gruesome things to you! With wire, and matchsticks, and like that."

"Excuse me, sir," Oscar said politely. "Do you speak English? *Parlez-vous français?*"

No response at all.

"We're not going to torture you, sir. We are civilized people here. We just want you to tell us why you were exploring our neighborhood with all these surveillance and arson devices. We're willing to be very reasonable about this. If you'll tell us what you were doing and who told you to do it, we'll let you go home."

No answer.

"Sir, I recognize that you're loyal to your cause, whatever it is, but you *are* captured, you know. You don't have to remain entirely mute under circumstances like this. It's considered entirely ethical to give your name, your number, and your network address. If you did that for us, we could tell your friends—your wife, your children— that you're alive and safe."

No answer. Oscar sighed patiently. "Okay, you're not going to talk. I can see that I'm tiring you. So if you'll just indicate that you're not *deaf* . . ."

The Regulator's heavy eyebrows twitched. He looked at Oscar, sizing him up for a bloodletting bowshot to the kidneys. Finally, he spoke. "Nice wristwatch, hand-some."

"Okay," Oscar breathed. "Let me suggest that we take our friend here and dump him into the Spinoffs building, along with those other Huey scabs. I'm sure they all have a lot of news to catch up on."

Gazzaniga was scandalized. "What! We can't send this character in there to rendezvous with those people! He's very dangerous! He's a vicious nomad brute!"

Oscar smiled. "So what? *We* have *hundreds* of vicious nomad brutes. Forget talking to this guy. We don't need him. We need to talk seriously to our own nomads. They know everything that he knows, and more. Plus, our friends actually want to defend us. So can we all knuckle down and get serious now? Boys, take the prisoner away."

After this confrontation, the Emergency negotiations rapidly moved onto much firmer ground: equipment and instrumentation. Here the nomads and scientists found compelling common interests. Their mutual need to eat was especially compelling. Burningboy introduced three of his technical experts. Greta commandeered the time of her best biotech people. The talks plowed on into darkness.

Oscar left the building, changed his clothes to shed any cling-on listening devices, then went into one of the gardens for a quiet rendezvous with Captain Burningboy.

"Man, you're a sneaky devil," Burningboy ruminated, methodically chewing on a long handful of dry blue noodles. "The tone of that meeting changed totally when you had that goon brought in. I wonder what they'd have done if he'd told 'em that we caught him two days ago."

"Oh, we both knew that Regulator was never going to talk," Oscar said. "I was reserving him for the proper political moment. There's nothing dishonest about revealing the facts within the proper context. After all, you did capture him, and he is a commando." They lowered their voices and tiptoed to avoid a dozing lynx. "You see, talking common sense to scientists just doesn't work. Scientists despise common sense, they think it's irrational. To get 'em off the dime, you need strong moral pressure, something from outside their expectations. They live with big intellectual walls around them—peer review, passive construction, all this constant use of the third person plural. . . ."

"I'm handing it to you, Oscar—the gambit worked great. But I still don't see why."

Oscar paused thoughtfully. He enjoyed his private chats with Burningboy, who was proving to be an appreciative audience. The Texan Moderator was an aging, disheveled outlaw with a long prison record, but he was also a genuine politician, a regional player full of southern-fried insights. Oscar felt a strong need to give the man a collegial briefing.

"It worked because . . . well, let me give you the big picture here. The really big, philosophical picture. Did you ever wonder why I've never moved against Huey's people inside this lab? Why they're still inside there, holding the Spinoffs building, barricaded against us? It's because we're in a netwar. We're just like a group of go-stones. To survive in a netwar, a surrounded group needs eyes. It's all about links, and perception, and the battle-space. We're surrounded inside this dome—but we're not *entirely* surrounded, because there's a smaller dome of enemies inside our dome. I deliberately threw that Regulator in there with them, so that now, that little subgroup has its own little nomad contingent, just like we do. You see, people instinctively sense this kind of symmetry. It works on them, on an unconscious level. It's meaningful to them, it changes their worldview. Having enemies inside the dome might seem to weaken us, but the fact that we can tolerate our own core of dissent—that actually strengthens us. Because we're not totalitarian. We're not the same substance all the way through. We're not all brittle. We're resilient. We have potential space inside."

"Yes?" Burningboy said skeptically.

"There's a vital fractal there. It's all about scaling issues, basically. Here we are, inside these walls. Outside our walls, Green Huey is lurking over us, full of sinister intent. But the President is lurking over Huey—and our new President is, in his own unique way, a rather more sinister person than the Governor of Louisiana. The President runs the USA, a nation that is all wounded and inward-turning now—a little world, surrounded by a bigger world full of people who grew bored with us. They no longer pay America to tell them that we are their future. And then beyond that world . . . well, I guess it's Greta's world. A rational, Einsteinian-Newtonian cosmos. The cosmos of

objective, observable facts. And beyond scientific understanding . . . all those dark phenomena. Metaphysics.
Will and idea. History, maybe."

"Do you really believe any of that junk?"

"No, I don't believe it in the way that I believe that
two and two are four. But it's doable, it's my working
metaphor. What can politicians ever really 'know' about
anything? History isn't a laboratory. You never step in the
same river twice. But some people have effective political
insight, and some just don't."

Burningboy nodded slowly. "You really see us from
way, *way* on the outside, don't you, Oscar?"

"Well, I've never been a nomad—at least not yet.
And I'll never be a scientist, either. I can recognize my
ignorance, but I can't be buffaloed by ignorance—I'm in
power, I have to act. Knowledge is just knowledge. But
the *control* of knowledge—that's politics."

"That wasn't the kind of 'outsiderness' I had in
mind."

"Oh." Oscar realized the truth. "You mean my personal background problem."

"Yup."

"You mean I have advantages because I'm outside
the entire human race."

Burningboy nodded. "I couldn't help but notice
that. Has it always been that way for you?"

"Yeah. It has. Pretty much."

"Are you the future, man?"

"No. I wouldn't count on that. I have too many
pieces missing."

Oscar knew that the situation had stabilized when a roaring sex scandal broke out. A teenage soldier accused a
middle-aged scientist of indecently fondling her. This incident caused frantic uproar.

Oscar found the scandal a very cheering development. It meant that the conflict between the Collaboratory's two populations had broken through to a symbolic, psychosexual, politically meaningless level. The public fight was now about deep resentments and psychic starvations that would never, ever be cured, and were therefore basically irrelevant. But the noise was very useful, because it meant that enormous quiet progress could now be made on every other front. The public psychodrama consumed vast amounts of attention, while the Collaboratory's truly serious problems had become background noise. The real problems were left in the hands of people who cared enough about them to do constructive things.

Oscar took the opportunity to learn how to use a Moderator laptop. He had been given one, and he rightly recognized this gesture as a high tribal honor. The Moderator device had a flexible green shell of plasticized straw. It weighed about as much as a bag of popcorn. And its keyboard, instead of the time-honored QWERTYUIOP, boasted a sleek, sensible, and deeply sinister DHIATENSOR.

Oscar had been assured many times that the venerable QWERTYUIOP keyboard design would never, ever be replaced. Supposedly, this was due to a phenomenon called "technological lock-in." QWERTYUIOP was a horribly bad design for a keyboard—in fact, QWERTYUIOP was deliberately designed to hamper typists—but the effort required to learn it was so crushing that people would never sacrifice it. It was like English spelling, or American standard measurements, or the ludicrous design of toilets; it was very bad, but it was a social fact of nature. QWERTYUIOP's universality made it impossible for alternatives to arise and spread.

Or so he had always been told. And yet, here was the impossible alternative, sitting on the table before him: DHIATENSOR. It was sensible. It was efficient. It worked much better than QWERTYUIOP.

Pelicanos entered the hotel room. "Still up?"

"Sure."

"What are you working on?"

"Greta's press releases. And I've got to talk to Bambakias soon, I've been neglecting the Senator. So I'm making some notes, and I'm learning how to type properly, for the very first time in my life." Oscar paused. He was eager to brief Pelicanos on the fascinating social differences he had discovered between the Regulators and the Moderators. To the undiscerning eye, the shabby and truculent proles could not be distinguished with an electron microscope—all their real and genuinely striking differences were inherent in the architecture of their network software.

An epic struggle had been taking place in the invisible fields of the networks. Virtual tribes and communities had been trying literally thousands of different configurations, winnowing them out, giving them their all, watching them die. . . .

"Oscar, we need to talk seriously."

"Great." Oscar pushed the laptop aside. "Level with me."

"Oscar, you're getting too wrapped up here. All the negotiations with the Emergency Committee, all the time you spend dickering with those NSC people who won't give you the time of day . . . we need a reality check."

"Okay. Fine."

"Have you been outside the lab lately? The sky is full of 'delivery aircraft' that never deliver anything to anyone. There are cops and roadblocks all over East Texas."

"Yeah, we're generating a lot of sustained outside interest. We're a big pop hit. Journalists love the mix here, it's very provocative."

"I agree with you that it's interesting. But that has nothing to do with our agenda. This situation was never in the plans. We were supposed to be helping Bambakias with the Senate Science Committee. The campaign krewe are supposed to be here *on vacation.* You were never supposed to become a spook who works part-time for the President, while you take over federal facilities with the help of gangsters."

"Hmm. You're absolutely right about that, Yosh. That was not plannable. But it was doable."

Pelicanos sat down and knotted his hands. "You know what your problem is? Every time you lose sight of your objective, you redouble your efforts."

"I've never lost sight of the objective! The objective is to reform American scientific research."

"Oscar, I've thought this over. I really hate this situation. For one thing, I don't much like the President. I'm a Federal Democrat. I wasn't *joking* when we were doing all that hard work for Bambakias and the Reform Bloc. I don't want to work for this President. I don't agree with the man's policies. He's a Communist, for heaven's sake."

"The President is not a Communist. He's a billionaire timber baron with a background in the reservation casino business."

"Well, the Communists are in his Left Tradition Bloc. I just don't trust him. I don't like his speeches. I don't like him picking fights with the Dutch when we ought to be putting our own domestic affairs in order. He's just not our kind of politician. He's cruel, and sneaky, and duplicitous, and aggressive."

Oscar smiled. "At least he doesn't sleep on the job, like the old guy did."

"Better King Log than King Stork, pal."

"Yosh, I know you're not a leftist, but you have to agree that the Left Tradition Bloc is a lot better than those total lunatics in the Left Progressives."

"That doesn't help! Bambakias would have trusted you implicitly—the President won't even give you a real post. He's never sent us anything but empty promises. He's left you exposed, he's hanging you out to dry. So, in the meantime, we're relying on these Moderators. And there's just no future in a gangster protection racket."

"Sure there is."

"No there isn't. The proles are worse even than the Left Progressives. They have funny slang, and funny clothes, and laptops, and biotech, so they're colorful, but they're still a mafia. This good old boy, Captain Burningboy . . . he's sucking up to you, but he's not what you think he is. You think he's a charming old coot who's a diamond in the rough, the kind of guy you could fit inside your krewe. He's not. He's an ultraradical cultist, and he definitely has his own agenda."

Oscar nodded. "I know that."

"And then there's Kevin. You haven't been paying enough attention to Kevin. You have put a bandit in charge of the police here. The kid is like a pocket Mussolini now. He's into the phones, he's in the computers, he's in the security videos, the place is saturated with his bugs. Now he's got a pack of tattletale snoop informants, some weird-sister gang of little old nomad ladies on the net in a trailer park, somewhere in the blazing wreckage of Wyoming. . . . The kid is off the rails. It just isn't healthy."

"But Kevin's from Boston, like we are," Oscar said. "Intense surveillance yields low rates of street violence. Kevin's getting the job done for us, and he never balks when we bend the rules. He was a really good personnel choice."

"Oscar, you're obsessed. Forget the nifty-keen social concepts and all the big-picture blather. Get down to brass tacks, get down to reality. Kevin works here because you're paying his salary. You're paying the salaries of all your krewe, and your krewe are the people who are really running this place. Nobody else has any salaries—all they do is eat prole food and work in their labs. I'm your accountant, and I'm telling you: you can't afford this much longer. You can't pay people enough to create a revolution."

"There's no way to pay people enough to do that."

"You're not being fair to your krewe. Your krewe are Massachusetts campaign workers, not miracle workers. You never explained to them that they had to become a revolutionary junta. This place has no real financial support. You don't even have a salary yourself. You don't even have an official post in the government. The Collaboratory is running off your capital."

"Yosh, there's always more funding. What's really interesting is governing without it! Managing on pure prestige. Consider the Moderators, for instance. They actually have a functional, prestige-based economy. It's all been worked out in fantastic detail; for instance, they have a rotating Australian electronic ballot system. . . ."

"Oscar, have you been sleeping at all? Do you eat properly? Do you know what you're doing here anymore?"

"Yes, I do know. It's not what we planned to do at first, but it's what has to be done. I am stealing Huey's clothes."

"You're in a personal feud with the Governor of Louisiana."

"No. That's not it. The truth is that I'm conducting a broad-scale struggle with the greatest political visionary in contemporary America. And Huey is years ahead of me. He's been cultivating his nomads for years now, winning their loyalty, building their infrastructure. He's set it up so that homeless drifters are the most technically advanced group in his state. He's made himself the leader of an underground mass movement, and he's promising to share the knowledge and make every man a wizard. And they worship him for that, because the whole structure of their network economy has been regulated that way, surreptitiously and deliberately. It's corruption on a fantastic scale—it's an enterprise so far off the books that it isn't even 'corruption' anymore. He has created a new alternative society, with an alternative power structure, that is all predicated on him: Green Huey, the Swamp King. I'm working here as fast and as hard as I can, because Huey has already proved to me that this works—in fact, it works so well that it's dangerous. America is on the ropes, and Green Huey is a smiling totalitarian who's creating a neural dictatorship!"

"Oscar, do you realize how crazy that sounds? Do you know how pale you look when you talk like that?"

"I'm leveling with you here. You know I always level with you, Yosh."

"Okay, you're leveling with me. But I can't do that. I can't live that way. I don't believe in it. I'm sorry."

Oscar stared at him.

"I've hit the wall with you, Oscar. I want some real food, I want a real roof over my head. I can't close my eyes and jump blind and take that kind of risk. I have a dependent. My wife needs me, she needs looking after. But you —you don't need me anymore. Because I'm *an accountant*! You're setting up a situation here where I have *no function*. No role. No job. There's nothing to account."

"You know something? That had never occurred to me. But wait; there's bound to be *some* kind of income transfer. There's scrap cash around, we're going to need bits of equipment and such. . . ."

"You're establishing a strange, tiny, alien regime here. It's not a market society. It's a cult society. It's all based on people looking deep into each other's eyes and giving each other back rubs. It's theoretically interesting, but when it fails and falls apart, it'll all become camps and purges just like the Communist Era. If you're determined to do that, Oscar, I can't save you. Nobody can save you. I don't want to be with you when the house of cards comes down. Because you will be going to prison. At best."

Oscar smiled wanly. "So, you don't think the 'congenital insanity' plea will get me off?"

"It's not a joke. What about your krewe, Oscar? What about the rest of us? You're a great campaign man-

ager: you really have a gift. But this is not an election
campaign. It's not even a strike or a protest anymore. This
is a little coup d'état. You're like a militia guru in a seces-
sionist compound here. Even if the krewepeople agree to
stay with you, how can you put them at that kind of risk?
You never asked them, Oscar. They never got a vote."

Oscar sat up straight. "Yosh, you're right. That's a
sound analysis. I just can't do that to my krewepeople; it's
unethical, it's bad practice. I'll have to lay it on the line to
them. If they leave me, that's just a sacrifice I'll have to
accept."

"I have a job offer in Boston from the Governor's
office," Pelicanos said.

"The Governor? Come on! He's a worn-out wind-
bag from the Forward, America Party."

"Forward, America is a Reformist party. The Governor is organizing an antiwar coalition, and he's asked me
to be treasurer."

"No kidding? Treasurer, huh? That's a pretty good
post for you."

"The pacifist tradition is big in Massachusetts. It's
multipartisan and cuts across the blocs. Besides, it has to be
done. The President is really serious. He's not bluffing. He
really wants a war. He'll send gunboats across the Atlantic.
He's bullying that tiny country, just so he can strengthen
his own hand domestically."

"You really believe that, Yosh? That's really your
assessment?"

"Oscar, you're all out of touch. You're in here all
night, every night, slaving away on this minutiae about the
tiny differences between nomad tribes. You're pulling all
the backstage strings inside this little glass bubble. But
you're losing sight of national reality. Yes, President Two
Feathers is on the warpath! He wants a declaration of war
from the Congress! He wants martial law! He wants a war
budget that's under his own command. He wants the

Emergency committees overridden and abolished overnight. He'll be a virtual dictator."

It instantly occurred to Oscar that if the President could achieve even half of those laudable goals, the loss of Holland would be a very small price to pay. But he bit back this response. "Yosh, I work for this President. He's my boss, he's my Commander in Chief. If you really feel that way about him and his agenda, then our situation as colleagues is untenable."

Pelicanos looked wretched. "Well, that's why I came here."

"I'm glad you came. You're my best and oldest friend, my most trusted confidant. But personal feelings can't override a political difference of that magnitude. If you're telling the truth, then we really have come to a parting of the ways. You're going to have to go back to Boston and take that treasury job."

"I hate to do it, Oscar. I know it's your hour of need. And your private fortune needs attention too; you've got to watch those investments. There's a lot of market turbulence ahead."

"There's always market turbulence. I can manage turbulence. I just regret losing you. You've been with me every step of the way."

"Thus far and no farther, pal."

"Maybe if they convict me in Boston, you could put in a good word with your friend the Governor on the clemency issue."

"I'll send mail," Yosh said. He wiped at his eyes. "I have to clean out my desk now."

Oscar was deeply shaken by the defection of Pelicanos. Given the circumstances, there had been no way to finesse it. It was sad but necessary, like his own forced defection from the Bambakias camp when he had moved to the President's NSC. There were certain issues that simply could not be straddled. A clever operative could dance on two stools at once, but standing on seven or eight was just beyond capacity.

It had been some time since Oscar had spoken to Bambakias. He'd kept up with the man's net coverage. The mad Senator's personal popularity was higher than ever. He'd gained all his original weight back; maybe a little more. His krewe handlers wheeled him out in public; they even dared to propel him onto the Senate floor. But the fire was out. His life was all ribbon cuttings and teleprompters now.

Using his newly installed NSC satphone, Oscar arranged a video conference to Washington. Bambakias had a new scheduler, a woman Oscar had never seen before. Oscar managed to get half an hour penciled in.

When the call finally went through he found himself confronting Lorena Bambakias.

Lorena looked good. Lorena, being Lorena, could never look less than good. But on the screen before him, she seemed brittle and crispy. Lorena had known suffering.

His heart shrank within him at the sight of her. He was surprised to realize how sincerely he had missed her. He'd always been on tiptoe around Lorena, highly aware of her brimming reservoirs of feminine menace; but he'd forgotten how truly fond he was of her, how much she represented to him of the life he had abandoned. Dear old Lorena: wealthy, sophisticated, amoral, and refined—his kind of woman, really; a creature of the overclass, a classic high-maintenance girl, a woman who was really *put together*. Seeing Lorena like this—all abraded in her sorrow —gave him a pang. She was like a beautiful pair of scissors that had been used to shear through barbed wire.

"It's good of you to call, Oscar," Lorena told him. "You never call us enough."

"That's sweet of you. How have things been? Tell me really."

"Oh, it's a day at a time. A day at a time, that's all. The doctors tell me there's a lot of progress."

"Really?"

"Oh, it's amazing what millions of dollars can do in the American health-care system. Up at the high end of the market, they can do all kinds of strange neural things now. He's cheerful."

"Really."

"He's *very* cheerful. He's stable. He's lucid, even, most of the time."

"Lorena, did I ever tell you how incredibly sorry I am about all this?"

She smiled. "Good old Oscar. I'm used to it now, you know? I'm dealing with it. I wouldn't have thought that was possible—maybe it isn't possible—but it's doable. You know what really bothers me, though? It isn't all the sympathy notes, or the media coverage, or the fan clubs, or any of that. . . . It's those evil fools who somehow believe that mental illness is a glamorous, romantic thing. They think that going mad is some kind of spiritual adventure. It isn't. Not a bit of it. It's horrible. It's banal. I'm dealing with someone who has become banal. My darling husband, who was the least banal man I ever met. He was so multifaceted and wonderful and full of imagination; he was just so energetic and clever and charming. Now he's like a big child. He's like a not very bright child who can be deceived and managed, but not reasoned with."

"You're very brave. I admire you very much for saying that."

Lorena began weeping. She massaged her eyes with her beautifully kept fingertips. "Now I'm crying but . . . Well, you don't mind that, do you? You're one of the people who really knew what we were like, back then."

"I don't mind."

Lorena looked up after a while, her brittle face composed and bright. "Well, you haven't told me how *you* are doing."

"Me, Lorena? Couldn't be better! Getting amazing things accomplished over here. Unbelievable developments, all completely fascinating."

"You've lost a lot of weight," she said. "You look tired."

"I've had a little trouble with my new allergies. I'm fine as long as I stay around air filters."

"How is your new job with the President? It must be exciting to be in the NSC when there's almost a war on."

Oscar opened his mouth. It was true; he was on the National Security Council, and there was a war in the works, and despite his tangential status and his deep disinterest in foreign affairs, he knew a great deal about the coming war. He knew that the President planned to send out a flotilla of clapped-out battleships across the Atlantic, without any air cover. He knew that the President was utterly determined to provoke his token war, whether the Congress could be talked into declaring one or not. He knew that in a world of precisely targeted cheap missiles and infinite numbers of disposable drone aircraft, the rust-bucket American fleet was a fleet of sitting ducks.

He also knew that he would lose his job and perhaps even face espionage charges if he revealed this to a Senator's wife on an NSC satphone. Oscar closed his mouth.

"I'm just a science adviser," he said at last. "The Senator must know a great deal more about this than I do."

"Would you like to talk to him?"

"That would be great."

Lorena left. Oscar opened his nomad laptop, examined the screen for a moment, shut it again.

The Senator arrived on-camera. He was wearing pajamas and a blue velvet lounge robe. His face looked plump, polished, and strangely shapeless, as if the personality behind had lost its grip on the facial muscles.

"Oscar!" Bambakias boomed. "Good old Oscar! I think about you every day."

"That's good to know, Senator."

"You're doing marvelous things over there with the science facility. Marvelous things. I really wish I could help you with that. Maybe we could fly over tomorrow! That would be good. We'd get results."

Lorena's voice sounded from off-camera. "There's a hearing tomorrow, Alcott."

"Hearings, more hearings. All right. Still, I keep up! I do keep up. I know what's going on, I really do! Tremendous things you're doing over there. You've got no budget, they tell me. None at all. Fill the place with the unemployed! Genius maneuver! It's just like you always said, Oscar—push a political contradiction hard enough, it'll break through to the other side. Then you can rub their noses in it. Great, great tactics."

Oscar was touched. The Senator was obviously in a manic state, but he was a lot easier to take when he was so ebullient—it was like a funhouse-mirror version of his old charisma.

"You've done plenty for us already, Senator. We built a hotel here from your plans. The locals were very impressed by it."

"Oh, that's nothing."

"No, seriously, your design attracted a lot of favorable comment."

"No, I truly mean that it's nothing. You should see the plans I used to do, back in college. Giant intelligent geodesics. Huge reactive structures made of membrane and sticks. You could fly 'em in on zeppelins and drop 'em over starving people, in the desert. Did 'em for a U.N. disaster relief competition—back when the U.S. was still in the U.N."

Oscar blinked. "Disaster relief buildings?"

"They never got built. Much too sophisticated and high tech for starving, backward third worlders, so they said. Bureaucrats! I worked my ass off on that project." Bambakias laughed. "There's no *money* in disaster relief.

There's no market-pull for that. I recast the concept later, as little chairs. No money in the little chairs either. They never appreciated any of that."

"Actually, Senator, we have one of those little chairs in the Director's office, here at the lab. It's provoking a lot of strongly favorable reaction. The locals really love that thing."

"You don't say. Too bad that scientists are too broke to buy any upscale furniture."

"I wonder if you'd still have those disaster plans in your archives somewhere, Alcott. I'd like to see them."

"*See* them? Hell, you can *have* them. The least I can do for you, after everything I've put you through."

"I hope you'll do that for me, Senator. I'm serious."

"Sure, have 'em! Take anything you want! Kind of a fire sale on my brain products. You know, if we invade Europe, Oscar, it probably means a nuclear exchange."

Oscar lowered his voice soothingly. "I really don't think so, Al."

"They're trifling with the grand old USA, these little Dutch creeps. Them and their wooden shoes and tulips. We're a superpower! We can *pulverize* them."

Lorena spoke up. "I think it's time for your medication, Alcott."

"I need to know what Oscar really thinks about the war! I'm all in favor of it. I'm a hawk! We've been pushed around by these little red-green Euro pipsqueaks long enough. Don't you think so, Oscar?"

A nurse arrived. "You tell the President my opinion!" the Senator insisted as the nurse led him away. "You tell Two Feathers I'm with him all the way down."

Lorena moved back into camera range. She looked grim and stricken.

"You have a lot of new krewepeople now, Lorena."

"Oh. That." She looked into the camera. "I never got back to you about the Moira situation, did I?"

"Moira? I thought we had that problem straightened out and packed away with mothballs."

"Oh, Moira was on her best behavior after that jail incident. Until Huey came looking for Moira. Now Moira works for Huey in Baton Rouge."

"Oh no."

"It got very bad for the krewe after that. Their morale suffered so much with the Senator's illness, and once Huey had our former press agent in his own court . . . well, I guess you can imagine what it's been like."

"You've lost a lot of people?"

"Well, we just hire new ones, that's all." She looked up. "Maybe someday *you* can come back to us."

"That would be good. The reelection campaign, maybe."

"*That* should be a real challenge. . . . You're so good with him. You were *always* so good with him. That silly business with his old architecture plans. It really touched him, he was very lucid for a minute there. He was just like his old self with you."

"I'm not just humoring him, Lorena. I really want those disaster relief plans. I want you to make sure that they're sent to me here. I think I can use them."

"Oscar, what are you really doing over there? It seems like a very strange thing. I don't think it's in the interests of the Federal Democrats. It's not a sensible reform, it's not like what we had in mind."

"That's true—it's certainly not what we had in mind."

"It's that Penninger woman, isn't it? She's just not right for you. She's not your type. You know that Moira knows all about you and Greta Penninger, don't you? Huey knows too."

"I know that. I'm looking after that. Although it's challenging work."

"You look so pale. You should have stayed with Clare Emerson. She's an Anglo girl, but she was sweet-

tempered and good for you. You always looked happy
when you were with her."

"Clare is in Holland."

"Clare is coming back. What with the war, and all."

"Lorena . . ." He sighed. "You play ball with a lot
of journalists. So do I, all right? I used to sleep with Clare,
but Clare is a journalist, first and last and always. Just
because she gives you softball coverage doesn't mean that
she's good for me. Don't send Clare over here. I mean it.
Send me the old architecture plans that Alcott did, when
he was a wild design student who had never made any
money. I can really use those. Do *not* send Clare."

"I don't want to see you destroyed by ambition,
Oscar. I've seen what that means now and it's bad, it's
worse than you imagine. It's terrible. I just want to see you
happy."

"I can't afford to be that kind of happy right now."

Suddenly she laughed. "All right. You're all right.
I'm all right too. We're going to survive all this. Someday,
we're going to be okay. I still believe that, don't you?
Don't fret too much. Be good to yourself. All right?"

"All right."

She hung up. Oscar stood up and stretched. She had
just been kidding about Clare. She was just teasing him a
little. He'd broken her out of her unhappiness for a little
moment; Lorena was still a player, she liked to imagine he
was her krewe and she was looking out for him. He'd
managed to give her a little moment of diversion. It had
been a good idea to make the phone call. He had done a
kindly thing for old friends.

Oscar began the liquidation of his fortune. Without Pelicanos to manage his accounts and investments, the time
demands were impossible. And, on some deep level, he
knew the money was a liability now. He was encouraging
thousands of people to abandon conventional economics

and adopt a profoundly alien way of life, while he himself remained safely armored. Huey had already made a few barbed comments along that line; the fact that Huey was a multimillionaire himself never hampered his sarcastic public outbursts.

Besides, Oscar wasn't throwing the money away. He was going to devote it all to the cause of science—until there was no money left.

The resignation and departure of Pelicanos had a profound effect on his krewe. As majordomo, Pelicanos had been a linchpin of the krewe, always the voice of reason when Oscar himself became a little too intense.

Oscar assembled his krewe at the hotel to clear the air and lay matters on the line. Point along the way: he was doubling everyone's salary. The krewe should consider it hazard pay. They were plunging into unknown territory, at steep odds. But if they won, it would be the grandest political success they had ever seen. He finished his pep talk with a flourish.

Resignations followed immediately. They took departure pay and left his service. Audrey Avizienis left; she was his opposition researcher, she was far too skeptical and mean-spirited to stay on under such dubious, half-baked circumstances. Bob Argow also quit. He was a systems administrator, and he made his grievances clear: pushy computer-security nonsense from Kevin Hamilton, and hordes of would-be netgods in the Moderators who created code the way they made clothes: handmade, lopsided, and a stitch at a time. Negi Estabrook left as well. There was no point in cooking for such a diminished krewe, and besides, the cuisine of road proles was basically laboratory rat chow. Rebecca Pataki also left. She felt out of place and half-abandoned, and she was homesick for Boston.

This left Oscar with just four diehard hangers-on. Fred Dillen the janitor, Corky Shoeki his roadie and new majordomo, and his secretary and scheduler, Lana Ramachandran. Plus, his image consultant, Donna Nunez, who

sensibly declared that she was staying on because in terms
of its image, the Collaboratory was just getting interesting.
Very well, he thought grimly; he was down to four people, he would just start over. Besides, he still had Kevin.
There were plenty of useful people walking around loose
within the Collaboratory. And he worked for the President.

He would ask the NSC for help.

Two days later, help arrived from the National Security
Council. The President's personal spooks had at last sent
military reinforcements to the Collaboratory. Military aid
took the form of a young Air Force lieutenant colonel
from Colorado. He was the very man who had been on
the graveyard shift when Oscar had been abducted, and
when Kevin had made his frantic phone call. In fact, it was
he who had ordered Oscar's armed rescue effort.

The lieutenant colonel was erect, spit-polished,
steely-eyed. He wore a full uniform with scarlet beret. He
had brought three vehicles with him to Texas. The first
contained a squadron of rapid-deployment ground troops,
soldiers wearing combat gear of such astonishing weight
and complexity that they seemed scarcely able to walk.
The second and third trucks contained the lieutenant colonel's media coverage.

The lieutenant enjoyed a glorious circuit of the Collaboratory, ostensibly to check it out for security purposes,
but mostly in order to exhibit himself to the awestruck
locals. Oscar tried to make himself useful. He introduced
the lieutenant colonel to his local security experts: Kevin,
and Captain Burningboy.

During the briefing, Kevin said little—Kevin
seemed rather embarrassed. Burningboy proved most
forthcoming. The Moderator captain launched into a detailed and terrifying recitation of the Collaboratory's strategic plight. Buna was a mere twenty kilometers from the

highly porous border with Louisiana. The murky swamps of the Sabine River valley were swarming with vengeful Regulators. Though the armed helicopter attack against the Regulator commandos had never become official news, the assault had provoked them to fury.

The threat to Buna was immediate and serious. The Regulators had swarms of airborne drones surveilling the facility around the clock. Huey had given up his plans to co-opt the facility. He wanted it abandoned, ruined, destroyed. The Regulators were more than willing to carry out Huey's aims. They were lethally furious that the Collaboratory was hosting Moderators.

This briefing enthralled the lieutenant colonel. Sickened by his desk job and embarrassed by the sordid coverup of his glorious attack, the man was visibly itching for a fight. He had come fully prepared. His all-volunteer squad of forest ninjas were lugging whole arsenals of professional gear: body armor, silenced sniper rifles, human body-odor sniffers, mine-proofed boot soles, night-fighting video helmets, even ultraspecial, freeze-dried, self-heating, long-range patrol rations.

The lieutenant colonel, having debriefed the locals on the ground, announced that it was time for a reconnaissance in force, out in the swamps. His media crew would not be neglected; their helicopters would serve as his comlink and impromptu air backup.

Oscar had some acquaintance with the lieutenant colonel through his NSC connections. Having finally met the man in person, he swiftly realized that the colonel was a clear and present danger to himself and every human being within firing range. He was young, zealous, and as dumb as a bag of hammers; he was an atavistic creature from the blood-soaked depths of the twentieth century.

Oscar nevertheless made his best professional effort. "Colonel, sir, those flooded woods in the Sabine River valley are tougher than you might expect. We're not just talking swamps here—we're basically talking permanent disaster areas. There's been a lot of severe flooding in the Sabine since the rain patterns changed, and a lot of the local farmland has gone back to wilderness. That's not the forest primeval out there. Those are deserted, toxic locales of no economic value, where all the decent lumber is long gone and there are poisonous weeds and bushes half the size of trees. It would be a mistake to underestimate those Regulators when they're on their native ground. Those Cajun nomads are not just native hunters and fishers and swamp dwellers; they're also very big on sylvan audio surveillance."

It was, of course, of no use. The lieutenant colonel, and his men, and his impressionable, airborne war correspondents, left on dawn patrol the next morning. Not a single one of them was ever seen again.

———————

Three days after this silent debacle, Captain Burningboy announced his own departure. He was now "General" Burningboy again, and having successfully retrieved his reputation, he felt it was time for him to leave.

Kevin threw a block party for the General, on the grounds of the police station. Greta and Oscar attended in full dress and, for the first time ever, as a public couple. They had of course been kidnapped as a couple, and rescued as a couple, so their appearance made perfect sense. It was also a boost for morale.

In point of sad fact, Greta and Oscar had very little to say to or do with one another at Burningboy's farewell party. They were both hopelessly preoccupied with the exigencies of power. Besides, Kevin's party featured a massive banquet of genuine food. After days on nomad biotech rations, the scientists and proles flung themselves on it like wolverines.

Oscar was pained to see Burningboy abandoning him. It seemed so unnecessary. Burningboy, who had been drinking heavily, took Oscar aside and explained his motives in pitiless detail. It all had to do with social network structure.

"We used to handle these things the way the Regulators do," Burningboy confided. "Promote the best, and segregate the rest. But they ended up with an aristocracy —the Sun Lords, the Nobles, the Respected, and down at the very bottom, all the lousy newbies. In the Moderators, we use balloting. So we have turnaround; people can spend their reputations, and lose them, and earn them back. Besides—and this is the killer point here—our technique prevents decapitation attacks. See, the feds are *always* after 'the criminal kingpins.' They always want 'the top guy in the outfit,' the so-called mastermind."

"I'll really miss these briefings of yours," Oscar said. It had been a long time since he had appeared in public with his full regalia of spats, cummerbund, and proper hat. He felt a million miles away from Burningboy, as if he were receiving signals from a distant planet.

"Look, Oscar, after thirty years of American imperial information warfare, everybody in the goddamn world understands counterinsurgency and political subversion. We *all* know how to do it now, we all know how to wreck the dominant paradigm. We're geniuses at screwing with ourselves and deconstructing all our institutions. We don't have a single institution left that works." Burningboy paused. "Am I getting too radical here? Am I scaring you?"

"No. It's the truth."

"Well, that's why I'm going to jail now. We Moderators have a kinda pet state magistrate out in New Mexico. He's willing to put me away on a completely irrelevant charge. So I'll be spending two or three years in a minimum security state facility. I think that once they've got me nice and safe in the slammer, I may be able to survive this thing you've done here."

"You're not telling me that you're actually going to prison, Burningboy."

"You should try it, amigo. It's the ultimate invisible American population. Prisons have everything that interests you. People with a lot of spare time. Weird economics, based on drugs and homemade tattoos. There's a lot of time to think seriously. You really do regret your old mistakes inside a penitentiary." Burningboy had an impossibly remote look now. Oscar was losing him; it was as if he were bound on a flower-decked Valkyrie ship for the shores of Avalon. "Besides, some of those poor evil bastards are so far gone that they actually have *bad teeth*. I can practice dentistry again, when I'm in stir. Did I ever tell you I used to be a dentist? That was before the caries vaccine came in and destroyed my profession."

Oscar had forgotten that Burningboy had once been a dentist. The man had earned a medical degree. Oscar was alarmed by this, not merely because the annihilation of the noble profession of dentistry was a stark barometer of America's social damage. It bothered him because he was forgetting important things about important people. Was he too old now, at twenty-nine? Was he losing his grip? Had he taken on too much? Maybe it was the way Burningboy dressed and talked. He was a dropout, a prole, a marginal. It was just impossible to take him seriously for more than a few instants.

"I have no regrets," Burningboy said, emptying his cocktail glass with a flourish. "I led my people into a lot of trouble here. That wasn't my idea—it was *your* damned idea—but they wouldn't have done it if I hadn't given it my big say-so. If you change hundreds of people's lives, you ought to pay a stiff price for that. Just to, you know, keep everybody from tryin' it. So I'm doing the honorable thing here. My people understand about prison."

"That is the honorable thing, isn't it? Doing time. Paying dues."

"That's right. I led the charge, and now I step aside. At least I won't end up like Green Huey."

"What do you mean by that?"

"I mean that Huey can't put it down, son. He can't put down the cross and take off the crown of thorns. He can't mosey off the stage and go sit quietly in the corner. He's the red-hot self-declared super-savior of the meek and downtrodden, and you can't pull a stunt like that in America without somebody shooting you. That's just the kind of thing we do in this country. Huey looks a mile high right now, but he's made out of meat. Somebody's gonna kill Huey. The lone nut sniper, a crowd of spooks outside the motorcade. . . ." He shot Oscar a sudden opaque look. "I just hope he doesn't get offed by somebody that I personally know."

"It would be very regrettable if the Governor came to harm."

"Yeah, right."

Oscar cleared his throat. "If you're leaving us, General, who's going to be in command here?"

"You are. You've always been in command here. Don't you get that yet? You need to wake up a little, son."

"Look, I don't give any orders. I just talk to the relevant parties."

Burningboy snorted.

"Okay, then let me rephrase my question. Who do I talk to, when I need to talk to the Moderators?"

"All right." Burningboy shrugged. "I'll introduce you to my anointed successor."

Burningboy led him inside the police station. From behind the locked door of the chief's office came a loud series of groans. Burningboy produced a swipecard from inside his medicine bag, and opened the door. Kevin had his bare feet up on his desk. He was receiving dual foot rubs from a pair of nomad women. He was very drunk, and wearing a silly party hat.

"All right, ladies," Kevin gurgled. "That'll be enough for now. Thank you so much. Really."

"Your metatarsals are really trashed," said the first masseuse, with dignity.

"Can we mark off a whole hour?" said the second.

"Oh, go ahead!" Kevin said royally. "Who's to know?"

"This is my successor," said Burningboy. "Our new security honcho. Captain Scubbly Bee."

"That's just great," Oscar said. "That's good news. Incredible. It's so wonderful I scarcely know what to say."

Kevin swung his oily feet from the desk. "I enlisted, man. I signed up with the mob. I'm a made guy, I'm a Moderator now."

"I understood that much," Oscar told him. "New alias and everything. 'Scubbly Bee,' am I right? What is that? Not 'Stubbly'?"

"No, Scubbly. Scubbly Bee." Kevin pointed to a nearby shredder. "I just trashed all my official ID. I can't tell you how great that felt. This is the best party I ever had."

"What's the significance of 'Scubbly Bee'? It must mean something of drastic importance in order to sound so silly."

Kevin grinned. "That's for me to know and you to find out, chump."

Burningboy shook Kevin's hand. "I'll be going soon," he said. "You keep your nose clean, all right, Captain? This is the last time I want to see you so drunk."

"I'm not all that drunk," Kevin lied. "It's mostly that intoxicating endorphin rush from my feet."

Burningboy left the office, throwing his arms over the willing shoulders of the two nomad women. Oscar sat down. "I hope you didn't destroy your voter registration, too."

"As if absentee voting in Boston is somehow gonna help us down here."

"He's really put you in direct charge over his own people inside the facility?"

Kevin yawned. "Y'know, when this party is over, I'm gonna have a serious talk with you, man. In the meantime, you need to eat something. Maybe even have a drink. After all, you're the guy who's paying for all this."

"I won't take much of your valuable party time, Captain Bee. This is just a friendly krewe-style chat."

"If we're going to be all friendly, then you'd better call me 'Scubbly.'" Kevin pulled his socks over his reddened, liniment-reeking feet, with a theatrical series of winces. "You've just *got to know* why he did that, don't you? You've *got* to be on top of developments, you can't even wait till morning to learn. Well, it's because he's setting me up, that's why. He's getting off the hot seat, and he's putting me right on it. See, he thinks the Regulators are gonna cross the border and come after us with everything they have. Because that's what he wants, that's his agenda. The Regulators will stomp this place, and then the Regulators will catch a truly massive counterreaction from the feds."

"That seems like a far-fetched gambit, doesn't it?"

"But that's the way he set this up, man. He didn't come here because he wanted to help your little pet scientists. You're too straight, you just don't understand these guys' priorities. They gave up on you a long, long time ago. They don't expect any law or justice from the U.S. government. They don't even expect the government to be sane. The whole federal system just detached itself from them and floated off into deep space. They think of the government as something like *bad weather*. It's something you just endure."

"You're wrong, Kevin—I understand all of that perfectly."

"When they want to take action, they take actions that matter to them. The other proles, that's who matters. They're like tribes who are wandering through an enormous hostile desert made of your laws and money. But the Moderators *hate* the Regulators. The Regulators are strong and scary now. They've got a state Governor as their big secret Grand Dragon Pooh-bah. They overwhelmed an Air Force base. The Moderators . . . all they own is a few dozen ghost towns and national parks."

Oscar nodded encouragement.

"Then *you* came along. All of a sudden there was a chance to take over this place. It's a federal science facility, a much *better* facility than a pork-barrel Air Force base. It has big prestige. Grabbing it is an intolerable insult to Regulator prestige, because their main man Huey built this place, and he thinks he owns it by right. He's nuts about green genetic gumbo and weird cognition crap. So that's why Burningboy helped you. And that's why he's getting out now, while the getting is good. He set a trap for the other side, and to his eyes, we're just poisoned bait."

"How do you know all this?"

Kevin opened a desk drawer. He removed a large and highly illegal revolver, and a bottle of whiskey. He sipped from the whiskey and then began placing hinge-lid cigar boxes on the polished face of his desk. "Because I heard him say so, man. Look at these things, would you?"

Kevin flipped open the first cigar box. It was full of pinned audio bugs, with neat handwritten labels. "You know how hard it is to fully debug a facility? It's technically impossible, that's how hard. There aren't any working 'sweeps' or 'monitors' for bugs—that's all crap! Any decent bug basically can't be detected, except by a physical search. So that's what I've been doing. I round up big gangs of Moderators with nothing better to do, and we go over every conceivable surface with fine-tooth combs. These bugs are like pubic crabs, they're a goddamn social disease. I've found bugs in here that go back fourteen and fifteen years. I made a special collection! Just look!"

"Very impressive."

Kevin flipped his cigar box shut and pointed at it solemnly. "You know what that is? It's *evil*, that's what it is. It's bad, it's just plain evil of us to do this to ourselves. We have no decency as a people and a nation, Oscar. We went too far with this technology, we lost our self-respect. Because this is media, man. It's evil, prying, spying media. But we want it and use it anyway, because we think we've got to be informed. We're compelled to pay total attention to everything. Even things we have no goddamn right or business paying any attention to."

Oscar said nothing. He wasn't about to stop Kevin while he was in a confessional mood.

"So I got rid of everybody else's bugs. And I installed my own. Because I'm finally the hacker who became the superuser. I didn't just crack the computers here. I've cracked this whole environment. I can access anything that goes on in here, anytime that I want. I'm a cop. But I'm more than a cop. I mean, being a cop would be traditional—a white Anglo guy imposing his idea of order on the restless natives, hell, every city in America was just like that once. And man, I was *thrilled to do it*. I loved myself, I thought I was magic. It's just amazingly interesting, like watching other people having sex. But you know, if you do that sixty or seventy times, it gets old. It just does."

"Does it really?"

"Oh yeah. And it has a price. I haven't gotten laid since I met you! I don't dare! Because I'm the Secret Master Policeman. I scare the crap out of any decent woman. Indecent women have their own agenda when they have sex with the secret police. And besides, I just don't have any time for my own needs! The Super Master Inquisitor is way too busy with everybody else's. I've got to run word scans on all my verbal tapes. Every time there's an incident somewhere I've got to peel the videos back. I got bugs with their batteries running down, people are findin' 'em and stepping on them. There's goblins lurking in the woods. There's spooks flying overhead. There's drunks, lost children, petty thieves. There's fire safety and car accidents. And every last one of those things is *my problem*. All of it. All of it!"

"Kevin, you're not planning to leave me, are you?"

"*Leave* you? Man, I was born for this. I got my every wish. It's just that it's turning me into a monster. That's all."

"Kevin, you don't look all that bad to me. Things aren't that bad here. This isn't chaos. The situation's holding."

"Sure, I'm keeping order for you. But it's not law and order, Oscar. There's order, but there is no law. We let things get out of control. We let it get all emergent and unpredictable. We let it fall back to ad hoc. I'm keeping order here because I'm a secret tyrant. I've got everything but legitimacy. I'm a spy and a usurper, and I have no rules. I have no brakes. I have no honor."

"There isn't anyplace for me to get you any of that."

"You're a politician, Oscar. But you gotta be something better than just that. You have got to be a statesman. You've got to find some way to make me some honor."

A phone rang in the office. Kevin groaned, picked up a laptop, and ran a trace with a function key. "Nobody is supposed to have this number," he complained.

"I thought you had all of that taken care of by now."

"Typical politician's remark. What I got is a series of cutouts, dummies, and firewalls, and you would not believe the netwar attacks those things are soaking up." He examined the tracing report on his laptop. "What the hell is this thing?" He answered the phone. "Yes?"

He paused and listened intently for forty-five seconds. Oscar took the opportunity to examine Kevin's office. It was the least likely police office he had ever seen. Girlie pinups, dead coffee cups, ritual masks, disemboweled telecom hardware driven into the walls with tenpenny nails. . . .

"It's for you," Kevin announced at last, and handed Oscar the phone.

Their caller was Jules Fontenot. Fontenot was angry. He'd been unable to reach Oscar through any conventional phone. He had finally been reduced to calling the Collaboratory's police headquarters through a Secret Service office in Baton Rouge. The runaround had irritated him greatly.

"I apologize for the local communications systems, Jules. There's been a lot of change here since you left us. It's good to hear from you, though. I appreciate your persistence. What can I do for you?"

"You still mad at Green Huey?" Fontenot rasped.

"I was never 'mad' at Huey. Professionals don't get mad. I was dealing with him."

"Oscar, I'm retired. I want to stay retired. I didn't ever want to make a call like this again. But I had to."

What was wrong with the man? It was Fontenot, all right, but his native accent had thickened drastically. It was as if the man were speaking through a digital "Cajun Dialect" vocoder. "To meck a caw lak diss . . ."

"Jules, you know that I always respect your advice. Your leaving the business hasn't changed that for me. Tell me what's troubling you."

"Haitian refugees. You get me? A camp for Haitians."

"Did you just say 'Haitians'? Do you mean black, Francophone people from the Caribbean?"

"That's right! Church people from Haiti. Huey gave 'em political asylum. Built a little model village for 'em, in the backwoods. They're living way back in mah swamps now."

"I'm with you, Jules. Disaster evacuations, Haitian refugees, charity housing, French language, that's all very Huey. So what is the problem?"

"Well, it's *somethin'*. It's not just that they're foreigners. Religious foreigners. Black, voodoo, religious, refugee foreigners who speak Creole. It's something lots weirder than that. Huey's done something strange to those people. Drugs, I think. Genetics maybe. They are acting weird. Really weird."

"Jules, forgive me, but I have to make sure that I have this straight." Oscar lifted his hand silently and began gesturing frantically at Kevin—Get This On Tape. Open Your Laptop. Take Notes! "Jules, are you telling me that the Governor of Louisiana is using Haitian refugees as human guinea pigs for behavioral experiments?"

"I wouldn't swear to that in a court of law—because I cain't get anyone to come out here and look! Nobody's *complaining* about it, that's the problem. They're the happiest goddamn Haitians in the whole world."

"It must be neural, then. Some kind of mood-altering treatment."

"Maybe. But it's not like any kind of dope I ever saw or heard tell of. I just don't have the words to properly describe this situation. I just don't have the words."

"And you want me to come and see it with you."

"I'm not saying that, Oscar. I'm just saying . . . well, the parish police are crooked, the state militia is crooked, the Secret Service won't listen to me anymore, and nobody even cares. They're Haitians, from a barren, drowning island, and nobody cares. Not a damn soul cares."

"Oh, believe me, I care, Jules. Trust me on that one."

"It's more than I can stand, that's all. I can't sleep nights, thinkin' about it."

"Rest easy. You have done the right and proper thing. I am definitely going to take steps. Is there a way that I can contact you? Safely, confidentially?"

"Nope. Not anymore. I threw all my phones away."

"How can I pursue this matter, then?"

"I'm retired! Hell, Oscar, don't let anybody know that *I* outed this thing! I live here now. I love this place. I wanna die here."

"Now, Jules, you know that's not right. This is a very serious matter. You're either a player, or you're not a player. You can't teeter along on the edge like this."

"Okay. I'm not a player." The phone went dead.

Oscar turned to Kevin. "Were you following the gist of that?"

"Who was that guy? Is he nuts?"

"That's my former krewe security chief, Jules Fontenot. He ran security for the Bambakias campaign. He happens to be a Cajun. He retired just before I met you, and he's been out in the bayou, fishing, ever since."

"And now he's calling you up with some cock-and-bull story about a scandal, and he's trying to lure you into the backwoods of Louisiana?"

"That's right. And I'm going."

"Hold on, cowboy. Think about this. What's more likely? That Huey is running weird atrocity camps in the bayou, or that your former friend the Cajun has just been turned against you? This is a trap, man. So they can kidnap you just like they tried before. They're gonna curb-stomp you and feed you to the alligators."

"Kevin, I appreciate that hypothesis. That's good, street-smart, bodyguard-style thinking. But let me give you the political angle on this. I know Fontenot. He was a Secret Service special agent. I trusted that man with my life—and with the Senator's life, the life of the whole krewe. Maybe he's plotting to kidnap and murder me now. But if Huey can turn Jules Fontenot into a murderous traitor, then America as we know it has ceased to exist. It would mean that we're doomed."

"So you're going into Louisiana to investigate these things he told you about."

"Of course I am. The only question is, how and under what circumstances. I'm going to have to give this project some serious thought."

"Okay, I'm going with you, then."

Oscar narrowed his eyes. "Why do you say that?"

"A lot of reasons. I'm supposed to be your bodyguard. I'm in your krewe. You pay me. I'm the successor of this Fontenot guy that you're so impossibly respectful of. But mostly—it's because I'm so sick and tired of you always being four steps ahead of me." Kevin slapped his desk. "Look at me, man. I'm a very smart, clever, sneaky guy. I'm a hacker. And I'm good at it! I'm such a net-dot-legend that I can take over federal science labs. I slot right into the Moderators. I even hang out with NSC agents. But no matter what I do, you always do something crazier. You're always ahead of me. I'm a technician, and you're a politician, and you're *always outthinking me*. You don't even take me seriously."

"That is *not true*. I know that you count! I take you with complete seriousness, Captain Scubbly Bee."

Kevin sighed. "Just make a little room for me in the back of your campaign bus, all right? That's all I ask."

"I need to talk to Greta about this development. She's my neural science expert."

"Right. No problem. Just a second." Kevin stood up and limped barefoot to a desktop computer. He typed in parameters. A schematic map of the Collaboratory appeared. He studied it. "Okay. You'll find Dr. Penninger in her supersecret lab in the fourth floor of the Human Resources division."

"What? Greta's supposed to be here at the party."

"Dr. Penninger hates parties. She bores real easily. Didn't you know that? I like doing favors for Dr. Penninger. Dr. Penninger's not like most women—you can talk to her seriously about stuff that matters. She needed a safe house in case of attacks, so I built her a cute little secret lab over in Human Resources. She fired all those clowns anyway, so there's plenty of room now."

"How do you know where she is at this very moment?"

"You've got to be kidding. I'm Security, and she's the lab's Director. I *always* know where the Director is."

After considerable ceremonial pressing of the flesh, Oscar left the party to find Greta. Thanks to Kevin's explicit surveillance, this wasn't difficult.

Kevin and his prole gangs had assembled a hole-in-the-wall workspace for Greta. Oscar punched in a four-digit code, and the door opened. The room was dark, and he saw Greta crouched over her dissecting microscope, its lights the only illumination. Both her eyes were pressed to the binocular mounts and both her hands were encased in step-down AFM dissection gloves. She had thrown a lab coat over her glamorous party gear. The room was as bare as a monk's cell, and Greta was utterly intent: silently and methodically tearing away at some tiny fabric of the universe.

"It's me," he said.

"Oh," she said. She looked up, nodded, and returned her attention to the lenses.

"Why did you leave the party?"

"Why shouldn't I? You weren't paying any attention to me."

Oscar was surprised, even mildly thrilled, to see Greta being coy. "We're in the Emergency Committee. You see me for hours and hours every day."

"We're never *together*. You've lost interest in me. You're neglecting me."

Oscar paused. He was certainly interested now. It occurred to him suddenly that he deeply enjoyed this part of a relationship. Women always seemed more interesting to him as objects of negotiation than they were as lovers or partners. This was a sinister self-revelation. He felt very contrite about it.

"Greta, I don't like to admit it, but you're right. Now that everyone knows we're lovers, we never have time for ourselves. We were together in a public situation tonight, and I tactlessly deserted you. I admit that. I regret it. I'm going to make it up to you."

"Listen to yourself. It's like you're addressing a committee. We're just two politicians now. You talk to me like a diplomat. I have to read speeches from the President that are full of lies. I don't get to work at anything that interests me. I spend my whole life in an endless political crisis. I hate administration. God, I feel so guilty."

"Why? It's important work. Someone has to do it. You're good at it! People respect you."

"I never felt this guilty when we were off in beach hotels having sleazy, half-violent sex. It wasn't the center of my life or anything, but it was really interesting. A good-looking, charming guy with hundred-and-one-degree core body heat, that's pretty fascinating. A lot more interesting than watching all my research die on the vine."

"Oh no, not you too," Oscar said. "Don't tell me you're turning on me now when I've put so much effort into this. So many people have left me now. They just don't believe it can work."

She looked at him with sudden pity. "Poor Oscar. You've got it all backward. That's not why I feel guilty. I'm guilty because I *know* it's going to work. Talking with those Moderators for so long . . . I really understand it now. Science truly is going to change. It'll still be 'Science.' It'll have the same intellectual structure, but its political structure will be completely different. Instead of being poorly paid government workers, we'll be avant-garde dissident intellectuals for the dispossessed. And that will work for us. Because we can get a better deal from them now than we can from the government. The proles are not so new; they're just like big, hairy, bad-smelling college students. We can deal with people like that. We do it all the time."

He brightened. "Are you sure?"

"It'll be like a new academia, with some krewe feudal elements. It'll be a lot like the Dark Ages, when universities were little legal territories all their own, and scholars carried maces and wore little square hats, and whenever the university was crossed, they sent huge packs of students into the streets to tear everything up, until they got their way. Except it's not the Dark Ages right now. It's the Loud Ages, it's the Age of Noise. We've destroyed our society with how much we know, and how quickly and randomly we can move it around. We live in the Age of Noise, and this is how we learn to be the scientists of the Age of Noise. We don't get to be government functionaries who can have all the money we want just because we give the government a lot of military-industrial knowledge. That's all over now. From now on we're going to be like other creative intellectuals. We're going to be like artists or violin-makers, with our little krewes of fans who pay attention and support us."

"Wonderful, Greta. It sounds great!"

"We'll do cute, attractive, sexy science, with small amounts of equipment. That's what science has to be in America now. We can't do it the European way, where there's all kinds of moral fretting and worrying about what technology will do to people; there's no fun in that, it's just not American. We'll be like Orville Wright in the bicycle shed from now on. It won't be easier for us. It'll be harder for us. But we'll have our freedom. Our American freedom. It's a vote of confidence in the human imagination."

"You *are* a politician, Greta! You've had a big breakthrough here. I'm with you all the way." He felt so proud.

"Sure—it might be wonderful, if it were somebody else doing this. I *hate* doing this to science. I'm deeply sorry that I'm doing it. But I'm on the cutting edge, and I just don't have any choice."

"What would you rather be doing?"

"What?" she demanded. "I'd rather be finishing my paper on inhibition of acetylcholine release in the hippocampus. It's all I ever wanted to do! I live and dream that someday this horrible mess will all be finished, and somehow, somebody will let me do what I want."

"I know that's what you want. I really understand

that now. I know what it means, too, Greta: it means I've
failed you."

"No. Yes. Well, it doesn't matter. The big picture is
going to work."

"I don't see how."

"I can show you." She found her purse and left the
room. A light came on. He heard water running. It occurred to Oscar that he had entirely forgotten the original
subject of his visit. Huey. Huey, and his purported refugee
camp full of Haitians. He was absolutely sure that Huey,
obsessed with Cognition as the Next Big Thing, had done
something ecstatic and dreadful. He knew it had something to do with Greta's neural work. Hellishly, Greta
herself had absolutely no interest in the practical implications of the things she did. She couldn't bear the strangling
intellectual constraints involved in having to care. She
couldn't abide the foul and endless political and moral
implications of the pure pursuit of knowledge. They
bored her beyond all reason. They just weren't science.
There was nothing scientific about them. The reactions of
society no longer made any sense. Innovation had burned
out the brakes. What *could* become of scientists in a world
like that? What the hell was to be done with them?

She entered the room. She'd given herself a rapid
little makeover at the bathroom sink. Her eyes were lined
in jagged black, her cheeks streaked in colored war paint.

He was stunned.

"I didn't invent this myself," she said defensively.
"Your image consultant did it for me—for the party tonight. I was going to wear it to the party for you, but it
was just too ridiculous. So I scraped it all off at the last
minute."

"Oh, that was a big mistake," he said, and laughed in
astonishment. "That is beautiful. That is truly hot. That is
beyond amazing. It is so transgressive. I can't believe what
I'm seeing."

"You're seeing a thirty-six-year-old Jewish woman who's made up like a crazy derelict."

"Oh no. The fact that it's *Greta Penninger,* that's what makes it work. That it's a Nobel Prize—winning federal lab Director who is still in her hose and a lab coat, and she's outed herself as an urban guerrilla." He bit his lip. "Turn around for me. Show me."

She spread her hands and whirled in place. She had a junk-jewelry headdress of linked beads clipped in the back of her head. "You like this, don't you? I guess it's not that bad. I don't look any weirder than the President does, do I?"

"Greta . . ." He cleared his throat. "You don't understand how well that works. That really works for me. I'm getting all hot and bothered."

She gazed at him in surprise. "Huh. My mother always said a good makeover would get a guy's attention."

"Take the lab coat off. In fact, take your blouse off."

"Wait a minute. Put your hands down."

"You know how long it's been? Absolutely forever. I can't even remember the last time."

"Okay! Later! In a bed! And when your face isn't that color."

He put his hand to his cheek. His skin was blazing. Surprised, he touched his ears. His ears were so hot they felt stir-fried. "Wow," he muttered. "I'm all overcome."

"It's just makeup."

"No it isn't. Now I know why Donna wanted to stay around here—now I know why Donna said that things were just getting interesting. That woman is a little genius. You can't claim that's just skin-deep. That's a lie, it's like saying that a vow of chastity and a nun's veil are just some words and some black cloth. Sure, it's just a symbol, but it puts you in a whole different moral universe. I'm having a major brain wave here."

"No, Oscar. I think you're having some kind of fit."

"This is going to work. This is *huge*. We've been

thinking way too small. We've got to break out of the box.
We're going to carry the war right to the enemy. Listen. I
need to go to Louisiana."

"What? Why?"

"We'll both go there together. We're great whenever
we're there. Louisiana really works for us. We'll go on a
triumphal tour of the state. We will throw Huey and the
Regulators totally on the defensive. We'll go in a fleet of
limos, with maximum media coverage. We'll hire campaign buses, we'll do a campaign tour. We'll get sound
trucks and copters. We will saturate the whole state. It'll
be totally romantic. We'll give scandalous, teasing interviews. You'll become a sexy science pop star. We'll do
pinups of you, T-shirts, bumper stickers, your own fragrance and lingerie. We'll build little Collaboratories
wherever we go. I've got all kinds of astounding plans
from Bambakias that we can put to use right away. We'll
lead a people's march on Baton Rouge. We'll picket the
statehouse. We'll beard Huey right in his den. We'll nail
him down and erase him."

"Oscar, you're having a fit. You're ranting."

"I am? Really?"

"We can't go to Louisiana. It's too dangerous. We
can't leave the Collaboratory now. We're having an Emergency here. People are afraid, they're deserting us every
day."

"Get more people."

"We can attract all the Moderators we want, but
there's no room for them here."

"Build extensions onto the lab. Take over the town
of Buna."

"Oscar, you scare me when you're like this."

He lowered his voice. "Do I?"

"A little." Her face was flushed beneath the war
paint.

His heart was pounding. He took a few deep breaths.
He was past being frantic now. He was leveling out; he

was cruising on a higher plane; he was exalted. "Darling, I'm going on a secret mission. I think it may be the crux of all our problems, but I may never come back. This may be the last private moment that we ever have together. I know I've upset you. I know I haven't been everything you expected. I may never see you again, but I'm leaving you with such a full and happy heart. I want to remember you looking like this, always. You are so special and dear to me that I can't express it. You're just such a brilliant, radiant creature."

She put her hand to her forehead. "Oh my God. I just don't know what to do with myself when you're like this. . . . You're just so *persuasive!* Oh well, never mind, come on with me, take your clothes off. There's plenty of room for us up here on the lab table."

11

After an extensive discussion of their options, Oscar and Captain Scubbly Bee decided to infiltrate Louisiana by covert means and in deep incognito. Kevin, boldly lying, told the local Emergency Committee that he was leaving for a recruitment drive. Oscar himself would not even officially leave Buna. He was replaced by a body double, a Moderator volunteer who was willing to wear Oscar's clothing, and to spend a great deal of time in a plush hotel room pretending to type on a laptop.

Their conspiracy swiftly assumed its own momentum. To avoid discovery, they decided to airmail themselves into Louisiana in a pair of ultralight aircraft. These silent and stealthy devices were slow, unpredictable, dangerous, painful, and nauseating—basically devoid of creature comforts of any kind. They were, however, more or less undetectable, and immune to roadblocks and shakedowns. Since they were guided by global positioning from Chinese satellites, the aircraft would arrive with pinpoint accuracy right on Fontenot's doorstep—sooner or later.

Kevin and Oscar next took the deeply melodramatic step of dressing themselves as nomad air bums. They borrowed the customary flight suits from a pair of Moderator air jockeys. These snug garments were riveted, fiber-filled cotton duck. They were protective industrial gear, painstakingly tribalized by much hand-stitched embroidery and a richly personal reek of skin unguent. Kevlar gloves, black rubber boots, big furry crash helmets, and shatterproof goggles completed the ensemble.

Oscar gave a few final Method-acting tips to his good-natured body double, and wedged himself into his disguise. He became a creature from an alien civilization. He couldn't resist the temptation to stroll around downtown Buna in his nomad drag. The result astonished him. Oscar was very well known in Buna; his scandalous personal life was common knowledge and the hotel he had built was locally famous. In the flight suit, goggles, and helmet, however, he was entirely ignored. People's eyes simply slid over him without the friction of a moment's care. He radiated otherness.

Kevin and Oscar had synchronized their departure for midnight. Oscar arrived late. His wristwatch was malfunctioning. He'd been running a mild fever for days, and the contact heat had caused the watch's mousebrain works to run fast. Oscar had been forced to reset his watch with its sunlight timer, but he had somehow botched it; his watch was jet-lagged now. He was running late, and it took far more effort than he had expected to climb to the roof of the Collaboratory. He'd never before been on the outside armor of the lab. In the sullen dark of a February night, the structure's outer boundary was windy and intimidating, a wearying physical trial of endless steps and hand rungs.

Winded and trembling, he finally arrived on the starry roof of the Collaboratory, but the best window of weather opportunity was already gone. Kevin, wisely, had already launched himself. With the help of a bored Moderator ground crew, Oscar strapped into his flimsy craft, and left as soon as he could.

The first hour went rather well. Then he was caught by a Greenhouse storm front boiling off the sullen Gulf of Mexico. He was blown all the way to Arkansas. Cannily reading thousands of Doppler radars, the smart and horribly cheap little vehicle darted sickeningly up and down through dozens of local thermals and wind shears, stubbornly routing itself toward its destination with the dumb persistence of a network packet. Blistered by the chafing of his harness, Oscar finally passed out, lolling in the aircraft's grip like a sack of turnips.

The pilot's lack of consciousness made no difference to the nomad machine. At dawn, Oscar found himself fluttering over the rainy swamp of the Bayou Teche.

The Bayou Teche was a hundred and thirty miles long. This quiet oxbow had once formed the main channel of the Mississippi River, some three thousand years in the past. During one brief and intensely catastrophic twenty-first-century spring, the Bayou Teche, to the alarm and horror of everyone, had once again become the main channel of the Mississippi River. The savage Greenhouse deluge had carried all before it, briskly disposing of floodproof concrete levees, shady, moss-strewn live oaks, glamorous antebellum plantation homes, rust-eaten sugar mills, dead oil rigs, and everything else in its path. The flood had ravaged the cities of Breaux Bridge, St. Martinville, and New Iberia.

The Teche had always been a world of its own, a swampy biome distinct and separate from the Mississippi proper and the rice-growing plains to the west. The destruction of its roads and bridges, and the consequent enormous growth of weedy swamp and marsh, had once again returned the Teche to eerie, sodden quietude. The bayou was now one of the wildest locales in North America—not because it had been conserved from development, but because its development had been obliterated.

On his fluttering way down, Oscar took quick note of Fontenot's new surroundings. The ex-fed had chosen to dwell in a scattered backwoods village of metal trailer homes, which were jacked up onto concrete-block columns and surrounded by outhouses and cheap fuel-cell generators. It was a Southern-Gothic slum for freshwater fishermen, a watery maze of wooden docks, lily pads, flatprowed straw-and-plastic bass boats. In the pink light of early morning, the bayou's reedy waters were a lush murky green.

Oscar arrived with impressive pinpoint accuracy— right onto the sloping roof of Fontenot's wooden shack. He swiftly tumbled from the building, falling to earth with an ankle-cracking bang. The now brain-dead aircraft shuddered violently in the morning breeze, tossing Oscar like a bug.

Luckily Fontenot limped quickly from his shack, and helped Oscar subdue his machine. After much cursing and a finger-pinching struggle, they finally had Oscar unbuckled and freed. They managed to fold and spindle the aircraft down to the size of a large canoe.

"So it really is you," Fontenot told him, puffing with exertion. He solemnly thumped Oscar's padded shoulder. "Where'd you get that goofy helmet? You really look like hell."

"Yeah. Have you seen my bodyguard? He was supposed to be here earlier."

"Come on inside," Fontenot said. Fontenot was not a man for metal trailer homes. His shack was an authentic wooden one, a broken-backed structure of cedar and board-and-batten, with gray wooden shingles on top, and spiderwebbed monster pilings beneath. The old shack had been dragged to the water's edge, and reassembled on-site without much professional care. The door squealed and shuddered off its jamb as it opened. Inside, the crack-shot wooden floors dipped visibly.

Fontenot's bare wooden parlor had rattan furniture, a large stout hammock, a tiny fuel-cell icebox, and an impressive wall-mounted arsenal of top-of-the-line fishing equipment. Fontenot's fishing gear was chained to the shack's back wall, and arranged with obsessive military neatness in locked plywood rifle cabinets. The nearest cabinet boasted a bright menagerie of artificial lures:

battery-powered wrigglers, ultrasonic flashers, spinning spoons, pheromone-leaking jellyworms.

"Just a sec," said Fontenot, thumping and squeaking into a cramped back room. Oscar had time to notice a well-thumbed Bible and an impressive litter of beer empties. Then Fontenot reappeared, hauling Kevin with one hand beneath his armpit. Kevin had been liberally bound and gagged with duct tape.

"You know this character?" Fontenot demanded.

"Yeah. That's my new bodyguard."

Fontenot dropped Kevin onto the rattan couch, which cracked loudly under his weight. "Look. I also know this kid. I knew his dad. Dad used to run systems for right-wing militia. Heavily armed white guys, with rigid stares and bad haircuts. If you're hiring this Hamilton boy as security, you must have lost your mind."

"I'm not exactly 'hiring him,' Jules. Technically speaking, he's a federal employee. And he's not just my own personal security. He's the security for an entire federal installation."

Fontenot reached into a pocket of his mud-stained overalls, producing a fisherman's pocketknife. "I don't even wanna know. I just don't care! It's not my problem anymore." He sliced through the duct tape and peeled Kevin free, finally ripping the tape from his mouth with a single jerk. "Sorry, kid," he muttered. "I guess I should have believed you."

"No problem!" Kevin said gallantly, rubbing his gummy wrists and showing a great deal of eye-white. "Happens all the time!"

"I'm all outta practice at this," Fontenot said. "It's the quiet life out here, I'm out of touch. You boys want some breakfast?"

"Excellent idea," Oscar said. A peaceful communal meal was just what they needed. Behind his pie-eating grin, Kevin was clearly measuring Fontenot for a lethal knife thrust to the kidneys.

"Some boudin," Fontenot asserted, retreating to a meager gas-fired camp stove in the corner. "Some aigs and ershters." Oscar watched Fontenot thoughtfully as the old man set about his cooking work, weary and chagrined. After a moment, he had it. Fontenot was in physical recovery from being a fed and a cop. The curse of spook work was finally leaving Fontenot, loosing its grip on his flesh like a departing heroin addiction. But with the icy grip of that long discipline off his bones, there just wasn't a lot left to Jules Fontenot. He was a one-legged Louisiana backwoods fisherman, strangely aged before his time.

The cabin filled with the acrid stench of frying pepper sauce. Oscar's nose, always sensitive now, began to run. He glanced at Kevin, who was sullenly picking shreds of duct tape from his wrists.

"Jules, how's the fishing in your bayou here?"

"It's paradise!" Fontenot said. "Those big lunkers really love the drowned subdivisions down in Breaux Bridge. Your lunker, that's a bottom-feeder that appreciates some structure in the habitat."

"I don't think I know that species, 'lunker.' "

"Oh, the local state fish-and-game people built 'em years ago. The floods, and the poisonings and such, wiped out the local game fish. The Teche was getting bad algae blooms, almost as bad as that giant Dead Spot in the Gulf. So, they cobbled together these vacuum-cleaner fish. Big old channel catfish with tilapia genes. Them lunkers get big, bro. *Damn* big. I mean to say, four hundred pounds with eyes like baseballs. See, lunkers are sterile. Lunkers do nothin' but eat and grow. While the lab boys were messing with their DNA, they kinda goosed the growth hormones. Now some of those babies are fifteen years old."

"That seems like a very daring piece of biological engineering."

"Oh, you don't know Green Huey. That's not the half of it. Huey's a very active boy on environmental issues. Louisiana's a whole different world now."

Fontenot brought them breakfast: oyster omelets and eerie sausages made of congealed rice. The food was impossibly hot—far beyond merely spicy. He'd slathered on pepper as if it were the staff of life.

"That lunker business was an emergency measure. But it worked real good. Emergency all over. This bayou would be a sewer otherwise, but now, the bass are coming back. They're working on the water hyacinth, they've brought back some black bear and even cougar. It's not ever gonna be natural, but it's gonna be real doable. You boys want some more coffee?"

"Thanks," Oscar said. He'd thoughtfully poured his first chicory-tainted cup through a gaping crack in the floorboards. "I have to confess, Jules, I've been worried about you, living here alone in the heart of Huey country. I was afraid that he might have found you here, and harassed you. For political reasons, you know, because of your time with the Senator."

"Oh, *that*. Yeah," Fontenot said, chewing steadily. "I got a couple of those little state militia punks comin' round to 'debrief' me. I showed 'em my federal-issue Heckler and Koch, and told 'em I'd empty a clip on their sorry punk asses if I ever saw 'em near my property again. That pretty much took care o' that."

"Well then," Oscar said, tactfully disturbing his omelet with a fork.

"Y'know what I think?" said Fontenot. Fontenot had never been so garrulous before, but it was clear to Oscar that, in his retirement, the old man was desperately lonely. "People are *different* nowadays. They buffalo way too easy, they lost their starch somehow. It has something to do with that sperm-count crash, all those pesticide hormone poisonings. You get these combinations of pollutants, all these yuppie flus and allergies. . . ."

Oscar and Kevin exchanged a quick glance. They had no idea what the old man was talking about.

"Americans don't live off the land anymore. They

don't know what we've done to our great outdoors. They don't know how *pretty* it used to be around here, before they paved it all over and poisoned it. A million wild-flowers and all kinda little plants and bugs that had been living here a jillion years. . . . Man, when I was a kid you could still fish for marlin. *Marlin!* People these days don't even know what a marlin was."

The door opened, without a knock. A middle-aged black woman appeared, toting a net bag full of canned goods. She wore rubber sandals, a huge cotton skirt, a tropical-flowered blouse. Her head was wrapped in a kerchief. She barged into Fontenot's home, took sudden note of Kevin and Oscar, and began chattering in Creole French.

"This is Clotile," Fontenot said. "She's my house-keeper." He stood up and began sheepishly gathering dead beer cans, while talking in halting French.

Clotile gave Kevin and Oscar a resentful, dismissive glance, then began to lecture her limping boss.

"*This* was your security guy?" Kevin hissed at Oscar. "This broken-down old hick?"

"Yes. He was really good at it, too." Oscar was fasci-nated by the interplay of Fontenot and Clotile. They were engaged in a racial, economic, gender minuet whose con-text was a closed book to him. Clearly, Clotile was one of the most important people in Fontenot's life now. Fonte-not really admired her; there was something about her that he deeply desired, and could never have again. Clotile felt sorry for him, and was willing to work for him, but she would never accept him. They were close enough to talk together, even joke with each other, but there was some tragic element in their relationship that would never, ever be put right. It was a poignant mini-drama, as distant to Oscar as a Kabuki play.

Oscar sensed that Fontenot's credibility had been seriously damaged by their presence as his houseguests. Oscar examined his embroidered sleeves, his discarded gloves, his hairy flight helmet. An intense little moment of culture shock shot through him.

What a very strange world he was living in. What strange people: Kevin, Fontenot, Clotile—and himself, in his dashingly filthy disguise. Here they were, eating breakfast and cleaning house, while at the rim of their moral universe, the game had changed entirely. Pieces swam from center to periphery, periphery to center—pieces flew right off the board. He'd eaten so many breakfasts with Fontenot, in the past life, back in Boston. Every day a working breakfast, watching news clips, planning campaign strategy, choosing the cantaloupe. All light-years behind him now.

Clotile forged forth sturdily and snatched the plates away from Kevin and Oscar. "I hate to be underfoot here when your housekeeper's so busy," Oscar said mildly. "Maybe we should have a little stroll outside, and discuss the reason for our trip here."

"Good idea," said Fontenot. "Sure. You boys come on out."

They followed Fontenot out his squeaking front door and down the warped wooden steps. "They're such good people here," Fontenot insisted, glancing warily back over his shoulder. "They're so real."

"I'm glad you're on good terms with your neighbors."

Fontenot nodded solemnly. "I go to Mass. The local folks got a little church up the way. I read the Good Book these days. . . . Never had time for it before, but I want the things that matter now. The real things."

Oscar said nothing. He was not religious, but he'd always been impressed by Judeo-Christianity's long political track record. "Tell us about this Haitian enclave, Jules."

"*Tell* you? Hell, telling you's no use. We'll just go there. We'll take my huvvy."

Fontenot's hovercraft was sitting below his house. The amphibious saucer had been an ambitious purchase, with indestructible plastic skirts and a powerful alcohol engine. It reeked of fish guts, and its stout and shiny hull was copiously littered with scales. Once emptied of its fisherman's litter, it could seat three, though Kevin had to squeeze in.

The overloaded huvvy scraped and banged its way down to the bayou. Then it sloshed across the lily pads, burping and gargling.

"A huvvy's good for bayou fishing," Fontenot pronounced. "You need a shallow-draft boat in the Teche, what with all these snags, and old smashed cars, and such. The good folks around here kinda make fun of my big fancy huvvy, but I can really get around."

"I understand these Haitians are very religious people."

"Oh yeah," nodded Fontenot. "They had a minister, back in the old country, doing his Moses free-the-people thing. So of course the regime had the guy shot. Then they did some terrible things to his followers that really upset Amnesty International. But . . . basically . . . who cares? You know? They're Haitians!"

Fontenot lifted both his hands from the hovercraft's wheel. "How can anybody care about Haiti? Islands all over the world are drowning. They're all going under water, they've all got big sea-level problems. But Huey . . . well, Huey takes it real personal when charismatic leaders get shot. Huey's into the French diaspora. He tried twisting the arm of the State Department, but they got too many emergencies all their own. So one day, Huey just sent a big fleet of shrimp boats to Haiti, and picked them all up."

"How did he arrange their visas?"

"He never bothered. See, you gotta think the way Huey thinks. Huey's always got two, three, four things going on at once. He put 'em in a shelter. Salt mines. Louisiana's got these huge underground salt mines. Underground mineral deposits twice the size of Mount Everest. They were dug out for a hundred years. They got huge vaults down there, caves as big as suburbs, with thousand-foot ceilings. Nowadays, nobody mines salt anymore. Salt's cheaper than dirt now, because of seawater distilleries. So there's no more market for Louisiana salt. Just another dead industry here, like oil. We dug it all up and sold it, and all we got left is nothing. Giant airtight caverns full of nothing, way down deep in the crust of the earth. Well, what use are they now? Well, one big use. Because you can't see nothing. There's no satellite surveillance for giant underground caves. Huey hid that Haitian cult in one of those giant mines for a couple of years. He was workin' on 'em in secret, with all his other hot underground projects. Like the giant catfish, and the fuel yeast, and the coelacanths . . ."

Kevin spoke up. " 'Coelacanths'?"

"Living fossil fish from Madagascar, son. Older than dinosaurs. They got genetics like fish from another planet. Real primitive and hardy. You nick off chunks from the deep past, and you splice it in the middle of next week— that's Huey's recipe for the gumbo future."

Oscar wiped spray from his waterproof flight suit. "So he's done this strange thing to the Haitians as some kind of pilot project."

"Yeah. And you know what? Huey's right."

"He is?"

"Yep. Huey's awful wrong about the little things, but he's so right about the big picture, that the rest of it just don't matter. You see, Louisiana *really is the future*. Someday soon, the whole world is gonna be just like Louisiana. Because the seas are rising, and Louisiana is a giant swamp. The world of the future is a big, hot, Greenhouse swamp. Full of half-educated, half-breed people, who don't speak English, and didn't forget to have children. Plus, they are totally thrilled about biotechnology. That's what tomorrow's world is gonna look like—not just America, mind you, the whole world. Hot, humid, old, crooked, half-forgotten, kind of rotten. The leaders are corrupt, every-body's on the take. It's bad, really bad, even worse than it sounds."

Fontenot suddenly grinned. "But you know what? It's doable, it's livable! The fishing's good! The food is great! The women are good-lookin', and the music really swings!"

They struggled for two hours to reach the refugee encampment. The hovercraft bulled its way through reed-beds, scraped over spits of saw grass and sticky black mud. The Haitian camp had been cannily established on an island reachable only by aircraft—or by a very determined amphibious boat.

They skirted up onto the solid earth, and left their hovercraft, and walked through knee-high weeds.

Oscar had imagined the worst: klieg lights, watch-towers, barbed wire, and vicious dogs. But the Haitian émigré village was not an armed camp. The place was basically an ashram, a little handmade religious retreat. It was a modest, quiet, rural settlement of neatly white-washed log houses.

The village was a sizable compound for six or seven hundred people, many of them children. The village had no electricity, no plumbing, no satellite dishes, no roads, no cars, no telephones, and no aircraft. It was silent except for the twittering of birds, the occasional clonk of a churn or an ax, and the distant, keening sound of hymns.

No one was hurrying, but everyone seemed to have something to do. These people were engaged in an an-cient peasant round of pre-industrial agriculture. They were literally living off the land—not by chewing up the landscape and transmuting it in sludge tanks, but by gar-dening it with hand tools. These were strange, museum-like activities. Oscar had read about them in books and seen them in documentaries, but he'd never witnessed them performed in real life. Genuinely archaic pursuits, like blacksmithing and yarn-spinning.

It was all about neatly tended little garden plots, swarming compost heaps, night soil in stinking wooden buckets. The locals had a lot of chickens. The chickens were all genetically identical. The birds were all the very same chicken, reissued in various growth stages. They also had multiple copies of a standard-issue goat. This was a hardy, bearded devil-eyed creature, a Nietzschean super-man among goats, and there were herds of it. They had big spiraling vines of snap beans, monster corn, big hairy okra, monster yellow gourds, rock-hard bamboo, a little sugar-cane. Some of the locals were fishermen. Sometime back, they had successfully landed a frightening leathery crea-ture, now a skeletal mass of wrist-thick fish bones. The skeleton sported baleen plates the size of a car grille.

The communards wore homespun clothes. The men had crude straw hats, collarless buttoned vests, drawstring trousers. The women wore ankle-length shifts, white aprons, and big trailing sunbonnets.

They were perfectly friendly, but distant. It seemed that no one could be much bothered with visitors. They were all intensely preoccupied with their daily affairs. However, a small crowd of curious children formed and began trailing the three of them, mimicking them behind their backs, and giggling at them.

"I don't get this," Kevin said. "I thought this was some kind of concentration camp. These folks are doing just fine here."

Fontenot nodded grudgingly. "Yeah, it was meant to be attractive. It's a Green, sustainable farm project. You bump people's productivity up with improved crops and animals—but no fuel combustion, no more carbon diox-ide. Maybe someday they go back to Haiti and teach ev-erybody to live this way."

"That wouldn't work," Oscar said.

"Why not?" said Kevin.

"Because the Dutch have been trying that for years. Everybody in the advanced world thinks they can reinvent

peasant life and keep tribal people ignorant and happy.
Appropriate-tech just doesn't work. Because peasant life is
boring."

"Yeah," Fontenot said. "That's exactly what tipped
me off, too. They oughta be jamming around us asking for
cash and transistor radios, just like any peasant always does
for a tourist from the USA. But they can't even be bothered to look at us. So, listen. You hear that kinda muttering sound?"

"You mean those hymns?" Oscar said.

"Oh, they sing hymns all right. But mostly, they
pray. All the adults pray, men and women. They all pray,
all the time. I mean to say, *all* the time, Oscar."

Fontenot paused. "Y'know, outside people do make
it over here every once in a while. Hunters, fishermen
. . . I heard some stories. They all think these folks are
just real religious, you know, weird voodoo Haitians. But
that ain't it. See, I was Secret Service. I spent years of my
life searching through crowds, looking for crazy people.
We're real big on psychoanalysis in my old line of work.
That's why I know for a fact that there's something really
wrong in the heads of these people. It isn't psychosis. It's
not drugs, either. Religion's got something to do with it
—but it's not *just* religion. Something has been done to
them."

"Neural something," Oscar said.

"Yeah. They know they're different, too. They
know that something happened to them, down in that salt
mine. But they think it was a holy revelation. The spirit
flew into their heads—they call it the 'second-born spirit,'
or 'the born-again spirit.' " Fontenot removed his hat and
wiped his brow. "When I first found this place, I spent
most of a day here, talking to this one old guy—Papa
Christophe, that's his name. Kinda their leader, or at least
their spokesman. This guy is a local biggie, because this
guy has really got a case of whatever-it-is. See, the spirit
didn't take on 'em all quite the same. The kids don't have

it at all. They're just normal kids. Most of the grown-ups are just kind of muttery and sparkly-eyed. But then they've got these apostles, like Christophe. The houngans. The wise ones."

Oscar and Kevin conferred briefly. Kevin was very spooked by Fontenot's story. He really disliked being surrounded by illegal alien black people in the middle of an impenetrable swamp. Visions of boiling iron cannibal pots were dancing in Kevin's head. Anglos . . . they'd never gotten over the sensation of becoming a racial minority.

Oscar was adamant, however. Having come this far, nothing would do for him but to interview Papa Christophe. Fontenot finally located the man, hard at work in a whitewashed cabin at the edge of town.

Papa Christophe was an elderly man with a long-healed machete slash in his head. His wrinkled skin and bent posture suggested a lifetime of vitamin deficiency. He looked a hundred years old, and was probably sixty.

Papa Christophe gave them a toothless grin. He was sitting on a three-legged stool on the hard dirt floor of the cabin. He had a wooden maul, a pig-iron chisel, and a half-formed wooden statue. He was deftly peeling slivers of brown cypress wood. His statue was a saint, or a martyr; a slender, Modigliani-like woman, with a serene and stylized face, her hands pressed together in prayer. Her lower legs were wrapped in climbing flames.

Oscar was instantly impressed. "Hey! Primitive art! This guy's pretty good! Would he sell me that thing?"

"Choke it back a little," Kevin muttered. "Put your wallet away."

The cabin's single room was warm and steamy, because the building had a crude homemade still inside it. Presumably, a distillery hadn't been present in the village's original game plan, but the Haitians were ingenious folk, and they had their own agenda. The still had been riveted together out of dredged-up automobile parts. By the smell of it, it was cooking cane molasses down into a head-bending rum. The shelves along the wall were full of cast-off glass bottles, dredged from the detritus of the bayou. Half the bottles were full of yellow alcohol, and plugged with cloth and clay.

Fontenot and the old man were groping at French, with their widely disparate dialects. Fed with Christophe's cast-off chips of cypress wood, the still was cooking right along. Rum dripped down a bent iron tube into the glass bottle, ticking like a water clock. Papa Christophe was friendly enough. He was chatting, and tapping his chisel, and chopping, and muttering a little to himself, all in that same, even, water-clock rhythm.

"I asked him about the statue," Fontenot explained. "He says it's for the church. He carves saints for the good Lord, because the good Lord is always with him."

"Even in a distillery?" Kevin said.

"Wine is a sacrament," Fontenot said stiffly. Papa Christophe picked up a pointed charcoal stick, examined his wooden saint, and drew on her a bit. He had a set of carving tools spread beside him, on a greased leather cloth: an awl, a homemade saw, a shaving hook, a hand-powered bow-drill. They were crude implements, but the old man clearly knew what he was doing.

They'd left their ragtag of curious children outside the cabin door, but one of the smaller kids plucked up his courage and peered inside. Papa Christophe looked up, grinned toothlessly, and uttered some solemn Creole pronunciamento. The boy came in and sat obediently on the earthen floor.

"What was that about?" Oscar said.

"I believe he just said, 'The monkey raised her children before there were avocados,'" Fontenot offered.

"What?"

"It's a proverb."

The little kid was thrilled to be allowed into the old man's workshop. Papa Christophe chopped a bit more, directing kindly remarks to the child. The rum dripped rhythmically into its pop bottle, which was almost full.

Fontenot pointed to the child, and essayed a suggestion in French. Papa Christophe chuckled indulgently. *"D'abord vous guetté poux-de-bois manger bouteille, accrochez vos calabasses,"* he said.

"Something about bugs eating the bottles," Fontenot hazarded.

"*Do* bugs eat his bottles?" Kevin said.

Christophe hunched over and examined his charcoal outline. He was deeply engrossed by his statue. For his own part, the little boy was fascinated by the sharp carving tools.

The kid made a sudden grab for a rag-coated saw blade. Without a moment's hesitation, the old man reached behind himself and unerringly caught the child by his groping wrist.

Papa Christophe then stood up, lifted the boy out of harm's way, and caught him up one-handed in the crook of his right arm. At the very same instant, he took two steps straight backward, reached out blindly and left-handed, and snagged an empty bottle from its shelf on the wall.

He then swung around in place, and deftly snatched up the brimming bottle from the coil of the still. He replaced the bottle with the empty one—all the while chatting to the little boy in friendly admonition. Somehow, Christophe had precisely timed all these actions, so that he caught the trickling rum between drips.

The old man then sauntered back to his work stool and sat down, catching the child on his skinny leg. He lifted the rum bottle left-handed, sampled it thoughtfully, and offered Fontenot a comment.

Kevin rubbed his eyes. "What did he just do? Was he dancing a jig backward? He can't do that."

"What did he say?" Oscar asked Fontenot.

"I couldn't catch it," Fontenot said. "I was too busy

watching him move. That was really strange." He addressed Papa Christophe in French.

Christophe sighed patiently. He fetched up a flat piece of planed pine board and his charcoal stick. The old man had a surprisingly fine and fluid handwriting, as if he'd been taught by nuns. He wrote, *"Quand la montagne brûle, tout le monde le sait; quand le coeur brûle, qui le sait?"* He wrote the sentence blindly, while he turned his head aside, and spoke pleasantly to the child on his knee.

Fontenot examined the charcoal inscription on the pine board. " 'When the volcano catches fire, everybody knows. But when the heart catches fire, who knows it?' "

"That's an interesting sentiment," Kevin said.

Oscar nodded thoughtfully. "I find it especially interesting that our friend here can write down this ancient folk wisdom while he talks aloud to that child at the very same time."

"He's ambidextrous," Kevin said.

"Nope."

"He's just really fast," Fontenot said. "It's like sleight of hand."

"Nope. Wrong again." Oscar cleared his throat. "Gentlemen, could we go out for a private conference please? I think it's time for us to move along to our boat."

They took Oscar at his word. Fontenot made his cordial good-byes. They left the old man's cabin, then limped their way silently out of the village, full of broad uneasy smiles for the inhabitants. Oscar wondered at the fate that had stuck him with two different generations of lame men.

Finally they were out of earshot. "So what's the deal?" Kevin said.

"The deal is this: that old man was thinking of two things at once."

"What do you mean?" Kevin said.

"I mean that it's a neural hack. He was fully aware of two different events at the same moment. He didn't let that little kid hurt himself, because he was thinking about that kid every second. And even though he was carefully working that hammer and chisel, he wouldn't let that bottle overflow. He was listening to the bottle while he was wood carving. He didn't even have to *look* at the bottle to realize it was full. I think he was *counting the drops*."

"So it's like he's got two brains," Kevin said slowly.

"No, he only has one brain. But he's got two windows open on the screen behind his eyes."

"He's multitasking, but with his own brain."

"Yeah. That's it. Exactly."

"How do you know that?" Fontenot asked, squinting skeptically.

"My girlfriend won the Nobel Prize for establishing the neural basis of attention," Oscar said. "Supposedly, that's years away from any practical application. Supposedly. Right? This is Green Huey at work here. I've been waiting for that shoe to drop for quite a while."

"How can you *prove* that a man is concentrating on two things at once?" Fontenot said. "How do you prove he's thinking at all?"

"It's difficult. But it's doable. Because that's what they're doing, all right. That's why they're never bored here. It's because they pray. They pray all the time—and I wouldn't be surprised if all that prayer wasn't serving some other purpose, too. I think it's some kind of relay between two separate streams of consciousness. You tell God what you're thinking every minute—and that's how you know it yourself. That's what Christophe was trying to tell us with the song-and-dance about the 'fiery heart.' "

"So it's like he's got two souls," Fontenot said slowly.

"Sure," Oscar said. "If that's the word you want to use. I sure wish Greta were here with her lab equipment, so we could nail this down." He shook his head regretfully. "That State of Emergency at the Buna lab has seriously stepped on our downtime together."

They'd now arrived at the hovercraft, but Fontenot showed no sign of leaving. His artificial leg was troubling him. He sat down on the hull of the hovercraft and removed his hat, breathing heavily. Kevin clambered over the back and sat inside the huvvy, propping up his aching feet. A pair of herons flew nearby, and something large and oily surfaced near a clump of tangled reeds.

"I don't know what to make of it," Fontenot confessed. He stared at Oscar, as if the revelation were all his fault. "I don't know what to make of *you* anymore. Your girlfriend won the Nobel Prize. A hacker is your security man. And you dropped on the roof of my house without a word of warning, dressed like a flying ape."

"Yeah. Of course." Oscar paused. "See, it all makes sense, if you get there step by step."

"Look, don't tell me any more," Fontenot said. "I'm in way too deep already. I don't want to play your game. I want to go home, and live here, and die here. If you tell me any more of this, I'm gonna have to take it to the President."

"I've got you covered on that issue," Oscar told him. "I work for the President. I'm with the National Security Council."

Fontenot was astonished. "You're in the Administration now? You work for the NSC?"

"Jules, stop acting so surprised at every single thing I say. You're starting to hurt my feelings. Why do you think I came here? How do you think I end up in situations like this? Who else could do this properly? I'm the only guy in the world who would walk into a neural voodoo cult in the middle of nowhere, and immediately figure out exactly what was going on."

Fontenot rubbed his stubbled chin. "So . . . Okay! I guess I'm with you. So, Mr. Super Expert Know-it-all, tell me something. Are we really going to have a war with Holland?"

"Yes. We are. And if I can get out of this damn swamp in one piece, and brief the President on my findings here, we're probably going to have a war with Louisiana."

"Oh my God." Fontenot groaned aloud. "It's beyond bad. It's the worst. It's the very worst. I knew I should have kept my mouth shut. I knew I shouldn't have outed this thing."

"No, it was the right thing to do. Huey's a great man, and he's a visionary, but Huey is around the bend. He's not just your standard southern-fried good-old-boy megalomaniac anymore. Now I know the full truth. These Haitians? They were just his proof of concept. Huey's done something weird to *himself*. Something very dark and neural."

"And you have to tell the President about that."

"Yes, I do. Because our President is not like that. The President is not insane. He's just a hard-as-nails, ambitious, strong-arm politician, who is going to bring law and order to this two-horse country, even if it means setting fire to half of Europe."

Fontenot considered this subject at length. Finally he turned to Kevin. "Hey, Hamilton."

"Yes sir?" Kevin said, startled.

"Don't let them kill this guy."

"I didn't want the job!" Kevin protested. "He didn't tell me how bad it was. Honest! You want the bodyguard job back? Take the damn job."

"No," Fontenot said, with finality. They climbed into the little boat, three men in a tub, and headed out into the bayou again.

"He did some great things for us," Fontenot said. "Of course, everything he ever did was always about Huey first. Huey was always item number one on the Huey agenda, everybody knew that. But he did good things for the people. He gave 'em good breaks that they hadn't had in a hundred years. It's still the future."

"Yeah," Oscar said, "Huey's got his own new order —but it isn't new, and it isn't order. Huey's a funny guy. He can crack a joke and pound the ol' podium, he'll buy everybody a drink and make public fun of himself. But he's got it all: total control over the legislature and the judiciary. A brownshirt militia on the rampage. His own private media network—his own economy, even. A blood-and-soil ideology. Secret retreats full of vengeance weapons. Huey kidnaps people. He abducts whole little populations, and makes them disappear. I suppose he does it all for the best of reasons, but the ends don't matter when you're using means like that. And now, he's dosed himself with some off-the-wall treatment that makes people permanently schizoid! He can't possibly get better after this. He can only get worse and worse."

Fontenot sighed. "Let me ask one favor. Don't tell anybody that I led you to this. I don't want any press. I don't want my poor neighbors knowin' that I sold old Huey out. This is my home. I want to die here."

Kevin spoke up. "You keep saying that this place is the future. Why do you want to die, old man?"

Fontenot looked at him with baggy-eyed tolerance. "Kid, *everybody* goes to the future to die. That's where the job gets done."

Oscar shook his head. "Don't feel guilty. You don't owe Huey any loyalty."

"We all owe him, dammit. He saved us. He saved the state. We owe him for the mosquitoes, if nothing else."

"Mosquitoes? What mosquitoes?"

"There aren't any. And we're in the middle of a swamp. And we don't get bit. And you didn't even notice, did you? I sure as hell notice."

"Well, what happened to the mosquitoes?"

"Before Huey came along, the mosquitoes were kicking our ass. Mosquitoes *love* the Greenhouse future.

When it got hotter and wetter, they came in tidal waves. Carrying malaria, dengue fever, encephalitis. . . . After the big Mississippi floods, mosquitoes boiled out of every ditch in the state. It was a major health emergency, people were dyin'. And Huey had just been sworn in. He just wouldn't have it, he said, *'Take action, get rid of 'em.'* He sent out the fogger trucks. Not insecticide, not that poison gas like before—DDT and toxins. That screwed up everything—not doable, everybody knows that. But Huey figured it out—he didn't gas the bugs, he gassed the *people*. With airborne antibodies. They're like breathable vaccinations. The people of Louisiana are toxic to mosquitoes now. Our blood literally kills them. If a mosquito bites a Cajun, that mosquito dies on the spot."

"Neat hack!" Kevin enthused. "But that wouldn't kill *all* the mosquitoes, would it?"

"No, but the diseases vanished right away. Because disease couldn't spread from person to person anymore. And the skeeters are going, too. See, Huey's gassing the livestock, wild animals, he's gassing everything that breathes. Because it works! Those bloodsuckers used to kill the people in job lots. For thousands of years they were a biblical plague around here. But Green Huey nailed 'em for good."

The hovercraft puttered on. The three of them fell thoughtfully silent.

"What's that bug on your arm, then?" Kevin said at last.

"Dang!" Fontenot swatted it. "Must have blown in from Mississippi!"

Oscar knew that his new allegations were extremely grave. Properly handled, this scandal would finish Huey. Handled badly, it could finish Oscar in short order. It might even finish the President.

Oscar composed what he considered the finest

memo of his career. He had the memo passed to the President—hopefully, for his eyes only. Oscar was unhappy at bypassing his superiors to the top of the chain of command, but he was anxious to avoid any further debacles from the paramilitary zealots of the NSC. Their killer helicopter attack during his kidnapping had probably saved his life, but true professionals simply didn't behave that way.

Oscar appealed to the President. He was calm, factual, rational, well organized. He pinpointed the locale of the Haitian camp, and recommended that human intelligence be sent in. Someone discreet, harmless-looking. A female agent would be a good choice. Someone who could thoroughly tape the place, and take blood samples.

For three days, Oscar followed his memo with a barrage of anxious demands and queries of the NSC higher-ups. Had the President seen his memo? It was of the greatest importance. It was critical.

There was no answer.

In the meantime, serious difficulties pressed at the Collaboratory. Morale was cracking among the civilian support staff. None of them were being paid anymore. None of the support staff enjoyed the prestige and glamour of the scientists, who were rapidly accustoming themselves to being followed by worshipful krewes of hairy-eyed Moderators. The civilian staff were miffed. The Collaboratory's medical staff were especially upset. They could get good-paying jobs elsewhere—and they could scarcely be expected to run a decent, ethical medical facility without a steady flow of capital and up-to-date supplies.

There was continued and intensifying Moderator/ Regulator feuding in the Sabine River valley. Scouting patrols by rival nomad youth gangs were degenerating into bushwhackings and lynchings. The situation was increasingly volatile, especially since the sheriffs of Jasper and Newton counties had been forced to resign their posts.

The good-old-boy Texan sheriffs had been outed on outrageous bribery scandals. Someone had compiled extensive dossiers on their long-time complicity in bootlegging, gambling, and prostitution—all those illicit delights that could be outlawed, but never made unpopular.

It didn't take genius to understand that civil order in East Texas was being deliberately undermined by Green Huey. Texas state government should have risen to this challenge, but Texas state government was well known for its lack of genius. The state held endless hearings on the shocking problem of endemic police corruption—apparently hoping that the riots would subside if fed enough paperwork.

The biggest wild card on the state border was the provocative presence of European and Asian news crews. America's hot war with the gallant, minuscule Dutch had made America hot copy again. Savage confrontations between armed criminal gangs had always been an activity that endeared America to its fans around the world. Dutch journalists had been banned in the USA—but French and German ones were everywhere, especially in Louisiana. The British were kind enough to suggest that the French were secretly arming Huey's Regulator gangs.

The prestige-maddened hotheads in the Regulators were thrilled to receive worldwide net coverage. Young Regulator goons lived for reputations and respect, since they had so little else. The military crisis was distorting the odd underpinnings of the Regulator attention-economy. Violent hotheads were vaulting through the ranks by their daring attacks on Moderators.

The Moderators, in Oscar's judgment, were a cannier and more ductile lot. Their networks were better designed and organized; the Moderators were cooler, less visible, far less confrontational. Still, it didn't take much pushing to render them murderous.

On the fourth day after sending his memo, Oscar received a curt message from the President. Two Feathers indicated, in a couple of lines, that Oscar's memo had been read and understood. Oscar was directly ordered not to speak further on the topic to anyone.

Forty-eight hours passed, and the scandal broke wide open. A squadron of U.S. helicopters had flown by night into the heart of Louisiana, where they rendezvoused in an obscure swamp village. Two of them promptly collided and crashed, crushing the homes of the sleeping natives, charring and killing innocent women and children. Undetermined numbers of the locals had been scandalously kidnapped by the abduction-crazed feds. Four federal spooks had been killed in the crash. Their bodies were paraded before Huey's European cameras, their zippy black flight suits top-heavy with aging cyber-gear.

This bizarre allegation simply hung there, misfiring, for another forty-eight hours. There was no formal reaction from the Administration. They simply declined comment on the issue, as if the demagogic raving of the Governor of Louisiana was too clownish for words. Public attention focused instead on the U.S. Navy, whose Atlantic armada was being launched against the Dutch in an archaic ritual of wind-snapping Old Glories. The gallant old warcraft wallowed out to sea from their half-drowned military dry docks. All eyes were on the War now—or at least, they were supposed to be.

Outside America, it was obvious to anyone, even the perennially suspicious Chinese, that a naval attack on the Dutch was an absurd and ridiculous gesture. It was the subject of amused lampoons in Europe. Only the Dutch seemed sincerely upset.

But the effect within America was profound. The nation was at War. Roused from its fatal lethargy by the cheering prospect of doing some serious harm, the Congress had actually declared a War. The result was instant, intense civil discord. Outflanked by the state of War, most of the Emergency committees promised to go quietly. A few defied the Congress and the President, risking arrest.

In the meanwhile, antiwar networks congealed and raged in the streets. They were sincerely disgusted to see the Constitution perverted, and the nation dishonored, for domestic political advantage.

Twenty-four more feverish hours of War ticked by. Then, the Administration accused the Governor of Louisiana of conducting unethical medical experiments on illegal aliens. This news arrived in the very midst of the martial fife-playing and drumbeating. It was a shocking distraction. But it was serious—bad, very bad, unbelievably bad. The surgeon general and the cabinet head of Health Services were wheeled out in public, burdened with grim looks, medical evidence, and terrifying cranial flip charts.

The PR attack on Huey was badly handled, amateurish, graceless even. But it was lethal. Huey had laughed off many other scandals, sidestepped them, passed the buck, silenced his critics, suborned them. But this scandal was beyond the pale. It was all about invisible, helpless, rootless people, deliberately driven out of their minds as an industrial process. That was just a little too close to home for most Americans. They couldn't live with that.

When his phone rang, Oscar was, for once, entirely ready.

"You little SCUMBAG!" Huey screamed. "You evil Yankee narc! Those people were *perfectly happy*! It was *heaven on earth*! And the feds came in the dark and kidnapped them! They *burned them alive*!"

"Good evening, Governor! I take it you've seen tonight's Administration briefing."

"You're FINISHED, you jumped-up little creep! I'm gonna make you sorry you were ever cloned! I made promises to those people, they were under my care. You outed them! I *know* it was you. Admit it!"

"Governor, of course I admit it. Let's be adults here. That news was bound to come out, whether I leaked it or not. You can't run two years of secret neural experiments on hundreds of human subjects and not have leaks. Scientists talk to each other. Even your pet scientists. Even nonpedigreed chicken-fried scientists who live down in salt mines doing gruesome things to foreigners. Scientists communicate their findings, that's just the way scientists are. So of course your pet goons in the salt mines leaked word to other neuroscientists. And of course I got wind of it. And of course I told the President. I *work* for the President." He cleared his throat. "Mind you, I didn't design that presentation tonight. If I had, it would have looked more professional."

He wondered if Huey would swallow this boldly prepared lie. He'd done his best to make it sound plausible. He'd done it in order to shield Fontenot, his real source. Maybe the deception would work. In any case it would surely distract and irritate Huey and his state-supported neuro quacks.

"You can't believe that racist poppycock they're handing out about my Haitians. Those folks aren't monsters! They're just very devout people with some strange drug practices. Blowfish zombie poisons, and all that."

"Governor, you're making me cry. Am I ten years old? Are you afraid I'm taping this? If you're not going to talk to me seriously, you might as well hang up."

"Oh no," Huey grunted. "You and I go back a little too far for that. I can always talk to *you*, Soap Boy."

"Good. I'm glad that our previous understanding still holds. Let's try to avoid cross-purposes, this time."

"At least I know that you can talk to the President. That son of a bitch won't return my calls! *Me*—the most senior Governor in America! I *know* that dumb bastard, I met him at Governors' conferences. Hell, I did him a whole lot of favors. I taught him everything he knows about proles and how you deal with 'em. 'Moderators'— what the hell is all that about? He's *killing my people*! He's *kidnapping* my people. You tell the President that he's crossed the wrong man. I'm not puttin' up with the strong-arm from the Featherweight. He got eighteen percent of the popular vote! You tell him that! You tell him Huey don't forget these things."

"Governor, I'll be glad to convey your sentiments to the President, but may I make a reasonable suggestion first? Shut up. You are finished. The President has you cornered. This thing you did with the Haitians was totally unconscionable! You've shot your own feet off in public."

"So I should have left them on their drowning island to be tortured to death."

"Yes, that's exactly what you should have done. Leave them alone. You don't own people just because you helped them survive. You want to blow people's minds by giving weird dope to uninformed experimental subjects? Go back to the 1960s and join the CIA! You're not God, Huey! You're just a damn Governor! You went way, *way* too far! And you can't wiggle out of this one, because your fingerprints are all over it—your *brain* prints are all over it!"

Huey laughed. "You just watch me and see."

"They're gonna demand that *you* go in for a PET-scan next, Huey. Then, they're going to find the dual synchronized waves of chemical gradients, and the shifting electrical patterns through the corpus callosum, and all that other boring neural crap that you and I are the only politicians in the world who have learned to pronounce properly! They're gonna out you as a bolt-in-the-neck monster. People are gonna Frankenstein you! You're gonna be barbecued by a torch-wielding mob. You're not just gonna be *politically embarrassed* by this. You're gonna *get killed*."

"I know all that," Huey said quietly. "Let 'em do their worst."

Oscar sighed. "Etienne—can I call you that? I feel that we know and understand one another so much better these days. . . . Etienne, please don't make people kill you. That can happen very easily, and it's just not worth it. Listen to me. I *sympathize* with you. I take a deep, lasting, personal and professional interest in politicians who happen to be monsters. Believe me, it doesn't get any better after this part. After this part, it just gets worse and worse."

"You know that I'm going to out you big-time for this, don't you? 'Colombian Clone Freak in Seaside Love Nest with Nobel Scientist.' "

"Etienne, I'm not *just* a Colombian clone freak. I am also a professional campaign adviser. Let me give you some very sincere campaign advice, right now. *Give up. Go away.* Just get yourself some cash out of the slush fund, and get your lovely wife if she really wants to come along, and go into exile. Go into self-imposed exile. You know? Leave the country. It happens. It's traditional. It's a legitimate political maneuver."

"I'm not gonna run away. Huey don't do that."

"Of course 'Huey do that,' dammit! Go aboard a nice French submarine—I know you got a dozen of 'em lurking offshore. Have 'em take you to a nice villa, on Elba, or St. Helena or something. Take a few pet bodyguards. It's doable! You eat well, you write the memoirs, you're tanned, rested, and ready. Maybe . . . maybe even, someday . . . if somehow things get much, *much* worse here in America . . . maybe you'll even look *good*. It sounds insane, but I'm not sure I can even judge anymore. Maybe, someday, deliberately imposing schizoid states of mind on unsuspecting human beings will become politically *fashionable*. But it sure as hell isn't now. Read tomorrow's opinion polls. You're toast."

"Kid, I'm Huey. *You're* toast. I can destroy you, and your ungrateful bitch girlfriend, and your entire research facility, which, in point of fact, is, and always will be, *my* research facility."

"I'm sure you can try that, Governor, but why waste the energy? It's pointless to destroy us now. It's too late for that. I really thought you had a better feel for these things."

"Son, you *still* don't get it. I don't need any 'feel' for it. I can do all that in my *spare time*—while I pat my head and rub my belly." Huey hung up.

———————————

Now the dogs of War were unleashed on the psychic landscape of America, and even as rather small dogs, with blunt, symbolic teeth, they provoked political havoc. No one had expected this of the President. An eccentric billionaire Native American—for a country exhausted by identity crisis and splintered politics, Two Feathers had seemed a colorful sideshow, an Oh-Might-As-Well candidate whose bluster might keep up morale. Even Oscar had expected little of him; the governorship of Colorado had never given Two Feathers much chance to shine. Once in the national saddle, however, Two Feathers was rapidly proving himself to be a phenomenon. He was clearly one of those transitional American Presidents, those larger-than-life figures who set a stamp on their era and made life horribly dangerous and interesting.

Unfortunately for Green Huey, the American political landscape had room for only one eccentrically dressed, carpet-chewing, authoritarian state Governor. Two Feathers had beaten Huey to the White House. Worse yet, he correctly recognized Huey as an intolerable threat that could not be co-opted. He was resolved to crush Huey.

A war of words broke out between the President and the rogue Governor. Huey accused the President of provocative spy overflights. This was true, for the sky over Louisiana was black with surveillance aircraft—feds, proles, military, Europeans, Asians, private networks, anyone who could launch an autonomous kite with a camera on board.

The President counteraccused the Governor of treacherous collaboration with foreign powers during wartime. This was also true, though so far the premier effect of the Dutch War had been to saturate America with curious European tourists. The Europeans hadn't seen anyone declare a War in absolute ages. It was fun to be a foreign national in a country at War, especially a country that sold bugging devices out of brimming baskets at flea markets. Suddenly everyone was his own international spy.

The President then upped the ante. He sternly demanded the swift return of all the federal weaponry stolen from the ransacked Louisiana Air Force base. He threatened unnamed, severe reprisals.

The Air Force weapons were, needless to say, not forthcoming. Instead, the Governor accused the President of plotting martial law and a coup d'état.

Huey's Senators launched a marathon procedural war within the U.S. Senate, with double-barreled filibusters. The President demanded impeachment proceedings against the two Louisiana Senators. He also announced criminal investigations of all of Louisiana's Representatives.

Huey called for the President to be impeached by Congress, and for antiwar activists to take to the streets in a general strike and paralyze the country.

Faced with the prospect of a general strike, the President counterannounced his unilateral creation of a new, all-volunteer, civil defense force, the "Civil Defense Intelligence Agency." On paper, this seemed a very strange organization—a national debating club of so-called "civil activists," loyal only to the President. The CDIA had no budget, and its head was an aging, much-decorated war hero, who happened to live in Colorado. He happened to know the President personally. He happened to be a very high-ranking Moderator.

A closer analysis showed that the "Civil Defense Intelligence Agency" *was* the Moderators. The CDIA was a gigantic prole gang with the direct backing of the nation's chief executive. At this point, a Rubicon was crossed. This stroke made it obvious that the Governor of Colorado had been cultivating his own prole forces for years. Huey had used his Regulator proles as a deniable proxy force, but the President was boldly bringing his own private mafia into the open, and brandishing it like a club. The President was a day late and perhaps a dollar short, but he had a great advantage. He was the President.

Now, for the first time, the President began to look genuinely powerful, even dangerous. This was a classic political coalition: it had worked in medieval France. It was the long-forgotten bottom of the heap, allied with the formerly feeble top, to scare the hell out of the arrogant and divisive middle.

The President's first deployment of his semilegal forces was against the now-illegal Emergency committees. This was a stroke of brilliance, because the Emergency committees were universally detested, and even more feared than the proles. Besides, the Emergency committees had lost all their legal backing, and were already on the ropes. Attacking a newly illegal force with a newly legitimized, formerly illegal force struck the American public very favorably. The maneuver had a nice unspoken symmetry to it. It was a player's move. The President's ratings went up sharply. He was accomplishing something tangible, where nothing had been accomplished in years.

The new CDIA, for its own part, revealed some impressive new tactics. The CDIA lacked the legal power to arrest anyone, so they pursued Emergency committee members with nonviolent "body pickets." These were armbanded bursars who methodically stalked committee members for twenty-four hours a day. This tactic was not difficult for a prole group. "Body picketing" was basically an intelligence stakeout, shadowing; but it was not surreptitious. It was totally open and obvious, and like all paparazzi work, it was extremely annoying to its victims.

The proles took to this job like ducks to water. They had always been organized much like intelligence agencies

—small, distributed, surreptitious networks, living on the fringes of society through shared passwords and persistent scrounging. But as a national goon squad, ordered from above, the prole networks suddenly coalesced into a rigid, crystalline substance. For the President's enemies, they became a human prison of constant surveillance.

Or so it seemed. It was still too early to tell whether the President's CDIA would have any staying power as a New Model Army. But the mere threat of its deployment sent a shock wave through the system. A new era was clearly at hand. America's Emergency was truly and finally over. The War was on.

Oscar followed these developments with great professional care, and reacted to catch the popular tide. He had Greta formally declare the Emergency over at the Collaboratory. There was no more Emergency. From now on, it was Wartime.

"Why are you doing this to us?" Greta demanded, in yet another bone-grinding late-night committee session. "What possible difference does it make?"

"It makes all the difference in the world."

"But it's all semantic! We're all the same people. I'm still the lab Director, God help me. And we still have the Emergency Committee as the only people who can run this mess."

"From now on, we're the War Committee."

"It's just symbolic!"

"No it isn't." Oscar sighed. "I'll explain it to you, very simply. The President has seized power in a time of crisis. He bypassed the Constitution, he undercut the Congress, he annihilated the Emergency committees. He did that by recruiting large gangs of organized social outcasts, who derive their new legitimacy strictly from him, and are loyal to him personally."

"Yes, Oscar, we know all that. We're not blind. And I'm very unhappy about what the President did. I certainly don't see why we have to imitate his radical, bully-boy tactics."

"Greta, the President is imitating *us*. That is exactly what *we* did, right here. The President is doing it because you and I got away with doing it! You're very popular because you did that, you're famous. People think it's exciting to seize power with prole gangs, and to throw all the rascals out. It's a very slick move."

Greta was very troubled. "Oh . . . Oh my God."

"I admit, this isn't great news for American democracy. In fact, it's bad news. It's terrible news. It might even be catastrophic news. But it's wonderful news for the lab. This news means that we're all much, much less likely to get arrested or indicted for what we've done here. You see? *We're going to get away with it*. It's a wonderful political gift from our chief protector and patron—the President. We're home free! All we have to do from now on is change our shirt whenever the President changes his shirt. From now on, we have protective coloration. We're no longer crazy radicals, on strike at a federal lab. We're loyal citizens who are fully and mindfully engaged in the grand experiment of our President's new social order. So from now on, that's why we're the War Committee."

"But we *can't* be the War Committee. We don't have our own war."

"Oh yes, we do."

"No, we don't."

"Just wait."

———————————

Two days later the President sent federal troops to Buna. The U.S. Army was finally responding to his orders, despite their deep institutional distaste for coercive violence against American citizens. Unfortunately, these soldiers were a marching battalion of Special Operations/Low-Intensity Conflict specialists.

The American military, at the historical tag end of

traditional armed conflict, knew that they had entered an era where the pen truly was mightier than the sword. The sword just wasn't much use in an epoch when battlefronts no longer existed and a standing army could be torn to shreds by cheap unmanned machinery.

So, the U.S. military had downgraded their swords and upgraded their pens. The President's U.S. Army Seventy-sixth Infowar and Social Adjudication Battalion were basically social workers. They wore crisp white uniforms, and concentrated on language skills, disaster relief measures, stress counseling, light police work, and first aid. Half of them were women, none of them had firearms, and, as a final fillip, they had been ordered into action without any federal funding. In fact, they were already four months behind on their salaries. They'd had to sell their armored personnel carriers just to make ends meet.

The Collaboratory was now seriously overcrowded. Poaching and eating the rare animals became a commonplace misdemeanor. With a battalion of five hundred mooching soldier/psychoanalysts, plus their camp-follower media coverage, the long-suffering Collaboratory was seriously overloaded. The interior of the dome began to fog over with human breath.

To keep the newcomers usefully occupied, Oscar deputized the Infowar Battalion to psychologically besiege Huey's loyalists, who were still stubbornly on strike, holed up in the Spinoffs building. They did this with a will. But the Collaboratory was beginning to resemble a giant subway.

The ideal solution was to build more shelter. The Moderators, in uneasy symbiosis with the feds, set up tents on the Collaboratory's spare ground outside the dome. Oscar would have liked to build annexes to the Collaboratory. Bambakias's emergency design plans suggested some quite astonishing methods by which this might be done. The materials were available. Manpower was in generous supply. The will to do it was present.

But there was no money. The Collaboratory was surrounded by the city of Buna, and its privately owned real estate. The city of Buna was still on friendly terms with the lab, even proud of them for having won so much publicity lately. But the lab couldn't commandeer the city by force of arms. Besides, all of Buna's available rental shelter had already been taken, on exorbitant terms, by European and Asian media crews, and nongovernmental civil-rights and peace organizations.

So they were stymied. It always boiled down to money. They just didn't have any. They had proved that the business of science could run on sheer charisma for a while, a life powered by sheer sense of wonder, like some endless pledge drive. But people were still people; they ran out of charisma, and the sense of wonder ate its young. The need for money was always serious, and always there.

Tempers frayed. Despite the utter harmlessness of the federal SO/LIC troops, Huey correctly took their presence on the border of Louisiana as a menacing provocation. He unleashed a barrage of hysterical propaganda, including the bizarre, and documented, allegation that the President was a long-time Dutch agent. As Governor, and as a timber businessman, the President had had extensive dealings with the Dutch, during happier times. Huey's oppo-research people had compiled painstaking dossiers to this effect.

It didn't matter. Only a schizoid with a case of bicameral consciousness could seriously contend that the President was a Dutch agent, when the President had just declared War on Holland. When the U.S. Navy was steaming for Amsterdam. When the Dutch were screaming for help, and getting none.

This spy allegation not only went nowhere, it convinced many former fence-sitters that Huey had utterly lost his mind. Huey was dangerous, and had to be pried from public office at all costs. And yet Huey held on, publicly drilling his state militia, conducting purges of his faltering police, swearing vengeance on a world of hypocrites and liars.

Oscar and Greta had reached the end of their rope. They began to argue seriously and publicly. They had had tiffs before, spats before, little misunderstandings; but after so many hours, days, weeks of difficult administration work, they began to have bruising public combats over the future of the lab, over the meaning of their effort.

The end of the Emergency and the beginning of the War necessitated the creation of yet another media environment. Oscar shut down the public loudspeakers that monitored Emergency Committee discussions. Wartime was about loose lips sinking ships, about blood, sweat, toil, and tears. It was time to stop propagandizing the people of the Collaboratory. They already knew where they stood and what was at stake. Now they had to defend what they had built; they should be in the trenches with shovels, they should be singing marching songs.

And yet they could do no such thing. They could only wait. The situation was out of their hands. They were no longer masters of their own destiny, they no longer held the initiative. The real struggle was taking place in Washington, in The Hague, in a flotilla of Navy ships somberly crossing the storm-tossed Atlantic, about as slowly as was physically possible. The nation was at War.

No sooner had they resigned themselves to their own irrelevance than the situation took a lethal head spin. The leader of the CDIA arrived in Buna. He was a Moderator from Colorado named Field Marshal Munchy Menlo. Munchy Menlo's original name was Gutierrez; in his distant youth, he had been involved in some nasty anti-insurgency shoot-'em-ups in Colombia and Peru. Munchy Menlo had become something of a lost soul in civilian life; he'd had drinking problems, he had failed at running a grocery. Eventually he'd drifted off the edge of the earth into Moderator life, where he had done very well for himself.

Field Marshal Menlo—he boldly insisted on retaining his "road name"—was a creature of a different military order than any Oscar had met before. He was plainspoken, bearded, and reticent, modest in his manner. He radiated a certain magnetism peculiar to men who had personally killed a lot of people.

With the outbreak of War, Oscar himself had had a promotion; he was now an actual, official member of the National Security Council. He had his own hologram ID card, and his own NSC letterhead proclaiming him to be a "Deputy Adviser, Sci-Tech Issues." Oscar was naturally the local liaison for Field Marshal Menlo. When the man arrived from Washington—on a lone motorcycle, and without any escort—Oscar introduced him to the War Committee.

Menlo explained that he had come on a quiet, personal reconnaissance. The new CDIA was considering a military attack across the Louisiana border.

The Collaboratory's War Committee met in full to hear Menlo out. There were fifteen people listening, including Greta, Oscar, Kevin, Albert Gazzaniga, all the Collaboratory's various department heads, along with six Moderator sachems. The Moderators were delighted at this news. At last, and with federal government backing, they were going to give the Regulators the sound, bloody stomping they deserved! Everyone else, of course, was appalled.

Oscar spoke up. "Field Marshal, while I can appreciate the merits of a raid on Louisiana—a lightning raid . . . a limited, *surgical* raid—I really can't see that a military attack on our fellow Americans gains us anything. Huey still has a grip on the levers of power in his state, but he's weakening. His credibility is in tatters. It's just a matter of time before internal dissent drives him out."

"Mmm-hmmm," said the Field Marshal.

Gazzaniga winced. "I hate to think what the global

media would make of American soldiers shedding American blood. That's ghastly. Why, it's civil war, basically."

"It would make us look like barbarians," Greta said.

"Economic embargo. Moral pressure. Net subversion, information warfare. That's how you handle a problem like this," Gazzaniga said with finality.

"I see," said the Field Marshal. "Well, let me bring up one small, additional matter. The President is very concerned about the missing armaments from that Air Force base."

They nodded. "They've been missing quite a while," Oscar said. "That scarcely seems like an urgent issue."

"It's not widely known—and of course, this news isn't to leave this room—but there was a battery of specialized, short-range, surface-to-surface missiles in that Air Force base."

"Missiles," Greta repeated thoughtfully.

"Aerial reconnaissance indicates that the missile battery is hidden in the Sabine River valley. We have some very good human intelligence that suggests that those missiles have been loaded with aerosol warheads."

"Gas warheads?" Gazzaniga said.

"They were designed for deploying gas," Menlo said. "Nonlethal, crowd-control aerosols. Luckily, their range is quite short. Only fifty miles."

"I see," said Oscar.

"Well," said Gazzaniga, "they're nonlethal missiles and they have a short range, right? So what's the big deal?"

"You people here in Buna are the only federal facility within fifty miles of those missiles."

No one said anything.

"Tell me how those missiles work," Greta said at last.

"Well, it's a nice design," Menlo offered. "They're stealth missiles, mostly plastic, and they vaporize in midair in a silent burst dispersion. Their payload is a fog: gelatin-coated microspheres. The psychotropic agent is inside the spheres, and the spheres will only melt in the environment of human lungs. After a few hours in the open air, all the microdust cooks down, and the payload becomes inert. But any human being who's been breathing in that area will absorb the payload."

"So they're like a short-term, airborne vaccination," Oscar said.

"Yes. Pretty much. That's well put. I think you've got the picture there."

"What kind of insane person builds things like that?" Greta said in annoyance.

"Well, U.S. military biowar engineers. Quite a few of them used to work at this facility, before we lost the economic war." Field Marshal Menlo sighed. "As far as I know, that technology has never been used."

"He's going to bomb us with those things," Oscar announced.

"How do you know that?"

"Because he's hired those biowar technicians. He must have picked 'em all up for a song, years ago. He's stuffed 'em down a salt mine somewhere. Psychotropic gas —that's just what he used against the Air Force base. And airborne vaccinations, he used that to kill mosquitoes. It all fits in. It's his modus operandi."

"We agree with that assessment," Menlo said. "The President asked him to give those gas weapons back. No go. So, he must mean to use them."

"What's the nature of this substance in the microspheres?" Greta said.

"Well, psychotropics seem likeliest. If they hit a place the size of Buna, you could have the whole town basically insane for forty-eight hours. But those microbeads could hold a lot of different airborne agents. Pretty much anything, really."

"And there's a battery of these missiles pointed at us, right now?"

Menlo nodded. "Just one battery. Twenty war-heads."

"I've been thinking," Gazzaniga announced, "if there was a limited, surgical raid . . . not by U.S. troops officially, but let's say, by some competent combat veterans disguised as irregular Moderators . . ."

"Completely different matter," said a department head.

"Exactly."

"Actually *defuses* the crisis. Increases the general security."

"Just what I was thinking."

"How long before you can attack, Marshal Menlo?"

"Seventy-two hours," the Field Marshal said.

But Huey had bombed them within forty-eight.

The first missile overshot the Collaboratory dome and landed in the western edge of Buna. A section of the city the size of four football fields was soaked with caustic black goo. The arrival of the bio-missile and its explosion were completely silent. It took until three in the morning for a partying German film crew in a local bed-and-breakfast to notice that the town's streets, roofs, and windows were covered with a finely powdered black tar.

The reaction was mass hysteria. The captive Haitians in Washington, DC, had been getting a lot of press lately. The attack of gas psychosis in the Air Force base had not been forgotten, either. The news from the Collaboratory's War Committee had, of course, immediately leaked to the public—not officially, but as rumor. Confronted with this black manifestation of their darkest fears, the people of Buna lost their minds. Fits of itching, burning, fainting, and convulsions were reported. Many of the afflicted claimed to have bicameral consciousness, or second sight, or even telepathy.

A courageous Collaboratory krewe donned emergency respirator gear and rushed to the site of the gas attack. They gathered samples and returned—barely able to make it through the panicked crowds at the Collaboratory's airlocks, townsfolk desperate for the safety of the airtight lab. There were ugly incidents at the gates, where families found themselves separated in the crowds, where women held their children up in the air and begged for safety and mercy.

By ten AM, a lab study of the black tar had revealed that it was paint. It was a black, nontoxic, nonremovable caustic polymer, in a fog of gelatin beads. There was no psychotropic agent at all. The insanity of the townsfolk had been entirely a case of mass suggestion. The missile was just a silent paint balloon, a darkly humorous warning shot.

The CDIA's raid across Louisiana's border was canceled, because the missile battery had been moved. Worse yet, twenty new dummy missile batteries had suddenly appeared in its place: on farms, in towns, roaming on shrimp trucks, all over Louisiana.

Despite the fact that scientific analysis had proved that the missile was paint, a large proportion of the population simply refused to believe it. The state and federal governments officially announced that it was paint; so did the city council, but people simply refused to accept this. People were paranoid and terrified—but many seemed weirdly elated by the incident.

In the days that followed, a thriving gray market sprang up for samples of the paint, which were swiftly distributed all over the country, sold to the gullible in little plastic-topped vials. Hundreds of people spontaneously arrived in Buna, anxious to scrape up paint and sniff it. A large number of miracle cures were attributed to use of this substance. People wrote open letters to the Governor of Louisiana, begging him to bomb their own cities with the "liberation gas."

Huey denied all knowledge of any missiles in Louisiana. He stoutly denied that he had anything to do with black paint. He made fun of the ridiculous antics of the war-crazed populace—which didn't require much effort —and suggested that it proved that the federal government had lost its grip. Huey's two Senators had both been purged from the Senate, which was behaving with more purpose than it had managed to show for years; but this allowed Huey to wash his hands of Washington entirely.

Huey's mood darkened drastically after his own bomb attack. One of Huey's trusted henchmen had planted an explosive briefcase inside the statehouse. Huey's left arm was broken in the explosion, and two of his state senators were killed. This was not the first conspiracy against Huey's life; it was far from the first attempt to kill him. But it was the closest to success.

Naturally the President was suspected. Oscar very much doubted that the President would have stooped to a tactic so archaic and crude. The failed assassination actually strengthened Huey's hand—and his hand came down hard on Louisianans, and on the Regulator hierarchy in particular. It was of course Louisianans who had the greatest reason to kill their leader, who in pursuit of his own ambitions had placed their state in a hopeless struggle against the entire Union. The Regulators in particular Huey's favorite fall guys—had a grim future ahead of them, if and when they faced federal vengeance. Regulators from outside Louisiana—and there were many such— were sensing which way the wind blew, and were signing up in droves for the quasi-legitimacy of the President's CDIA. Huey had been good to the proles, he had made them a force to be reckoned with—but even proles understood power politics. Why go down in flames with a Governor, when you could rise to the heights with a President?

The missile attack had one profound and lasting consequence. It jarred the Collaboratory from its sense of helplessness. It was now quite obvious to everyone that the

War was truly on. The black paint had been the first shot, and the likelihood was quite strong that the city of Buna would in fact be gassed. The prospect of choking in a silent black fog while surrounded by neighbors turned into maniacs—this prospect had clarified people's minds quite wonderfully.

The Collaboratory was airtight. It was safe from gas; but it couldn't hold everyone.

The obvious answer was to launch an architectural sortie. The fortress should be extended over the entire city.

Construction plans were immediately dusted off. Money and rights-of-way were suddenly no problem. Locals, wanderers, soldiers, scientists, Moderators, men, women, and children, they were one and all simply drafted into the effort.

All these factions had different ideas of how to tackle the problem. The gypsy Moderators understood big-top tents and teepees. The people of Buna were very big on their bio-agricultural greenhouses. The SO/LIC soldiers, who were trained in environmental disaster response, were experts at sandbags, quonset huts, soup kitchens, latrines, and potable water supplies. For their own part, the techies of the Collaboratory flew into a strange furor over the plans of Alcott Bambakias. The scientists were long-used to the security of their armored dome, but it had never occurred to them that the rigid substance of their shelter might become cheap, smart, and infinitely distensible networks. This was architecture as airtight ephemera: structure like a dewy spiderweb: smart, hypersensitive, always calculating, always on the move. There seemed to be no limit to the scale of it. The dome could become a living fluid, a kind of decentered, membranous amoeba.

It would have seemed sensible to weigh the alternatives carefully, hold safety hearings, have competitive bids submitted, and then, finally, engage in a major building project. The mayor of Buna, a well-meaning middle-aged woman who had made a bundle in the greenhouse-flower industry, made a genuine effort to "assert control."

Then two more paint bombs arrived. These were better-aimed. They hit the Collaboratory dead on—it was a large target—and splattered the glass sky with black muck. The dome's interior light became dim and scary, the temperature dropped, the plants and animals suffered, and the people were grim and enraged. Confronted with this direct insult, their will to resist stiffened drastically. It was personal now—they could see the evil slur against them, hovering above their heads.

All debate stopped. There was no longer time for talk, and the decision was a fait accompli. Everyone simply began contributing everything they could all at the same time. They dropped all other efforts. When projects overlapped or interfered, they simply tore the little one down and built the more ambitious one. The town of Buna as people had previously known it simply ceased to exist. The dome metastasized; it sent out giant filmy buttresses on Daliesque walking stilts. The greenhouses of Buna linked together spontaneously into endless ramparts and tunnels. City blocks transmuted overnight into gleaming fields of plastic soap bubbles. Airtight brick crypts and bomb shelters sprang up everywhere, like measles.

Huey chose this moment to launch a well-documented outing attack on Oscar and Greta. There was no denying it this time. It was sordid and painful, but Huey's timing could not have been worse. In a time of peace, it would have been politically disastrous to learn that a Machiavellian campaign adviser (of dubious genetic heritage) had fiendishly installed his girlfriend as the quasi-dictator of a federal science facility, while she paid him off with sexual favors in a Louisiana beach house.

In Washington, the news caused some alarm; pundits issued some obligatory tut-tutting; elderly male scientists were interviewed, who declared that it was truly a shame to see a woman sleep her way to the top. But in Buna, the

War was on. The revelation, which was no revelation to anyone in Buna, was a war romance. All was instantly forgiven. Oscar and Greta were practically pitched into each other's arms by the sheer pressure of public goodwill.

Ancient social boundaries snapped under the strain of war. Wartime affairs broke out like chicken pox: scientists, Moderator women, dashing European journalists, chicken-fried Buna locals, even the military was having sex. It was just too much to ask of human beings that they work shoulder to shoulder and cheek by jowl under the constant expectation of a mind-crushing gas attack while, somehow, avoiding sex with strangers.

Besides, their leaders were doing it. It was happening. It was a suddenly public declaration of their society's unsuspected potency. Of course they were breaking the rules; that was what every sane person was doing, that was what the effort was all about. Of course the lab's Director was having hot sex with the genetically warped politician. She was their painted Joan of Arc, the armored bride of the science wars.

People even made jokes about it. The jokes were loyally relayed to Oscar by Fred Dillen, one of his last remaining krewe members, who had been trained to understand that political jokes were valuable.

Fred presented him with a Greta-and-Oscar political joke.

"See, Greta and Oscar have sneaked off to Louisiana to have sex in the middle of a swamp. So they hire a bass boat and they paddle way out in the middle of nowhere where there aren't any spies or bugs. So they're getting it on inside the boat, but Oscar gets overexcited, and he falls in the water. And he doesn't come back up.

"So Greta paddles back alone, and tries to get some help from some swamp Cajuns, but there's just no sign of Oscar. So she waits for a whole week, and finally the Cajuns come over to see her again. 'Well, Dr. Penninger, we got some good news and we got some bad news.'

" 'Give me the bad news first.'

" 'Well, we found your boyfriend the genetic freak, but we're afraid he drowned.'

" 'Oh, that's bad news. That's terribly bad news. It's awful. It's the very worst.'

" 'Well, it's not all bad; when we dredged him up outta the mud, we came up with two big gunnysacks of big blue crabs!'

" 'Well, at least you found his poor body. . . . Where have you put my boyfriend?'

" 'Well, beggin' your pardon, ma'am, but we never done so good on the crabs before, so we figured we'd leave him down there just one more day!' ''

That was a pretty good political joke for such a small community—especially when its subtext was analyzed. Like most political jokes, it was all about displaced aggression, and it was the aggression against him that was being fed to the crabs here. The joke was popular, and it was a signifier. And the punch line was very clear: he was going to get away with it. People didn't fear or hate him the way they feared and hated Huey. He was both a politician and a monster, and yet people, in an odd and marginal way, had come to sympathize with him.

Oscar had reached the peak of his public reputation. Proof of this came when the President was asked about the sex scandal—and about Oscar's role within the NSC. Here was the President's main chance to drop him overboard and silently feed him to the swamp crabs; but the President chose otherwise. The President pointed out— properly enough—that a man couldn't be expected to do anything about the fact that he was the illegal product of a South American mafia genetics lab. The President said that it smelled of hypocrisy to hold such a man to persnickety standards of sexual correctness—especially when other public figures had deliberately chosen to warp their own brain tissue. The President further declared that he himself was "a human being." And that, "as a human being," when he saw lovers persecuted, the spectacle "stuck in my craw."

The press conference then returned to the hotter issue of the Dutch War, but the President's aside went over very well. Certain demographic segments were becoming alarmed with the President's relentless strong-arm tactics and his feral pursuit of domestic opponents. This sudden revelation of a sentimental softer side was an excellent tactical play.

Oscar had reached a great career moment. The President had publicly played the Oscar card. In thinking the matter over, Oscar knew what this meant. It meant that he was burned. He had had his moment in this poker round, he had thumped down like a minor trump on the green baize. If played again, he would be dog-eared. Time to shuffle back into the pack.

So: thus high, but no higher. The lethal subtext of the President's statement had made that clear to him. He was useful, he was even cute; but on some profound level, he was not trusted. He would never become a pillar of the American state.

Within Buna, Oscar had less and less of a role. He had been an agitator, and instigator, and a gray eminence, but he could never be king. Greta could leverage her own fame now. She had issued a public appeal for aid and assistance, and like a boozy cry to "come to Montmartre," the cry brought a tidal wave of national response. Bombs or no bombs, Huey or no Huey, President or no President, Buna was going to become a Greenhouse metropolis. The place was an intellectual magnet for every species of dreamer, faker, failed grad student, techie washout, downsized burnout; every guru, costumed geek, ditzy theorist, and bug collector; every microscope peerer, model-rocket builder, and gnarly simulationist; every code-dazed hacker, architectural designer; everyone, in short, who had ever been downgraded, denied, and excluded by their society's sick demand that their wondrous ideas should make commercial sense.

With all this yeast gathered in one place, the very earth would rise. Some who arrived were enemies. Arsonists burned the city's greenbelt; the sappy pines blew up like Roman candles and a ghastly pall of smoke polluted Texas for miles downwind. But when those flames died, the new society moved onto the blackened acres and consumed them utterly. In the grinding hoppers of the biohackers, trees digested more easily when partially cooked. The ash contained vital minerals. A scorched and blackened forest was a natural phoenix nest for the world's first genuine Greenhouse society.

12

The U.S. Navy arrived off the shores of the Netherlands. The War had reached a point of crisis. In order to have something to do, the American armada announced a naval blockade of shipping in the ports of Rotterdam and Amsterdam. Since large sections of those cities were already underwater, this was not a crushing economic threat.

Still, there seemed very little else that the Navy could do. They hadn't brought any land troops or tanks with which they could physically invade Holland. The battleships had long-range naval guns, with which they might easily devastate major cities, but it seemed unthinkable that the United States would physically blast civilians in a nation offering no organized military resistance.

So, after enormous fanfare and intense press coverage, the hot War with Holland was revealing its rickety underpinnings as a phony war. The President had whipped the nation into frenzy, and strengthened his own hand, and ended the Emergency. He had made his pet proles into a nationwide dandruff of cellular-toting miniature Robespierres. That was an impressive series of accomplishments, more than anyone had dared to hope for. Now the smart money had it that the War would soon be folded up and put away.

The smart money took the unlikely personage of Alcott Bambakias. The junior Senator from Massachusetts had chosen this moment to make a long-expected tour of the Buna National Collaboratory.

The Senator was much improved mentally. The rainbow of neural treatments had finally reached an area of his emotional spectrum where Bambakias could lodge and take a stand. He was quite simply a different man now. The Senator was heavier, wearier, vastly more cynical. He described his current mental state as "realistic." He was making all his quorum calls, and most of his committee assignments. He made far fewer speeches these days, picked far fewer dramatic fights, spent far more time closeted with lobbyists.

Oscar took it upon himself to give the Senator and Mrs. Bambakias a personal tour of the works in Buna. They took an armored limousine. With the Dutch War stalling visibly, it seemed somewhat less likely that Huey would launch any paint bombs.

However, this had not stopped the construction frenzy in Buna. On the contrary, it had liberated them from any pretense that they were sheltering themselves from gas. With thousands of people continuing to pour in, with guaranteed free food, free shelter, and all the network data they could eat, the city was tautly inflated with boom-town atmosphere. One group of zealots was constructing a giant plastic structure roughly the size and shape of the Eiffel Tower, which they had dubbed the "Beacon of Cosmic Truth." Other hobbyists had taken smart geodesics and airtight skins to a logical extreme, and were building aerostats. These were giant self-expanding airtight bubbles, and if they could get the piezoelectric musculature within the tubing to work properly, the things would engorge themselves to the point where they could literally leave the surface of the earth.

Oscar couldn't fully contain his enthusiasm for these marvels, and he sensed that Bambakias and Lorena could use some cheering up. Bambakias looked much better— he was clearly lucid now, perhaps even cured—but stress had taken a permanent toll on Lorena. She'd put on weight, she'd sagged, she looked preserved rather than put-together. In her husband's company she offered Oscar mostly bright monosyllables.

Bambakias was doing all the talking, but it wasn't his usual bright and tumbling rhetoric.

"The hotel was good," he said. "You did very well with the hotel. Considering all the local limitations."

"Oh, we enjoy the hotel. I still sleep there most nights. But it doesn't begin to compare to the scale of what's been done to the town."

"They're not doing it right," Bambakias said.

"Well, they're amateurs."

"No, they're worse than amateurs. They're not following code. They're not using certified and tested materials. All these tents and pylons, in untested combinations —a lot of them are going to collapse."

"Yes, surely, Senator—but it only took them a few days to put them up! If they go bust, they'll just build more."

"I hope you're not expecting me to take personal responsibility for this. I sent you those plans, but I never expected them to be executed. Once I abandon my intellectual property to all and sundry, I can't be expected to be responsible for other people's exploitation of it."

"Of course not, Senator! These were Emergency conditions, War conditions . . . you know, there *is* an upside to this. This isn't permanent structure, and it isn't in classic form, but it's remarkably popular."

Bambakias brightened a little. "Really."

"The people who are living under these things . . . they're not architecture critics. A lot of them are people who haven't had much shelter of any kind for many years. They're really *impressed* to see nomad architecture pushed to these mind-boggling extremes."

"That isn't 'nomad architecture.' It's ultrascale emergency relief."

"That's an interesting distinction, Alcott, but let me just put it this way: it's nomad architecture now."

"I think you'd better listen to him, darling," Lorena put in faintly. "Oscar always has very good instincts about these things."

"Oh yes, instincts," Bambakias said. "Instincts are wonderful. You can live off instincts, as long as you don't plan to live very long. How long do you expect all this to last, Oscar?"

" 'This'?" Oscar said delicately.

"Whatever it is that you've created here. What is it, exactly? Is it a political movement? Maybe it's just one big street party. It certainly isn't a town."

"Well . . . it's a little difficult to say exactly where all this will go. . . ."

"Maybe you should have thought that through a bit more thoroughly," Bambakias said. It clearly irked the man to have to discuss the matter, but he was taking it as a painful duty. "You know, I'm a ranking member of the Senate Science Committee. It's going to be a little difficult explaining these developments to my colleagues back in Washington."

"Oh, I miss that Science Committee every day," Oscar lied.

"You know, developments here remind me of the Internet. That old computer network, invented by the American scientific community. It was all about free communications. Very simple and widely distributed—there was never any central control. It spread worldwide in short order. It turned into the world's biggest piracy copy machine. The Chinese loved the Internet, they used it and turned it against us. They destroyed our information economy with it. Even *then* the net didn't go away—it just started breeding its virtual tribes, all these nomads and dissidents. Suddenly they could organize in powerful new ways, and now, finally, with the President taking their side . . . who knows? Do you see my parallel here, Oscar? Does it make sense to you?"

Oscar was increasingly uncomfortable. "Well, I never said what happened here was entirely without precedent. The great secret to creativity is knowing how to hide your sources."

"You stole these ideas from Huey. You stole Huey's clothes, didn't you?"

"Time-honored tactic, Alcott!"

"Oscar, Huey is a dictator. He's a man on horseback. Do I understand this 'prestige economy' business? It seems to run entirely on instinct. They spend all their time doing each other little volunteer community services. And they rank each other for it. Eventually somebody pops out of the mix and becomes a tribal big shot. Then they're required to do what he says."

"Well . . . it's complicated. But yes, that's the basics."

"They really just don't fit in the rest of American society. Not at all."

"It was designed that way."

"I mean they don't have any way to properly *deal* with the rest of society. They don't even have proper ways to deal with each other. They have no rule of law. There's no Constitution. There's no legal redress. There's no Bill of Rights. They don't have any way to deal with the rest of us, except through evasion, or intimidation. When one network meets another that's set up along different lines, they feud. They kill each other."

"Sometimes."

"Now you've made these people aware of their mutual interest with the scientific research community. Another group of people who basically live outside the state, outside of economics. One wants freedom of inquiry, and the other wants freedom from physical want, and neither of them has any sense of responsibility to the rest of us. In fact, the rest of us have given up expecting anything from them. We no longer hope that science will give us utopia, or even a real improvement. Science just adds more factors to the mix, and makes everything more unstable. We've given up on our dispossessed, too. We have no illusion that we can employ them, or keep them docile with more bio-bread, or more cyber-circuses. And now you've brought these two groups together and they've become a real coalition."

"I'm with you, Senator. I'm following the argument."

"What now, Oscar? What are they going to do now? What becomes of the rest of us?"

"Hell, I don't know!" Oscar shouted. "I just saw Huey doing it, that's all. We were in a feud with Huey— you *pushed* me into the feud with Huey! The lab was broke, it was halfway in his pocket already, and he was just going to rack them up. They would just . . . become his creatures. I didn't want them to be his creatures."

"What's the difference? If they're still creatures."

"The difference? Between me and Green Huey? Okay! At last a question I can answer! The difference between me and Huey is that whatever Huey does is always about Huey. It's always about Huey first and foremost, and it's always about the greater glory of Huey. But the things that I do will never, ever be about me. They aren't allowed to be about me."

"Because of the way you were born."

"Alcott, it's worse than that. I wasn't even born at all."

Lorena spoke up. "I think you two boys should stop all this. You're going in circles. Why don't we get something to eat?"

"I don't mean to wound his feelings," Bambakias said reasonably. "I'm just looking at the structure critically, and I'm pointing out that there's nothing holding it up."

Lorena folded her arms. "Why pick on Oscar, for

heaven's sake? The President sent a newspaper-boat navy across the Atlantic, and there was nothing holding that up either. The War will be over in Washington soon. It can't go on, it's a stage show. Then the War will be over here too. They'll just fold all this up, and we'll find some other distraction. That's the way life is now. Stop fussing about it."

Bambakias paused thoughtfully. "You're right, dear. I'm sorry. I was getting all worked up."

"We're supposed to be on vacation here. You should save some energy for the hearings. I want some chowder, Alcott. I want some étouffée."

"She's so good to me," Bambakias told Oscar. Suddenly he smiled. "I haven't gotten so worked up in ages! That really felt good."

"Oscar always cheers you up," Lorena told him. "He's the best at that. You should be good to him."

───────────

The Senator and his wife wanted Louisiana cuisine. That was a legitimate request. They took a fleet of limos, and the Senator's large krewe, and their media coverage, and the Senator's numerous bodyguards, and the entire caravan drove to a famous restaurant in Lake Charles, Louisiana. They took a great deal of pleasure in this, because it was an excellent restaurant, and they were certain that Huey would quickly learn of their raid.

They ate well and tipped lavishly, and it would have been a lovely meal, except that the Senator was on his mood stabilizers, so he no longer drank. The Senator's wife drank rather too much. They also brought along the new senatorial press secretary in the krewe; and the new press secretary was Clare Emerson.

Then the caravan returned ceremoniously to the hotel in Buna, and the bodyguards drew great, quiet sighs of relief. The Senator and his wife retired, and the bodyguards set up their night patrols, and the media krewe went out looking for trouble and action at some Moderator orgy under some enormous dewy tent. Oscar, who had exhausted himself avoiding Clare, found himself maneuvered into a situation where he and his former girlfriend had to have a sociable nightcap together. Just to show that there were no hard feelings. Though the feelings were extremely hard.

So Clare had a glass of hotel Chablis, and Oscar, who didn't drink, had a club soda. They sat at a small wooden table while music played, and they were forced to talk privately.

"So, Clare. Tell me all about Holland. That must have been fascinating."

"It was, at first." She was so good-looking. He'd forgotten how beautiful she was. He'd even forgotten that he'd once made it a habit to court beautiful women. As a member of the Bambakias krewe and a press player in Washington, Clare was far better put-together than she had ever been as a newbie Boston political journo. Clare was still young. He'd forgotten what it meant to date young, beautiful, brilliantly dressed women. He'd never gotten over her. He hadn't given himself enough time. He'd just shelved the issue and sought out a distraction.

Her lips were still moving. He forced himself to pay attention to her words. She was saying something about finding her cultural roots as an Anglo. Europe was full of Yankee defectors and émigrés, bitter, aging white men who clustered in beer cellars and moaned that their country was being run by a crazy redskin. Europe hadn't been all romance for Clare. The part of Europe that was drowning fastest didn't have much romance for anyone.

"Oh, but a war correspondent, though. That seems like such a career opportunity."

"You're enjoying this, aren't you?" she said. "You enjoy torturing me."

"What?" He was shocked.

"Didn't Lorena tell you all about my little Dutch misadventures?"

"Lorena doesn't tell me about her krewe activities. I'm not in the Bambakias circle anymore. I scarcely have a krewe of my own, these days."

She sipped at her wine. "Krewes are pitiful. They're disgusting. People will do anything for a little security nowadays. Even sell themselves into servitude. Any rich person can scare up their own loyal gang, just for the asking. It's feudalism. But we're so wrecked as a country that we can't even make feudalism work."

"I thought you liked Lorena. You always gave her such good spin."

"Oh, I loved her as copy. But as my boss . . . well, what am I saying? Lorena's great to me. She took me on when I was down, she made me a little player. She never outed me on the Dutch thing. I have a classy job in Washington, I have nice clothes and a car."

"All right. I'll bite. Tell me what happened in Holland."

"I have bad habits," Clare said, staring at the tablecloth. "I got this impression that I could sleep my way into good stories. Well, it worked great in Boston! But Den Haag is not Boston. The Dutch aren't like Americans. They can still concentrate. And their backs are against the wall." She twisted a lock of hair.

"I'm sorry to hear that you met with a setback. I hope you don't think I'm angry with you because our affair ended badly."

"You *are* angry with me, Oscar. You're furious. You resent me and you hate me, but you're just such a player that you would never, ever show that to me. You'd dump me if you had to, and you *did* dump me, but at least you couldn't be bothered to crucify me. I made a real mistake, thinking that all politicians were like you."

Oscar said nothing. She was going to spill it all very soon. More words wouldn't make it come any faster.

"I got a hot lead on a scandal. I mean a major Cold War scandal, huge, big. All I had to do was wheedle it out of this Dutch subminister of something-or-other. And he was gonna come across for me. Because he was a Cold War spook, and he knew that I knew that he was a spook, and I was a journalist, which is halfway to spookiness, really. And he was hot for me. But that was okay, because, you know, if you put your mind to it, you can get these things out of men. It's a mentor thing. They're like your uncle, or maybe your professor, and you don't know the ropes, and they're going to teach you the ropes. And all you have to do is let them tie you up with the ropes just a little." She had another sip.

"Clare, why would I be judgmental about that? These things happen. It's reality."

"You know, we don't understand that here in America. We don't get it that we're the eight-hundred-pound gorilla of climate politics. We're so out of sync that we still measure in pounds and inches. We think it's funny that we're having a War with a bunch of little people with tulips and wooden shoes. We're like spoiled children. We're like big fat teenage pop stars cruising around in our two-ton pink Cadillac blasting our stereo and throwing our beer empties everywhere. We don't get it that there are serious, civilized people who spend their time in downtown Amsterdam watching hookers in public sex cages in a city saturated with dope, and the sex doesn't touch them, and the dope doesn't touch them, because they are very determined, and they are very cold."

"Are they cold people, the Dutch?"

"Cold and *wet*. And getting wetter. All the time."

"They tell me the Navy is considering knocking some holes in their dikes with artillery blasts."

"You'd know that, being NSC, wouldn't you?"

A chill like dry ice wafted between them. Oscar almost sensed a swirl of congealing fog.

Clare leaned back in her chair. "It smells funny in

Buna. Doesn't it? All these tents and gas shelters. That big dome smells weird. It's like they never change their underwear."

"This isn't Boston, it's the Gulf Coast. You think it smells funny inside here, you should walk around outside for a while."

"Too many mosquitoes."

Oscar laughed.

Clare frowned. "You don't have to know what happened to me in Holland. I just got in too deep, that's all. I got away from there, and I was lucky to get away, that's my big story. I'm lucky Lorena has such a big heart."

"Clare . . . it's just a shame. War is a hard game and even a toy war has casualties. I wouldn't have wished that on you for anything."

"You *told me* that. You *warned* me about it. Remember? And I told you that I was a grown-up. We were working in this dinky little Boston election where the guy had seven-percent approvals. We were like kids in a sandbox. I thought it was so upscale and important, and it all seems so innocent now. And here you've done this incredible thing and I . . . well, I work for the Senator now. So I guess that's all right."

"It's the breaks."

"Oscar, why aren't you more of a scoundrel? I'm all burned out on men. And you're like this slimy pol who always gets his way, and I thought I'd be all burned out on you, but when I saw you tonight . . . well, it all came back to me."

"What came back?"

"You and me. That you're this cute guy who was always sweet and polite to me, and gave me his house pass and taught me about funny old modern art. My old flame. The dream boyfriend. I really miss you. I even miss the satin sheets and your skin temperature."

"Clare, why are you telling me this? You know I'm involved with another woman now. For heaven's sake, everyone in the world knows I'm involved with Greta Penninger."

"Oscar, you can't be serious about that. Her? She's a rebound type. No, she's not even that. Oscar—don't you get it? People *make jokes* about you and her. She's funny-looking. She's *old*. She has a big nose and no ass. She *can't* be any fun. I mean, not like the kind of fun we used to have."

He conjured up a smile. "You're really jealous! Shame on you."

"Why would you go for her? She just had something that you wanted."

"Clare, even though you're a journalist, I really don't think that's any of your business."

"I'm saying wicked things because I'm sad, and I'm jealous, and I'm lonely, and I'm sorry. And I'm getting really drunk. And you dumped me. For *her*."

"I didn't dump you. You dumped me, because I was out of town, and you wouldn't fly down and join me, and you decided that it was a better career move to go live with our country's worst enemies."

"Oh, well, *that's* better," Clare said, and wrinkled her nose at him, and grinned a little. "I guess I'm getting through to you, finally."

"I did my level best to make it work out for us, but you wouldn't let me do it."

"Well, it's too late now."

"Of course it's too late."

She looked at her watch. "And it's getting pretty late tonight, too."

Oscar glanced at his mousebrain watch. The thing had just dampened his wrist with liquid waste, and it was nowhere near the correct time. It was sometime around midnight. "You'd better sleep this off, if you're going to make the Senator's flight back to Washington."

"Oscar, I have a better idea. Stop toying with me.

Let's just do it. This is my only night here, this is our big chance. Take me upstairs, let's go to bed."

"You're drunk."

"I'm not too drunk to know what I'm doing. I'm just drunk enough to be a lot of fun. You've been looking at me all night. You know I can't stand it when you look at me with those big brown puppy-dog eyes."

"There's no future in that." He was weakening.

"Who cares about the future? It's about old times. Come on, it's practically just as bad, just 'cause you want it so much."

"It's not just as bad. It's worse to do it. It's the worst of all. When the volcano burns, everyone knows it, but when the heart is in flames, who knows it?"

She blinked. "Huh?"

Oscar sighed. "I just don't believe you, Clare. I'm a smooth talker and I know how to please, but as a male specimen, I'm just not that overwhelming. If I were, you'd have never left me in the first place."

"Look, I already said I was sorry. Don't rub it in. I can *show* you how sorry I am."

"Who sent you here, really? Are there bugs in your purse? Are you wearing a wire right now? You got turned, didn't you? They turned you, in The Hague. You're a foreign agent. You're a spy."

Clare went very pale. "What is this? Have you cracked up? All this paranoia! You're talking like the Senator at his worst!"

"What am I, a useful idiot? There's a war on! Mata Hari was Dutch, for Christ's sake."

"You think they'd let me work for a Senator, if I was a Dutch spy? You don't know what Washington's like these days. You don't know a damn thing about anything."

Oscar said nothing. He watched her with lethal care.

Clare gathered the rags of her dignity. "You really

insulted me. I'm really hurt. I have a good mind to just get up and leave you. Why don't you call me a cab?"

"Then it's the President, isn't it?"

Her face went stiff.

"It is the President," he said with finality. "It's me and Greta Penninger. The situation's a little out of hand down here. It'd be better for domestic tranquillity if the girlfriend and I came to a sudden parting of our ways. Then it would all work out. That would put a nice healthy dent in the local morale. The Moderators would slide right into his private espionage network, and the scientist would go back to her lab, and the slimy pol who can't keep his hands off women would be outed to everybody as just another slimy pol."

Clare lifted a napkin and wiped her eyes.

"You go back and tell your agent-runner that I don't work for the President because he's a nice guy. I work for him because the country was up on blocks, and he got the country moving. I'm loyal to him because I'm loyal to the country, and it's going to take more than a nightingale to push me off the playing board. Even if it's a very pretty nightingale that I used to care about."

"That's enough, I'm leaving. Good night, Oscar."

"Good-bye."

————————————

Bambakias left Texas the next morning with all his krewe, including Clare. Oscar was not outed. No recorded tapes of the conversation showed up. There were no blaring net-flashes about his tête-à-tête with a former girlfriend. Two days passed.

Then there was big news on the War front.

The Dutch were giving up.

The Dutch Prime Minister made a public statement. She was small and bitter and gray. She said that it was hopeless for an unarmed country like the Netherlands to resist the armed might of the world's last military superpower. She said that it was impossible for her people to face the environmental catastrophe of having the country's dikes bombarded. She said that America's ruthless ultimatum had broken her country's will to resist.

She said that the Netherlands was surrendering unconditionally. She said that the country was declaring itself an open country, that her tiny military would lay down its arms, that they would accept the troops of the occupier. She said that she and her cabinet had just signed documents of surrender, and the Dutch government would voluntarily dissolve itself at midnight. She proclaimed that the War was over, and that the Americans had won, and she called on the American people to remember their long tradition of magnanimity toward defeated opponents.

The speech took eight minutes. And the War was over.

For a strange historical instant, the United States went mad with joy, but the madness subsided with remarkably few casualties. Their long trials had made the American public peculiarly resilient. No more than eight hours passed before the first net pundits began to explain why total victory had been inevitable.

Total victory had its merits. There was no resisting the overwhelming prestige of a hero President. His favorables shot into the high nineties and hung there as if nailed to a mast.

The President was not caught napping by this development. He wasted no time: scarcely an hour; scarcely a picosecond.

He commandeered domestic airlines by executive order. There were swarms of American troops in every Dutch airport by morning. The Yankee soldiery, dazed and jet-lagged, were met by a courteous and chastened Dutch populace, waving homemade American flags. The President declared the War over—barely bothering to have a docile Congress certify this—and declared the arrival of a new American era. This epoch was to be henceforth known as the Return to Normalcy.

Like a sorcerer slamming swords through a barrel, the President began to bloodlessly reshape the American body politic.

The Normalcy manifesto was a rather astonishing twenty-eight point document. It stole the clothes of so many of America's splintered political parties that they were left quite stunned. The President's national plan for action bore only the slightest resemblance to that of his party platform, or that of his supposed core constituency in the Left Tradition Bloc. The President's idea of Normalcy had something in it to flabbergast everyone.

The dollar would be sharply devalued and made an open global currency again. A general amnesty would free from parole anyone whose crimes could be considered remotely political. A new tax structure would soak the ultra-rich and come down brutally on carbon-dioxide production. Derelict and underused buildings would be nationalized en masse, then turned over to anyone willing to homestead them. Derelict cities and ghost towns—and there were many such, especially in the West—would be scraped clean from the face of the earth and replanted in fast-growing trees. Roadblocking was henceforth to be considered an act of piracy and to be punished without mercy by roving gangs of the CDIA, who, since they were all former roadblockers of the most avid temperament, could be expected to know just how to put an end to the practice.

A constitutional amendment was offered to create a new fourth branch of government for American citizens whose "primary residences were virtual networks." America's eight hundred and seven federal police agencies would be streamlined into four. There was a comprehensive reform plan for the astoundingly victorious American military.

There was also a new national health plan, more or less on a sensible Canadian model. This would never work. It had been put there deliberately, so that the President's domestic opposition could enjoy the pleasure of destroying something.

———————

The President's fait accompli was not to be resisted—least of all by the state of Louisiana. Recognizing the hurricane power of this turn of events, Green Huey bent with the wind.

Huey resigned his office as Governor. He begged the people's forgiveness and shed hot tears on-camera, expressing deep regret for his past excesses, and promising a brand-new, hundred-percent, federally approved Normalcy Cooperation Policy. His lieutenant governor also resigned, but he was not missed, as he had always been the most colorless of Huey's stooges.

Huey's supine State Senate swiftly installed an entirely new Governor. She was a spectacular young black woman from New Orleans, a former beauty queen, a woman of such untoward and astonishing lithe beauty (for a state chief executive, at least) that the world's cameras simply could not keep their lenses off her.

The new Governor's first act as chief executive was to issue blanket pardons to all members of the former state government, including, first and foremost, Green Huey. Her second act was to formalize Louisiana's state relationships—"formal and informal"—with the Regulators. The Regulators would henceforth be loyal local members of a statewide CDIA, directly modeled on the federal agency that the wise President in his infinite mercy had imposed on the American Republic. It was pointed out that some Haitian guests of the State of Louisiana were still being held by their federal captors, and the new Governor, being of Haitian extraction herself, asked that they be granted clemency.

An enterprising news team—obviously tipped off— managed to locate and interview some of the Haitian subjects, who had been waiting out the days and hours in their federal medical kraal. The Haitians, having been ripped from their homes and medically probed from stem to stern, naturally expressed a devout wish to return to their swamp compound. It was a very poetic set of pleas, even when crossing the boundaries of translation. But at the end of the day, they were just Haitians, so no one felt much need to pay attention to their wishes. They stayed in their illegal-migrant slammer, while the President waited for the ex-Governor's next shoe to drop.

On the issue of the Buna National Collaboratory and its frenetic reformers, the President did and said precisely nothing. The President apparently had bigger and better matters on his mind—and this President was in a position to see to it that his interests seized and held the limelight.

With the sudden and stunning end of the War, the mad immigration into Buna slowed to a crawl. Then, it began to reverse itself. People had seen enough. The gawkers, and the fakers, and the most easily distracted trendies, began to realize that a glamorous, noncommercial, intellectual-dissident Greenhouse Society was simply not for everyone. Living there was going to involve a lot of work. The mere fact that money was not involved did not signify that work was not involved; the truth was the exact opposite. This congelation of science and mass economic defection was going to require brutal amounts of dedicated labor, constant selfless effort, much of it by necessity wasted on experiments that washed out, on roads that were better not taken, on intellectually sexy notions that became blinding cul-de-sacs.

Beneath the fluttering party streamers, there was going to be serious science in Buna: "Science" with a new obsessive potency, because it was art pour l'art, science for its own sake. It was science as the chosen pursuit of that small demographic fraction that was entirely consumed by intellectual curiosity. But the hot air of revolutionary fervor would leak from their bubble, and the chill air of reality would leave it somewhat clammy, and unpleasant to the touch.

Work on the newly renamed Normalcy Committee, by its very nature, somehow lacked the brio attendant on Emergency and War. The work had always been exhausting, but the attendees had rarely been bored.

Now Greta and Oscar were discovering brief moments when they could think for themselves. Moments when they could speak, and not for public consumption. Moments when business took the rest of the Committee quorum elsewhere. Moments when they were alone.

Oscar gazed around the empty boardroom. The place looked the way his soul felt: drained, overlit, empty, spattered with official detritus.

"This is it, Greta. The campaign's finally over. We've won. We're in power. We have to settle down now, we have to learn to govern. We're not the rebels anymore, because we can't lead any strikes and marches against ourselves. We can't even rebel against the President: he's benignly ignoring us in a classically passive-aggressive fashion, he's giving us rope. He's going to see if we make it, or if we hang ourselves. We've got to deal with reality now. We have to consolidate."

"I've been waiting for you to tell me that. To tell me that I'm finally off the hook. No more Joan of Arc."

"I painted you as Joan of Arc because that's the kind of image that a candidate needs when she's leading a heroic crusade. You're not Joan of Arc. Joan of Arc was a fifteen-year-old female military genius who heard voices in her head. You don't have voices in your head. All that noise you had to listen to all this time, that wasn't the crying of angels, that was a very gifted and clever public relations campaign. Joan of Arc got burned at the stake.

She was toast. I didn't set this up so that you would be toast. I don't want you to be toast, Greta. Toast isn't worth it."

"So what *do* you want from me, Oscar? You want a Joan of Arc who somehow gets away with it all. A schizoid peasant girl who successfully builds a grand castle, and becomes, what, a French duchess? A peasant duchess in beautiful brocade robes."

"And with a prince, too. Okay?"

"What prince really wants or needs Joan of Arc? I mean—for the long term."

"Well, the obvious candidate would have been Gilles de Rais—but that guy clearly lost his perspective. Never mind that; historical analogy only carries us so far. I'm talking about you and me now. We're at the end of the road. This is finally it. Now we have to take a stand. We have to settle."

Greta closed her eyes, drew a few deep breaths. The room was silent except for the subtle hiss of the air filter. Stress made her allergies worse; she carried her air filters around like handbags now. "So, at the end, this is all about you and me."

"Yes, it is."

"No it isn't. Let me tell you all about you and me. When I first saw you, I was totally skeptical. I wasn't looking for any trouble. But you just kept making these little passes at me. And I thought: what is he doing? He's a political operative. I have nothing this guy wants. I'm just wasting my life on this board, trying to get proper equipment. I wasn't even managing to accomplish *that*. But then it occurred to me, this remote speculation: this guy is actually hot for me. He thinks I'm sexy. He wants to sleep with me. It really is that simple."

She took a breath. "And I thought: that is really a bad idea. But what's the worst that can happen to me? They find me in bed with this character, and I'll get a scolding and they'll throw me off the board. Wonderful!

Then I can go back to my lab! And besides: look at him! He's young, he's handsome, he writes funny notes, he sends big bouquets. And there's something so different about him."

She looked at him. Oscar was not missing a word. He felt he'd been waiting for this all his life.

"I fell in love with you, Oscar. I know that's true, because you're the only man that I ever felt jealous about. I never had that kind of emotional luxury before. I love you, and I marvel at you as my favorite specimen. I really love you for what you truly are, all the way down, all the way through. And we had a lovely fling. I took the plunge and I wasn't afraid to do it, because when it's all said and done, you have one huge, final, saving grace. Because you're temporary. You're not my destiny. You're not my prince. You're just a visitor in my life, a traveling salesman."

Oscar nodded. "Now we're getting somewhere."

"Really?"

"It's totally true. I've *always* been temporary. I can give advice, I can run campaigns, I can come and go. I can have brief affairs, but I can't make anything stick! My foster dad picked me up on an impulse. Dad had four wives and a zillion girlfriends: every woman in my childhood rushed by me on fast forward. I have a permanent fever. I have to reinvent myself every morning. I built a business, but I sold it. I built a house, but it's empty. I built a hotel, but I can't run it. I built a coalition here, I built a whole new society, I built a city to house it in with a lighthouse beacon, and loudspeakers blaring and pennants waving, but I *still* don't get to stay. I'm its founding father, I'm the prince, but I still don't belong. I just don't get to stay."

"Oh, good Lord."

"Am I making sense to you here?"

"Oscar, how can *I* stay? I can't go on like this, I'm all burned out. I did what I had to do, I can't say that you used me. But *something* used me. History used me, and it's using me all up. Even our affair is used up now."

"We should do the right thing, Greta, we should declare ourselves. Let's take a stand together. I want you to marry me."

She put her head in her hands.

"Look, don't do that. Listen to me. This can be made to work. It's doable. In fact, it's a genius move."

"Oscar, you don't love me."

"I love you as much as I will ever love anyone."

She stared at him in astonishment. "What a brilliant evasion."

"You'll never find another man who's more attentive to your interests. If you find some other man that you want to marry, leave me for him! I'm not afraid of that happening. It'll never happen."

"God, you're such a beautiful talker."

"It's not dishonest. I'm being very honest. I'm making an honest woman of you. I'm finally taking a stand, I'm committing myself. Marriage is a great institution. Marriages are great symbolic theater. Especially a state marriage. It was a war romance, and now it's a peace marriage, and it's all very normal and sensible. We'll make it a festival, we'll invite the whole world. We'll exchange rings, we'll throw rice. We'll put down roots."

"We don't have roots. We're network people. We have aerials."

"It's the right and proper thing to do. It's necessary. In fact, it's the only real way that the two of us can move on from here."

"Oscar, we can't move on. My marrying you can't stick a whole community together. Making two people legitimate, that doesn't make their society legitimate. It's not a legitimate thing. I'm a war leader, and a strike leader —I was Joan of Arc. Nobody ever elected me. I rule by force and clever propaganda. The real powers here are you and your friend Kevin. And Kevin is like any outlaw who takes power: he's a scary little brute. He brings me big dossiers, he bullies people and spies on them. I'm sick of all that. It's turning me into a monster. It can't go on, it's not right. There's no future in it."

"You've been thinking a lot about this, haven't you?"

"You *taught* me how to think about it. You taught me how to think politically. You're a good tactician, Oscar, you're really clever, you know all about people's kinks and weaknesses, but you don't know about their integrity and their strength. You're not a great strategist. You know all the dirty tricks with go-stones in the corner, but you don't comprehend the whole board."

"And you do?"

"Some of it. I know the world well enough that I know that my lab is the best place for me."

"So you're giving up?"

"No . . . I'm just quitting while I'm ahead. Something is going to work here. Something of it will last. But it's not a whole new world. It's just a new political system. We can't close it off in an airtight nest, with me as the Termite Queen. I have to quit, I have to leave. Then maybe this thing will shake down, and pack down, and build something solid, from the bottom up."

"Maybe we'll do better than that. Maybe I *am* a great strategist."

"Sweetheart, you're not! You're streetwise, but you're young, and you're not very wise. You can't become King by marrying your pasteboard Queen, someone you created by marching a pawn down the board. You shouldn't even want to be King. It's a lousy job. A situation like this doesn't need another stupid tyrant with a golden crown, it needs . . . it needs the founder of a civilization, a saint and a prophet, somebody impossibly wise and selfless and generous. Somebody who can make laws out of chaos, and order out of chaos, and justice out of noise, and meaning out of total distraction."

"My God, Greta. I've never heard you talk like this before."

She blinked. "I don't think I ever even *thought* like this before."

"What you're saying is completely true. It's the hard cold truth, and it's bad, it's impossibly bad, it's worse than I ever imagined, but you know, I'm glad that I know it now. I always like to know what I'm facing. I refuse to admit defeat here. I refuse to pack up my tent. I don't want to leave you, I can't bear it. You're the only woman who ever really understood me."

"I'm sorry that I understand you well enough to tell you what you just can't do."

"Greta, *don't give up on me*. Don't dump me. I'm having a genuine breakthrough here, I'm on the edge of something really huge. You're right about the dictatorship problem, it's a dirt-real, basic, political challenge. We've worked ourselves to the bone now, we're all burned out, we're all bogged down in the little things. Daily tactics won't do it for us anymore, but abandoning it to its own devices is a cop-out. We need to create something that is huge and permanent, we need a higher truth. No, not higher, *deeper,* we need a floor of granite. No more sand castles, no more improvising. We need genius. And you're a genius."

"Yes, but not that kind."

"But you and I, we could do it together! If we only had some time to really concentrate, if we could just talk together like this. Listen. You have totally convinced me: you're wiser than I am, you're more realistic, I'm with you all the way. We'll leave this place. We'll run off together. Forget the big state marriage and the rings and the rice. We'll go to . . . well, not some island, they're all drowning now. . . . We'll go to Maine. We'll stay there a month, two months, we'll stay a year. We'll drop off the net, we'll use pens and candlelight. We'll really, seriously concentrate, without any distractions at all. We'll write a Constitution."

"What? Let the President do that."

"That guy? He's just more of the same! He's a social-ist, he's gonna make us sane and practical, just like Europe. This place isn't Europe! America is what people created when they were sick to death of Europe! Normalcy for America—it isn't keeping your nose clean and counting your carbon dioxide. Normalcy for America is *technological change*. Sure, the process ran away with us for a little while, the rest of the world pulled a fast one on us, they cheated us, they want the world to be Rembrandt canvases and rice paddies until the last trump of doom, but we're off our sickbed now. A massive rate of change *is* normalcy for America. What we need is *planned* change—Progress. We need Progress!"

"Oscar, your face is getting really red." She reached out.

He jerked his wrist back. "Stop trying to feel my pulse. You know I hate it when you do that. Listen to me carefully, I'm making perfect specimen sense lab-table really love me. I'm doing this all for you, Greta. I'm totally serious, we can do it tomorrow morning. A long sabbati-cal together in Maine, at some lovely romantic cabin. I'll have Lana rent us one, she knows all about it."

Her eyes widened. "What? Tomorrow? Lana? Wil-derness? We can't just abandon romantic Clare Lana Ramachandran little Kama Sutra girl."

Oscar stared. "What did you say?"

"I'm sorry. I didn't mean to say that about Lana. Lana can't help how she feels about you. But I'm not sorry I said it about Clare. You were having drinks with her! Kevin told me."

Oscar was stunned. "How did we get onto this sub-ject?"

An angry flush rose up Greta's neck. "I *always* think about it—I just never say it out loud! Clare, and Lana, and the Senator's wife, and Moira, all these painted pointed glamour women with their claws . . ."

"Greta, stop that. Trust me! I'm asking you to marry me. Moira! Get it through your head. This is for real, this is permanent and solid. Tell me once and for all, will you marry Moira?"

"What? Moira's one of your krewewomen, isn't she? She came over to make amends."

"But Moira works for Huey! When did you see Moira?"

"Moira came to my office. She brought me a brand-new air filter. She was very nice."

Oscar stared in mounting horror at the air filter at his elbow. He was so used to them now. They were everywhere, and so innocuous. They were cleansing Trojan fog horse biowar gas miasma. "Oh, Greta. How could you take a gift from that woman?"

"She said it was *your* gift. Because it smells of roses." She patted the box, and then looked up in pain and bewilderment, and a dawning and terrible knowledge. "Oh, sweetheart, I thought you knew. I thought you knew everything."

———————————

The Collaboratory was, by design, equipped to deal with biological contamination. They had to shut down the entire Administration building. The gas from the booby-trapped air filter was of particularly ingenious design, micronized particles the size and shape of ragweed pollen. The particles stuck to the nasal tract like a painless snort of cocaine, whereupon their contents leaked through the blood-brain barrier, and did mysterious and witchy things.

Oscar and Greta, having wearily crammed themselves into decontamination suits, were carried red-faced and stumbling to the Hot Zone's clinic. There they were ritually scrubbed down, and subjected to gingerly examination. The good news was immediate: they were not dying. The bad news took longer to arrive. Their blood pressure was up, their faces were congested, their gait and posture were affected, they were suffering odd speech disabilities. Their PET-scans were exhibiting highly abnormal loci of cognitive processing, two wandering hot blobs where a normal human being would have just one. The primal rhythm of their brain waves had a distinct backbeat.

Oscar had been slowly and gently poisoned as he was making the speech of his life. This foul realization sent him into a towering animal rage. This reaction revealed yet another remarkable quality of his poisoned brain. He could literally think of two things at once; but it stretched him so thin that he had very little impulse control.

A nurse suggested a sedative. Oscar cordially agreed that he was feeling a bit hyperactive, and accented this by screaming personal insults and repeatedly kicking the wall. This behavior produced a sedative in short order. Dual unconsciousness resulted.

By noon, Oscar was conscious again, feeling sluggish yet simultaneously hair-trigger. He paid a visit to Greta, in her separate decontamination cell. Greta had passed a quiet night. She was now sitting bolt upright in her hospital bed, legs folded, hands in her lap, staring straight into space. She didn't speak, she didn't even see him. She was wide-awake and indescribably, internally busy.

A nurse stood guard for him, while Oscar stared at her with bittersweet mélange. Bitter; sweet; bitter / sweet: bittersweet. She was exalted, silent, full of carnivorous insight: Greta had never looked more like herself. It would have been a profanation to touch her.

Accompanied by his nurse, Oscar tottered back to his cell. He wondered how the effect felt for Greta. It seemed to hit people differently. Maybe there were as many ways to think doubly as there were to think singly.

When he closed his eyes, Oscar could actually feel the sensation, somatically. It was as if his overtight skull had a pair of bladders stuffed inside, liquid and squashy, like a pair of nested yin-yangs. One focus of attention was somehow in "the front" and the other in "the back," and when the one to the front revolved into direct consciousness, the other slipped behind it. And the blobs had little living eyes inside them. Eyes that held the nascent core of other streams of consciousness. Like living icons, awaiting a mental touch to launch into full awareness.

Kevin stepped into the cell. Oscar heard him limping, was fully aware of his presence; it took a strange little moment to realize that he should take the trouble to open his eyes and look.

"Thank God you're here!" he blurted.

"That's what I like," Kevin said, blinking. "Enthusiasm."

With an effort, Oscar said nothing. He could restrain his urge to blurt his thoughts aloud, if he really put his mind to it. All he had to do was press his tongue against the roof of his mouth, clench his teeth, and breathe rhythmically through his nose.

"You don't look so bad," Kevin said analytically. "Your color's a little high, and you're holding your neck like a giraffe on speed, but you don't look crazy."

"I'm not crazy. Just different."

"Uh-huh." Kevin took a disinfected metal chair and eased his aching feet. "So, uhm, sorry about the security screwup, man."

"These things happen."

"Yeah. See, it was all those Boston people from the old Bambakias krewe: that was the problem. The Senator's wife . . . she went way out of her way to tell me I was supposed to let it slide with the press secretary. You and this press babe being the former romantic item, and all that. Great, I thought, better really bury this one; but then, in comes this Moira Matarazzo woman who was the Senator's *former* press secretary. . . . See, I just lost track. That's all. Just plain couldn't keep up with it all. All these Boston krewepeople, and former krewepeople, and krewepeople of the former krewepeople; look, *nobody* could keep track of that crap. Hell, I don't even know if *I'm* your krewepeople anymore."

"I get the picture, Kevin. That's a by-product of what's basically a semifeudal, semilegal, distributable-deniable, net-centered segmented polycephalous influence sociality process."

Kevin waited politely for Oscar's lips to stop moving. "For what it's worth, I've got Moira's movements tracked. Into the dome, into the Administration building, out of the dome . . . I'm practically sure that she didn't leave any of those tasty little time bombs for the rest of us."

"Huey."

Kevin laughed. "Well, of course it was Huey."

"It just seems so pointless and small of him to do this to us *now*. After the war's over, after he's out of office. When I was getting ready to leave all this."

"So you really meant it about leaving us, then."

"What?"

"I overheard. I forgot to mention that I ran the tapes of the poisoning incident. That romantic discussion that you and Dr. Penninger were having as you were being gassed."

"You have that conference room bugged?"

"Hey, pal, *I'm* not brain-damaged. Of course I have the conference room bugged. Not that I have time to listen to every damn room that I bug around here. . . . But hey, when there's a terrorist biowar incident taking place in one, you bet I run the tapes back and listen. I do pay attention, Oscar. I'm a quick study. I make a pretty good cop, really."

"Never said you weren't a good cop, you big-mouthed incompetent."

"*Holy* cow, there it is again. . . . Did you know that you actually have *two different voices* when you say contradictory stuff like that? I need to run a stress analysis there, I bet that could screw up vocal IDs." Kevin leaned back in his chair and put a sock-clad foot on Oscar's bed. Kevin was taking developments rather easily, Oscar thought. Then again, Kevin had witnessed this phenomenon among the Haitians. He'd had time to get used to the concept.

"*Sure* I've had time to get used to the concept," Kevin said. "It's obvious. You mutter things aloud to yourself, just so you know what you're thinking. I recognize the syndrome, man. Big deal! I got used to your *other* personal background problem. . . . Oscar, haven't we always been on good terms?"

"Yeah."

"I have to tell you, it really hurt my feelings when Dr. Penninger said I was a 'scary little brute.' That I 'bullied people' and 'spied on them.' And you didn't stick up for me, man. You didn't tell her a thing."

"I was proposing marriage to her."

"Women," Kevin grunted. "I dunno what it is with women. They're just not rational. They're creepy little Mata Hari sexpots carrying poison gas bombs. . . . Or maybe they're like Dr. Penninger down the hall, the Rigid Ice-Queen of Eternal Light and Truth. . . . I just can't understand what it takes to please that woman! I mean, system-crackers like me, we have *everything in common* with scientists. It's all about hidden knowledge, and how you find it, and who gets to know it, and who gets the rep for finding out. That's all there is to science. I *loved* working for her, I thought she was really *getting it*. I bent absolutely double for that woman, I did anything she ever asked me —I did favors for her that she never even knew she got. I *looked up* to her, dammit! And what do I get for all my loyal service? I scare her. She wants to purge me."

Oscar nodded. "Get used to the idea. This is a clean sweep. Huey took us out. It's decapitation. I can barely talk now. I can barely walk. And Greta, she's in some kind of wide-awake schizoid catatonia hebephrenia trance nonverbal. . . ."

"A little adjective trouble there, man, but no problem, I take your point. Either I seize power myself now, and try to run the whole shebang as a secret-police state. Or else I just . . . I dunno . . . airmail myself back to Boston. End of the story. It all makes a nice hacker brag, though, right? Kind of a good bar story."

"You can't hold this place together alone, Kevin. People don't trust you."

"Oh, I know that, man. You distribute all the big favors yourself, and you use me as your heavy guy to intimidate people. I know that I was the heavy guy. My dad was the heavy, too. The Founding Fathers are a bunch of dead white males; the guys on Mount Rushmore are all scary Anglo guys now. We're the heavies. I was used to the role. Hey, I was glad to have the work."

"I want you to help me now, Kevin."

"Help you what, pal?"

"To get out of here."

"No problem, boss. I'm still Captain Scubbly Bee. Hell, I was working hard on being *Colonel* Scubbly Bee. I can get you outside this place. Where you want to go?"

"Baton Rouge. Or wherever Huey is hiding."

"Oh ho! Not that I doubt your judgment now, man, but I have a really great countersuggestion. *Boston*, okay? The good old muddy water! Beacon Hill, Charlestown, Cambridge. . . . You and I, we're actually *neighbors*, man. We live on the same street! We could *go home* together. We could have a real beer, inside a real Boston bar. We could take in a hockey game."

"I need to talk to Huey," Oscar said flatly. "I have a big personal problem with him."

Green Huey had gone into semiretirement. He was doing a lot of ceremonial ribbon-clipping these days. It was a little difficult doing all this public apple-polishing while surrounded by a militant phalanx of Regulator bodyguards, but Huey enjoyed the show. The ex-Governor had always been good for a laugh. He knew how to show the people a good time.

Oscar and Kevin dressed like derelicts, vanished through the social membrane, and began to stalk the Governor. They traveled by night in the sorriest hotels; they slept in roadside parks in newly purchased military-surplus tents. They burned their IDs and wore straw hats and gum boots and overalls. Kevin passed as Oscar's minder, a lame guy with a guitar. Oscar passed as Kevin's somewhat dim-witted cousin, the one who mumbled a lot. Oscar bran-dished an accordion. Even in a land that had once favored accordion music, they were mostly avoided. It was a frightening thing to see two mentally incompetent side-walk buskers, with battered folk instruments, who might at any moment burst into song.

Oscar had finally lost his temper with Huey. He was of two minds about the matter. Oscar was always of two minds about everything now. On the one hand, he wanted to publicly confront the man. And on the other, he simply wanted to murder him. The second concept made a lot of sense to Oscar now, since killing political figures was not uncommon behavior for mentally ruined drifters with nothing left to lose. He and Kevin had seri-ous discussions about the issue. Kevin seemed to waver between pro and con. Oscar was pro and con at the same time.

Their strategic problem was dizzyingly multiform. Oscar found it extremely hard to stop thinking about it, since he could contemplate so many different aspects of the issue all at once. Killing Huey. Maiming Huey, per-haps breaking Huey's arms. Reducing him to a wheel-chair, that had appealing aspects. Blinding Huey had a certain biblical majesty to it. But how? Long-range sniping was not a pursuit for amateurs who had never handled firearms. Handguns would surely entail almost instant arrest. Poison sounded intriguing, but would require advance planning and extensive resources.

"You're NSC, aren't you?" Kevin told him, as they bagged out in the tent to the sound of crickets, blissfully far from the sinister fog of urban surveillance. "I thought they trained you guys to do awful things with the juice of cigars."

"The President doesn't order assassinations of his domestic political opponents. If he were outed for that, he'd be impeached. That's totally counterproductive."

"Aren't *you* one of the President's agents?"

It was wise of Kevin to point this out. Oscar recognized that he'd been getting a little tangled in the proliferating vines of his cognitive processes. Next day they stopped at a greasy spoon outside the town of Mamou, and called the NSC from a satellite pay phone.

It took quite some time for Oscar's immediate superior to answer a random pay-phone call on a deeply insecure line from the heart of Cajun country. When he came on, he was livid. Oscar announced that he had been poisoned, was non compos mentis, had suffered a complete mental breakdown, could no longer be considered responsible for his actions, was no longer fit for public service, and was therefore resigning from his post, immediately. His superior ordered him to fly to Washington for a thorough medical assessment. Oscar told him that this was not on his agenda as a newly private citizen. His superior told Oscar that he would be arrested. Oscar pointed out that he was currently in the center of the state of Louisiana, where the locals were profoundly unfriendly to federal agents. He hung up. It had been a lot to say. His tongue felt sore.

Kevin was getting into the swing of things. He suggested that it might be a good idea to similarly break all ties with Senator Bambakias. They went out for a leisurely brunch of red beans and rice, and returned to find the original pay phone swarming with Regulator goons in fast pickup trucks. They tried to earn a little money with their guitar and accordion, and they were told to get lost.

They hitchhiked from Mamou to Eunice, and made another pay-phone call, this time to the Senator's office in Washington. The Senator was no longer in Washington. Bambakias had gone on a fact-finding mission to the newly conquered Netherlands. In fact, the entire Senate Foreign Relations Committee had set up shop in The Hague, in a vacated Dutch government building. Oscar apologized, and was about to hang up, when the Senator himself came on the line. He'd been paged from across the Atlantic, and he had woken from a sound sleep, but he was anxious to talk.

"Oscar, I'm so glad you called. Don't hang up! We've heard all about the event. Lorena and I are just sick about it. We're going to pin this thing on Huey. I know that it means outing me on the Moira debacle, but I'm willing to face the music there. Huey can't go on savaging people like this, it's atrocious. We can't live in a country like that. We have to take a stand."

"That's very good of you, Senator. Courageous principled apologize it was all my fault anyway."

"Oscar, listen to me carefully. The Haitians have survived this thing, and so can you. Neurologists around the world are working on this problem. They're very angry about what was done to Dr. Penninger, it's a personal affront to them and their profession. We want to fly you into Den Haag, and try some treatments here. They have excellent hospitals here in Holland. In fact, their whole infrastructure is marvelous. Roadblocks absolutely unheard-of. These government facilities here are top-notch. The Foreign Relations Committee is getting more work done here in Den Haag than they have in a year in Washington. You have resources, Oscar. There's hope. Your friends want to help you."

"Senator, even if you do help Greta, I'm a special

504   B r u c e   S t e r l i n g

case. I have a unique genetic background, and neural Colombian conventional medical useless."

"That's not true! You've forgotten that there are
three Danish women here in Europe who are basically
sisters of yours. They've heard about your troubles, and
they want to help you. I've just met them, and I've talked
to them personally. Now I think that I understand you
better than I ever have before. Tell him, Lorena."

The Senator's wife took the phone. "Oscar, listen to
Alcott. He's talking perfect sense to you. I met those
women too. You're the pick of the litter there, that's very
obvious; but they do want to help you anyway. They're
sincere about it, and so are we. You're very important to
us. You stood by Alcott and me in our darkest days, and
now it's our turn, that's all. Please let us help you."

"Lorena, I'm not insane. Huey's been like this for at
least two years, and Huey's not insane either. It's just a
profoundly different mode of cognition. Sometimes I have
a little trouble getting issues to clarify, that's all."

Lorena's voice went distant suddenly. "Talk him
down, Alcott! He's using real English now!"

Bambakias came on, in his richest and most intent
baritone. "Oscar, you are a professional. You're a player.
Players don't get angry. They just get even. You have no
business wandering around in Louisiana, with an Anglo
terrorist hacker who has a police record. That is just not a
player's move. We're going to nail Huey for this; it'll take a
while, but we'll pin him down. Huey made a fatal error—
he poisoned a member of the President's NSC. I don't
care if Huey's got a skull full of turbochargers and after-
burners. Insulting Two Feathers by gassing one of his staff
was a very stupid move. The President is a very hard man
—and most directly to my point, he's proved himself a far
better politician than the ex-Governor of a small Southern
state."

"Senator, I'm listening. I think there's something to
what you say."

Bambakias exhaled slowly. "Thank God."

"I hadn't really thought much about Holland before. I mean, that Holland has so much potential. I mean, we *own* Holland now, basically, don't we?"

"Yes, that's right. You see, Holland is the new Louisiana. Louisiana is yesterday's news! You and I were right to get involved in Louisiana earlier, there was a serious difficulty there—but as a rogue state, Louisiana is a sideshow now. It's the Dutch who are the real future. They're a serious, well-organized, businesslike nation, people who are taking methodical, sensible steps about the climate and environment. Believe it or not, they're ahead of the United States in a lot of areas—especially banking. Louisiana is over the top. They're not serious. They're visionary crawdad-eating psychos. We need serious political organization now, a return to normalcy. Huey is yesterday's man, he's out of the loop. He's a fast-talking loon who throws technological innovation here and there—as if randomly spewing a bunch of half-baked ideas can increase the sum of human happiness. That's sheer demagoguery, it's craziness. We need common sense and political stability and sensible, workable policies. That's what government is for."

Oscar swirled this extraordinary statement over in his mind. He felt thoughts and memories sifting like a soft kaleidoscope. "You're really *different* now, aren't you, Alcott?"

"I beg your pardon?"

"I mean this regimen you've been through. It's completely changed you as a person. You're realistic now. You're sensible and prudent. You're boring."

"Oscar, I'm sure that you have some kind of interesting insight there, but this isn't the time for chatter. We need to stick to the point. Tell me that you'll come to Den Haag and join us. Lorena and I, we feel that we're your family—we're in lieu of your family, at a time like this.

You can come here to Holland, and take your place in our krewe, and we'll set you all straight. That's a promise."

"All right, Senator, you've convinced me. You've never gone back on your word to me, and I'm very touched by that pledge. I can see I've been impulsive. I can't go off half-cocked. I need to think these things all the way through."

"That's great. I knew I could make you see sense, I knew I could cheer you up. And now, I think we've talked too long on this phone. I'm afraid this line isn't secure."

Oscar turned to Kevin. "The Senator says this phone isn't secure."

Kevin shrugged. "Well, it's a random phone, man. It's a big state. Huey can't be tapping every last one of 'em."

Two hours later they were arrested on a roadside by Louisiana state police.

———————————

Green Huey was at a cultural event in Lafayette. He and part of his corps of semilegal good old boys were whooping it up on a hotel balcony, overlooking the folk festival. There was a monster fandango taking place, in near silence. At least a thousand people were engaged in a kaleidoscopic square dance. They were all wearing headphones with positional monitors, and some code within the silent music was directing their crowd flow. They seemed free and controlled at the same time, regimented but spontaneous, bacchanalian but exquisitely channeled.

"Y'know, I really dote on these grass-roots folk events," Huey said, leaning on the curvilinear iron of the hotel's balcony rail. "You Yankee boys are young and spry, you ought to give it a chance sometime."

"I don't dance," Kevin said.

"Pity about the big sore feet on the Moderator here," Huey said, squinting in the sunlight and adjusting his new straw hat. "I dunno why you brought ol' Limpy Boy along anyhow. He's no player."

"I was propping the player up," Kevin said. "I was wiping the drool off his chin."

Oscar and Kevin were wearing white plastic prison overalls. Their hands were neatly cuffed behind their backs. They'd been dragged onto the balcony in full sight of the crowd below, and the people seemed completely unperturbed to see them. Perhaps Huey spent large amounts of his retirement time chatting with handcuffed prisoners.

"I was thinking you'd *call* first," said Huey, turning to Oscar. "I thought we had an understanding there—that you'd always call me up and clear the air when we had one of our little contretemps."

"Oh, we were hoping for a personal audience, Governor. We just got a little distracted."

"The guitar and the accordion gambit, that was especially good. You actually play the accordion, Oscar? Diatonic scales, and all that?"

"I'm just a beginner," Oscar said.

"Oh, you'll be surprised how easy it is to play music now. Dead easy. Play while you sing. Play while you dance. Hell, play while you dictate financial notes to a spreadsheet."

"Cutting his hands free would be a good start," Kevin suggested.

"They must have some awful soft jails up in Massachusetts, to have Limpy Boy here crackin' wise so much. I mean, just 'cause we had you two boys stripped, and scrubbed, and checked under fingernails, and had a nice long look up every orifice that opens, and some that don't. . . . That don't mean I'm gonna cut the hands loose on the Hacker Ninja Boy here. He might have a blowgun up his finger bones, or sumpin'. You know there's been five attempts on my life in the past two weeks? All these Moderator jaspers gunnin' for ol'

Huey . . . they all wanna be Colonel This or Brevet
General That; I dunno, it sure gets tiresome."

"Maybe we shouldn't stand here in the open air,
then," Oscar said. "There have been a lot of people anxious to kill me, too, and it would be a shame to see you
catch a stray bullet."

"That's why I got all these guards, son! They're not
as bright as you are, but they're a lot more loyal. You know
something, Soap Boy? I like you. I enjoy these homemade
scientific efforts that don't work out commercially, but
just refuse to stay down. I took a serious interest in you; I
even got skin samples. Hell, I got a square yard of your
skin, livin' down there in a salt mine. Got enough of your
skin to stretch on a dang drumhead. You're quite a specimen, you are. You're a real gumbo thing—little o' this,
little o' that. There are chunks of you that are upside
down, stretched all backward, duplicated . . . and *no introns,* that's the cool part. I didn't know a man could even
live without introns."

"I couldn't recommend it, Governor. It has some
technical drawbacks."

"Oh, I know you're a little frail, Brainy Boy. I was
tryin' to take it easy on you. Ran a lot of medical tests on
that DNA of yours. Didn't want to hurt you or nothin'."
Huey squinted. "You're with me here, aren't ya? You're
not all confused or anything."

"No, Governor. I can follow you. I'm really concentrating."

"You don't think I'm funnin' you about your DNA,
do you? I mean, just 'cause I'm a coonass, that don't mean
I can't hack DNA, bubba."

"Just as long as you don't try cloning him as an
army," Kevin said.

"Got my own army, thanks." Huey raised one arm
of his linen jacket and patted his bulky armpit. "Man
needs a whole dang army just to stay alive these days, sad
to say." He turned to Oscar. "That's the problem with

these pesky Moderators. They're prole gangs all right, your basic army-of-the-night. All day long, it was power-to-the-people this, and revolutionary justice that. Really mountin' up, though, y'know? Getting somewhere serious. Finally we get a chance to make our own rules and give the common man a real break."

Huey snorted. "Then all of a sudden along comes a new President, who deigns to take a little royal notice of 'em. Throws 'em a dog biscuit, maybe even two. They're fallin' all over themselves, they're salutin' his socks, they're salutin' his shorts. They're killin' their own brothers for the Man. Makes you sick."

"The Man is a player. He's got talent, Huey."

"What the hell! The man's a Dutch agent! He sold out the country to a foreign power! You don't think the Dutch gave up that easy, do ya? Without one single shot being fired? This is the *Dutch* we're talking about! When they get invaded, they flood their own country and die in the ditches with big pointy sticks in their hands. They gave up easy because they planned that whole damn gambit from the get-go."

"That's an interesting theory, Governor."

"You should talk to the French about this theory sometime. They're real big on theory, the French. The French know the score. We entertain 'em, they think Americans are natural clowns, they think our worst comedians are funny. But they're scared of the Dutch. That's the problem with modern America. We pulled up our borders, we're all parochial now. We don't know what's goin' on. Hell, we used to lead the whole world in science . . . lead 'em in everything. Country like France gets along great without science. They just munch some more fine cheese and read more Racine. But you take America without science, you got one giant Nebraska. You got guys living in teepees. Well, at least the teepee boys still want somethin'. Give *them* the science. Let *them* work it out."

"That's an even more interesting theory."

"Oh, well, *yeah*. You BELIEVE ME on that one," the Governor boomed. "You stole my damn clothes, you sorry kid! You stole my science facility. You stole my data. There was just one damn thing left that you didn't know about, one damn important thing you didn't know how to steal! So that's what I *gave* to ya."

"I see."

"You can't say that Huey ain't generous. You outed me on everything you possibly could. Chased me up and down in the press. Sicced a Senator on me. Turned the President against me. You're a busy guy. But you know something? You don't have any SPIRIT, boy! You don't have any SOUL! You don't BELIEVE! There's not one fresh idea in your pointy head. You're like a dang otter raidin' a beaver's nest, you're like this streamlined thing that kills and eats the beaver's children. Well, I got big news for you, Soapy. You're a genuine beaver now."

"Governor, this is truly fascinating. You say you've studied me; well, I've studied you. I learned a lot. You're a man of tremendous energy and talent. What I don't understand is why you carry out your aims in such absurd, tacky, uncivilized ways."

"Son, that one's dead easy. It's because I'm a dirt-poor, dirt-ignorant hick from a drowning swamp! Nothin' came easy for us twenty-first-century hicks. Nothing is *elegant* here. They took all our oil, they cut our timber, they gillnetted our fish, they poisoned the earth, they turned the Mississippi into a giant sewer that killed the Gulf for five hundred miles around. Then hurricanes started comin' and the seas rose up to get us! What the hell did you expect from us, when you were up in Boston polishing the silver? We Cajuns need a future just like anybody else. We been here four hundred years! And we didn't forget to have children, like the Cabots and the Lodges did. If you had a workin' brain in your head, you'd have blown off that sorry architect and come down here to work for *me*."

"I didn't like your methods."

"Hell, you *used* enough of 'em. You used damn near every one. Hell, I ain't particular about any methods. You got a better method for me, spit it out! Let's talk it over."

"Hey, Huey," Kevin said. "What about me? I have methods too."

"You're last year's news, Mr. Whitey. You're the hired help now, you're lucky to have a damn job. Lemme talk to the Genetic Wonder here. We're talking cognition now. This is for grown-ups."

"Hey, Huey!" Kevin insisted. "My methods still work. I outed you on the Haitians. I figured that one out, I flew people over your border."

Huey's brow wrinkled in distaste. "My point is," Huey said to Oscar, "we're in the same boat now. If I'd just kept hold of that Collaboratory, I could have spread a new cognition on a massive scale. In fact, I'm *still* gonna do that—I'm gonna make the people of this state the smartest, most capable, most creative people on God's green earth. You put a serious crimp in my production facilities—but hell, that's all history now. Now you've got no real choice but to help ol' Huey. Because you been hanging on to power by the skin of your teeth, cadgin' favors, hiding your past. Now you're a freak twice over. But! If you come on over to Huey now—and if you bring along your loving girlfriend, who's the source of all this goodness in the first place, and is in the same boat as you —then you get a brand-new lease on life. In fact, the sky's your limit."

"First I'd have to get my temper back, Etienne."

"Oh, pshaw! Real players don't get angry. Why get all ticked off at me? I actually *accept* you. I *love* your god-damn background problem. See, I finally got you all figured out. If America settles down and gets all normal, then you're on the outside for good. You're always gonna have your nose pressed up against the glass, watchin' other folks drink the champagne. Nothing you do will last. You'll be a sideshow and a shadow, and you'll stay one till you die. But, son, if you get a big head start in the coming revolution of the human mind, you can goddamn *have* Massachusetts. I'll give it to ya."

"Hey, Huey! Yo! Were you always this crazy, or did the dope do it?"

Huey ignored Kevin's interruption, though his scowl grew deeper. "I know you can attack me for this. Sure, go ahead and do it. Tell everybody what a freak you are now. Tell everybody that your Senator's former lover —and Moira's now in France, by the way—took revenge on you, for the dirty trick that you pulled to cover his sorry ass. Step out in public like the fire-eatin' boy, and nicely set fire to yourself. Or else, just see sense and come on board with me! You'll be doin' just exactly what you did before. But instead of just fast-talkin' people into a new way of life—hell, words never stick anyhow—you can *blast* 'em into it. When you do that to 'em, they don't go back, son. Just like you're never going back."

"Why would I make thousands of people into sideshow freaks? Why should everyone be as unhappy as I am?"

"Nothin' unhappy about it! The science really works! It works just great!"

"Hey, *Huey*! Give it up, dude! I *know* this guy. You'll *never* make *him* happy! He doesn't know what the word means! You can't get away with this, man—you've made him *twice as bad*!"

Huey had lost patience. He gestured absently for his bodyguards. A pair of pistol-toting goons emerged from the gilded shadows of the elegant room behind the balcony. Kevin fell silent.

"Get his hands free," Huey told the bodyguard. "Get him a coat and hat. He's a player. We're talking seriously now."

The bodyguard freed Oscar's hands. Oscar began rubbing his wrists. The bodyguard threw someone's dark jacket over Oscar's prison coveralls.

Huey sidled a little closer. "Oscar, let's talk turkey now. This thing is a great gift. Sure, it's a little tough on you at first, like ridin' a bicycle. It's multitasking, that's its very nature. I'm not saying it's perfect. Nothing technical is ever perfect. It's a very real-world thing. It speeds up your heartbeat—has to speed up the chip a little. And it *is* multitasking, so you do get certain operations that kinda hang. . . . And others that pop up suddenly. . . . And every once in a while, you get two streams of thought going that get kinda stuck; so you freeze there, and you have to drop your working memory. But you just give the old head a good hard shake, and you boot right back up again."

"I see."

"See, I'm really leveling with you here. This isn't snake oil, this is the McCoy. Sure, you have some language problems, and you do tend to mutter sometimes. But, son . . . *you're twice the man you were*! You can think in two languages at once! If you work at it, you can do amazing things with both your hands. And the best of all, boy—is when you get two good trains of thought going, and they start *switching passengers*. That's what intuition is all about—when you know things, but you don't know how you know. That's all done in the preconscious mind —it's thought that you don't know you're thinking. But when you're really bearing down, and you're thinking two things at once—ideas bleed over. They mix. They flavor each other. They cook down real rich and fine. That's inspiration. It's the finest mental sensation you'll ever have. The only problem with *that* is—sometimes those ideas are so confounded great, you have a little problem with impulse control."

"Yes, I've noticed that little impulse problem."

"Well, son, most people hide their light under a

bushel and they never act on impulse. That's why they end up buried in unmarked graves. A real player's got initiative, he's a man of action. But sure, I admit it: the impulse thing is a bug. That's why a major player needs good counselors. And if you don't *have* a top-of-the-line, raccoon-tailed political adviser, maybe you can *make* yourself one."

"Heeeey!" Kevin screeched. He had given up on Huey; he had suddenly turned his attention to the crowd below. "Hey, *people*! Your Governor's gone nuts! He uses poison and he's gonna turn you into crazy zombies!"

The bodyguards seized Kevin's pinioned arms and began to pummel him.

"They're torturing me!" Kevin screamed in anguish. "The cops are torturing me!"

Huey turned. "Goddammit, Boozoo, don't punch him in public like that! Haul him inside first. And, Zach, stop using your damn fists every time. Use your sap. That's what it's for."

Despite his bound arms, Kevin wasn't going quietly. He spun in place, began hopping up and down. His howls were of little use, for the crowd below was rapt inside the embrace of their headphones. But not all of them were dancing, and some were looking up.

Boozoo pulled a sap from within his clothing. Kevin aimed a clumsy kick. Boozoo half stepped back, tripped over the foot of a second guard, tangled suddenly in the spindly legs of a white iron balcony chair. He tumbled backward, landing with a crash. The second bodyguard tried to leap forward, tangled with the struggling Boozoo, and fell to his knees with a squawk.

"Aw *hell*," Huey grumbled. He swiftly reached into his own jacket, removed a chromed automatic pistol, and absently emptied a shot into Kevin. Struck high in the chest and with his hands still bound, Kevin catapulted backward, smashed into the railing, and tumbled to the earth below.

Deeply surprised, Huey walked to the railing, craned his head, and stared down. The pistol still gleamed in his grip. The crowd below him saw the gun, and billowed away in fear.

"Uh-oh," the Governor blurted.

––––––––––––––––

"I still don't know what to do with him," the President said. "He murdered a man in broad daylight in front of a thousand people, but he still has his adherents. I'd love to jail him, but Jesus. We've put so many people through the prison system that they're a major demographic group."

Oscar and the President of the United States were having a stroll through the White House garden. The Rose Garden, like the White House itself, was swept for bugs with regularity. It didn't help much. But it helped some. It was doable, if they kept moving.

"He always lacked a sense of decency, Mr. President. Everyone knows Huey went too far, even in Louisiana. They'll wait until he's dead before they name some bridges after him."

"What do you think of Washington now, Oscar? It's a different city now, don't you agree?"

"I have to admit, Mr. President: it bothers me to see foreign troops stationed in the capital of the United States."

"I agree with you there. But that solved the problem. People burrowing into the streets, barricading whole neighborhoods . . . no major government can survive in a capital like that. I can't order American troops to pursue these people with the rigor it requires to break decentered network gangs. But the Dutch will clean the streets if it takes ten years. They'll tough it out."

"It is a different city now, sir. Much tidier."

"You could live here, couldn't you? If the salary were right? If the White House krewe looked after you."

"Yes, sir; I like to think that I could live anywhere that duty called."

"Well, it isn't Louisiana, at least."

"Actually, Mr. President, I'm very fond of Louisiana. I still keep up with developments there. It's a bellwether state in many, many ways. I had some very fulfilling moments in Louisiana. I've come to think of it as my second home."

"Really."

"You see, the Dutch got so hard and desperate when the seas came up. I think Louisiana is on to something. I'm starting to think there's a lot to be said for simply lying down in the ooze."

The President stared. "Not that you yourself plan to do a lot of oozing."

"Only on occasion, sir."

"In an earlier discussion, Oscar, I told you that if you followed orders at the Collaboratory I'd find a post for you in the White House. There have been some interesting developments in your career since then, but none that give me any reason to doubt your ability. This is not an Administration for bigotry—or for scandal—and now that we have some grasp of constitutional coherency again, I'm going to cut the spook-and-cowboy business back to a dull roar. I'm actually governing this country now—even if I sometimes have to employ Dutch troops—and when I leave the Oval Office, I intend to leave a country that is sane, responsive, decent, and well behaved. And I think I have a role for you in that effort. Would you care to hear about it?"

"By all means, sir."

"As you're well aware, we still have *sixteen goddamn political parties* in this country! And I don't intend to face reelection with a pipsqueak party like the Soc-Pats behind me. We need a massive shake-out and total political reconsolidation. We need to shatter all these calcified partisan lines and establish a workable, practical, sensible, bipolar system. It's going to be Normalcy versus everything else."

"I see, sir. Much like the old days. So are you left-wing, or right-wing?"

"I'm *down*-wing, Oscar. I have my feet on the ground, and I know where I stand. Everyone else can be up-wing. They can all be up in the air, scattering crazy, high-tech, birdbrained ideas, and the ones that fall to ground without shattering, those will belong to me."

"Mr. President, I congratulate you on that formulation. You have a window of opportunity here where you can try anything that you please, and that formulation sounds doable."

"You think so? Good. This is your role. You will be a White House congressional liaison to interface with the current party structure. You'll shake the radicals and crazies out, and agglomerate them into the up-wing."

"I'm not down-wing, sir?"

"Oscar, there *is* no down-wing without the up-wing. It doesn't work unless I mold my own opposition. The up-wing is crucially important to the game plan. The up-wing has to be brilliant. It has to be genuinely glamorous. It has to be visionary, and it has to almost make sense. And it has to never, ever quite work out in real life."

"I see."

"I'm particularly concerned about that prole/scientist coalition. Those people have the bit between their teeth. They are already shaking down industries by threatening to research them. They're the only truly novel and vigorous movement on the political landscape right now. They cannot possibly be inside my camp. I can't buy them off. I can't sweet-talk them. They're inherently radical, because they're our century's version of the main motive force that transformed Western society during the past six centuries. To destroy them would be criminal, it would lobotomize the country. But to give them their head is insane."

The President drew a deep breath. "Because the spin-offs of their research built American capitalism, wrecked American capitalism, made the seas rise, poisoned the topsoil, wrecked the ozone layer, scattered radioactivity, filled the skies with contrails and the land with concrete, caused a population boom, caused a reproductive collapse, set Wyoming on fire . . . no, it's even worse than that. It's much, much worse. Now they've got our brains laid out like a virgin New World, and every last human being is a backward, undeveloped Indian. Someone has to deal seriously with these people. I suspect that you are just the man."

"I think I understand you, sir."

"They don't have any grasp of political reality, but they're going to blow the doors off the human condition unless something is done with them. I'm thinking: something subtle. Something attractive. Something glamorous, something that would make them behave less like Dr. Frankenstein and more like artists do. Modern poetry, that would be excellent. Costs very little, causes intense excitement in very small groups, has absolutely no social effect. So, I'm thinking mathematics. Nothing practical, just something totally arcane and abstract."

"You can't trust abstract mathematics, sir; it always turns out to be practical."

"Computer simulation, then. Extremely, *extremely* time-consuming, complex, and detailed simulations that never do any harm to reality."

"I think that's a lot more likely to produce your intended result, sir, but frankly, no one in the sciences takes cybernetics seriously anymore. That line of research is all mined out, it's intellectually dowdy. Even bio-studies and genetics have been mostly metabolized by now. It's all about cognition now, sir. That's the last thing left to them."

"You must have suffered from that. Maybe you can

convince them to try something much more pretty. With more sheer wonder in it."

"Mr. President, there is one issue here. Aren't you asking me to infiltrate them and betray them?"

"Oscar, I'm asking you to be a politician. It's not our business to blow the damn doors off the human condition. That's not in our job description. The job is to establish justice, ensure domestic tranquillity, and promote the general welfare. A job we politicians signally failed to do. You know something? It's not a pretty thing to watch a nation go crazy. But it happens. To great countries sometimes, the greatest peoples on earth. Japan, Germany, Russia, China . . . and we Americans have just had a bad, bad spin in the barrel. We're still very groggy. We were lucky. It could be the fire next time."

"Sir, don't you think the scientific community— such as it is—should be *told* all this? They're citizens too, aren't they? They're rather bright people, if a little narrowly focused. I don't really think that deceiving them is a tactic that can prosper in the longer term."

"We're all dead in the longer term, Oscar."

"Mr. President, this really is a dream job that you're offering me. I recognize its importance, I'm very impressed by your trust. I even think I might have the ability to do it. But before I engage in something that is this— what can I call it? So Benthamite/Machiavellian—I need you to tell me something. I need you to level with me on one issue. Are you in the pay of the Dutch?"

"The Dutch never paid me a thing."

"But there was an arrangement, wasn't there?"

"In a manner of speaking . . . I'd have to take you out to Colorado. I'd have to show you the timber. You know, ever since we Native Americans got into the drug and casino businesses, we've been buying back little bits of this great country of ours. Mostly the cheap ones, the parts too ruined for any commercial use. If you leave them alone long enough, seven generations, sometimes they come back a little. But they'll never come back the same way. Extinction is permanent. A futuristic swamp full of homemade monsters really isn't the same as a native wetlands. We really did kill the buffalo, and the native flowers, and the native grasses, and the primeval forests, and we did it for a cheap buck, and it's gone forever. And that's bad. It's very bad. It's worse than we can ever repay. It's like a hideous war crime. It haunts America like genocide haunts Germany, like slavery haunts the South. We turned our brother creatures into toys. And the Dutch are right about that. All the people whose homes are drowning are dead right, morally right, ethically right, physically right. Yes, we Americans spewed more greenhouse gas than anyone else in the world. We are the single biggest problem. So yes, I intend to implement some Dutch policies in this country. Not every last one of them, the ones that I think make most sense. And that change would never, ever happen by them conquering us. It could only happen by us conquering them."

"Then you *are* a Dutch agent."

"Oscar, we *own* them. They surrendered. We're a large and slowly drowning country that defeated a small and quickly drowning country. That's reality, it's the world, it's what we live in."

"Mr. President, I agree with you. I'm glad that I know the truth now. It's a shattering truth that just destroyed every ambition I have ever had, but I'm glad that I know the truth. It's the highest value I have, as the person that I am, and I won't surrender it. I don't want your job."

"Well, you'll never work in this town again, son. I'll have to fix it that way."

"I know that, Mr. President. Thank you for your courtesy."

The Mississippi River had cut New Orleans in half, but if anything, the flooding had added to the city's raffish charm. The spectral isolation of the French Quarter was only intensified by its becoming an island; there was an almost Venetian quality to it, intensified by the gondolas.

The official parades down Canal Street were well policed, but it was very loud on Bourbon Street, where spontaneous crowds accreted, with no raison d'être other than entertaining one another.

Greta stepped away from the green and peeling window shutters. "It's so good to be here," she said.

Oscar enjoyed the Mardi Gras crowds. He felt at ease as the only sober being in a huge, jostling mess of flat-footed drunks. Among them, but never quite of them. It was the story of his life. "You know, I could have gotten us onto one of those parade floats. Throwing out beads and bangles and free software. That looked like fun."

"Noblesse oblige," she murmured.

"It's a local krewe thing. Very old, very New Orleans. The local debs booked up all their dance cards in the 1850s, but they tell me that cadging a float ride is doable. If you know who to know."

"Maybe next year," she told him. A subtle rap came at the door's mahogany paneling. Hotel staffers in white jackets and boutonnieres arrived with a rattling sandalwood pushcart. Oysters, shrimp, iced champagne. Greta left for the bedroom to change for dinner. The locals silently busied themselves at the linen table, lighting the candelabrum, opening the bottle, brimming the glasses. Oscar patiently escorted them back to the hall. Then he clicked off the light.

Greta returned and examined the candelabrum. She was dressed in deep brown antebellum lace and a feathered vizard. The mask really worked for him. He loved the mask. Even in the thickest sprawl of Mardi Gras she would be a striking creature.

"Chocolate truffles?" she said eagerly.

"I didn't forget. Later." Oscar lifted his champagne flute, admired the golden bubbles, set it back down.

"You still don't drink, do you?"

"You go ahead. I'll just admire it. With half an eye."

"I'll just have a sip," she said, licking her long upper lip below the feathered edge of the mask. "I have this little problem with impulse control. . . ."

"Why let that slow you down? This is Mardi Gras."

She sat. They dabbed a bit at their shrimp cocktails. There were deadly little crystal plates of horseradish. "Did I tell you that I had a cellular cleansing done?"

"You're kidding."

"I resented it, you know. That I hadn't chosen to do it to myself. And then, there was the blood pressure, the stroke risk. So, I had my brain tissue cleaned out."

"How was it? Tell me."

"It all felt very normal. Very flat. Like living in black and white. I had to go back again, I don't care anymore, I just had to." She put her long pale hands on the tabletop. "What about you? Can you stop?"

"I don't want to stop it. It works for me."

"It's bad for you."

"No, I love bicamerality. That's what I really like about our little gift and affliction. All those other troubles, humanity's stinking little prejudices, the race thing, the ethnic thing. . . . It's not that they disappear, you know. That's too much to hope for. They never disappear, but the new problems screw them up so much that the old problems lose center stage. Besides, now I can multitask. I really can do two things at once. I'm much more effective. I can run a business full-time while I work full-time for legalization."

"So you're making money again."

"Yes, it's a thing I tend to do." Oscar sighed. "It's the basic American way. It's my only real path to legitimacy. With serious money, I can finance candidates, run court challenges, set up foundations. It's no use wandering around the margins with our bears and tambourines, dancing for pennies. Cognition will become an industry soon. A massive, earthshaking, new American industry. Someday, the biggest ever."

"You're going to turn my science into an industry? When it's illegal now, when people think it's crazy just to mess with it? How is that supposed to happen?"

"You can't stop me from doing it," Oscar told her, lowering his voice. "No one can stop me. It will come on very slowly, very gently, so quietly that you hardly feel it at first. Just a gentle lifting of the veil. Very tender, very subtle. I'll be taking it away from the realm of abstract knowledge, and bringing it into a real and dirty world of sweat and heat. It won't be ugly or sordid, it'll seem lovely and inevitable. People will want it, they'll long for it. They'll finally cry out for it. And at the end, Greta, I'll possess it totally."

A long silence. She shivered violently in her chair, and the feathered mask dipped. She couldn't seem to meet his eyes. She lifted a silver oyster fork, probed at the quiescent gray blob on her plate, and set the fork back down. Then she looked up, searchingly. "You look older."

"I know I do." He smiled. "Shall I put my mask on?"

"Is it all right to worry about you? Because I do."

"It's all right to worry, but not during Mardi Gras." He laughed. "You want to worry? Worry about people who get in my way." He swallowed an oyster.

Another long silence. He was used to her silences now. They came in flavors; Greta had all kinds of silences. "At least they let me work in the lab now," she murmured. "There's not much danger they'll ever put me in power again. I wish I were better at my work, that's all. It's the only thing I regret. I just wish I had more time and that I were better."

"But you're the best that there is."

"I'm getting old, I can feel it. I can feel the need leaving me, that devouring gift. I just wish that I were better, Oscar, that's all. They tell me I'm a genius but I'm always, always full of discontent. I can't do anything about that."

"That must be hard. Would you like me to get you a private lab, Greta? There would be less overhead, you could run it for yourself. It might help."

"No thank you."

"I could build a nice place for you. Someplace we both like. Where you can concentrate. Oregon, maybe."

"I know that you could build an institute, but I'm never going to live in your pocket."

"You're so proud," he said mournfully. "It could be doable. I could marry you."

She shook her masked head. "We're not going to marry."

"If you gave me just a week, once a quarter. That's not much to ask. Four weeks a year."

"We couldn't stand each other for four whole weeks a year. Because we're driven souls. You don't have the time for a real marriage, and neither do I. Even if we did, even if it worked, you'd only want more."

"Well, yes. That's true. Of course I would want more."

"I'll tell you how it would work, because I've seen it work. You could be the faculty wife, Oscar. I'll still put in my eighty-hour weeks, but you can look after me, if I'm ever around. Maybe we could adopt. I'll never have any time for your kids either, but I'd feel guilty enough to get them Christmas presents. You could look after the house, and the money, and maybe the fame, and you could cook for us, and who knows. Probably you would live a lot longer."

"You think that sounds bad to me," he said. "It doesn't sound bad. It sounds very authentic. The problem is, it's impossible. I can't keep a family together. I can't settle down. I've never seen it done. I wouldn't know how to sit still. I've had affairs with three different women since last August. I used to line my women up one at a time. I can't manage that anymore. Now I multiplex them. Giving you a ring and a bridal veil, that wouldn't change me. I realize that now, I have to admit it. It's beyond me, I can't control it."

"I despise your other women," she said. "But then, I think of how they must feel, if they ever learn about me. At least that's some comfort."

He winced.

"You haven't ever made me happy. You've just made me complicated. I'm very complicated now. I've become the kind of woman who flies to Mardi Gras to meet her lover."

"Is that so bad?"

"Yes, it's bad. I feel so much more pain now. But, I feel so much more awake."

"Do you think we have a future, Greta?"

"I'm not the future. There's another woman out there tonight, and she's all dressed up and she's very drunk. Tonight she's going to have sex with her guy, and when she ought to be smart, she'll just say 'oh, the hell with it.' She'll get pregnant at Mardi Gras. *She's* the future. I'm not the future, I've never been the future. I'm not even the truth. I'm just the facts."

"I must be human after all," Oscar said, "because I only get the facts in little bits."

"We won't ever marry, but someday we'll be past this. Then I could walk with you on the beach. Feel something for you, just as a person, in some quieter, simpler way. If I have anything to give like that, it will be at the very end of my life. When I'm old, when the ambition fades away."

Oscar rose and went to the glass doors. It was a very bitter thing to tell him, because he felt quite sure that she would in fact be doing that thing, in her old age. Wisdom and communion. But she would be doing it with someone else. Never with her lover. With a worshipful grad student, maybe a biographer. Never with him. He stepped outside, shot his cuffs, and leaned out on the opulent grille of the balcony.

A large organized group was methodically working their way down Bourbon Street, under the blue and white banner of an extinct multinational bank. The revelers, grim and unsmiling, were neatly dressed in sober three-piece tailored suits and polished shoes. Most groups of this sort would throw cheap beads at the crowds, but the proles had cut all suppositions short: they were simply throwing away wads of cash.

"Look at these characters," Oscar called out.

Greta joined him. "I see they're in their holiday gear."

A five-dollar bill attached to a fishing weight came flying up from street level, and bounced from Oscar's shoulder. He picked it up. It was genuine money, all right. "They really shouldn't be allowed to do this sort of thing. It could cause a riot."

"Don't be grumpy. I feel better now, it's all right. Let's go and break the bed now."

She lured him into the bedroom. The damp air sang with erotic tension. "Shall I keep the mask on?"

He took his jacket off. "Oh yes. The mask is definitely you."

He set to work on her in a particularly levelheaded and elaborate fashion. During their long separation he had had enough time to imagine this meeting. He had formed a multilevel erotic schemata with a number of variable subroutines. The sheets were soaked with sweat and the veins were standing out on her neck. With a strangled cry she tore the mask from her eyes, tumbled out of bed with a thump, and hurried out of the room.

He followed her in alarm. She was digging desperately in her purse. She came up with a pencil stub.

"What's . . ." he began gently.

"Shhh!" She began scribbling frantically at the back leaf of a New Orleans travel guide. Oscar found a cotton bathrobe, put it over her shoulders, found his pants, sipped half a bottle of cold mineral water. When his temples stopped throbbing he returned to the balcony.

There were extraordinary scenes down on Bourbon Street. Their balcony, divided into segments, stretched the length of the little hotel and there were four women and three other men on it. There was a bizarre interplay between the people up on the balconies and the crowds at street level.

Women were showing their breasts to crowds of strangers, in exchange for plastic beads. Men were hoarsely yelling for the spectacle and throwing the beads as bribes. Women in the streets would display themselves to the men on the balconies, and the women on the balconies would display themselves to men on the streets. There was no groping, no come-ons; cameras would flash and gaudy necklaces would fly, but there was a ritual noli-me-tangere atmosphere to these exchanges. They were strangely old and quaint, like an elbow-link in a square dance.

A pretty redhead in the balcony across the way was tormenting her crowd of admirers. She would kiss her boyfriend, a grinning drunk in a devil suit, and then lean out with an enormous dangling swath of gold, green, and purple beads around her neck, and she'd teasingly pluck at the hem of her blouse. The men below her were booing lustily, and chanting their demands in unison.

After torturing them to a frenzy, she slung the beads over her shoulder and bared her torso. It was worth the wait. Slowly the stranger deliberately caressed her own nipple. Oscar felt as if he had been fish-hooked.

He went back into the hotel room. Greta had leaned away from her scribbling. Her face was pale and thoughtful now.

"What was all that?" he said.

"A strange thing." She put her pencil down. "I was

thinking. I can think about neurology while I have sex now."

"Really?"

"Well, it's more like *dreaming* about neurology. You had me all excited, and I was right on the edge . . . you know how you can sort of hang there where it's wonderful, right on the edge? And I was thinking hard about wave propagation in glial cells. Then suddenly it came to me, that the standard calcium-wave astrocyte story is all wrong, there's a better method to describe that depolarization, and I almost had that idea, I almost had it, I almost had it, and I just got *stuck* there. I got stuck there on the edge. I couldn't get loose and I couldn't quite come and the pleasure kept building up. My head started roaring, I was almost blacking out. And then it came all over me, in a tremendous rush. So I had to jump out of bed to write it down."

He stepped to the table. "So what does it look like?"

"Oh"—she shoved the paper away—"it's just another idea. I mean, now that I can see it down on paper, there's really no way that a glial syncytium can behave like that. It's a clever notion but it's not consistent with the tracer studies." She sighed. "It sure felt good though. When it happened. My God, did that ever feel good."

"You're not going to do that every time, though."

"No. I just don't have that many good ideas." She looked up, her lips still swollen from the grip of his teeth. "Don't you think of something else, too?"

"Well, yes."

"What?"

He drew a little nearer. "Other things that I can do with you."

They climbed back into bed. This time, she did black out. He didn't notice her deep slide from consciousness, because her body was still moving rhythmically, but her eyes had rolled up in her head. When she began to speak to him, he blacked out at once.

"Are you with me?" she whispered blindly.

"Yes, I'm here," he said, struggling to speak through his body's gasping. They had merged now, together, from areas of cognition so low and so blind to conscious awareness that they were barely able to manifest themselves. But they had chosen a good moment to take the mind's central stage. Their sweating bodies began to slow, to melt together gently into deep relaxation. It was all very easy now, a vast moonlit Pacific of sexuality, washing some distant shore. They could breathe together.

When they woke, it was ten PM. Streetlights crept through the blinds to stripe the ceiling. Greta stirred and yawned, prodded his bare ankle with her foot. "It's sweet to have these little naps, after."

"We seem to be making a habit of passing out."

"I think dreaming is good for us." She pulled herself out of bed. "Shower . . ." Her voice faded as she padded off. "Oh, they have a bidet! That's great."

He followed her in. "We'll wash now. We'll get dressed," he told her cheerfully. Lovemaking was behind them now, always tensely awaited but maybe just a little bit of a burden, in retrospect. Still, he felt good about it. They were all purged, the tension had sung out of them; they were having fun together. "We'll put on our masks, we'll go out and have some coffee. I'll take your picture in the street, it'll be fun."

"Good plan." She examined her smashed hairdo in the mirror, and grimaced. "One martini too many. . . ."

"You look great. I feel good, I feel so happy now."

"Me too." She stepped into the shower and set it to hiss.

"It's a holiday," he said absently. "We'll just have our little holiday now, we'll live for the moment, we'll be just like real people."

When they were dressed, they stepped onto the balcony. The balcony was crowded now, with many friendly strangers. As Greta appeared, she was instantly greeted from the streets below with howls of male demand.

Greta's eyes grew wide with shock behind her feathered mask. "Good Lord," she said. "I always knew that's what men want from you, but to have them just standing there, publicly *yelling* it. . . . I can't believe this."

"You can show yourself off if you like. They'll give you beads for it."

She thought about it. "I might just do it if *you* went down into the street, and yelled up at me."

"That's a distinct possibility. Let me get my camera first."

She smiled wickedly. "You'll have to throw me my beads, though, mister. And they'll have to be very nice ones."

"I enjoy a challenge," Oscar said.

A string of green-and-gold beads flew up to strike at Greta. She batted at the necklace, tried to catch it, missed. In the street below them, a tall middle-aged man with a mustache below his mask was jumping up and down, and bellowing at her. He was waving both arms frantically, as if trying to signal an airliner.

"Look at that clown," Oscar said, grinning. "He's really smitten."

"He's got a girlfriend already," Greta said.

The man and his smiling girlfriend fought their way valiantly through the passing crowd, until they had wedged themselves directly below the balcony.

"Dr. Penninger!" the man shouted. "Hey, show us your brain!"

"Oh, hell, that's torn it," Oscar said angrily. "They're paparazzi."

"Hey, Oscar!" the man shouted lustily. He pulled off his mask. "Look, look!"

"Do you know that man?" Greta said.

"No . . ." Oscar stared suddenly. "Hey! I do! It's

Yosh! It's Yosh Pelicanos." He leaned over the balcony, doubling over to shout down. "Yosh! Hi!"

"Look here!" Yosh shouted giddily, pointing to the masked and costumed brunette at his side. "Look, it's Sandra!"

"What is he talking about?" Greta said.

"That's his *wife*," Oscar marveled. "It's his wife, Sandra." He cupped his hands to his mouth and shouted, "Sandra! Hello! Good to meet you!"

"I'm all better!" Sandra shrilled. "I'm so much better now."

"That's great!" Oscar yelled. "That's marvelous! Come on up, Yosh! Come up and have a drink with us!"

"No time!" Pelicanos shouted. His wife was being swept away by the pressure of passersby. Pelicanos caught her hand and shielded her for a moment. Sandra seemed a little unsure of herself in the crowd; not too surprising, considering her nine years in a mental hospital.

"We have to go make love now," Sandra shouted, with a shy and radiant smile.

"God bless you, Dr. Penninger!" Pelicanos shouted, waving his mask and retreating. "You're a great genius! Thank you for being alive! Thank you for being you!"

"Who were those people?" Greta demanded. "Why did you invite them up?"

"That was my majordomo. And his wife. His wife was a schizophrenic."

"That was his wife?" She paused. "Oh, well, then it must have been NCR-40 autoimmune syndrome. Attention therapy deals with that really well now. She'll be just fine.

"Then he'll be fine, too."

"He looked all right, once he calmed down. Kind of goodlooking, even."

"I almost didn't recognize him. I'd never seen him happy before." Oscar paused. "*You* made him happy."

"Well, maybe I get the credit." She smiled. "I didn't

mean to make him happy. Science gets the credit for things science never meant to do. Science isn't a better effort just because it sometimes helps humanity. But on the other hand, that must mean that science isn't really any worse for causing mankind harm."

"I'm not sure I follow you there. That's not political thinking."

She had a long sip of champagne. The men in the street were still yelling for her attention, but she regally ignored them. "Look at me," she told him suddenly. She smoothed her feathered mask against her face with her long fingers. Within the owlish cowl of brown feathers, her eyes moved suddenly, in two different directions.

Oscar jumped. "Wow! How'd you do that?"

"I can do it now. I practiced. I can even *see* two things at once. Watch me." Her eyes rolled in their white sockets, like a chameleon's.

"Good God! You did that just by thinking about it?"

"It's the life of the mind."

"I can't believe it. No, look at me again. Use both your eyes. Now use one eye. Good Lord, that's the most shocking thing I've ever seen in a human face. The hair's standing up on my neck. Do it for me again, sweetheart. My God! I've got to get a camera."

"You're not scared? I never showed anyone else."

"Of course I'm scared! I'm petrified. It's wonderful. Why am I the only guy in the world who knows how sexy that is?" He laughed delightedly. "You blew my mind! Come and kiss me."

About the Author

BRUCE STERLING is the author of the nonfiction book *The Hacker Crackdown,* as well as the novels *Holy Fire, Heavy Weather, Schismatrix,* and *Islands in the Net.* With William Gibson he co-authored the acclaimed novel *The Difference Engine.* He also writes popular science and travel journalism. He lives with his wife and two daughters in Austin, Texas.

WILLIAM GIBSON / BRUCE STERLING

THE DIFFERENCE ENGINE

LONDON, 1855: Steam-powered Babbage Engines are run by an elite group of "clackers." When paleontologist Edward Mallory, on the verge of his greatest achievement, finds himself in possession of a box of punched Engine cards, he finds out how fleeting fame can be—because someone wants those cards badly enough to kill for them....

_____ 29461-X   THE DIFFERENCE ENGINE $6.99/$9.99